Mind's Eye
Law of the Night

SABBAT GUIDE

Credits

Written by: Justin Achilli, Bruce Baugh, Clayton Oliver, Ree Soesbee
Developed by: Cynthia Summers
Edited by: Rich Ruane
Previously published material has appeared in: Laws of the Night, MET: The Camarilla Guide, The Guide to the Sabbat,
Art direction by: Aaron Voss
Art by: Laura Robles
Front and back cover design by: Aaron Voss
Layout and typesetting by: Aaron Voss
Playtesters: Matthew Skipper, Brett Murphy, Richard Stratton

735 Park North Blvd.
Suite 128
Clarkston, GA 30021
USA

© 2000 White Wolf Publishing, Inc. All rights reserved. Reproduction without the written permission of the publisher is expressly forbidden, except for the purposes of reviews, and for blank character sheets, which may be reproduced for personal use only. White Wolf, Vampire the Masquerade, Vampire the Dark Ages, Mage the Ascension, World of Darkness and Aberrant are registered trademarks of White Wolf Publishing, Inc. All rights reserved. Werewolf the Apocalypse, Wraith the Oblivion, Changeling the Dreaming, Hunter the Reckoning, Werewolf the Wild West, Mage the Sorcerers Crusade, Wraith the Great War, Trinity, Mind's Eye Theatre Journal, Oblivion, Kindred of the East Companion, and Laws of the Hunt are trademarks of White Wolf Publishing, Inc. All rights reserved. All characters, names, places and text herein are copyrighted by White Wolf Publishing, Inc.

The mention of or reference to any company or product in these pages is not a challenge to the trademark or copyright concerned.

This book uses the supernatural for settings, characters and themes. All mystical and supernatural elements are fiction and intended for entertainment purposes only. Reader discretion is advised.

For a free White Wolf catalog call 1-800-454-WOLF.

Check out White Wolf online at

http://www.white-wolf.com; alt.games.whitewolf and rec.games.frp.storyteller
PRINTED IN THE UNITED STATES.

Contents

CHAPTER ONE: RECRUITMENT	4
CHAPTER TWO: CAINE'S OWN	28
CHAPTER THREE: MAKING A MONSTER	58
CHAPTER FOUR: THE WAY AND THE TRUTH	74
CHAPTER FIVE: CAINE'S ARMORY	96
CHAPTER SIX: MIDNIGHT DANCES	138
CHAPTER SEVEN: URBAN LEGENDS	182

Chapter One: Recruitment

Abandon All Hope, Ye Who Enter Here

The Final Nights are strange and terrible times for the Sabbat. They hurl themselves at the strongholds of their enemies, the Camarilla, with a ferocity that belies the desperation beneath. These are the nights that have been whispered of in the prophecies of the *Book of Nod*. This has been foreseen as the end times. And worst of all, their most terrible fears — of the hunger of the Antediluvians and the horror of Gehenna — would seem to be finally borne out.

Racked from within by fractious sect politics and beset from without by enemies of all stripes, the Sabbat pits itself in direct opposition to the Camarilla. There is no Masquerade here, no cowering from mortals who are fit only for service or food, no boot-licking to elders who haven't earned the respect they believe due them. The Sabbat's children revel in their vampiric natures, believing full well that vampires are meant to rule the night as the ultimate predators. Even as it battles the Camarilla for territory and the hearts of young vampires who chafe under the elders' talons, the sect glories in being the best monster it can be.

Prophecy and the crumbling strength of the Camarilla would seem to be on their side. If these are indeed the Final Nights, and the time of darkness approaches, the Sabbat should celebrate, but they instead fight with all the strength they can muster. It is precisely because prophecy and fears are at last coming to light that the sect fears the approach of the end times, and why it calls on its strength to the last vampire.

What This Book Is (and Isn't)

This book details the innermost workings of the monstrous Sabbat. From their rituals to the strange Disciplines their members command, from the ghastly revenant families to the workings of the *antitribu*, here all is revealed.

What you have in your hands is not meant to be a stand-alone volume. There's a lot in the original **Laws of the Night** that you'll need to play Sabbat (such as character creation, Disciplines and the basic rules). Other items, such as the elder levels of Disciplines such as *Auspex* or *Obfuscate*, are found in **The Camarilla Guide.** You may also find the tabletop **Guide to the Sabbat** handy for more information regarding the sect's history and internal chemistry.

A Friendly Warning

Repeat after me: "I am not a vampire. I am not a bloodthirsty creature of the night. I do not have supernatural powers. If I ever start to confuse the boundaries of the game and real life, I will put down the game and not endanger other people." Repeat this until you believe it.

Consider this the official "You're not a vampire — behave yourself" warning. There may not be an Inquisition, but there are certainly mortals out there who will hunt you down if you start believing your own propaganda — they're called teachers, police officers, clergy and parents, and White Wolf supports them heartily. The major rules of **Mind's Eye Theatre** are more important than ever when playing a Sabbat chronicle. It can be exciting and more than a little scary to delve into the dark parts of your psyche; the problem is when art and life start blurring too much.

The abyss is definitely looking back at you. Don't get out of hand.

Welcome to the Family

Welcome to the Sabbat. Described as an apocalyptic blood cult, a coven of death-obsessed leeches, crusaders fighting an endless civil war and a hodge-podge of blood-drinking psychotics, the Sabbat is all of this and more.

For the Sabbat, to be a vampire means being a weapon in the Great Jyhad, an unending holy war on the ancient, cannibalistic monsters who passed on the Curse of Caine during the Biblical nights. The Antediluvians — and their mindless servants in the Camarilla — seek to bring about the end of the world and destroy the race of Cainites. The Sabbat rages against this fate; they have better things to do than die at the fangs of their bloodthirsty sires. The world belongs to *them*, not to the ancient evil that sleeps beneath the land.

The Great Jyhad is a matter of the sect against the world. Although the members of the Sword of Caine aren't above internecine intrigue, blatant rivalry or treachery, in the end the Sabbat must come first. Martyrs and zealots, the Sabbat's children hurl themselves fangs-first at their enemies, falling upon on their foes in scores and rending them like a pack of wolves. It's a no-holds-barred war, and rulership of the night is the prize.

In truth, however, the sect is more than this. Though neither mindless fiends nor demonic apostates, vampires of the Sabbat *do* tread dangerously close to becoming such monsters. Having forsaken the ways of mortals, Sabbat

vampires understand that they are damned, creatures of the Beast. Rather than rail against their natures and pine for what they once were, they flaunt their monstrosity: They have become more than human, and are yet cursed for daring to move beyond the boundaries of the kine.

Of course, this means the sect is as incestuously self-serving as any other group of "Kindred" — a term of weakness among the Sons and Daughters of Caine. In the modern nights, the sect is racked with corruption, festering from within, yet denying its own collapse with a passion unmatched by other vampires anywhere.

The High Price of Unlife

At a casual glance, the Sabbat would seem to be a haven for miscreants, thugs and cackling, self-indulgent deviants. Such is not the case. Indeed, nightly unlife for the Sabbat is so fraught with hellish peril that those members of the sect who *are* psychotic murderers and rapine blood-gluttons have become so to survive the incredible stresses they face.

The Sabbat suffers no end of internal schisms. Elder members of the sect, hundreds of years old and perhaps even present at its formation over half a millennium ago, have radically different outlooks from the younger Sons and Daughters of Caine. Most young Sabbat have spent fewer than 25 years as Cainites. As such, the Sabbat is a fractious entity, divided from within and beset from without. The Sabbat does not generally have Cainites who are analogous to ancillae — the sect is comprised primarily of neonates, who do most of the nightly fighting and dirty work, and a handful of potent elders who have managed to turn the sect to their own ends by indoctrinating the young Cainites and convincing them to serve their whims. This isn't to say that the elders don't believe in the grand struggle, but rather that they observe it as it suits them. Elders of five centuries have too much at stake to risk fighting against the Antediluvians personally. Better to hurl a pack of howling neonates at their enemies and survive to continue the war on another night.

Hypocrisy plays a great role in the Sabbat. The sect is simultaneously righteous and venal, spiritual and base, patriotic and selfish. A Sabbat Cainite may have no qualms about hunting and destroying a Camarilla Kindred for his oblivious service to the Ancients — but it may have to wait until after she's finished gutting the mortal vessel who accidentally strayed across her path. Like a late-era Rome, the Sabbat has a strong, consistent philosophy that individual corruption all too often pushes aside.

The History of the Sabbat

The sect's history prior to the momentous Cainite event known as the Convention of Thorns is shrouded in mystery. Some Sabbat claim legacies of monstrosity and predation, wandering the Old World as a death cult. Others claim the sect never truly existed prior to the Anarch Revolt, and instead took the form of roving packs, not unlike the packs of the modern nights. Still others claim that the very name defines the sect's origin — a loose confederation of witches and self-avowed monsters claiming servitude to Hell.

Despite the conflicting theories as to the sect's origin, one fact remains relatively reliable: The Sabbat came into being sometime after the Anarch

Revolt. When the rebellious neonates of Clans Lasombra and Tzimisce destroyed their Antediluvians, the elders knew their iron rule had come to an end and that Cainite society would never be the same.

After innumerable bloody skirmishes, the anarchs gained ground on their elders and sires. With the victory of the Tzimisce and Lasombra still fresh in many minds, Cainite struggles plagued Europe. Young vampires turned to open revolt, and elders met their ends nightly, sometimes taking their childer with them. Aided by the mercenary Assamite clan, the anarchs left no stone unturned in their war on the hated elders. Although no other clans managed to achieve the same success over their Ancients that the Tzimisce and Lasombra did, it wasn't for lack of trying.

As the bloodshed of the Anarch Revolt reached new heights, a critical mistake was made: Mortals discovered that monsters loomed in their midst. After a desperate appeal to Rome, humankind entreated the Pope to turn the Inquisition against the night-walkers and blood-drinkers that had sought to lord it over them for so long. Even more horrifying, the Church agreed, and the combined might of the witch-hunters added a new and terrifying dimension to the chaotic soup that were those nights. The war ground on, looking more and more like a stalemate.

In the midst of this, certain powerful elder vampires, among them a Ventrue named Hardestadt (who had been believed to be the first elder to fall to the anarchs), chose to throw their lots together, believing that unity would give them the necessary strength. Under their combined might, the tide began to turn. Hardestadt and his collective, called the Camarilla, called for all "Kindred" to parley. In the English town of Thorns, the anarchs and the Camarilla sat down to a written accord, known as the Convention of Thorns, which promised to restore order and sanctity to the race of Cainites.

Not every anarch gave up so easily, however. The treaty offered little to remedy the situation that had caused the strife in the first place. Furthermore, Clan Assamite suffered the brunt of punishment for the war. Enraged, a war party of anarchs and rogue Assamites rampaged through Thorns, leaving the town burning behind them. The sect that would become the Sabbat committed itself to its immortal course of action that night.

In the years that followed, the vampires of the newly formed Sabbat took their war against the Camarilla. The Inquisition continued to claim victims, and Cainites drew lines in the sand to mark their allegiances. The end result, though, was a guerrilla bloodbath. Puppet rulers fell, knightly orders crumbled, and havens burned like winter hearth-fires.

With the discovery of the New World, the Sabbat saw a new empire for the taking, and the sect flourished while the Camarilla huddled in Europe. Soon, though, they faced opposition, as disenfranchised young Camarilla vampires arrived, hoping to carve out legacies for themselves away from the ironbound holdings of European elders. Before long, the Camarilla-Sabbat war had reached the shores of the Americas.

Not long afterward, the Lasombra and Tzimisce fell to warring amongst themselves for the rapidly depleting resources of the New World. The continent was huge and underdeveloped, its cities few and far between, and

rare was the Cainite who wished to attempt surviving in the wilds. Cities became commodities while the clans fought each other for the dwindling communities of kine that sustained their existence. During the struggle, the Camarilla quietly spread through the New World. By the time the Sabbat realized that they had been surrounded and, in fact, overtaken, it was too late.

Sabbat vampires are nothing if not survivors, however, and despite the obstacles of the Camarilla's encroachment, the sect persevered. Establishing strongholds in Canada (for which certain Sabbat vampires' ties to the Native Americans proved immensely helpful) and Mexico (where impoverished conditions and corrupt governments allowed the society of the undead to flourish), the Sabbat effectively blocked in the Camarilla.

Finally, now painfully aware that their actions had cost them more territory, the Sabbat vampires put their differences to rest... for a short time. Convening in New York, which the sect had managed to hold against all the best efforts of the Camarilla, high-ranking Sabbat reconsidered their commitment to the sect's causes. Not content to merely sign a goodwill agreement as they had before, Sabbat vampires took a long, hard look at what was important to the Sword of Caine. An unheard-of congregation of Sabbat committed to document the Code of Milan, a collection of tenets that composed Sabbat ideology supposedly since the establishment of the sect. Additionally, the assembled vampires submitted a few addenda to bring the code up to date in light of recent affairs.

Documents of Import

Although the Sabbat is predicated upon freedom and the Great Jyhad against the Antediluvians, politics inevitably find their way into the affairs of the Sword of Caine. Over the course of their existence, several important agreements have come to have meaning to the Cainites of the sect. The Convention of Thorns, which ended the Anarch Revolt, is seen by many Cainites as not only the article that resulted in the formation of the Camarilla, but also the Sabbat. The Purchase Pact enforced a previously inconceivable unity to the sect after one of its debilitating civil wars. The Code of Milan asserted what it meant to be Sabbat, and the responsibilities that the sect determined should accompany its freedoms.

The Convention of Thorns

Many years have passed since the start of our current conflict, now called the Anarch Movement. Be it known that on this night of 23 October, 1493, the Jyhad has ended. The time for self-destruction is over.

This concordat, bound in the Covenant of Caine by sacred vow, represents an unyielding, vigilant truce between the Kindred known unto themselves as the Anarchs, the Clan Assamite, and the freestanding Kindred bound under the title of Camarilla. Henceforth, the parties shall be recognized by faction as the Anarchs, the Assamites, and the Camarilla.

Each of the parties agrees to the responsibility of maintaining peace. Each shall lay its censures on any who breech or oppose this sacred Agreement. Accounting will be made of all parties for violations by them to either the letter or spirit of this Agreement. This document is binding under the social code of

all Children of Caine by the accepted Lextalionis of all Cainites as it has passed through the ages. All Kindred are entreated to accept and gain solace from this peaceful accord.

Be it known that the Anarchs will enjoin with the Camarilla as an accepted part, making it whole. Anarchs are expected to work peacefully to achieve their own ends. They must become defenders of all, and they shall receive full entitlement to all rights and privileges belonging to all Camarilla Kindred. All Anarchs shall be accepted back unto their elders and their formerly denounced clans without any fear of reprisal. Only the most vicious of atrocities shall not be forgiven. These shall stand written for the justicars to hear within one year, after which all allegations are no longer valid. All Anarchs shall reclaim all remaining and rightful property confiscated from them. In return they must turn over any war gains taken during the conflict by giving them to their sires or any recognized clan elder.

Know also that if the Anarchs are further warred on, this open Jyhad invalidates their responsibility to maintain peace with their attacker. They may act freely without fear of reprisal from inactive members of the Camarilla. Anarchs are guaranteed the freedom to act as they please, short of breaching the *Masquerade* imposed for the protection of all Kindred from the kine.

It is also noted that any member of any other self-proclaimed sect must openly declare this before his elders and renounce this relation. Failure to do so will result in the destruction of any deemed guilty. No Kindred may be sent knowingly to his death by an elder or sire, unless the security of clan or Camarilla outweighs the possible loss of unlife.

From this night forward, the Assamites shall henceforth no longer commit diablerie on members of other clans. The Assamites must commit themselves to this acceptance by a mark of assurance placed on them in the form of a Thaumaturgical limitation. All members of the Assamites shall become unable to drink freely of the vitae of other Kindred from now unto forever. In addition, the Assamites shall pay the Brujah elders of Spain two thousand pounds of gold, in ransom of the five Assamite elders captured committing diablerie. Also, the Assamites may no longer participate in blood hunts.

Be it also know that the Assamites are guaranteed complete independence from Camarilla demands. The Assamite fortress, Alamut, shall be free from further assaults. Assamites are also granted, out of respect for their beliefs, the freedom to commit diablerie within their own clan without restraint and the right to commit diablerie on all Kindred not recognized as holding membership within the Camarilla.

It is rendered that all parties involved and all showing allegiance to any of these parties shall be held responsible for all aspects of this Convention brought forth here, in the neutral Kingdom of England, outside the hamlet of Thorns, near the town of Silchester. May Caine hold truth and peace for us all.

Terms of the Purchase Pact

Let it be know that forthwith, the Sabbat exists as a free entity, though the price of that freedom comes in the form of the sacrifice of certain rights.

On this, the 19th of September, 1803, all Sabbat of good faith and conscience do hereby suspend all grievances with other Sabbat.

Any Sabbat found in open violation of this agreement — e.g., any Sabbat making open war on another for the purposes of his own betterment at the expense of the sect — is hereby declared forsaken, and may be hunted for the blood in his veins. Such abandonment must be pronounced by a duly recognized bishop, archbishop or other elder member of the sect.

In this we are united. In this we are Sabbat.

Signed,

Regent Gorchist

Witnessed,

Cardinal Radu Bistri

Priscus Livia Boleslav Czernzy

Archbishop Enrique Albertos Marquez

Bishop Federic Montaigne

The Code of Milan

By the solemn word of Regent Gorchist, this is the one true Code of Milan, revised from the original manuscript this night, December 21, 1933. Out of the ashes of our great war may this peace reign everlasting.

An oath of allegiance has been sworn by the regent and the consistory in the presence of all faction leaders and 50 other witnesses to faithfully follow all regulations imposed by this code in leading the Sabbat. This revised Code of Milan is agreed on by all Sabbat factions, including those of Cardinals Huroff, Bruce de Guy, Agnes and Charles VI; and Archbishops Beatrice, Una, Tecumseh, Giangaleazzo, Toth, Aeron, Marsilio, Rebecca, Julian and Salluccio. All other factions must pledge themselves in support of this revised Code of Milan or claim separation from the Sabbat.

These are the statutes comprising the Code of Milan:

I. The Sabbat shall remain united in its support of the sect's regent. If necessary, a new regent shall be elected. The regent shall support relief from tyranny, granting all Sabbat freedom.

II. All Sabbat shall do their best to serve their leaders as long as said leaders serve the will of the regent.

III. All Sabbat shall faithfully observe all the *auctoritas ritae*.

IV. All Sabbat shall keep their word of honor to one another.

V. All Sabbat shall treat their peers fairly and equally, upholding the strength and unity of the Sabbat. If necessary, they shall provide for the needs of their brethren.

VI. All Sabbat must put the good of the sect and the race of Cainites before their own personal needs, despite all costs.

VII. Those who are not honorable under this code will be considered less than equal and therefore unworthy of assistance.

VIII. As it has always been, so shall it always be. The Lextalionis shall be the model for undying justice by which all Sabbat shall abide.

IX. All Sabbat shall protect one another from the enemies of the sect. Personal enemies shall remain a personal responsibility, unless they undermine sect security.

X. All sect members shall protect Sabbat territory from all other powers.

XI. The spirit of freedom shall be the fundamental principle of the sect. All Sabbat shall expect and demand freedom from their leaders.

XII. The *Ritus* of Monomacy shall be used to settle disputes among all Sabbat.

XIII. All Sabbat shall support the Black Hand.

Addenda to the Code of Milan

Observed by all witnessing parties present on this night, December 21, 1933, and hereafter upheld.

XIV. All Sabbat have the right to monitor the behavior and activities of their fellow sect members in order to maintain freedom and security.

XV. All Sabbat possess the right to call a council of their peers and immediate leaders.

XVI. All Sabbat shall act against sect members who use the powers and authority the Sabbat has given them for personal gain at the expense of the Sabbat. Action shall be taken only through accepted means, approved by a quorum of prisci.

Modern Nights

Some say the Sabbat has matured remarkably in the intervening years. Indeed, it has become a force to be reckoned with, claiming or reclaiming cities long held by the Camarilla and using sieges and crusades with deadly efficiency. This singularity of vision seems to have overcome at least a modicum of the sect's disorganization. Additionally, the sect as a whole is considerably younger than the Camarilla, able to adopt modern technology with a speed that terrifies its stodgy counterpart. Whatever the reason, the sect has scored some astounding coups and become a legitimate contender for the Camarilla's eroding power.

Not surprisingly, the Sabbat exercises a great deal of influence over Third World nations and the most squalid cities of the world. There, amid the hives of homeless and faceless juicebags, Sabbat vampires feed with impunity and build their own private empires. In modernized parts of the world, the Sabbat is careful to cover its tracks. While scorning the Masquerade of the Camarilla (at least in theory, if not in practice), the Sabbat's leadership realizes that the threat of organized and technologically advanced human resistance is too dangerous to provoke. Thus, in cities of Europe and North America, the Sabbat takes some pains to cover its tracks, though its methods — intimidation and murder — are far cruder than the (usually) subtle machinations of the Camarilla. With its limited contact in mortal circles, the Sabbat suffers in modern cities; for now, the Camarilla's influence in many human institutions remains one of their greatest banes.

North America

Canada and the United States are perhaps the most successful staging ground for the Sabbat. The sect has recently redoubled its efforts along the East Coast of the United States, solidifying its dominance in Miami, Washington DC, Baltimore, Philadelphia and Atlantic City. Likewise, Detroit, Mexico

City and Montreal have become ever more important jewels in the sect's crown. Concerned Sabbat see these cities as paper tigers, however, as the sect's former supremacy in New York City eroded completely after a successful Camarilla coup. Supporters of the war movement hasten to note that the cities of Atlanta, Richmond, Boston and Raleigh-Durham have recently fallen or are in serious contention. Nightly, the sect tightens its grip on the Midwestern states, hoping to crack the Camarilla like a nut between the combined might of Mexico and the East Coast territories.

South America

In a continent overrun with feudal, balkanized vampiric domains, the Sabbat holds only limited sway. Most of the Cainites of South America support private domains backed up by small coteries of influential allies. Although major cities are always prime targets for the Sabbat, the economics of South American countries do not hold the appeal of North America and Europe, so they are often considered secondary targets due to their combined lack of financial power and (incorrectly) importance to the Jyhad. In fact, the neutral attitudes of South America make many of the cities a perfect middle ground for meetings with members of other sects or organizations. When a Camarilla or independent vampire needs to make arrangements with the Sabbat, it's as likely as not to happen here, often rubbing elbows with war criminals, expatriates and other exiles of the mortal world. Sabbat vampires in South America are disorganized and fractious. The cities are largely independent, and the given presence of Sabbat in any city is usually limited to a single pack.

Europe

As the home of the elders of the Camarilla and the birthplace of the Sabbat, Europe is prime ground for the sect's more subtle warfare. Here, the Sabbat still fights to overthrow the decrepit "Kindred" of latter nights. Unfortunately, the presence of many powerful and paranoid elders makes it difficult at best to besiege cities, and the Camarilla is quick with retribution against any perceived attack. As a result, the Sabbat has only limited influence in Europe, primarily in Spain and Italy where the Lasombra clan still holds its traditional sway.

Many of the Sabbat in Europe are quite old; indeed, some vampires claiming to have been involved in the fabled Anarch Revolt still give counsel in the European nations. As a result, upward mobility in the sect is limited here. Despite the Sabbat's rallying cries of freedom and equality, young European Cainites chafe at finding themselves unable to rise in position because older and more cunning vampires already hold the reins of power. Eastern Europe, with the Russian territories and the former Ottoman provinces, is almost a separate continent as far as vampires are concerned. Here, the hoary Tzimisce ply the ancient ways of their clan, some even still existing as feudal overlords ruling from crumbling castles. Sabbat vampires of the Old World generally look on their compatriots in the Americas with disdain, often considering them crude and barbaric.

Africa and the Middle East

With the fierce rivalry between the Followers of Set and the Serpents of the Light, Africa does occupy some of the Sabbat's attention. However, the Setites remain too deeply entrenched in their homeland for the Sabbat to confront them effectively. The Middle East, encompassing northern parts of Africa and some Far Eastern sections of Europe, is an exception to the Sabbat's otherwise minimal presence in the Dark Continent. As the traditional home of the Assamites, countries like Turkey and Saudi Arabia are fortifications of strength for the Black Hand. The shifting allegiances of religious factions also make fertile ground for recruitment; once the Blood has become involved, it is often a simple matter to turn fervent loyalty from a holy mortal cause to an unholy immortal one.

Australia

As a marginally independent territory, the Sabbat finds Australia frustrating. The princes of the area either pay lip service to the Camarilla or hold completely independent cities. Consequently, the Sabbat has pushed its attacks on Australia, as evidenced by rising crime and political unrest. Without reinforcements from outside, the cities of Australia may soon fall to the Sabbat presence, but many major outposts — Sydney and Melbourne in particular — remain remarkably free of Sabbat influence.

Asia

The Far East remains shrouded in mystery to the Sabbat. The native vampires have little or no interest in contact or cooperation, and none seem to fear the Antediluvians. Even when using the underground smugglers who deign to transport Cainites (albeit at ridiculously high prices), the Sabbat finds itself balked by the enigmatic locals and their disdain for the sect's ruthless nature. Because of Asia's huge mortal population (primarily in China and India) and financial markets (Japan and Korea), the Sabbat is quite interested in establishing power in this region. Aside from a single agent in Hong Kong and a pack in Tokyo, though, there are no active Sabbat in Asia. All attempts to gain ground in the region have failed miserably, with agents disappearing or dying before achieving any goals. Direct assaults with large packs of cannon fodder meet horrible ends as Cathayans seem to melt out of the shadows and overwhelm them with powers never seen before. Asia is a deathtrap for the Sabbat, and the sect seethes with frustration at these failures.

The Structure of the Sword of Caine

Although it is sometimes difficult to distinguish from the outside, the Sabbat observes an organized hierarchy. The sect has leaders and followers, as it must to be anything other than an anarchic mob.

Like any philosophical gathering of vampires, the Sabbat is not ruled so much as it is led. Even the most august Cainites of the sect do what they do out of devotion to the Great Jyhad. Leadership among the Sword of Caine, however, is a capricious thing. At the higher echelons, Sabbat vampires tend to lose touch with the young Cainites who make their lofty positions possible. At lower levels of the organization, a ductus' or priest's decisions sometimes

have more meaning than those of a city's archbishop. In the end, the Sabbat's rabid self-sufficiency damns it as the disorganization endemic to a sect sworn to uphold freedom prevents it from maintaining consistency.

Despite their seemingly fanatical devotion to the sect, members of the Sabbat are individuals first and foremost. Sabbat vampires struggle with the same problems as the other undead. Hunters, fellow Cainites, the mysterious other creatures who stalk the night and even savvy kine who catch on to a vampire's depredations all conspire against the Sabbat as violently as they would any other threat. Although they scoff at labeling it thus, the vampires of the Sabbat maintain a necessary "Masquerade"; the sect isn't stupid, and its leaders know that they cannot achieve success if the sect falls to its enemies before it can muster for the Great Jyhad.

In response to the need for stability, the Sabbat supports specific titles and positions to serve its interests. Any vampire who has managed to acquire one likely has the power, in one form or another, to support the claim. The Cainites of the Sabbat also remember slights as vividly as any Camarilla harpy or anarch dissident — intra-sect politics are no less vicious than those of the Camarilla even though the Sabbat pretends to be above such petty matters. Cainites at various stations almost universally owe some fellow Sabbat favors, nurse rivalries with others and manipulate all the resources at their disposal toward making things difficult for their foes while gaining (or erasing) debts sworn to others.

The Sabbat respects these offices, by and large. In theory, this organization provides a foundation for the sect — the hierarchy is supposedly one based on merit and achievement. In practice, however, the structure is only as strong as its weakest member. Vain elders sometimes demand near fealty from the Cainites below them, and young Cainites rankle within the hierarchy of a sect that claims to revile such things. The Sabbat may well be its own greatest enemy as many of the battles take place in the cold hearts and devious minds of the sect's members.

The Regent

The regent of the Sabbat supposedly coordinates the master plan of the sect, much like a mortal dictator or corporate president. Supported by a consistory of other powerful vampires, the regent holds little sway over the sect as a whole, however. Young Sabbat often make a big show of rejecting this hypocritical figure of authority as elder Sabbat flout her rule for their own personal gain. In the end, the regent may demand service, fealty and respect, but she had best be able to back it up as the Sabbat has no lack of wide-eyed megalomaniacs who would not hesitate to usurp the position for themselves.

The Cardinals

Cardinals have the responsibility of handling sect interests over large geographical regions. Archbishops report directly to them and are, according to the hierarchy, responsible to them. Also, cardinals coordinate the Sabbat in their own cities — a city in which a cardinal makes his haven sometimes does not have an archbishop or bishop.

The Prisci

As advisors, sages and chamberlains to the Sabbat, the prisci make up the majority of the consistory, the "cabinet" that assists the regent in matters of war and policy. The title carries no temporal power; these Sabbat are not enforcers or warlords. Rather, the prisci offer their unique insight to other members of the sect, particularly the regent, cardinals and archbishops.

The Archbishops

Archbishops handle the administration of Cainite affairs in individual cities, often by wielding this title as preeminent in the city. Most often appointed by cardinals, archbishops bear the responsibility for all vampires underneath them, and they must see to the support of the city in the Sabbat's best interests. Of course, the Sabbat's best interests are not necessarily the best interests of the mortals of a given city — indeed, they're often quite at odds. Thus, the archbishop's position is one of balance: He must keep the city hospitable to the Sabbat and yet prevent it from becoming a wasteland by allowing the local Cainites to abuse it at their whim.

The Bishops

Not every Sabbat city has an archbishop to oversee the Cainite concern. Those that don't typically host a council of three to five bishops, depending on the city's size. Like the archbishops, bishops maintain Sabbat influence in their cities. Likewise, they lead the spiritual growth of the vampires therein.

The Ducti

As leaders of individual packs, the ducti attend to the operational matters of their packmates. The title of ductus is a loose distinction, recognizing the most accomplished member of a pack. They work closely with pack priests to coordinate attacks, grow sect and pack influence and act as liaisons to the bishops and archbishops.

The Priests

Priests are charged with the spiritual growth of their packmates. Many priests hail from Clan Tzimisce, but anyone of any clan may become a priest with the proper instruction. As the ductus' second-in-command, the pack priest conducts all of the pack's *ritae* and sometimes creates a few that are unique to it. All packs have a priest; some rare large packs even have two. Should the ductus be eliminated, the priest becomes the pack leader *pro tem*, until a bishop or archbishop (or in some cases, the pack itself) appoints a new leader.

The Templars

Sometimes known as paladins, the templars are bodyguards appointed by a bishop or greater Sabbat. Although they have no formal organization, gaining the title of templar is a great honor for a Cainite. It conveys the obvious favor of a sect leader, makes the individual a symbol of strength in the Sabbat and endorses her fighting skills.

True Sabbat

As the most populous group of Sabbat, the True Sabbat are members of the sect who have proven themselves to their sires, packs or superiors and earned the privilege of continued existence and service to the sect. Once a Cainite has received her Creation Rite, she is considered True Sabbat.

The Clans and the Antitribu

While the Sabbat may have fewer members than its rival sect, the Camarilla, those Cainites hail from a greater variety of clans. In nights past, Clans Lasombra and Tzimisce made up the majority of the sect. In the modern nights, though, mass Embraces and new groups joining the sect have skewed those numbers a bit. While the Lasombra and Tzimisce still maintain some numerical superiority, the *antitribu* or "anti-clans" have certainly come into their own.

These *antitribu* have turned away from the clans into which they were originally Embraced. Most have no love for their parent clans — the *antitribu* went their own way, and few harbor any illusions of future reconciliation, particularly with Gehenna imminent. In most cases, the reasons for the clan schisms have been lost to centuries of ill will, and few Cainites bear such resentment as do the *antitribu* for their progenitors.

More information on them appears in Chapter Two (with the exception of the Tzimisce and Lasombra, who are covered in **Laws of the Night**).

Factions of the Sabbat

The Sabbat is hardly a unified entity, as its history, cosmopolitan makeup and penchant for personal freedom illustrates. The sect is home to numerous splinter groups who have united under the Sabbat's banner to achieve their own ends (which sometimes correspond with those of the sect) or to direct the greater body of the sect. In the chaos of the Sabbat, it is not unlikely to find members of these factions among the packs, though by no means does every member of the Sabbat support a faction — most simply support the Sword of Caine itself. Nonetheless, these factions claim a great number of members, and some have become integral to the existence of the Sabbat itself.

The Black Hand

The Black Hand is best described as a sect within a sect; a unique group of vampires distinct from all other Sabbat. The Black Hand (also known simply as the Hand or, less frequently, the *manus nigrum*) is not a wholly independent sect, however, as all Hand members are also loyal members of the Sabbat. The Black Hand consists of vampires of many different clans, but it draws most of its membership from the Assamite and Gangrel *antitribu*. It also includes many militant vampires, for whom clan is often a tertiary concern at best, as they pursue the Sabbat's ideal of freedom.

Conceived as a special militia, the Black Hand is, at its simplest, a military force at the disposal of Sabbat leaders. Like a true army, the Hand specializes in numerous aspects of warfare, from intrigue and intelligence to assassination to outright physical combat. The Black Hand seldom remains active for any long period of time, instead sending small, focused units or packs to attend to the issue at hand. Indeed, very few vampires can even remember a time when the whole of the Hand acted simultaneously at all. Sabbat elders seem to prefer this arrangement, and some secretly fear that this sect-within-a-sect would attempt a coup if kept active for too long. Throughout its history, however, the Black Hand has always served the Sabbat with unwavering loyalty. Many Sabbat credit the Black Hand with the cohesion of the sect through difficult times. Indeed, the Black Hand remained solvent during two Sabbat civil wars, enabling the sect to maintain influence in cities that would have otherwise fallen to the Camarilla.

Members of the Black Hand bear a distinguishing mark — the faction brands its members with a permanent, mystical sigil on the palms of their right hands. Once the vampire receives this mark, she has become a true member of the Black Hand and must heed the group's call whenever she receives it. Although members may conceal the brand (which spies for the group often do to keep from revealing themselves), they may never remove it. Membership in the Black Hand lasts until the vampire meets her Final Death.

The Sabbat Inquisition

Taking its cue from the mortal Spanish Inquisition, the Sabbat Inquisition is a political faction charged with rooting out heretics and infernalists. Of course, the faction resembles the mortal Inquisition in other ways as well: If it labels someone an infernalist, the accusation is unlikely to be denied, and the faction makes a practice of using similarly torturous tactics. As it possesses the power to depose bishops, archbishops, pack priests and ducti, the Sabbat Inquisition is a political entity as well. It stands on the cusp of becoming a political tool, but has yet to do so, largely because its members are devout in their duties and respond poorly to attempts at manipulation.

The Sabbat Inquisition has recently doubled in size, from 15 to 30 members, largely owing to its success. All members of the Inquisition are respected and trusted (and powerful...) members of the Sabbat. Cells of Inquisitors travel to all Sabbat-held territories, presiding over trials and delivering punishments against accused Sabbat. Despite its success in exposing infernalists, however, the Inquisition has acquired a reputation for cruelty, no mean feat among those who willingly label themselves monsters.

The Inquisition has unprecedented power, able to move and accuse as it will. Nomadic Inquisitors usually travel in groups of five, accompanied by a pair of templars. Although their success leaves the Sabbat better for its interference, the Inquisition has made few friends. Many bishops and archbishops resent the Inquisition's presence, as the Inquisitors tend to disrupt the usual affairs of the sect and dig up dirt on *all* Cainites in a given city. Rumors claiming antagonism between the Black Hand and the Inquisition rise and circulate with alarming frequency. The Sabbat expressly forbids members of one faction from joining the other, and some suspect this rivalry has resulted from the Inquisition's recent successes coupled with growing complaints of the Hand's impotence.

The Loyalists

The Loyalist faction claims that it is the legacy of the "true" Sabbat, those vampires who shook off the yoke of their elders and seized their freedom for themselves. Other Sabbat tend to dismiss Loyalists as anarchists, sociopaths and spoiled childer who want the benefits of the Curse of Caine without the responsibilities.

The Loyalists' philosophy is simple: Each vampire is her own master. The freedom to do as one wills belongs to each vampire, whether she wants to destroy the Antediluvians or go on a rampage through a suburban mall. In practice, few Loyalists stoop to such recklessness as they know local law enforcement would hunt them down, most likely at the behest of other vampires who actually value their secrecy.

The night no longer belongs to the Sabbat, Loyalists contend. Sect is irrelevant given the modern state of affairs; Sabbat packs are as powerless as Camarilla neonates or rabid anarchs because of the apathy and antagonism of their elders. As the original anarchs and *antitribu* did in the nights of the Anarch Revolt, Loyalists do what they do because they believe they must. Loyalists accept anyone into their ranks, and they have no codes or secret rituals to identify themselves to one another.

Lesser Factions

Smaller in power and number, lesser factions exist among the Sabbat to help the sect and themselves. These lesser factions come and go, springing up almost overnight and then falling out of favor or being wiped out in some grandiose but doomed war effort. Some of the longer-standing intra-Sabbat factions include the following.

The Status Quo

As their name suggests, things are good enough for the Status Quo. Made up primarily of Lasombra, Tzimisce and key members of the Black Hand, the Status Quo accepts the nature of vampires and knows that change is relatively impossible. The Great Jyhad continues, for better or worse, and shaking the foundations of the Sabbat serves only to distract it from its greater goal. The Status Quo does not want to increase the authoritarianism of the sect — its members aren't after hoarding power for themselves because it promotes rebellion in the lower ranks. At the same time, increasingly unreasonable demands from overly vociferous Loyalists and concerned Moderates serve only to agitate other members of the sect, and a compromise must be struck.

Moderates

The Moderates oppose what they see as increasing rigidity intruding into the sect. Edicts such as the Purchase Pact and the revised Code of Milan limit the rights of individual Sabbat for the good of a few. While not as vehement as the Loyalists, Moderates nonetheless oppose the encroachment of "rules and guidelines" that have no place among such creatures as vampires. The faction rests between Loyalist dogma and Status Quo conservatism, acknowledging the need for order and structure, but not adherence to arbitrary codes that offer no benefit to offset their inconvenience. Moderates generally oppose sieges and crusades (though they usually follow orders), and they do not hesitate to question those in charge if an order seems foolish or reckless.

Ultra-Conservatives

Predictably composed of the eldest members of the Sabbat, most of whom belong to Clans Lasombra and Tzimisce, the Ultra-Conservatives favor centralization and authoritarianism, hoping to turn the Sabbat into a military force against the Antediluvians and the Camarilla. The time for freedom is over, claim the Ultra-Conservatives. Gehenna looms around the corner, and it's time to stabilize the Sabbat, lest it fail utterly. Ultra-Conservatives favor strong leaders and Monomacy, ritually removing weak leaders through duels. The Black Hand seems to be slowly leaning toward support of the Ultra-Conservatives, but it remains characteristically quiet when confronted with the issue.

Old World Tzimisce

Not every Tzimisce supports the Sabbat wholeheartedly. Indeed, when it comes to the arcane Tzimisce of the Old World, few support it at all. Of course, aligning oneself against the Sabbat is a good way to end up facing down a pack of self-important rabble who want to strike at the elders for the good of the Sabbat and all that rubbish, so it's often easier to join the society yet abstain from its meetings. Most keep to themselves, maintaining castles on ancestral lands like *voivodes* of old.

The Order of St. Blaise

In Europe during the 14th century, the Church established an auxiliary of 14 saints to protect the plagued masses. One of the 14, St. Blaise, was known for his ability to heal throat maladies. It became wide practice during this time that devotees would have their throats blessed by a pair of crossed candles on February third. Cainites active in the Church found it particularly ironic that those same blessed throats would provide a sacred meal for vampires. Vampires of the Order of St. Blaise lead dangerous unlives, integrating themselves into the hierarchy of the Roman Catholic Church. Through careful manipulation of Church resources and "good works" done at the community level, members of the order influence aspects of their cities in ways most Sabbat traditionally neglect. By establishing herds in soup kitchens and exempting certain buildings from tax status, the Order of St. Blaise expands the Sabbat's power locally. Indeed, most Sabbat cities, rife with murder, rape and skyrocketing crime rates, see an increase in Church attendance, brought about by desperate mortals' attempts to find any salvation they can in the World of Darkness.

Children of the Dracon

A bizarre knightly order of Tzimisce vampires, the Children of the Dracon seem to bear more Hellenic features than the Slavic heritage of Clan Tzimisce suggests. The Children seem to be a cultural division, almost a bloodline, but the distinction is more artificial than a true deviation in the vitae. The exact agenda of the Children of the Dracon is unknown, but they seem to be at intellectual odds with the rest of the Tzimisce. Perhaps this is due to some past transgression, or perhaps it lies in the difference of mortal stock from which the

vampires were originally drawn. Whatever the case, the Children of the Dracon do not antagonize the other Tzimisce so much as they take a consistent role of Devil's Advocate. If the Tzimisce favor a siege, the Children posit the values of holding back; if the Fiends support the Inquisition, the Children argue against giving any faction too much power. Although this seems arbitrary, the Children seem to see themselves as the warders of their brothers. Apparently, sometime in the mists of history, a Tzimisce made a decision that affected the entirety of his clan (perhaps resulting in the clan's odd weakness). The Children of the Dracon have sworn to make the Tzimisce consider the full gravity of their actions… or perhaps atone for them.

Infernalists

Infernalists — devil-worshippers, Satanists, followers of the Path of Evil Revelations — are not truly a faction within the Sabbat. Rather, they are a sickness that plagues it. Infernalists have no formal structure as they rarely associate with one another. The business of trafficking with demons is downright medieval — the infernalist is a lone conjurer, dealing with devils for his own forbidden knowledge. The practice of infernalism runs contrary to everything the Sabbat believes in. While most infernalists see themselves as taking a shortcut to power, the truth is that they are selling themselves into demonic servitude. To the Sabbat, such servitude is completely counter to the ideas of freedom to which the sect swears. The Inquisition's leading purpose is the tracking of these creatures, and woe to the fool whose infernal master deserts him as his foes close in.

The Pack

Vampires are by and large solitary creatures at heart. Sabbat do not practice solitude — the nights are too dangerous to face completely alone without trustworthy comrades. For them, the pack becomes a strange mix of gang, family and platoon unit.

Packs are typically organized with a single ductus to lead the group's nightly activities, a priest to tend to spiritual needs and three to seven members. A pack's purposes may vary, from spying to computer hacking to breaking the Masquerade in Camarilla cities to frontline fighting in the Jyhad. The Sabbat may create some packs for such specific purposes of hunting relics or bringing down Lupines.

For a Sabbat vampire, the pack is *everything*. It is a surrogate family, bound together through ties of blood and reinforced through the Vaulderie. When all hell's breaking loose, your pack will be always at your back. This isn't to say that such families aren't dysfunctional — some packs' dysfunction could fuel talk shows for years — but there is some degree of mutual sympathy that runs through the dynamic, or they would have no reason to stay together.

There are two types of packs — nomadic and established. Nomadic packs are just that — often roaming the countryside in campers, on motorcycles, or stealing their transportation when the mood strikes them. Many are on scouting missions while others just prefer the freedom of wandering. Founded packs, on the other hand, choose a specific city to maintain a haven in, often serving the local bishop and keeping the mortals in line. Whatever they do,

packs usually set up a communal haven (usually outfitted with a fantastic array of traps and escape routes), which has living quarters for each pack member and communal rooms for running rituals or storing weapons.

The Creation Rites

Most Kindred only see the "shovelhead" method of the Creation Rites, where a new vampire is thwacked on the back of the head with a shovel, buried in a grave and then must dig her way out. Packs only use such means during times of Jyhad, when speed is of the essence and the childer are useful as cannon fodder. Away from crusades, the Sabbat take as much care in selecting their childer and giving the Embrace as any other vampire. However, such new vampires must prove themselves before becoming True Sabbat. Without the Creation Rites, the new vampire is not a vampire in the eyes of the Sabbat: Her pack may feed from her or order her into battle, and she is generally at their mercy.

Rites vary, but a priest always presides (or a higher authority if the initiate is an elder's childe). The sire determines what form the rites should take, for it is he who decides if the childe should even receive the rite. Among Brujah *antitribu* or other violent groups, the rites may be similar to gang-style initiations. The Kiasyd may turn the childe loose in a strange library and order her to find a new piece of lore for her sire. A Toreador *antitribu*'s rites could be a masterfully executed flaying or blood-sculpture while a Malkavian *antitribu* requires the initiate to cast an augury from the entrails of a still-living woman. Failure almost guarantees destruction — the childe has embarrassed the sire, who is unlikely to want a reminder of such, but success means the vampire becomes a True Sabbat, another monster unleashed upon the night.

A Sabbat Lexicon

The vampires of the Sabbat have evolved their own specialized patois, much of which takes into account their holy war on the Antediluvians and the attendant rituals and practices that follow it. Particularly old Sabbat vampires even recall terms and phrases that have long since passed into history. Although many of these terms are in common use among Sabbat vampires, some of them take on different meanings colloquially, given the lack of formal communication among sect members. Vampires who would "talk the talk" are advised to be aware of everything they say and what it means.

Abbot — A vampire or ghoul charged with the maintenance of a pack's communal haven.

Antitribu — Literally, "anti-tribe" or "anti-clan." The *antitribu* are vampires who have turned their backs on their "parent" clans and now espouse the policies of the Sabbat instead. One notable exception to this rule is the Lasombra *antitribu*, who have abandoned the Sabbat in favor of independent or Camarilla unlives. Parent clans hold their *antitribu* in low regard, especially the Lasombra.

Archbishop — A vampire who serves as the leader of a city under the Sabbat's influence. Not every Sabbat-held city claims an archbishop; some have councils of bishops.

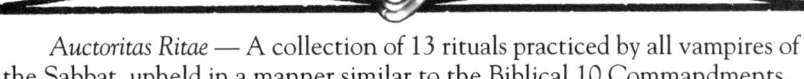

Auctoritas Ritae — A collection of 13 rituals practiced by all vampires of the Sabbat, upheld in a manner similar to the Biblical 10 Commandments.

Bishop — A vampire who serves or advises an archbishop, or a vampire who maintains Sabbat influence in a city with the aid of others of equal status. Those who are in the know liken bishops to the primogen of the Camarilla.

Black Hand — The secret militia of the Sabbat. Some references allude to another organization with the same name. The "true" meaning of this term, if there is one, is a matter of much uncertainty, even among those who claim to be members.

Blood Feast — A victim or group of victims, bound and suspended upside down. Said victims serve as refreshment at Sabbat functions.

Brave — A vampire participating in a war party.

Cainite — A vampire. Sabbat vampires use this term in places where other vampires would use the term *Kindred*. Sabbat vampires accept and claim descent from Caine, while the Camarilla largely claims him to be a myth.

Cardinal — A Sabbat vampire who oversees the influential affairs of a large territory. A group of archbishops, who govern the affairs of local cities, attends each cardinal.

Chief — The leader of a war party.

Code of Milan — An oft-referenced but rarely seen document developed as a code of conduct for Sabbat vampires. Some Sabbat scoff at it, claiming that codifying the sect's behavior runs counter to everything the Sabbat stands for.

Column — A permanent pack of Black Hand members, usually nomadic.

Communal Haven — A single haven shared by an entire pack.

Consistory — The body of advisors to the regent, composed of key prisci and cardinals.

Convention of Thorns — The treaty that supposedly ended the Anarch Revolt and resulted in the formation of the Sabbat.

Coven — A pack of Sabbat that makes a permanent haven in a city; used to differentiate between founded packs and nomadic packs. Most Sabbat cities host numerous covens in addition to providing "hospitality" to a seemingly endless stream of nomadic packs.

Creation Rites — The special ritual marking a Sabbat vampire as becoming a true member of the sect. The Creation Rites differ from the Embrace in that anyone can be Embraced, but until he receives the Creation Rites, the recruit is not a member of the Sabbat (and thus, not considered a vampire…).

Daughters and Sons (of Caine) — All vampires. A similar term with the same meaning is "brothers and sisters."

Ductus — The leader of a Sabbat pack. This title is a highly subjective one, sometimes held by the meanest thug in a pack, sometimes acquired through ritual combat or genuine merit. The ductus decides the logistical affairs of her pack, though the wise ductus gives careful ear to her packmates' voices.

Esbat — A weekly meeting held by a pack, whether nomadic or founded. Central to the esbats are the *auctoritas* and *ignoblis ritae* as well as discussions of events that affect the pack.

Festivo dello Estinto — The "Festival of the Dead," a grand celebration held during the second week of April in Sabbat cities. All covens attend the festival, as do any nomadic packs that can make it.

Fire Dance — A ritual and rough celebration in which Sabbat vampires prove their loyalty and bravery by jumping through raging fires. Many Sabbat war efforts and other events begin with fire dances.

Founded Pack — A coven; a pack of Sabbat vampires that maintains a permanent haven in a city.

Great Jyhad — The war for supremacy in the New World, begun in the 17th century and arguably raging during the modern nights.

Hand — The Black Hand.

Headhunter — A Sabbat vampire who collects the skulls of his fallen foes as trophies. Some headhunters collect only vampire skulls while others collect Lupine skulls, mortals' skulls or the skulls of witch-hunters. Sabbat consider these trophies great honors, according to the degree of difficulty associated with claiming them.

Horseman — A nomadic Sabbat vampire, thought to have been inspired by the Four Horsemen of the Apocalypse.

Hulul — The figurehead of the Assamite *antitribu*, rumored to be ritually destroyed every 100 years.

Ignoblis Ritae — The rituals practiced by individual Sabbat packs to reinforce unity, loyalty and the causes of the Sabbat. These rituals vary from pack to pack, and the Sabbat considers them less important individually than the *auctoritas ritae* because they are not universally practiced. Some Sabbat members observe no *ignoblis ritae* at all.

Jyhad — The eternal conflict with other vampire sects. Sabbat use this term more loosely than other vampires because almost all struggle is a holy war from the Sabbat point of view. In her mind, a Sabbat takes part in the Jyhad any time she fights.

Kindred — Non-Sabbat vampires. Most Sabbat use this term derisively, considering Camarilla vampires to be their inferior and laughing at their "big, happy family" of vampires who cower from humankind. Many Sabbat also apply the term "Kindred" sarcastically to vampires of independent clans, whom they perceive as too selfish or foolish to take up the cause against the Antediluvians.

Loyalist — A Sabbat vampire who refuses to acknowledge leaders among the sect out of loyalty to its original goals. Loyalists believe that to be truly loyal to the Sabbat, they must have total freedom. Most Sabbat view Loyalists as agitators and dissidents, and their packmates and the elders watch them warily. Much of the Sabbat's terrifying reputation among other vampires may stem from the actions of particularly fervent Loyalists.

Monomacy — A ritual duel between vampires of the Sabbat, held under formal rules. This duel is a traditional Sabbat means of settling disputes, and it often results in the Final Death of one of the participants.

Nomadic Pack — A pack that travels constantly in its duties to the Sabbat. Nomadic packs maintain no permanent havens, but they sometimes keep bolt-holes and emergency havens throughout the regions they travel. Nomadic packs may also stop in cities for indeterminate periods of time, but they eventually return to the roads.

Nomads — Members of nomadic packs.

Pack — A group of Sabbat who have sworn the Vaulderie to one another. A Sabbat may belong to only one pack at a time — usually the one that enacted her Creation Rites — though she may have ties of blood to other packs from her past.

Paladin — A Sabbat vampire who serves another important vampire as an assassin or bodyguard. Also known as templars, most Sabbat fear paladins for their disciplined martial prowess. The sect forbids paladins to hold membership in the Black Hand.

Palla Grande — A grand and terrible festival held on All Hallows Eve, when all Sabbat vampires in a city gather to celebrate and revere the sect. It often takes the appearance of a masquerade ball, and the sect sometimes invites humans as guests — or refreshments.

Paths of Enlightenment — The belief systems followed by the majority of the members of the Sabbat in place of Humanity. Paths of Enlightenment are moral codes that serve to anchor the Sabbat vampire against her ravening Beast, though some paths encourage "riding" the Beast rather than controlling it. The most common paths practiced by the Sabbat include the Path of Caine, the Path of Cathari, the Path of Death and the Soul, the Path of the Feral Heart, the Path of Honorable Accord, the Path of Lilith and the Path of Power and the Inner Voice. Some Sabbat follow the Path of Evil Revelations, though these vampires are hunted by the Sabbat Inquisition as heretics and traitors to the sect.

Priest — The leader of Sabbat *ritae* in a given pack. The spiritual leader of a pack, the priest is (theoretically) below the ductus in "rank," though this is not true of every pack.

Prior — An abbot (*vide*).

Priscus — A Sabbat vampire, often quite advanced in age and/or generation, who advises the regent and cardinals. Plural *prisci*.

Recruit — A vampire Embraced against her will, usually in the interests of providing cannon fodder for the sect's conquests.

Regent — The "leader" of the Sabbat, insofar as the sect recognizes one. Only one regent exists at a time.

Sabbat — 1. The vampiric sect that opposes the Camarilla and the machinations of the Antediluvians.

2. A vampire belonging to the sect. Usage: *You'll never meet a tougher Sabbat than Kassius.*

3. A group of vampires belonging to the sect. Usage: *That last festival was a nightmare! We must have had 30 or 40 Sabbat all running around like their bishops told them to go berserk.*

True Sabbat — A Sabbat who has proven himself to the sect and has received the Creation Rites.

Vaulderie — A mingling of the blood of all vampires in a pack, which is then consecrated by the pack priest and consumed by all members of the pack.

Vinculum — A "blood tie" that creates an artificial loyalty to another member of one's pack, like a minor blood bond. Vinculi result from partaking in the Vaulderie.

Vulgar Argot

The Sabbat is a violent, hostile, youthful sect, and the young ones' language reflects as much. Hereafter are some of the (more printable) terms Sabbat vampires casually drop. Many of these terms have roots in modern slang, but with an added meaning for vampires. Some even transcend the boundaries of sect and may be used anywhere.

Bat — An elder vampire of the Sabbat, who often has little in common with younger members of the sect.

Bitch — A probationary pack member or a Sabbat of lesser status than the speaker.

Chica — A female Sabbat vampire.

Costello — Dismissive term for the Camarilla. Some suspect this term to have arisen after a mispronunciation of "Sabbat."

Counting Coup — Taking the head of a fallen foe as a trophy (see *Headhunter*). This practice is sometimes called "scalping."

Crowley — A derogatory or dismissive term for followers of the Path of Evil Revelations, or vampires who make ostentatious shows of evil for its own sake. These individuals are also known as *Ozzys* or *Mansons* by some packs.

Did — Killed. Usage: *On that last ride through Dallas, we did everyone — the highway patrolman, that van full of campers and even a Lupine. It was a mess.*

Dog — A Lupine. In certain circles, dog also means an infectious carrier of blood-borne diseases (short for plague dog).

Go Down — A vampire who, usually out of habit, perversity or derangement, commits sexual acts regardless of his own vampiric impotence. Also known by a host of other charming epithets including *dick, handjob, hummer,* etc., usually custom-tailored to the specifics of the vampire in question's behavior.

Headache — Accidentally killing while feeding. Usage: *It was hilarious — Melissa gave the bishop's favorite vessel a headache, and now she's feeding and watering his horses upstate.*

Injun or Indian — A member of a nomadic pack.

Juice — Blood.

Keg — A "member" of a Blood Feast. Some packs refer to these individuals as *pints* or *longnecks*.

Pimp — A vampire charged with gathering vices for packmates. The pimp may procure drugs, alcohol, prostitutes, children or any other indulgences for fellow vampires (or mortals…).

Pipes — An exceptional failure or an object of derision. Usage: *Gavin loves the blood-tattoos Maris did for him, but I think they're the pipes.*

Poet — A member of the Goth subculture, especially one who "dresses like a vampire." Also known as *Shelleys* or *Byrons*.

Shovelhead — A Sabbat vampire created during a siege or other event that necessitated the "quick and dirty" mass Embrace. Also known as a *Thwack* or a *Clang* (after the sound a shovel to the head makes, presumably). The latter are sometimes used as verbs.

Tongue — Sabbat propaganda or Sabbat proselytizer, often spread among the anarchs of Camarilla cities.

V — A vampire.

Vato — A male Sabbat vampire.

Witch — Irreverent term for a pack priest, best used out of earshot of the individual in question.

OLD FORM

Despite its war on the elders, the Sabbat claims some members who are quite advanced in age themselves. These vampires recall the nights when the Sabbat was born and have carried over or adopted phrases as old as they are. Beware the vampire who speaks in the tongue of the Sabbat elders, for she is surely formidable and wicked beyond belief.

Angellis Ater — The "black angels" of Clan Lasombra, often young vampires who embrace the stereotypical and shallow evils of the modern night in blatant attempts to become monsters.

Kamut — A nomadic pack of Sabbat formed for a specific purpose, such as hunting Lupines, scouting Camarilla cities or exposing heretics.

Lacheur — A young Sabbat, particularly an insolent one. May be used to refer to any young vampire in some cases.

Manus Nigrum — A mysterious subsect of the Sabbat, or one entirely independent about which very little is known. Younger vampires refer to this group, apparently erroneously, as the Black Hand.

Revenants — Individuals who are born as ghouls. Revenants are families of ghouls that have existed for so long with the blood of their undead masters in their veins that it now passes on to each of their descendants as well. The vampires of Clan Tzimisce seem to use revenants most often, and they are often held in suspicion by others who know of their natures.

Shakari — The eldest vampires among the Assamite *antitribu*.

Sword of Caine — The Sabbat.

Voivode — The leader of Clan Tzimisce. Some vampires postulate that there is no single *voivode*, and the title is one of inscrutable significance to only the Fiends themselves.

Chapter Two: Caine's Own

The Sabbat is a very diverse sect, with representatives from almost every major clan within its ranks. Although most Sabbat hail from the ranks of Clans Lasombra and Tzimisce (see **Laws of the Night**), as many as half come from the ranks of the antitribu or "anti-clans" that have turned their backs upon their progenitors. Additionally, a few strange bloodlines have arisen in the sect, with no connection to outside clans or bloodlines. In this way, the sect prepares itself for the coming Gehenna and the continual Great Jyhad of the Antediluvians by arming themselves with soldiers of many capabilities.

Assamite Antitribu

Since the Sabbat's formation, the Assamite *antitribu* have played an important role in the sect and have become some of the most feared warriors of the Sword of Caine. Assamite *antitribu* typically place more emphasis on following the ideals of their clan than on upholding the sect's purposes, though many of their beliefs coincide. The Angels of Caine seek to bring themselves closer to Caine, whom mainstream Assamites regard as a cursed and corrupt infidel. For some reason, the two clans seem to have guarded respect for each other, for which no one outside can give a plausible reason. Assamite *antitribu* claim superiority over their independent brethren, whom they despise for accepting the Camarilla's punishment during the Treaty of Thorns. Even though the curse has since been broken, feelings on the matter have not changed.

Like their brethren, Sabbat Assamites excel at assassination and stealth. Assamite *antitribu* make up a potent martial force for the sect, which would lose a good deal of discipline and focus without them. Many attain significant status in the sect and rise to prominence as templars, pack leaders and members of the deadly Black Hand. Assamite *antitribu* rarely assume the responsibilities of pack priests, though many ducti hail from the clan, especially if combat or assassination is their pack's purpose. Some Assamite *antitribu* form single-clan packs, but may also be found in more cosmopolitan groups.

Although ardent supporters of the Sabbat and not as fanatical about their beliefs as the independent Assamites, the Angels of Caine are often insular and dismissive of those from other clans. The legacy of the Sabbat Assamites is one of bloodshed and ritual, and those Cainites not of the clan who observe their rites rarely walk away without a shudder, if at all. Every 100 years, they destroy one of their own prominent members, the *hulul*, as a gesture of favor to their dark father, and many of their practices are similarly grim in nature.

Roleplaying Hints: You are a sword in the war of vengeance waged against the "Kindred," their masters and anyone foolish enough to get in the way. You are not a mindless killer, though — wanton murder has no place in the war of the righteous. You rarely attempt to "convert" others; forcing your principles upon those who do not wish to accept them is vain and futile. Caine will recognize his own when he returns.

Disciplines: *Celerity, Obfuscate, Quietus*

Advantage: Members of this clan of death-bringers have a legacy of success. Most Sabbat Cainites respect these vampires based on the simple fact that the Assamite *antitribu* chose to Embrace them: Only the most potent mortals receive such. All Assamite *antitribu* gain the Sabbat Status of *Feared*.

Additionally, like members of their parent clan, Sabbat Assamites often train in the ways of violence even before receiving the Curse of Caine. Assamite *antitribu* gain either one *Melee* Ability *or* one *Brawl* Ability at no additional cost during character creation.

Weakness: The Sabbat Assamites have the same weakness as their progenitor clan — indeed, they never lost it, for they never succumbed to the Tremere's curse. Members of this clan frequently become addicted to the blood of other vampires. When a Sabbat Assamite tastes vampiric vitae, she must make a *Self-Control/Instinct* Test with a four-Trait difficulty. If she fails, the taste is not enough, and she takes as much blood as she can, maybe even draining the vessel. Even if the Cainite succeeds in the test, the hunger should be roleplayed to the best of the player's ability.

BLOOD BROTHERS

Created through vile Tzimisce and Tremere magic in the castles and chantries of the Old World, the Blood Brothers are an artificial "bloodline" of soldiers and servants. Extensive experimentation in blood bonding resulted in a brutal collective of vampires linked by communal thought. Although the bloodline is known as the Blood *Brothers*, a few rumors circulate concerning female members, but without evidence the talk remains just that.

Blood Brothers are built around a hive-mind, sharing thoughts and experiences vicariously through other members of their "circles." This allows them to work effectively even at a distance. The bloodline excels at security, sabotage and coordinated attacks. The Frankensteins also practice an unpleasant Discipline that allows them to take advantage of their mental links and even extend them into physical permutations — they may share limbs or heal the wounds of other circlemates.

Blood Brothers are almost never members of packs. Rather, their packs are their immediate circles of other Blood Brothers, all of whom typically undergo Tzimisce fleshcrafting to make themselves look exactly alike (unsettling and confusing their opponents). Very few Blood Brothers have any degree of personal drive; they were created to serve unquestioningly. This has the secondary effect of removing their capacity for critical thought, making it difficult for them to outwit their enemies. This does not make the Blood Brothers stupid or dense; they just work better at simple, clearly defined tasks.

With the disappearance of the Tremere *antitribu*, Blood Brothers have become increasingly rare in the modern nights. Few Tzimisce know the complete ritual necessary to create them, and even the Fiends tend to prefer their revenants to the single-minded Frankensteins. Still, a focused circle of Blood Brothers is not a foe to be taken lightly, especially in battle.

Roleplaying Hints: Do what you are told. When you ask questions, they relate to the completion of your responsibilities, not the purpose or validity of them. Your master knows best, and your reason for existing is to aid him in achieving his greater goals.

Note: Obviously, with so little room for individual thought and characterization, the Blood Brothers do not usually make good choices for ongoing player characters. The bloodline is best used by Storytellers as a plot device or simple (but very determined…) rivals.

Disciplines: *Fortitude, Potence, Sanguinus*

Advantage: Blood Brothers are chosen for their hardiness. Due to their hale bodies and mystical origins, Blood Brothers become even tougher upon their "Embrace" (see below). During character creation, Blood Brother characters receive an additional two endurance-related Physical Traits, such as *Enduring, Resilient, Stalwart* or *Tough*.

Weakness: Blood Brother vitae is sterile. Created by mystical rituals, they are not Cainites in the literal sense of the word and they

may not Embrace mortals (though they may create ghouls). If a Blood Brother attempts to sire a childe (why would his master tell him to do this?), the mortal simply dies. Note that with the loss of the Tremere *antitribu*, few Cainites know how to create Blood Brothers, and the number of circles is shrinking.

The hive-mind and common creation ritual do have their detriments. Blood Brothers share each others' declivities as well as their strengths: Any Blood Brother's Negative Physical or Social Traits may be bid against any other member of his circle in challenges.

Brujah Antitribu

During the Anarch Revolt, many young Brujah readily took up the cause. Several clan elders denounced the anarchs after a brief dalliance with the revolutionary ideology. The Brujah anarchs saw this as another of the elders' betrayals and treacheries against the young childer of Caine and now nurse an eternal grudge against those elders who joined the Camarilla. Most Sabbat Brujah are very supportive of their sect, unlike the fractious and indolent Brujah of the Camarilla. Not only do they support the sect with enthusiasm, they have an active vision that Sabbat ideology (or propaganda, as their rivals suggest) serves to unify.

Brutes often take the roles of soldiers, enforcers and other "muscle" for the Sabbat, which suits them just fine. Sect leaders suspect that the Sabbat Brujah are likely the most numerous non-Lasombra or Tzimisce members of the sect, mainly because they take what they want when they want it — even with regard to potential childer. Many Sabbat see the Brujah *antitribu* as little more than common thugs, but the clan sees itself as adherents of the Sabbat's original philosophy — freedom.

Dismissing the Brujah *antitribu* as brutish punks has been the downfall of more than one Cainite. The Brutes have all the passion and drive of their counterparts in their parent clan, which the Sabbat focuses toward its own ends. An inspired Sabbat Brujah will go to any length for his cause, which may well be the sect's welfare. For every simple-minded bruiser in the clan, another may have been Embraced for her cunning mind, her social acumen or even for her contacts among the gangs and reform groups with whom the Brutes surround themselves. Like the Camarilla Brujah, the Brujah *antitribu* are more than leather-jacketed adolescents.

Recently, many Brujah *antitribu* have lost faith in the Lasombra and Tzimisce leaders, and they have made many of their own coups, unsanctioned crusades and victories. Many members of the clan support the Loyalist faction, and a few calm themselves long enough to contribute something of worth to the Black Hand or Inquisition or become paladins. The Brutes are, quite possibly, the future of the sect.

Roleplaying Hints: You're a vampire, dammit, so you may as well act like it! The world is yours, and no elder's puppets are going to take that from you. Talk and planning have their place, but the Final Nights are the time for action! You may be undisciplined or utterly calculating, but one thing is true in every case: Those who stand idly by never make the change that's necessary to winning the war.

Disciplines: *Celerity, Potence, Presence*

Advantage: Sabbat Brujah may be vocal firebrands, reasoned intellectuals or bare-knuckled hooligans, like their Camarilla kin, but

they tend to be less involved with the influential side of things. Instead of a bonus Influence Trait, Sabbat Brujah may take a second Ability during character creation, free of cost, to reflect the time they spend "doing things the hard way." Brujah may select two Abilities from the following group: *Politics, Academics, Brawl* and *Streetwise*, or any combination.

Weakness: Brujah *antitribu* suffer the same short tempers and blind rages of their parent clan, as their blood carries the same passion for challenge. Sabbat Brujah suffer one-Trait penalties on tests of *Self-Control/Instinct*.

Gangrel Antitribu

Like the bestial vampires of legend, the Gangrel *antitribu* display the Sabbat's animalistic side. Whether the predatory City Gangrel or the untamed Country Gangrel, Sabbat Gangrel are tireless hunters whose skill in the pursuit of prey knows no peer. Like animals, they are consummate stalkers, reveling in the thrill of the hunt and gorging themselves on the blood of their victims.

Gangrel *antitribu* have two distinct bloodlines, with two very different tastes in the modern nights. The Country Gangrel still somewhat resemble their parent clan, shunning society and prowling the nights alone. They conjure images of the vampires of legend, assuming animal forms and commanding hordes of animals. The Country Gangrel serve the Sabbat as nomadic scouts, calling upon the beasts to retrieve information and their martial prowess to shred their enemies.

Most assume their counterparts, the City Gangrel, to have diverged from their forebears during the Industrial Revolution, as cities grew larger and more autonomous from the resources of the countryside. A few of the New World Sabbat Gangrel made havens in the cities, becoming the monsters of urban legend. No less feral than their Country Gangrel siblings, City Gangrel prefer the asphalt jungle of streets and buildings to the deadly lands beyond.

Although they are disorganized, territorial and solitary, the Hunters nonetheless provide the sect with a degree of spirituality. Their close ties to their bestial sides make them ideal warriors in the Great Jyhad, for what animal wants to be consumed by another? Also, many of the New World Gangrel who joined the Sabbat had some connection to the Native American tribes indigenous to the land. These Cainites understand the primal forces of the land and may often be found as ducti or priests of nomadic packs. Indeed, the Hunters are often the backbone to most of the sect's traveling covens.

In recent nights, since the defection of the "mainstream" Gangrel from the Camarilla, the Sabbat has seen many converts to their cause from their rival sect. Although the defectors remain tight-lipped about the event that drove them away, it seems to have given them a new conviction for the Sabbat's cause.

Roleplaying Hints: Cainites are as much Beast as they are Man, and you embody this fact. Your unlife depends upon your instincts — let the Lasombra scheme and the Tzimisce indulge their perversities; they have lost touch with what it means to be a vampire. Whether you are a feral monster or a refined predator, you indulge your more primitive nature to survive.

Disciplines: *Animalism, Fortitude, Protean* (Country Gangrel); *Celerity, Obfuscate, Protean* (City Gangrel)

Advantage: As they embrace their animalistic natures, the Gangrel of the Sabbat are knowledgeable of the ways of beasts, so they gain one *Animal Ken* Ability at no extra cost during character creation.

Gangrel *antitribu* often feel the same wanderlust as their parent clan. As such, they often spend (or have spent) some period of their unlives alone and away from the comforts of permanent havens. They gain one *Survival* Ability during character creation at no extra cost.

Weakness: After frenzies, the Beast leaves a mark of its passage on the Gangrel *antitribu*. When a Gangrel experiences a frenzy, she acquires an animalistic feature and a Negative Social Trait — *Bestial, Feral* or *Repugnant* — in the aftermath. These Traits may not be removed except by exceptional means (such as powerful magic or *Vicissitude*, though they may be hidden by certain powers of *Obfuscate*). The character may gain no more than five Negative Traits in this manner. Indeed, some Sabbat Gangrel barely resemble the human stock from which they came....

Harbingers of Skulls

This enigmatic cult of necromancers has only recently joined the Sabbat, which they claim to have done solely for the purpose of vengeance. Members of the bloodline are almost all of advanced age, and many speak of returning from exile in the realms of the Underworld. As they tell the tale, a murderous band of sorcerers hunted them for their blood in nights long past, driving them to extinction to serve their own desires for power.

Other members of the sect describe the Lazarenes as aloof and guarded. Some even allude to the Harbingers as paranoid, or perhaps tainted by madness after whatever ordeal that consumed them for so long. Only a few of these Cainites are known to exist, but they have accumulated an inordinate amount of power and voice in the sect for such a short period of membership. The Black Hand, the Inquisition and the consistory all have members of the Harbingers among them.

The Harbingers of Skulls wield death-magic as effectively as any Giovanni, perhaps more so for their time in the Underworld. The sect regards the Lazarenes' Necromancy as a great benefit, allowing them a resource that the Camarilla has yet to explore. Some speculate this may be the Harbingers' sole purpose in the Sabbat — new power in exchange for favors to be collected later.

The Embrace bestows upon the Harbingers the appearance of emaciated cadavers, which they often heighten by flaying the skin from their heads (hence their name). Whether they do this as a form of self-mutilation or simply to terrify their rivals is unknown. Also, the bloodline has a formal and extensive system of ritual that relies on masks — prominent members wear ornate headdresses, while lesser members have simpler masks.

Roleplaying Hints: Revenge is a dish best served cold, and yours has chilled for centuries. The Sabbat is a tool and nothing more; its political agenda is secondary, but as long as you assist the sect, you collect favors that you can call upon as you need them. You don't care who knows this; the Cainites of the Sabbat have no illusions regarding your mercenary nature. To them you are an ally, and to you they are weapons to turn upon your hated foes.

Note: Vampires of advanced age comprise this bloodline, and they are often not a viable option for player characters. Storytellers should feel free to restrict this bloodline to Storyteller characters or elder games.

Disciplines: *Auspex, Fortitude, Necromancy*

Advantage: The Harbingers of Skulls are no strangers to the realms of politics, and are certainly not above using *Necromancy* to unearth secrets for blackmail material. During character creation and at no extra cost, a Harbinger of Skulls may take any permutation of three of the following Traits: Sabbat Status, one *Influence* or a trivial boon. For example, a player may choose for his character to possess one Sabbat Status Trait and two *Church* Influence Traits, or two Sabbat Status Traits and one trivial boon.

Weakness: As the Harbingers of Skulls resembles corpses, they are as visually unpleasant as the most twisted Nosferatu. They suffer a similar Weakness: Every Harbinger possesses the Negative Social Traits *Ghastly* x 3 whenever they reveal their true forms. These Traits may never be removed by Free Traits or Experience Traits (though they may be hidden by *Obfuscate*). They may never possess Traits relating to appearance such as *Gorgeous* or *Seductive*. Harbingers may not initiate Social Challenges, though they may defend against them normally.

NEW TRAIT: GHASTLY

The *Ghastly* Trait exists to illustrate the negative social connotations of the Lazarenes' appearance. They are not so twisted as the Nosferatu, but rather more macabre and cadaverous, so the Trait *Repugnant* doesn't apply.

Ghastly is a Negative Trait related to Appearance. The visage of *Ghastly* characters unsettles everyone around them, resulting in fearful first impressions and strained interactions thereafter. *Ghastly* characters simply look too morbid for others to interact with comfortably.

Kiasyd

An inscrutable line of fey-blooded Cainites, the Kiasyd are small in number and seem to have few active relations with the Sabbat, though the sect maintains that they are members. The Kiasyd are scholars and masters of hidden lore. They generally prefer to observe rather than taking an active role in the sect's efforts. Most Kiasyd don't like to resort to physical action against an opponent, preferring enigmas and battles of wits instead. They value their knowledge and private collections, and seem to enjoy the role of "eccentric sage" that others ascribe to them. While a Kiasyd's haven is always open to her bloodline peers, Weirdlings tend to be territorial, and most cities are haven to only one, if any. They also seem to dislike competing with each other for knowledge, which makes their small numbers even more understandable; many maintain impressive collections of scrolls, books, rituals and Cainite lore.

Regarding the Kiasyd's origins and membership in the Sabbat, many theories involve Lasombra influence. Whether the Keepers have some agreement with the Kiasyd or whether one line begot the other in nights long past is unknown. In the end, most Sabbat know of them as fell curiosities and masters of secrets that are often best left uncovered.

Kiasyd almost never join covens and adopt the lifestyle of the nomads even less frequently. They are the loremasters and keepers of secrets, tied to their havens, from which they research hoary mysteries. Every now and then, a young Kiasyd accompanies a pack on some errand or asks their protection when searching for a particular artifact, but most are loath to leave their sanctums.

The few Kiasyd that are known beyond mere shadowy reputation are elders, and the consistory may even consult with these Cainites for their counsel. To the sect's foot soldiers, however, the Weirdlings are transitory and legendary, stories exchanged over the fires of the *ritae*. Still, every now and then, one emerges from his lair to utter some cryptic warning or charge a bishop with an inscrutable quest.

Roleplaying Hints: Unlife is not something to be frivolously wasted on battle or conquest. The curse of immortality can be a blessing if it is used to unravel the mysteries of the world. Still, ruthlessness has its place, and one should not hesitate to use the powers at one's command. After all, the young Cainites are thirsty, and the blood of elders, Kiasyd or otherwise, is always on their minds. Keep them in their place with the odd bit of lore and a healthy dose of fearful respect.

Note: Because of their elder natures and sheer rarity, Kiasyd are best used as Storyteller characters.

Disciplines: *Dominate, Mytherceria, Obtenebration*

Advantage: The Kiasyd often spend their unlives in search of secrets, and much of the bloodline's concept of prestige balances upon how much a given member knows. To reflect this undying thirst for knowledge, Kiasyd gain two *Lore* Abilities of their choice during character creation at no extra cost. This often takes the form of *Kindred Lore* as it is most useful, but a few Kiasyd have uncovered the practices of the Lupines or puzzled out the riddles of the Wild Ones.

Weakness: The Weirdlings seem to have some tie to the fae — cold iron causes them pain and discomfort. Simply being in the presence of iron causes the Kiasyd to suffer a one-Trait penalty on *Self-Control/Instinct* tests. Any damage inflicted upon a Kiasyd by an iron weapon is considered aggravated.

Malkavian Antitribu

The violent, dangerous nature of the Sabbat offers no solace for the fractured minds of the Malkavians. Indeed, Sabbat Malkavians are often more deranged and psychotic than their Camarila counterparts. Still, the old maxim of method lying beneath madness often proves true for the Sabbat — the seemingly incomprehensible actions of the Malkavians confound the sect's foes, and more than one conflict has been won at the hands of a Malkavian tactician.

Still, chaos is a dangerous element, and it festers in the minds of the Malkavian *antitribu*. At varying points lucid and manic, Sabbat Malkavians are no more reliable than others of their mad line as insanity takes its toll on them. Malkavians of the Sabbat tend to have vicious edges to their insanity, and the clan claims a number of serial killers, mass murderers, cannibals and other unpleasant aberrations found less frequently elsewhere. Many have no fear of Final Death while others claim that madness is the legacy of unclouded vision and hurl themselves into the jaws of the enemy.

Like the Gangrel *antitribu*, Malkavian *antitribu* exist forever close to their Beasts, though it does not manifest in such an animalistic fashion. The Beast of a Sabbat Malkavian is a more cerebral entity, revealing itself in strange behavior, random actions and unquenchable bloodlusts. For all the good they do, they do an equal amount of ill, which the sect accepts as part of the devil's deal they have made with madness. The Malkavian *antitribu*'s greatest enemies are themselves.

The Freaks are not without their usefulness, however. By and large, the sect accepts mysticism more readily than the Camarilla. As such, the Sabbat Malkavians also occupy the roles of prophets, diviners and interpreters of omens. Those lucid enough to offer insight sometimes find themselves taking on the responsibilities of pack priests or even ducti. As the madness of their line warps each Freak in a different fashion, they have no universally accepted status in the sect — some are so rabid as to be destroyed a few nights after their Embrace, while others rocket through the hierarchy in an astonishingly short time.

Roleplaying Hints: The truth is ugly — so ugly, perhaps, that most people would rather look away than see it plainly. You suffer no such delusion, however; the truth has warped you in its own unique way, but you know its nature. Or perhaps you don't — perhaps Fate has played the ultimate trick upon you and lied to you very successfully. Still, if that's the case, who would know unless they had the strength to observe it themselves? That's what you tell yourself. That's how you abate the fever in you mind each night: Even if you're completely wrong, you're still less wrong than the ones who can't bear to learn.

Disciplines: *Auspex, Dementation, Obfuscate*

Advantage: Malkavian insanity is the price of insight, or so the clan maintains. Whether or not this is true, Sabbat Malkavians experience bursts of clarity to which other Cainites seem nigh oblivious. During character creation, Malkavian *antitribu* gain one extra *Awareness* Ability at no extra cost.

Sabbat Malkavians share the mysterious connection to the network of fractured minds known as the "madness network." Sometimes their insight is

the result of their uncommon vision, but it is also the product of the whispered voices that travel ceaselessly through the minds of all Malkavians.

Weakness: Afflicted by the curse of insanity, every Malkavian *antitribu* suffers from some form of derangement, which the player chooses during character creation. This derangement may never be removed or permanently cured, though Willpower Traits may temporarily overcome it.

Additionally, the Sabbat breeds unrest and lessens a Malkavian *antitribu*'s control over the Beast (whether through lack of discipline or too much indulgence in monstrousness). A Sabbat Malkavian may not spend a Willpower Trait to control herself during a frenzy — she must ride it through to the end.

Nosferatu Antitribu

Elders of the sect suspect that the Nosferatu *antitribu* joined the Sabbat less out of hatred for their sires than out of something lurking beneath the clan's own veil of secrecy. Nosferatu of the Sabbat seem to be on the best terms with their Camarilla counterparts of all the clans of the Sword of Caine, but why? As expected, the Nosferatu and their *antitribu* close ranks when asked about it — the problem is theirs alone.

The Nosferatu *antitribu* are as hideously deformed as their Camarilla counterparts, making their havens in the sewers under their cities, forming clutches and broods and kingdoms of filth. Some Nosferatu *antitribu* even revel in their hideousness, tormenting Cainite and kine alike with their displays of vileness. In other cases, perhaps because of their disfigurements, Sabbat Nosferatu have become arguably the most humane (but not necessarily *human*) of the *antitribu*. Because of this, some ignorant Sabbat consider the Nosferatu *antitribu* weak or apathetic to the sect — until they step into the sewers and observe the nightmare pits that comprise the Nosferatu's havens.

Like most Camarilla Nosferatu, the Nosferatu *antitribu* maintain extensive networks of information. Many Cainites turn to the Creeps because, "They know everything," or so goes the sentiment. Of course, the Nosferatu *antitribu* don't deny this, for such seems to be their lot in unlife. After all, one rises (or sinks) to meet her own fate.

Nosferatu of the Sabbat form nests of Cainites in the sewers beneath a city, again like their Camarilla counterparts. These subterranean warrens often hide varieties of vermin and other beasts associated with the clan — rats, scuttling insects, feral dogs and cats, and the like. Whether the Sabbat Nosferatu's packmates join them in these dank tunnels or deal with them on less disgusting territory, they know that the monsters who make up the Creeps are just as twisted on the inside as they are on the outside.

Roleplaying Hints: Sabbat, Camarilla, whatever. That doesn't matter too much. What's important is knowing what people need you to know because that puts them in your debt. Unlike the other clans, you *fear* your Antediluvian rather than hating it blindly because the ancient tales of your clan tell that it has loosed a horde of hunters upon you. The more people who owe you favors, the more people upon whom you can call to tell you what *they* know, the more aware you'll be when the end of the world arrives. And just maybe you'll be able to survive it.

Disciplines: *Animalism, Obfuscate, Potence*

Advantage: When one is a hideously disfigured monster, one either dies quickly or adapts to her environment. The Nosferatu *antitribu* are hale Cainites, tough and determined. Every Sabbat Nosferatu gains one free *Stealth* Ability and one free *Survival* Ability during character creation.

Weakness: The other side of wretched ugliness, and the most significant, is the toll it takes upon one's social capabilities. No Nosferatu *antitribu* may ever acquire the Traits *Gorgeous*, *Alluring* or *Seductive* unless they use magical means or a Discipline. Additionally, Nosferatu *antitribu* suffer the Negative Social Traits *Repugnant* x 3 when they show their visage, and these Traits may never be removed without some outstanding circumstance. Sabbat Nosferatu may not call for a Social Challenge (except intimidation), though they may defend against them normally.

Panders

Although not truly a clan (no Antediluvian is believed to have founded the bloodline), the Panders have made a place for themselves despite their inauspicious origins. Like Caitiff — which, for all practical purposes, they are — any vampire who joins the Sabbat and has no known clan becomes a Pander as do childer Panders Embrace. A broad spectrum of Cainites comprise the Panders, most of whom are young and rowdy. Haughty Cainites should beware, however; Panders are True Sabbat, not just a proving ground for embarrassing childer.

The Panders came to be recognized during the late 1950s. Impressed with the efforts of the rabble leader Joseph Pander, the elders of the Sabbat rewarded his sect-loyal followers with formal recognition, though a few members of the more "legitimate" clans harbor great resentment over this fact. Most Panders recognize their situation, though, and accept their humble role with resolve. Indeed, in any Sabbat conflict, Panders out to prove themselves generally populate the front lines. Joseph himself is still believed to stalk the modern nights, though conspiracy theories and assassination rumors abound.

Panders lack the organization and identity of the other clans; they truly are a motley crowd. Unlike many of the other clans, however, they carry the Sabbat cause close to their unbeating hearts. With the Sabbat's gesture of recognizing the Mutts, it has earned a loyal ally. In practice, though, Panders almost invariably get saddled with the worst responsibilities. Savvy Panders accept these dubious honors as tests of mettle, while the slower ones simply do what they're told because that's the way to avoid a beating.

Most Panders know that theirs is a position of convenience for the sect. They understand that the recognition they have received is just a bone that the sect leaders have thrown them. Despite these differences, however, many Panders earn their pack's respect and join the ranks of the templars or the ducti. Many Loyalists also claim Pander heritage, but this seems to come more often as a result of their low social status rather than any sincere loyalty to nebulous Cainite "freedom." Still, Panders love to adopt a cause, giving them purpose in the Final Nights.

Roleplaying Hints: This is the Sabbat: If you don't prove you're worth something, then you're not. Proving yourself can take any form — maybe you're a smooth diplomat, maybe you know all the right people, or maybe you're just really good at putting the hurt on Cainites who need it, but whatever it is, you do it well. After all, you have to — if you're no good, you're going to end up as a pile of ashes. You can't rely on the elders because they only indulge you so long as you're useful. In a vampire's world, you have to rely on yourself.

Disciplines: Any. Panders have no specific clan Disciplines, choosing and learning Disciplines as per Caitiff (see **Laws of the Night**, p. 63 and 124).

Advantage: Panders have no innate advantage.

Weakness: The benefit of having no advantage is that the Panders also have no inherent disadvantage — the blood of Caine is so polluted, weak or subverted in them that they carry none of the traditional banes or benefices of the clans. Note that few Panders ever achieve any significant degree of Sabbat Status, however. Also, because their blood is so diluted, no Pander may begin the game lower than Ninth Generation.

Ravnos Antitribu

According to the spotty oral history of the clan, a faction of Ravnos Cainites split from their Gypsy heritage after the formation of the Sabbat. Sabbat vampires didn't torment each other with complex Hindu dharma riddles or deny that the Beast was a part of them. The Sabbat became a haven for these young defectors who became the first Ravnos *antitribu*.

Over the years, the Rogues have distanced themselves from the sect, helping when it suits them and otherwise generally doing whatever they please. Many Sabbat wonder why they claim membership in the sect at all. The Ravnos *antitribu* maintain that it is for their own identity: They no longer observe the ways of their original clan and have freed themselves from their elders' games. Isn't that the purpose of the Sabbat?

Of all the Sabbat clans, the Ravnos *antitribu* are perhaps the most unlike their parent clan. Most of the other *antitribu* split along philosophical lines or as a result of elder-neonate tensions. The Sabbat Ravnos, however, grew culturally apart from their foreparents. Although still possessed of the wanderlust often exhibited in other Ravnos, the *antitribu* have Embraced far and away from the ethnic roots that unite the parent line. Few Rogues have any relationship to Middle Eastern or "Gypsy" heritage — they have no universal ethnic stock. Sabbat Ravnos Embrace whomever they believe would be a promising childe, which varies by whatever criteria the prospective sire applies. This has taken its toll on the clan — Sabbat unlife has turned its Ravnos vicious and hardy.

The nomadic opportunities afforded by the Sabbat suit the Ravnos *antitribu*. The idea of a permanent haven holds little appeal for a Sabbat Ravnos, though he is less likely to feel stultified by such than his independent counterparts. Ravnos *antitribu* also observe a traditional code of conduct for dealing with their clanmates. This code may be difficult for those outside the clan to follow, but a Ravnos' word is his law. The road is not the place to lose one's companions, especially after the cannibal rage that briefly eclipsed the clan so recently (see **Laws of the Night**, pp. 54-55).

Roleplaying Hints: You do what you want and if it helps the Sabbat, so much the better. That way, they owe you something, or at least that's how you see it. Your sire's sire may have joined the sect to escape the old clan's games, but you know the score — the Sabbat's just like any other group of Cainites, full of liars and bastards looking out for their own desires. And since you know that, you have no problems upholding those ideals yourself; after all, it's not like you're pretending you're better than anyone else.

Disciplines: *Animalism, Chimerstry, Fortitude*

Advantage: Sabbat Ravnos know the value of learning the ins and outs of the low-life. Whether they travel each night or they settle down into a comfortable haven, Ravnos *antitribu* cultivate the contacts and opportunities necessary to keeping their unlives safe. During character

creation, a Ravnos *antitribu* may take a *Contacts* Trait or *Street* Influence at no additional cost.

Also, their nomadic tendencies instill in them a keen sense for how to survive in less than ideal situations. Sabbat Ravnos also receive an additional *Survival* or *Stealth* Ability at no extra cost.

Weakness: Blood is stronger than politics and the Ravnos still suffer the same urges for vice as their parent clan. Each Ravnos *antitribu* has a passion for a "signature crime," whether theft, murder, con games or even the blood of inebriated vessels. Any time the Ravnos *antitribu* faces his vice of choice, he must indulge it unless he succeeds at a three-Trait *Self-Control/Instinct* test.

Caine's Own

SALUBRI ANTITRIBU

The Salubri *antitribu* have only recently joined the Sabbat, though they have established themselves as fervent opponents of the Camarilla, whom they blame for the destruction of their clan progenitor. Although they care little for the ideals of the Sabbat, they claim membership in the sect out of necessity rather than true support. The Sabbat is happy to take any allies it can find, and the Salubri *antitribu* know how greatly the Sabbat hates the Camarilla.

The Sabbat Salubri make proud boasts regarding their effectiveness, claiming that they have eliminated the Cainites responsible for slaying their founder. Driven by vengeance, the Salubri *antitribu* operate as furious warriors, though their own private grudges easily distract them. Most Sabbat consider them useful in times of war, but oppressively self-righteous when not in combat. To the Sabbat Salubri, this is fine — unlife is an endless torment, ending only in glorious death or bloody vengeance.

The Furies are as much a cult of personality as they are a bloodline. Unlike most other Cainite families, Sabbat Salubri have a body of propaganda that is less reflective of their members' personalities and more a result of the indoctrination most of the bloodline's sires teach their childer. The eldest of the group, Adonai, is very much a spiritual leader to the Furies, stoking their righteous frenzies as the Final Nights approach.

Most Sabbat Salubri are young and have gained very little status in the sect while others die before being able to make a name for themselves. Some few find a place among the templars or Inquisition, but their numbers are too small to see them spread very evenly across the sect's hierarchy. A few Sabbat believe that they are products of the Final Nights, while others believe them to be simple, angry young Cainites reacting against the millennial *fin de siecle*.

Roleplaying Hints: First and foremost comes the fight against the Camarilla, in which the Sabbat is nothing but a convenient ally. Whether or not you know the specifics of *why* the fight is so dire (which not every Salubri *antitribu* does), you know that the cause is justified. The bloodline is almost a cult or religion, so fiercely does it believe in its own cause and the need for atonement. This fervor serves you well, for it gives you purpose when you rise for the night.

Disciplines: *Auspex, Fortitude, Valeren*

Advantage: In studying their past, the Sabbat Salubri acquire some knowledge of the world's supernatural mysteries. During character creation, each member of the bloodline gains one free *Occult* Ability at no extra cost.

The bloodline places great emphasis on accepting one's vampiric nature. If the player chooses to have his character assume a Path of Enlightenment at character creation, he gains one Morality Trait, free of charge. This may not take a beginning character above three Morality Traits at the beginning of the game, however.

Weakness: Angry, impassioned creatures, the Salubri *antitribu* must take the blood that sustains them from fallen enemies or otherwise by force. Blood that is freely offered to them does not give them any Blood Trait benefit — they must take their sustenance in the heat of passion.

Additionally, the Salubri *antitribu* are few in number, and their spectrum of generations is not very broad. All Salubri *antitribu* must begin the game between 10th and 12th Generation.

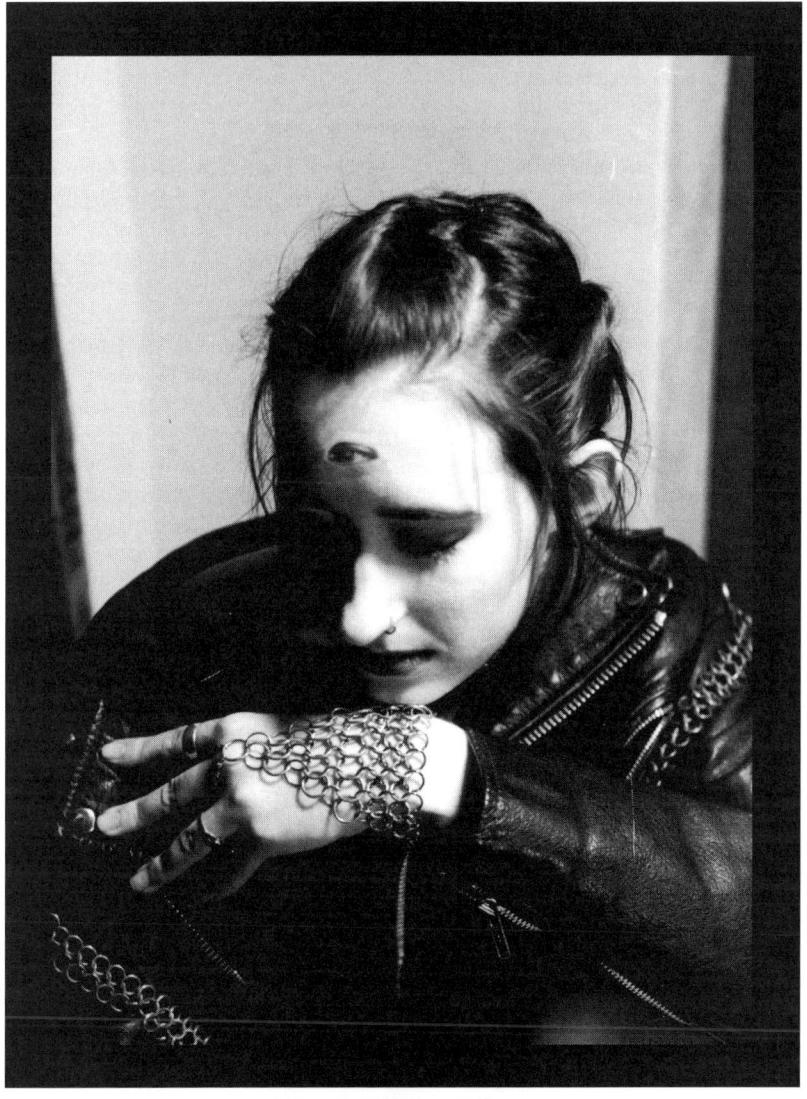

Serpents of the Light

The Serpents of the Light are a renegade cult of the Followers of Set. The Serpents bear little connection to their parent clan: While many Setites trace their lineages to Egypt, the Serpents claim they originated in the West Indies. Some Cainites propose that the first Serpents were orphaned Setites who agreed with the political ideology of the Sabbat.

The formative Serpents sought protection from their hostile forebears in the ranks of the Sabbat, and the animosity between the Serpents of the Light and the Setites grew nightly afterward until the Serpents proclaimed total independence from the Followers of Set. Most modern Serpents recognize that the Setites would have destroyed them if not for the Sabbat's support, and they pledge their undying loyalty to the sect in return.

The Followers of Set despise the Serpents, and the Serpents return the favor. Hatred between the two factions runs deep; indeed, the Setites consider the Serpents heretics. Likewise, the Serpents of the Light believe the Followers of Set to be traitors to the Cainite race for their reverence an undead vampire god. The two groups take great pains to torment each other, waging nocturnal war across the continents. Serpents of the Light oppose the other Antediluvians as well, pointing to a cultic *voudoun* prophecy similar to the Gehenna foretold in the *Book of Nod*. As such, their ideology makes them ideal Sabbat members.

While the Cobras may differ in philosophy from their parent clan, their means are very similar. Serpents of the Light remain very active in vice trade, not only to garner their own influence, but to "fight fire with fire," opposing the Setites with their own methods. Drugs, prostitution, smuggling and other staples of organized crime draw the Cobras, which they use to bring their victims under their sway. In fact, for such a small and specialized bloodline, the Serpents of the Light have significant influence over the contacts with whom they interact.

Roleplaying Hints: Manipulation by seduction is your tool of choice, after which you discern your mark's weakness — be it drugs, sex, power or whatever — and bring your victim under your influence. You generally prefer to operate under cover or away from the sight of others, extending your influence through minions and dupes without identifying yourself and drawing attention. You have a "fight fire with fire" attitude when it comes to conflict with the Setites and, when you encounter it, the Camarilla.

Disciplines: *Obfuscate, Presence, Serpentis*

Advantage: Like their parent clan, the Serpents of the Light involve themselves in the underworld and its vice markets. Of course, they do this for good reason: Their vitality depends upon it. To reflect their connections with the criminal culture and those peripheral to it, each Serpent of the Light gains one extra *Streetwise* Ability at no

additional cost during character creation. Also, the Serpent may take one Influence at no extra cost from the following list: *Political*, *Street* or *Underworld*.

Weakness: As vampires — especially those who hail from a dark god of the Egyptian underworld — Serpents of the Light are creatures of the night, despite their name. They are very sensitive to light, even from the dimmest and most artificial source. Exposure to sunlight causes them to suffer an additional health level of damage. Other sources of bright light (such as spotlights, flares, halogen street lights, etc.) inflict a one-Trait penalty for all actions undertaken in the light.

Caine's Own

Toreador Antitribu

In the early nights of the sect, the Toreador *antitribu* played an instrumental role in bringing the Sabbat together. Much of what took place after the Convention of Thorns did so with the guidance of Toreador anarchs who would later lead the sect. The nascent Toreador *antitribu* established much of the sect's structure as well as outlining many of the sect's beliefs.

The Perverts have adopted roles not too dissimilar from the Lasombra — they are often leaders, and many find themselves assuming the roles of ducti, priests or political organizers. Theirs is a legacy of aristocracy and artisanship, twisted by the bloodsports and depravity that consume the Sabbat. In many ways, they embody the hypocrisy that plagues the sect; they simultaneously crusade for the sect and indulge themselves in the excesses that leadership makes available.

In the modern nights, the Toreador *antitribu* follow similar ideals as their Camarilla siblings, though their appreciation for "beauty" has grown to include pain and depravity. How is a rose, sonnet or portrait more enrapturing than a masterfully executed flaying, reason the Toreador *antitribu*? What is beauty, if not subjective?

Of all Sabbat, Toreador *antitribu* have probably the most interaction with mortals. They move in the kine's most fabulous cliques, plying their trade in art and society, taking blood and amassing favors from the rich and effete. Like Camarilla Toreador, the Perverts are socialites of the most deadly order, moving wickedly yet quietly through the mortal throng like hunting sharks.

Roleplaying Hints: You are the life of the party and the death that walks through it. Cainites and kine alike are but toys in your games, and you play them off each other with consummate skill. Whether spreading a vicious rumor over flutes of champagne or stripping the skin from a now-tedious paramour, you balance your monstrous passion with cunning. Your ministrations can be tender or agonizing, but that call is yours to make.

Disciplines: *Auspex, Celerity, Presence*

Advantage: Because they must move through the ranks of society with ease, Toreador *antitribu* often learn the concepts and concerns of the people with whom they meet. Every Toreador gains any combination of two Traits from the following: *Academics, Crafts, Performance* or *Subterfuge* (she may take two separate Traits or the same one twice) at no extra cost.

Weakness: While art and beauty mesmerize the Toreador, the Toreador *antitribu* have come to be fascinated by pain and displeasure. Whether their own or that of others, discomfort

veritably hypnotizes the Sabbat Toreador. When confronted with a scene of pain or the opportunity to do harm (no matter how inconsequential), the Toreador *antitribu* must indulge the dark passion, or else spend a Mental Trait to free herself from the temptation. This may be as simple as making a callous remark or as grave as torture or murder.

VENTRUE ANTITRIBU

Centuries ago, according to the Ventrue *antitribu*, members of their clan were knights and aristocrats, masters of statecraft and diplomacy. After the Anarch Revolt and the formation of the Camarilla came the Renaissance, and the Ventrue changed with the times. Rather than remain nobles, they pursued financial interests, joining the merchant class. They abandoned nobility and the right of kings to rule.

So say the Ventrue *antitribu*. The Ventrue anarchs who had opposed their elders during the revolt had chafed under the dominance of their aged sires. As mortal society evolved, these elders tightened their grip on their holdings, preventing younger and more able Ventrue from achieving what was rightfully theirs. The Ventrue had given up true nobility for common greed. The Ventrue anarchs maintain that their leaders had failed, tempted by wealth and power. Thus, Ventrue *antitribu* see their Camarilla siblings as failures, and they have assumed the roles of Cainites' saviors to atone for this.

The Ventrue *antitribu* have adopted a vampiric code of honor. They are warriors of the modern nights, sworn to stop the Ancients and ruin the hedonistic Camarilla. The Sabbat's original purpose — to oppose corrupt elders who would pave the way for the Antediluvians' return through their indolence — drives the clan, many of whom are Embraced from once-prominent mortal families. Others hail from still-strong families and possess a twisted sense of nobility. The Crusaders claim to shoulder a great burden, much like their parent clan. They went *antitribu* because they believed the Camarilla Ventrue to have taken the wrong path.

Taken at face value, the Crusaders have lofty causes that reflect everything noble the Sabbat claims to stand for. In the end, though, they are still vampires, and members of the Sword of Caine as well. Their purpose may briefly seem noble, but they support the Sabbat to the end. They believe mortals to be vessels, suitable only for food and childer. Gehenna may come, but Cainites, as tools of God's vengeance and the Devil's will, should dominate the Children of Seth.

Roleplaying Hints: You bear the task of paving the way for the childer of Caine to their proper place. After the Antediluvian threat has been destroyed, you will help usher in a new era of Cainite supremacy. Until then, however, you must fight tirelessly. To accept anything else is to take the path of the disgraced Ventrue of the Camarilla, and that's not a failure you're willing to accept.

Disciplines: *Dominate, Fortitude, Presence*

Advantage: Their passionate dedication to their cause has given the Ventrue *antitribu* a powerful reputation among the Sons and Daughters of Caine. At the beginning of the game, Ventrue *antitribu* gain one Sabbat Status Trait from the following list at no additional cost: *Respected, Righteous, Passionate* or *Feared*.

Crusaders come from hale stock, with skills necessary for the Great Jyhad. Also at no additional cost, a Ventrue *antitribu* player may take

one of the following Abilities for her character during character creation: *Academics, Finance, Leadership, Melee* or *Politics*.

Weakness: Like their counterparts in the Camarilla, Sabbat Ventrue suffer selective tastes when it comes to the matter of feeding. Ventrue may take only blood that meets the exacting requirements of their restriction (though they may Embrace as normal). This comes into play not only during the course of the game, in which the character may take sustenance only from his prey group, but also at the beginning of the game — Ventrue *antitribu* begin play with one less Blood Trait than other vampires of their generation.

Chapter Three: Making a Monster

The following is a brief description of character creation, adapted **from Laws of the Night,** for Sabbat characters. The lists of Attributes, Abilities and Merits and Flaws are by no means complete — for more detailed information on character creation, see **Laws of the Night.**

Step One: Inspiration

Arguably the most important step in character creation is the formation of the basic concept. Every vampire was once a normal human, after all, with hopes, fears, dreams and ambitions. Once Embraced, the character brings her particular views to her new unlife. These strengths and weaknesses shape the character's Traits, capabilities and limitations. The first step in creating a character is to come up with a basic idea of the person. Don't worry about details now; think more in terms of broad brushstrokes. Create the person *before* you create the vampire.

Clan

With a base concept in mind, determine your character's clan. Did he arrive by a mass Embrace (which wasn't too picky about a particular breed)? Did the clan select her for certain qualities (a savage outlook on life? her ruthless dealings with other people)? The choice of clan influences a character's development heavily. The clan also determines the sorts of Disciplines, strengths and weaknesses innate to the character.

There are few or no Caitiff in the Sabbat. While those born without a clan are common (given the rampant siring that occurs during certain rituals and times of war), they have banded together as a clan of their own — the Panders. If you wish to play a true Caitiff, outside the Pander clan, you will need a very good reason to have been excluded from the "family."

Nature and Demeanor

To define a character's personality, choose an Archetype. Each Archetype lists an underlying motivation, a reason for a character to behave in specific ways. The Archetypes described here are, by no means, the final list of personalities; Storytellers can suggest and approve any further number of Archetypes. Bear in mind that the more "humane" Natures or Demeanors are simply inappropriate: Those without the stomach for the job rarely survive.

A character's Nature is her innermost persona, the true basis of her motives. By contrast, the Demeanor is the public face, the one a character shows to everyone else. On occasion, Nature and Demeanor may be the same. In the Sabbat, an individual's Demeanor is most likely very close to her true self — the Sabbat has little time for duplicity. Also, your pack will be aware of your Nature, even if you attempt to hide it from others.

Listed below are a number of Sabbat-specific Archetypes. Of course, feel free to use Archetypes listed in **Laws of the Night** or to create your own with approval from your Storyteller.

Capitalist — You are the ultimate mercenary, with a keen understanding of how to manipulate others.

Chameleon — You can blend into any situation, able to pass yourself off as anything. You have no true loyalties.

Creep Show — You strive to shock and disgust, to intimidate and control others.

Daredevil — You love taking risks and will seize any opportunity to do so.

Dark Pioneer — You can't change the traditions of the past, but you can be the force that drives the future.

Dark Poet — You want to share the beauty of darkness with the rest of the world.

Drunk Uncle — When things are going well, you're everyone's best friend. When they are going poorly, you're their worst nightmare.

Enigma — Your actions are bizarre, uncontrolled; your erratic behavior is considered insanity by those you meet.

Eye of the Storm — Despite your calm outward appearance, you surround yourself with chaos and death.

Guru — You seek enlightenment and cling to your idealism, trying to convert others.

Recruiter — It makes sense to build your side up before trying to tear theirs down.

Sadist — You exist to inflict pain and suffering. Killing is too easy — they have to know pain.

Sociopath — All inferior beings should be eradicated. You have no remorse or compassion. You are a machine.

Stalker — The chase is all; the capture and feeding is almost anticlimactic.

Sorority Sister — You do whatever the "in" crowd does, and you do it better.

Torturer — Pain isn't a profession for you — it's a calling.

Paths of Enlightenment

Every vampire struggles with the Beast Within, the predatory drive of hunger that pushes Cainites to acts of fury, desperation and horror. Only by clinging to a moral compass can a vampire resist the slide into total depravity.

Vampires of the Sabbat feel that Humanity is a lesser path, and seek alternate means of controlling their Beasts. The Paths of Enlightenment have existed for as long as many Sabbat can remember, guiding those who follow them away from Wassail. Those who follow these Paths have no Humanity left; the Paths espouse utterly alien (albeit wholeheartedly vampiric) beliefs and morals. The Sabbat insists on placing its recruits on Paths so that they are more suited to leave mortal society behind and accept their new existence.

At this step in character creation, decide on your Morality. As strange as it might sound, many Sabbat neonates (usually the very young) take their early years still clinging to their Humanity; they simply haven't had the time or experience to completely cast off all their mortal side, but those who cling for too long don't survive long enough to change. However, Sabbat past their neonate years are often on a Path of Enlightenment, guided by their priests or mentors. Paths of Enlightenment are not for beginning players; they are utterly inhuman codes of behavior that demand intense roleplay. Consult your Storyteller if you're unsure what your character should follow.

Details of the various Sabbat Paths are listed in Chapter Four.

Step Two: Attributes

Natural capabilities use Attributes for descriptions. You determine your character's natural talents, selecting whether your character is to be physically adroit, mentally agile or socially adept. Once you've decided on your character's inherent strengths, you should describe exactly the sorts of exceptional characteristics she possesses. In your primary area of Attribute development, choose seven Traits; in your secondary, choose five; in your tertiary area, select three Traits.

New Attributes

Attributes are descriptors of a character's natural talent and capabilities. In the Sabbat, some Attributes are considered a good mark of a sect member, while more "humane" ones are considered a liability.

Physical Attributes are the character's general health, dexterity, stamina and general physical capability. The Sabbat values individuals who are good fighters, and strong workers.

A character's Social Attributes are a definition of her personality, her internal capacity to interact with others and her ability to lead and to follow. The Sabbat typically chooses only the most ruthless and aggressive personalities, bringing hardened killers and other amoral individuals into the sect. While the Sabbat does occasionally choose individuals who are beautiful, smooth and competent, the sect encourages certain behaviors and morals.

Mental Traits define the character's capacity for learning and reasoning. The Sabbat typically does not value most types of study, but they do support occult education and tactical training.

Laws of the Night gives many examples of Traits that a player may choose to represent the character's Mental, Social and Physical Attributes. The Traits listed below are intended to add to those and define more Sabbat-specific character Traits. Some of the Traits listed in **Laws of the Night** are recopied here, under different areas (*Callous*, for example, is considered to be a desirable Trait in the Sabbat, whereas *Empathetic* is Negative). Only those Traits listed below are considered to have "changed sides," although as always, your Storyteller is the final arbiter of what is appropriate. For the Sabbat chronicle purposes, the character receives a *Bestial* (not *Callous*) Trait when he frenzies and acquires a Negative Trait.

If you're going to have a mixed chronicle, then you may not wish to expand your system with these optional Traits. It's not fair to make players try to guess at Negative Traits they've never seen before. However, if you're running a strictly Sabbat chronicle, then feel free to encourage your players to use these more "Sabbat-oriented" Traits.

Physical

Strength-related: *Vicious*
Dexterity-related: *Fierce*
Stamina-related: *Deadly, Savage*
Miscellaneous Physical: *Aggressive*

Aggressive: You are familiar with fighting, and eagerly match your opponent strike for strike.
Uses: Combat

Deadly: An indomitable strength of body, able to continue fighting despite damage.
Uses: Combat. *Fortitude* tests. Second challenges or challenges after being wounded.

Fierce: Driven by your will to win, swift movements are easy for you.
Uses: Fighting an obviously superior enemy.

Savage: You possess brutal intensity and an instinct for slaughter that rivals the most ferocious animals.
Uses: Brute force. *Fortitude* challenges. Combat

Vicious: You have a powerful urge to destroy, coupled with the wiry strength of a predator.
Uses: Second or subsequent challenges. Dirty fighting

Negative Physical

Frail: You are fragile and easily broken. You always come out of a fight looking like you got the worst of it — even if you didn't.
Slow: The opposite of the *Quick* and *Nimble* Traits. You lack muscular coordination and are always a half-beat behind the rest.
Soft: You lack the physical strength to carry out arduous tasks.

Social

Charisma-related: *Intense, Threatening*
Manipulation-related: *Callous, Cruel, Manipulative*

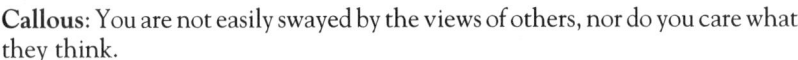

Callous: You are not easily swayed by the views of others, nor do you care what they think.
Uses: Defending against *Presence* powers. Testing to perform an inhumane act.

Cruel: With refined viciousness, you have the ability to precisely target the weaknesses of others.
Uses: *Presence* or intrigue. Challenges used to control or harm others.

Intense: You have an unnerving presence that draws the attention of others.
Uses: Commanding the actions of others. *Intimidation* challenges. Inspiring fear.

Manipulative: You can easily convince others in such a manner that they rarely notice your intentions.
Uses: *Dominate* and *Dementation* challenges. Gauging the abilities and mental prowess of others.

Threatening: Your presence actively makes others uncomfortable.
Uses: Goading or insulting someone. Intimidation. *Dread Gaze* challenges.

Negative Social

Empathetic: Able to identify and commune with the emotions of others. In the Sabbat, the ability to feel strong emotions other than fear or hatred is disapproved and treated with scorn. Your "soft" ways earn you the ridicule of others.

Kind: You still retain much of your Humanity, and for that, you are treated harshly by the other members of the Sabbat. Your actions disgust everyone around you.

Meek: It is difficult for you to make your presence known, and you are often overlooked for honors or advancement. Further, your mild nature makes it difficult for you to enter combats; you often hesitate before acting.

Mental

Perception-related: *Analytical*
Intelligence-related: *Focused*
Wits-related: *Insidious*
Miscellaneous Mental: *Depraved, Inhumane*

Analytical: You believe in a strict mental regimen that guides your thoughts.
Uses: *Auspex* challenges. Investigation. Noticing clues or anything out of place.

Depraved: Your mind works in strange, unpleasant ways.
Uses: Resisting *Dominate* challenges. Making a mental defense.

Focused: You are fixated on a course of thought, and no distraction can drive you from it.
Uses: Defending against emotion-related attacks. Maintaining concentration despite distractions.

Inhumane: You are capable of acting without emotional shackles.
Uses: Killing. Performing any action that would be considered brutal or violent

Insidious: You are a master liar and conniver; few suspect you, and your betrayals are devastating.

Uses: Infiltration. Disguise. Changing someone's mind.

Negative Mental

Deceitful: Occasional mistruths, minor adjustments to the facts and misleading others all seem like second nature to you.

Squeamish: You have difficulty grasping the brutality of the world; everything is dirty, foul or uncomfortable.

Unstable: Your mind is constantly teetering on the edge, and *anything* could upset the careful balancing act.

Step Three: Advantages

No character begins play completely out of the void. A character has skills and knowledges, perhaps the ones that landed her the Embrace or ones she learned later. Furthermore, vampiric powers, called Disciplines, flow from the blood of all Cainites, granting them superhuman capabilities. Collectively, these Advantages are learned or developed benefits over and above one's raw potential.

A Sabbat character may not choose Backgrounds (although these may be purchased with Free Traits and with experience) at this time, but does receive an additional basic Discipline level.

Choosing Abilities

Select five Abilities that represent your character's education and training. Whether learned in mortal days or honed after death, Abilities set your character apart by letting her attempt tasks that less skilled compatriots cannot understand or complete. You can choose an Ability multiple times, if desired, to show greater expertise. Note that your Storyteller may restrict some Abilities. Sabbat-specific Abilities are listed on page 60.

Choosing Disciplines

Select four Disciplines. You must select them in the order listed (that is, you must take the first Basic level before taking the second Basic level in any given Discipline), and you can only take the Basic levels at this time. All four of these Disciplines must come from your clan's Disciplines, but you may take more than one level in any. If you are a Pander, you may simply choose any three Basic Disciplines desired, but your Storyteller may restrict you to the eight most common Disciplines — *Animalism*, *Auspex*, *Celerity*, *Dominate*, *Fortitude*, *Obfuscate*, *Potence*, *Presence* — unless you have an exceptional reason for learning a more specialized power.

Step Four: Last Touches

At this stage, you should note your character's total number of Blood Traits, Willpower Traits and Path Traits. Note that Paths of Enlightenment still use Virtue Traits, which come in three categories: *Conscience / Conviction* Traits, *Self-Control / Instinct* Traits and *Courage* Traits. You get seven Traits to split among these categories. Each category must range from one to five total Traits. For greater detail on each of these Trait categories, see **Laws of the Night**.

Morality Traits

While your Virtue Traits represent your ability to hold off against the Beast, your Morality Traits show how closely you adhere to your chosen code of ethics. A high rating in your Morality Traits indicates that you set high standards for yourself, but you risk losing ground to the Beast even with relatively trivial violations of your chosen morals. Low Morality Traits indicate that you are close to losing control to the Beast forever.

Your starting Morality Trait total equals the average of your *Conscience / Conviction* and *Self-Control / Instinct* Traits, rounded up. During character creation, you may choose to lose one Morality Trait in exchange for gaining two Free Traits. You may do so only once — losing a Morality Trait counts as taking two Negative Traits. Be warned though, that doing so is a dangerous course; a low Morality Trait total practically guarantees disintegration into Wassail, the final frenzy.

Negative Traits, Derangements and Flaws

Some characters have particular weaknesses or shortcomings. Others just never developed in some fashion or suffered injuries that set back otherwise strong attributes. Negative Traits represent these. Though Negative Traits are not required, they can represent a deficiency or injury in your character.

In addition to Negative Traits, you can choose derangements for your character. A derangement represents some sort of mental instability or neurotic behavior. Taking a derangement counts as two Negative Traits and thus grants you two Free Traits, but you may only take one derangement at character creation (or one extra, in the case of Malkavians, who all start with one).

Representing specific deficiencies or drawbacks aside from inherent weaknesses common to many people, Flaws showcase particular problems. As with Negative Traits, Flaws grant additional Traits to the user. Each Flaw is rated in terms of its value, ranging from one to seven Traits. The higher the value, the more debilitating the Flaw. A character may total up to seven Traits of Flaws.

Free Traits and Merits

Because no two Cainites are alike, each character gets five Free Traits. Additional Free Traits are earned from Negative Traits, Flaws or derangements taken earlier, or by removing Morality Traits. One Negative Trait grants a single Free Trait. A derangement or Morality Trait is worth two Free Traits and Flaws have variable values listed individually. For details on how to spend your Free Traits, see **Laws of the Night**.

Purchasing Merits is one way to spend Free Traits. Merits represent special bonuses and capabilities beyond the norm. Each Merit is rated in terms of its Trait value. To take a Merit, you must expend Free Traits equal to the Merit's value. You can take no more than seven Traits of Merits, total (though some older vampires may have more).

Step Five: Spark of Life

Your character is more than a summation of Traits and adjectives. At this stage, take the concepts that you've emphasized and develop a story for your character. Why did your character learn certain things? What circumstances

made her grow and change? Think about the sort of person that you're playing and the motives of the individual. For more specific details, see the suggestions given in **Laws of the Night**.

SONS AND DAUGHTERS OF CAINE

Sabbat characters have a few other particulars that must be addressed during creation. What is her political leaning? What Path of Enlightenment does she follow? Is she involved in the sect's spiritual side, or is she just this side of a rampaging monster?

There are two types of "people" that become members of the Sabbat: those who were considered by their sires to be good additions to the sect and those who survived mass Embrace by some fluke. When you start creating your Sabbat character, take some time to decide what brought him to his sire's attention. Did he happen to be in the wrong place at the wrong time, or was he watched for several months or even years? Your character's mortal life can be a good place to begin the character creation process, even if a large part of it was purged during his Creation Rites — it may help you with determining if he was brought in with a purpose or as cannon fodder.

The process of Embrace is meant to winnow the weak from the strong. A potential member is Embraced, then "shoveled" (slammed on the back of the head with a shovel and buried in a grave which she may have dug herself) and then forced to dig herself out with her own hands. If she survives this test, she is considered a False Sabbat member. Traditionally, the period during which a member of Sabbat is considered "False" is strewn with tests of strength and savagery. These tests serve to drive out any humanity that the character retains as well as to teach her Sabbat values. Many False Sabbat do not survive this time of testing, either destroyed for weakness or caught by an enemy. How did your character survive her testing? Is she still False Sabbat, still proving herself?

Even after becoming *Proven*, the new True Sabbat must carve a place for herself in the local hierarchy. The Sabbat's pecking order is ruthless, and any character unable to stand her ground will be crushed beneath the heel of those more powerful or cunning. Did she have a position, only to lose it, or is she uninterested in the sect's ladders of power? Did she suffer when someone else fell from grace?

POLITICS

The political stance a member of the Sabbat takes is no less important than her Path of Enlightenment or clan. Central to this political debate are the dual and opposing roles of the two main Sabbat ideals: freedom and loyalty to the sect. The rest are just details.

The struggle over ideology continues to pull the Sabbat in different directions and is perhaps their greatest internal enemy, affecting even how a particular Sabbat views status, who she will take orders from and even if she will take orders at all. Thus, knowing what political faction your character belongs to can be as central as her Nature in determining how she reacts to a situation.

Loyalists represent the far left wing within the Sabbat; in a way, they can be thought of as the Sabbat's "anarchs." Loyalists believe that the only way to

be loyal to the Sabbat is to follow the original principle of the Anarch Movement — that all vampires must be free and ultimately responsible for their own actions. Orders, rules and regulations that restrict the freedom and responsibility of the vampire must be removed.

The **Moderates** represent the vast middle ground of the Sabbat; roughly three-quarters of the sect is divided between them and the Status Quo. Many *antitribu* belong to the Moderates. Many Moderates have contacts with all of the factions and generally have the most flexibility. Neither far left nor far right, they believe in balance but tend to favor the side of freedom.

The **Pander Movement** represents what the Moderates could become if they changed their focus from greater freedom to greater power. Not all Panders share this mindset, but other moderates from other clans tread very close to their philosophy of convenience over ideals. The Panders focus on doing whatever is necessary to gain as much power and authority within the Sabbat; if it means supporting the Status Quo one week and allying with the Loyalists the next, they'll do so to save their skin.

The **Status Quo** represents the system of leadership and authority that has kept the Sabbat together since the last destructive Sabbat civil war. The current hierarchy of the Sabbat is a testament to the Status Quo as it is their vision made flesh. The Status Quo literally seeks to keep things the way that they are and work within their current systems, believing that allowing members a looser rein will compromise the secrecy and security of the sect.

The **Ultra-Conservatives** represent the far right hand of the equation and are the smallest faction in the Sabbat. Leaders that are weak need to be culled, and Sabbat that break the Code or disobey critical orders need to be purged before the sect falls to the Antediluvians.

Jumping into political factions during character creation can be confusing, particularly if you've never played in a Sabbat chronicle before. If this is the case, consider playing a freshly minted Sabbat (newly *Proven* or False), and let the game's action guide your choice of politics.

Paths

The Sabbat has the reputation of being bloody and nonhuman, and that reputation is deserved. The majority of the vampires in the Sabbat do not follow the ethics of the Camarilla, having long ago spurned Humanity in favor of their more monstrous selves. The Paths of Enlightenment, like those presented in **Laws of the Night**, are alternate codes of morality, meant to help a vampire control his Beast. While moral quandaries still face the vampires of the Sabbat, they are of a different nature. Listed below is a list of the most common Paths in the Sabbat; more detailed information on these paths can be found in Chapter Four. All Paths value *Courage*, but differ in other Virtues they prize.

Path of Caine

Virtues: *Conviction* and *Instinct*

Comprised of ancient scholars and mystics, the Path of Caine seeks for the keys to the enigma of vampiric existence, believing Caine to be the progenitor and paragon of all vampires.

Path of Cathari

Virtues: *Conviction* and *Instinct*

Cathari vampires believe in the old Albigensian heresy — that the forces of Light and the forces of Darkness are at continual odds with each other, and in the end, only one will triumph. They consider themselves the servants of Darkness and spread wickedness, believing that they are aiding Darkness and testing Light.

Path of Death and the Soul

Virtues: *Conviction* and *Self-Control*

Those on the Path of Death and the Soul are cold, emotionless beings that devote their lives to the study of death and its consequences. To understand the purpose of existence, they say, one must know what motivates and drives the immortal soul.

Path of the Feral Heart

Virtues: *Conviction* and *Instinct*

To hunt, to kill, to be the ultimate predator — these are the goals of those who follow the Path of the Feral Heart. They believe that vampires are the ultimate hunters, and that their purpose in unlife is to accept the predator that exists within their hearts.

Path of Honorable Accord

Virtues: *Conscience* and *Self-Control*

The Path of Honorable Accord was created to represent the ideals set down in the Code of Milan and to give a voice to the laws that govern the Sabbat. Its followers are expected to be hospitable to other Sabbat members and uphold leaders that work toward the goals of the Sabbat.

Path of Power and the Inner Voice

Virtues: *Conviction* and *Instinct*

Those on this Path see the exercise of power and control as the best reason for Cainite unlife. They believe that Cainites have been set above mortals, and they must accept their existence as superior beings. In doing so, they strive to control their own souls through harsh discipline and ruthless strength.

Path of Evil Revelations

Virtues: *Conviction* and *Instinct*

Some vampires revel in their evil natures, but the Corruptors go one step further — they actively sell themselves to the infernal forces and seek others for sacrifice. Vampires are already damned, they reason — one might as well be on the winning side.

Path of Lilith

Virtues: *Conviction* and *Instinct*

This Path is considered heretical by most Cainites of the Sabbat. These vampires follow the doctrines and dictates outlined by Lilith, the Dark Mother of Noddist teachings. The Bahari consider themselves children to a greater power, and they learn through surviving trial and pain.

Abilities

The Sabbat is an ever-changing arena of war and personal power. Members are expected to be knowledgeable in a vast array of subjects, from the sect's history and traditions to battle tactics against the Camarilla's pawns. These are the tricks of the trade, the hard-earned rewards of those who survive in the sect. Abilities aid the outcome of actions, give the character knowledge and an understanding of the world around her and describe how competent a character is in her chosen fields.

The Abilities listed in the **Laws of the Night** are all applicable to the Sabbat venue; those listed below are additional Sabbat-only Abilities.

Blindfighting

Many Sabbat games and Monomacy ritual fights require use of this Ability. *Blindfighting* means you are practiced at fighting without the aid of your eyes. You've learned to use your instincts, hearing and innate hunter nature instead of sight. You may use this Ability to retest in any *Brawl* challenge that occurs in the dark or while blindfolded.

Fire Dancing

You can enter a trancelike state that relieves you from Rötschreck and allows you to leap bonfires and burning coals during Fire Dance rituals. You do not get nervous around fire if you take the time to sit apart and meditate for five minutes before encountering the flames closely. However, unless a fire is specifically built as a ritual bonfire, you still suffer the same Rötschreck as anyone else.

Fortune-telling

Tea leaves, Tarot cards, runes, I Ching sticks, a swinging pendulum or entrails — these are the tools you call upon to read the future. Whether or not you have the actual psychic chutzpah to do this is up to the Storyteller, but at the very least, you can put on a good show and part the gullible from their money. Using *Fortune-telling* requires you to specify at least one divination method and may require Social Challenges to pull off a good performance.

Rituals

You know the rituals and *ritae* of the Sabbat and can perform them whenever the occasion requires. This Ability is vital to being a pack priest: Unless the character performing the *ritae* has this knowledge, the *ritae* will fail. This Ability is not simply the knowledge of such rituals, but is a spiritual, almost supernatural ability to perform them. This Ability is typically taught to pack priests and other spiritual leaders, and a Sabbat who is not a priest but possesses such knowledge may come under scrutiny.

Torture

You know how to inflict pain and are efficient at doing so. This Ability allows you to retest any Physical Challenge when you are in a torture situation — i.e., when you have already caused pain to your opponent and are continuing to inflict pain (not damage). Regular combat is not an appropriate use of this Ability; this can be used for retesting when inflicting pain on your opponent either during an interrogation or when using Disciplines.

Vamp

You can use your seductive means to get any information from anyone. Your advances could make a sailor blush, and you know how to tailor them to the individual. Remember, however, that you will still need to spend blood in order to make yourself appear human to ordinary sight and touch. This Ability can be used in appropriate *Presence* retests, as well as in unique interrogation circumstances. Bear in mind that vampires on Paths of Enlightenment may not spend blood to make themselves appear more human, and many vampires find the idea of such base acts to be no better than animals coupling (benefits aside).

Backgrounds

Sabbat do not receive free Backgrounds at character creation and must purchase all Backgrounds. Examples and definitions of character Backgrounds can be found in **Laws of the Night**, although they will have a slightly different slant in a Sabbat chronicle. Remember that Backgrounds like *Allies*, *Contacts* or *Influence* mean interaction with mortals on some level, and most Sabbat consider mortals inferior — tolerated at best, or no better than food at worst. While it's not inconceivable that a Sabbat vampire might somehow still have ties to the mortal world, such ties are best kept hidden — after all, who would want it known that he actually *needs* mortals for anything? If you're going to have them, give some thought to how you acquired these Backgrounds and how you keep them up.

Status

Sabbat status and dynamics are very different from those of the Camarilla. The fundamental systems are different, as are the means and uses of Status within the Sabbat. Sabbat may use Status to force another sect member to back down or bid it in a Social Challenge in place of a normal Social Trait. Characters can ignore Status, but only at the price of not being able to use their Status for the rest of the session. Status is accrued by actions, accomplishments or taking up positions within the sect that carry a certain amount of prestige.

See more on Status and its uses in Chapter Six.

Derangements

The derangements listed here seem to be peculiar to the Sabbat; indeed, many of the sect's members suffer some form of instability, whether from the trauma of the Embrace or some other event. A Malkavian *antitribu* may select her initial derangement from this list or from the more "common" ones found in **Laws of the Night**.

Berserk

You have tremendous difficulty controlling your anger and frustration. When confronted with stressful situations, you often lose control, lashing out at those unfortunate enough to cross your path, whether friend or foe. The bloodlust and violence of the Sabbat suits you well; indeed, the sect seems to breed this kind of madness. You must win two Simple Tests to avoid frenzy.

Blood Addict

You are addicted to the blood of your pack. It gives you a physical and emotional high that can't be beat. For every period of six hours you go without consuming pack vitae, you lose one Physical Trait until you get your fix. When you wake, you are down one Physical Trait until you get pack blood.

Blood Sweats

When you're stressed, you get so nervous and agitated that your state of mind affects your body. Much like a mortal may become jumpy and break out in cold sweats, you become likewise ill at ease. The "sweat" in your case, however, is blood that works its way to your skin. This blood is very obvious in your sleeping environs, not to mention staining your clothes and making you a disturbing sight to vampires and mortals alike. Blood sweats cause you to begin play each night an additional point down in your Blood Pool. In addition, the blood is quite obvious (your clothes are stained not long after changing, and you "perspire" continuously), and you're often nervous and twitchy.

Blood Taste

You hate the taste of blood. Your body craves it, but you think it tastes disgusting. You go out of your way to feed on drunks (the alcohol helps kill the taste), even hanging out in mortal bars. The Vaulderie is torture; one person's blood is bad enough by itself, but the blood of a whole pack let out to go stale in the air like that is really vile. You must win or tie a Static Test each time you participate in the Vaulderie to see if you spit out the blood. If you fail the test, you must burn a Willpower Trait if you wish to keep the noxious fluid in your mouth.

Creation Memory

High stress, especially violence, usually triggers plaguing memories of your Creation Rites. Whenever you see a Storyteller, hear a specific word or encounter a certain type of event, your thoughts will immediately return to the time of your creation, and you feel a pressing need to share these memories with whoever is around. Characters may play this derangement as anything from a near-frenzy to the burning desire to tell anecdotes. You are down one Mental Trait whenever you lapse into these memories.

Gluttony

Gluttonous vampires have difficulty taking their sustenance in moderation. Why stop when one is merely sated? Why not drink in the heady vitae until there is no more? This derangement is particularly prevalent among elder vampires who have indulged their vices for so long that they lack the ability to control their hunger. Vampires suffering from this derangement must spend a Willpower Trait when they wish to stop feeding. A gluttonous vampire automatically frenzies when confronted with the sight, smell or taste of blood when hungry (blood pool is at 3 or less), and may be continuously "snacking", despite not needing more (such overeating may lead to many episodes of bloat, where an overfull vampire sheds blood tears and has pronounced ruddy skin).

Obsession

You are obsessed with someone in your pack. You have a permanent Vinculum of 10 for her and can't shake the desire to be constantly in her business and affection. You try to suck up as much of her attention and blood as you can to prevent others from getting what you crave.

Pack Feeding

You believe you can no longer feed on mortals or vampires other than those in your pack and become ill when vitae from other sources passes into your system. Your Vinculum ratings are at two higher than whatever the results of the night's Vaulderie. No one is sure if this is a psychological condition or

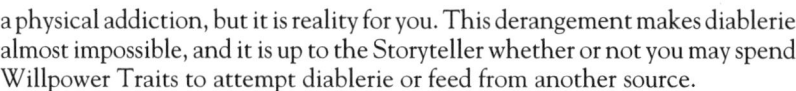

a physical addiction, but it is reality for you. This derangement makes diablerie almost impossible, and it is up to the Storyteller whether or not you may spend Willpower Traits to attempt diablerie or feed from another source.

Paranoid of Ancients

Everyone and everything that is not expressly Sabbat is a tool of the Antediluvians and dedicated to your personal destruction. All of your loyal comrades are doomed along with you. You are suspicious and wary of anything outside the sect and will not infiltrate the Camarilla for fear of being subliminally taken over by their ancient masters. You insist that those who have made contact outside the sect be purified to be sure they have not been overcome by the influences of the Ancients themselves.

Passion Player

While you strongly dislike and refuse to take part in torture, you believe that killing is your divine duty. Camarilla vampires avoid killing because they disrespect their Creator's wishes. They hide behind the Masquerade even when they do kill, though it is God's will for them to reveal themselves as the angels of death that they are. Each time you kill, you make sure your victim knows exactly what you are first.

Phobia

Something in your past affected you deeply. It may be the sight of a shovel or the feeling of cold water around your body, but you have an instinctual trigger that causes you to frenzy. If this trigger affects you, you must test as if for Rötschreck. This *Phobia* frenzy, if entered, does not cause any lasting Negative Traits.

Ritual Freak

The more rituals your pack performs, the happier you are. You insist on Vaulderie at least twice a night, once at rising and once before sleep. You encourage others to participate in rituals before every anticipated combat and after every unanticipated one. You believe a Sabbat priest should bless everyone who ventures into the Camarilla's realm, whether to fight, cause trouble or infiltrate, and purify them upon each return.

Merits and Flaws

Physical

Early Riser (1 Trait Merit)

No one can explain it, but you seem to have the ability to exist on less rest than your fellow packmates do, tending to rise at least one hour before everyone else. You always seem to be the first to rise and the last to go to bed, even if you've been out until dawn. While your packmates may still be groggy, you're awake and aware. You may awaken early, or remain awake late, with no need to expend Willpower during the first or last hour of light to stay awake.

Vulnerability to Silver (2 Trait Flaw)

To you, silver is as painful and as deadly as the rays of the sun. You suffer aggravated wounds from any silver weapons (bullets, knives, etc) and the mere touch of silver objects pains you. Further, you are one Trait down when in contact with the metal.

Lazy (3 Trait Flaw)

You avoid anything that requires effort on your part. For any actions that require preparation, there's a good chance you didn't properly prepare. You are down one Trait for any spontaneous actions (including combat, unless it is part of a planned offensive).

Infertile Vitae (5 Trait Flaw)

During your Embrace, something went horribly wrong, causing your blood to mutate under the stress of dying and rising again. All those you try to Embrace die. No matter what you do, you may not create any childer. You can still use your blood in the Vaulderie or for any other vampiric need, including making ghouls. Blood Brothers may not take this Flaw.

Social

Sanctity (2 Trait Merit)

This Merit is sometimes called the halo effect; everyone considers you pure and innocent, though not necessarily naive. You have a saintlike quality that is hard to pinpoint but cannot be denied. You are trusted, even if you are not trustworthy. At the Storyteller's discretion, you tend to receive lesser punishments for wrongdoing, and most Cainites and humans like you. You are two Traits up when initiating non-aggressive social challenges.

Special Responsibility (1 Trait Flaw)

Shortly after your Embrace, you volunteered for some task in order to gain respect and approval from your pack members. Now, you wish you had never opened your damn mouth! While no one gives you any special credit for performing this duty, you would lose much respect from the pack if you were to stop. The Storyteller should work out the nature and details of your duty in advance. Ideas can range from lending money to pack members to acting as pack messenger or possibly a constant responsibility to gather victims for Blood Feasts. You must define your duty before beginning play, and if you refuse to perform your duty at any time, you are stripped of one Status per game session until you resume your duty.

Mental

Introspection (1 Trait Merit)

You have keen insight into your own psyche, making you concretely aware of the motives of all your actions. You also have incredible insight into the underlying motives behind the actions of others. You are two Traits up when attempting to use the *Subterfuge* Ability to discover the Negative Traits of someone with the same Nature or Demeanor as yours or when attempting to perceive that character's aura.

Flashbacks (6 Trait Flaw)

You managed to make it through the Creation Rites, but not wholly intact. The most insignificant thing can throw you into a different mood or state of mind. Your behavior is extremely unpredictable. Because of your precarious emotional state, your Willpower fluctuates. At the beginning of each session, make a Simple Test with your Storyteller (no Traits risked). If you succeed, you may participate in the night's game as normal. If you fail, however, you may only spend a single Willpower during the session. You may still use your total number of Willpower for Tests, but may only spend one Willpower Trait during the session. You may test again at the beginning of the next night to see if you have regained your wits.

Chapter Four: The Way and The Truth

Paths of Enlightenment

The Sabbat view of the Cainite condition rejects all ties to humanity. Vampires are dead, won't ever be alive again and now exist in a realm of experience wholly unlike anything mortals know. While this rejection opens up many possibilities for Sabbat vampires, it doesn't free them from the basic facts of their own nature. Each Sabbat vampire, just like each Camarilla and independent vampire, must keep the Beast in check. Reveling in one's capabilities as a hunter is one thing; losing all capacity for thought forever, doomed to feed mindlessly until someone destroys the brute that once was a vampire, is another.

Harsh experience shows the Sabbat that vampires retain the need for some code of ethics, principles to guide and limit their behavior. Many junior members of the Sabbat and a handful of elders continue to follow the Path of Humanity. They're not very good at it, but it does keep them a pace or two back from the brink of Wassail. A great many Sabbat neonates perish in a few months or years; Sabbat priests often refrain from teaching any Path at all until their new recruits show signs of surviving to become something more than cannon fodder. Some vampires take immediately to a Path with an instinctive drive from the moment of their creation while others never feel the need to give up Humanity altogether.

Progress on any Path of Enlightenment takes deliberate effort. The Paths are *supposed* to be inhuman. Each one exalts an aspect of Cainite nature, history or alleged destiny instead of some aspect of human nature. No mortal instinct or doctrine really prepares a vampire to follow a Path. By definition, following a Path means not acting in a human or humane manner.

The Paths can make real trouble in a LARP. Storytellers must prepare to spend some time watching players and reining in self-indulgent acts of random violence and disruption. It's far more difficult to identify with characters well

advanced on a Path than with characters of high Humanity. Specific parts of various Paths do connect to elements of human experience, but the overall synthesis of each is unique and inhuman. Players and Storytellers who cooperate with each other in maintaining an awareness of what the Paths mean in practice and thinking about what the events of each scene imply for adherents of the various Paths get the reward of an engaging, rich, satisfying game despite the reduced intuitive identification.

At the outset, Storytellers must make it clear that the Paths are *not* license to run wild. Indeed, the upper levels of each Path restrict a character's power of choice far more than Humanity does. A vampire who commits to a Path sets aside many emotions, desires and values to pursue a very limited set of goals. Paths that include *Instinct* as one of the Virtues *require* their adherents to enter frenzy, and merely make it possible to maintain limited control in some turns. Vampires find, as they advance along their Paths, that their choices of goals, of friends and associates, and of every other aspect of their existence become highly focused. The Paths close doors of choice at every step; characters and players alike should think carefully.

The Path of Caine

Followers of the Path of Caine, or Noddists, focus on Caine as the first and perfect vampire. All deficiencies of the Cainite condition stem from vampires' distance from Caine. A Noddist has two duties: to study every available scrap of information about Caine and the nature of vampires (including the duty to uncover more information) and to apply that knowledge to purging human limitations on the way to achieving vampiric completion.

Noddists believe that academic study only takes them so far. It's good to read history, autobiographies and the like, but to really appreciate another vampire's experience requires more. Specifically, it requires diablerie. A Noddist who drains the essence of another vampires gets the victim's whole essence and sees the world, briefly, through another's eyes, sharing another's memories and thinking another's thoughts. Noddists never undertake diablerie lightly. It's a sacred moment on the step to unity with Caine's perfect state; it requires preparation beforehand and serious contemplation afterward.

Cainite occultists created the Path of Caine in the 16th century. Ironically, they drew precisely the sort of inspiration from mortal affairs — in particular, the Enlightenment and its emphasis on reason anchored in historical study — that their Path rejects. The Camarilla's relentless advocacy of Humanity as the only safe moral code rankled the first Noddists. They had to acknowledge that most Paths force vampires into behavior that invites mortal reprisal but didn't want to accept the Camarilla's solution. Thus the Path of Caine includes its own version of the Masquerade while allowing (even encouraging) what the Camarilla abhors.

At any given time, only a handful of vampires pursue the Path of Caine. It's rigorous and scholarly. Vampires who focus on the (un)life of the mind seldom flourish in the Sabbat, and very few non-Sabbat vampires would accept some of the Path's key tenets. Noddist scholarship doesn't always happen in cloistered laboratories: Noddists lead war parties, act as bishops and roam with wandering packs, all in the effort to understand Caine's life as a warrior, leader and wanderer. Modern Noddists often say that the Final Nights are a time of active scholarship, with passive book study waiting for calmer times to return.

Vampires on the Path of Caine practice *Conviction* and *Instinct*.

The Ethics of the Path

- Study Caine's history and act as much like Caine as you can.
- The Beast is one more part of your nature. Increase your will and instinct so that you can master it just like the rest of yourself.
- Take the vitae of unworthy vampires and study the insights their sacrifice offers you. Make yourself worthy through wise action.
- Purge whatever remains of your lost Humanity. Develop the potential in you now.
- Test your own limits, and test others with suitable challenges. Find out what vampires can do so that you know what goals to set for yourself.

Following the Path

Noddists tend to be better educated and more reserved than the vampires around them, although some Noddists lived without interest in scholarly matters and developed their love of learning after the Embrace. They study Caine for practical reasons: They want to make the best possible use of their condition. Theory only matters when it guides action, either suggesting a line of research or guiding the choice between alternative courses of action. Assamite *antitribu* often favor the Path of Caine as the equivalent of the Path of Blood without the cowardice. Serpents of the Light, Toreador *antitribu* and Ventrue *antitribu* make up most of the rest of the Path's followers. They often gravitate to positions of spiritual leadership. Their comrades in the Sabbat generally view them as haughty and vain.

Noddists stay out of most Sabbat politics. Power structures don't interest them — Caine was above all hierarchy, after all. As priests, Noddists make very even-handed instructors, seeing the potential for perfection in every vampire along with the need to begin with whatever talents a vampire has right now. All Noddists like to share their insights with others so that as many vampires as possible can achieve unity with Caine.

The research aspects of the Path of Caine encourage vampires to develop *Occult* and *Lore* Abilities of all kinds. Since the Path also encourages practical action, Noddists often study *Survival*, *Melee* and *Athletics*. Proselytizers find *Expression*, *Subterfuge* and *Leadership* useful.

Most Noddists frown on the Disciplines that don't appear in the common texts of the *Book of Nod*, preferring Disciplines that enhance innate abilities: *Auspex*, *Celerity*, *Fortitude*, *Potence* and *Presence*. Some Noddists shun esoteric Disciplines like *Thaumaturgy* and *Serpentis* while others study them as interesting sidelights that simply aren't as important as the core Disciplines attributed to Caine himself.

The First Impulse

Some vampires, fresh from a shovel party, crawl from their graves filled with a determination to be the perfect vampire, since vampires they must be. Other vampires, recruited more selectively, accept the Embrace for its promise of power. They want to have it all, everything the Cainite condition makes possible. The Sabbat's spiritual advisors recognize this drive for vampiric perfection as an indication that the new recruits might flourish on the Path of Caine.

\	Path of Caine Hierarchy of Sins
Traits	Violations
Five	Failing to engage in study (academic or active) each night, whatever the circumstances; failing to instruct others in the Path of Caine
Four	Befriending or associating with mortals; showing disrespect to other Noddists (and non-Noddists diligently studying Caine)
Three	Resisting frenzy rather than riding with it; succumbing to Rötschreck
Two	Failing to diablerize a "humane" vampire; failing to regularly test one's limits in Abilities and Disciplines
One	Neglecting an opportunity to pursue lore about vampirism; denying vampiric needs (by refusing to feed, showing compassion or failing to learn about one's own abilities)

The Path of Cathari

Followers of the Path of Cathari, who call themselves Albigensians or Gnostics, hold to a mystical tradition which identifies two Gods. The pure and good God of Light made everything spiritual while the corrupt and evil God of Darkness made everything material. The idea surfaced again and again among believers in Classical and medieval times: Zoroastrianism and Manicheism made the two Gods equal while Gnostic groups within Judaism and Christianity declared the God of Darkness doomed to ultimate destruction. In the 12th and 13th centuries, the Cathar heresy's version of this dualist view of the world displaced mainstream Christianity in southern France. The Albigensian Crusade marked its violent end — the Bishop of Citeaux gave the famous advice "Kill them all; God will know His own" to the soldiers who then slaughtered every suspected heretic. The idea surfaced in future centuries, but never as successfully as during the Cathar era.

Some desperate Cathars accepted local vampires' offer of shelter or escape and were Embraced. As the truth of their new condition sank in,

those Cathars who didn't give themselves up to the sun set about systematically defining their place in the world. Vampires are the perfect creatures of Darkness, their spirit locked in flesh forever and their existence confined to the hours when darkness rules. They therefore took up the burden of being the foremost servants of Darkness. They test the weaknesses of Light: Anything that they can destroy deserves to perish. Since former Cathars created the Path as an actual codified doctrine, it bears the name of Cathari. Older vampires who'd already developed similar views adopted the practice without necessarily endorsing the name, and even in the Final Nights, followers of the Path still argue about its most proper title.

The Path of Cathari directs adherents to engage in every form of vice and indulgence… but not capriciously. Cathari vampires fight on the front lines of the cosmic war. They must tempt every child of the Light, then destroy all who prove weak or uncommitted. Private sins don't matter to the Cathari, only the sins that lead others to fall. Some Cathari believe that in the last moment of history, the Light will prevail and they'll be destroyed like Darkness itself. They accept this and focus on doing their duty in the meantime so that what remains in that final moment will stand strong, tested and purified. Other Cathari believe the outcome of the cosmic war is in doubt and that if Darkness wins, it deserves to.

Cathari do not kill anyone lightly. An imposed death interrupts the process of a soul's collapse from within, unlike suicide, being shot while resisting arrest or any of the deaths that come from a falling mortal's own actions. Cathari practice mastering frenzy to avoid strengthening the forces of Light with the ill-timed removal of a new recruit to Darkness. Sometimes a follower of this Path decides, after calm reflection, that a mortal or Cainite must die to further the overall course of the war. The Gnostic then kills deliberately and coolly, trying to derive as little pleasure from the process as possible. Like the mortal dualists they once were, the Cathari teach that souls reincarnate. They want to make sure that people reincarnate badly rather than well, which means letting corruption flourish fully.

Vampires on the Path of Cathari practice *Conviction* and *Instinct*.

The Ethics of the Path

- Sin gloriously. Indulge every capacity of your senses, reveling in the potential of the material world. The world is corrupt, and it is yours to rule.
- Lead others into temptation. Everyone who succumbs is your lawful prey.
- Embrace the most passionate mortals. Strengthen Darkness with the fire of conviction and desire.
- Fate made you what you are. Accept your destiny — fulfill it, don't try to flee it.
- Until the final victory of Light or Darkness, all souls reincarnate. Mortals return so you can kill them again and again. If you meet Final Death, you'll return as mortal yourself and may not earn your current status again.

Following the Path

Cathari take satisfaction in their role as masters of the world. They move freely and easily through mortal society. Nothing human beings do surprises old Cathari: There are no new sins, only new applications of the same failings. Cathari almost all agree that Darkness' triumph grows nearer every night.

The Path of Cathari calls its practitioners to deal with others. Almost all Cathari emphasize Social Attributes and Abilities. *Subterfuge* and *Streetwise* let Cathari find their next victims and set up the targets' falls. *Finance* and *Bureaucracy* help out when Cathari aim for the upper classes. A handful of scholarly Cathari — almost all of whom either practiced the path's various pre-Albigensian forms or are the childer of such old Cathari — study the historical and theological context of the Path and rely on *Academics* and *Occult*.

Cathari favor the Disciplines that let them corrupt and control others. *Dominate* and *Presence* are essential. Not many Cathari get the opportunity to learn *Chimerstry*, but those that do treasure it. *Animalism's* ability to interfere with sentient souls pleases the Cathari; only the most profoundly dedicated followers of the Path worry about winning the souls of animals to Darkness.

The First Impulse

Some people leave the living world gladly. Whether they expressed their loathing loudly (perhaps supported with firepower) or lived with quiet curses, they hated humanity and everything beneath the sun. People like this accept vampirism, eager for the chance to separate themselves from the daylight world and bring it all down. They're natural adherents of the Path of Cathari if they'll accept training about how to transmute raw hatred into specific ethical precepts.

Path of Cathari Hierarchy of Sins

Traits	Violations
Five	Acting with prudence, temperance or restraint; showing trust.
Four	Withholding the Embrace from passionately wicked (or virtuous!) mortals; resisting frenzy.
Three	Acting against another follower of the Path; killing in passion.
Two	Refraining from indulging in any interesting vice.
One	Arbitrary killing (rather than letting a victim destroy himself); encouraging others to restrain their impulses.

The Path of Death and the Soul

Necronomists — followers of the Path of Death and the Soul — study that part of themselves (and others) which remains aware after vital processes stop. Vampiric unlife illuminates normal death and life because it is poised in between them, making clear the boundaries and contours that normally remain hidden by simple death. After isolating the distinctly mortal components of existence, Necronomists can then grasp the true form of spirit.

Necronomists reject both the immortality of ghosts and the endless undead existence of vampires. They seek spiritual mastery, not mere disengagement, and freedom from all mortal and vampiric limits. Everything in the universe begins with spirit — the truly enlightened soul might include everything that is within its existence and rewrite the book of the world to suit itself.

According to Necronomists, the heart anchors the soul in its body. Vampire hearts are so vulnerable precisely because vampires shed so much of the armor of mortal life. A vampire's soul withdrew at Embrace from most vital functions to concentrate itself in the heart. Small wonder that a simple wooden stake can destroy such potent force. The Path of Death and the Soul encourages experimentation to overcome this limitation along with all others.

Vampires on the Path of Death and the Soul practice *Conviction* and *Self-Control*.

The Ethics of the Path

- Death releases the soul. Understand how and why this process works.
- Everything material reflects preexisting spiritual patterns. Discover those patterns and learn how the world truly works.
- Do not fear Final Death. Like all others, your soul is immortal and will endure in some form you do not yet know.
- Reason and emotion both express the soul's underlying state beneath all expression finite beings understand. Discover each soul's unique composition by studying how it manifests in behavior.
- Everything contains a piece of the truth, however disguised. Pierce every veil of myth and ignorance.

Following the Path

Tzimisce scholars developed this Path in antiquity; it's the oldest of the common Sabbat Paths by at least a thousand years. It replaces conventional morality with a drive that contains both intellectual and emotional elements, guiding behavior without endorsing human assumptions. (After all, still-living beings can scarcely understand existence without life.) During the Inquisition and Enlightenment, the Path picked up accretions from new scientific and occult theories, undergoing revision at the same time several other Paths got started. Most of its practitioners belong to the Sabbat, but not all. It appeals to a minority of studious vampires who reject all sect affiliation as mere distraction from the real great work of Cainites.

Necronomists seek to isolate soul manifestations by making them pure and intense. Everything must be extreme: all-consuming rage, blinding pain, overwhelming love and utterly dispassionate reason alike all illuminate the soul. Necronomists generally devote themselves to studying a few manifestations at time, then moving on when they feel they've mastered that realm of existence. Outsiders regard Necronomists as obsessive even by Sabbat standards since a dedicated Necronomist generally loses interest in everything but her current topic. When concerned with leadership, strategy and the like, Necronomists make excellent leaders. The rest of the time they exist on the fringes of Sabbat society; Necronomists currently studying pain often serve as torturers, but most Necronomist research simply doesn't matter to the vampires around them.

Unless they're experimenting on themselves to understand emotional states better, Necronomists present an icily rational and detached demeanor. They know that passion clouds perception, and while they find others' confusion fascinating, they don't want to confuse themselves.

Tzimisce (both of the main clan and the Old Clan) generally lead Necronomist groups. Most of their followers come from the ranks of Malkavian and Toreador *antitribu*, although the Path appeals to a handful of vampires in every clan. Harbingers of Skulls often pursue this Path in solitary study.

Almost all followers of the Path of Death and Soul make Mental Attributes primary. They learn as much *Occult*, *Academics*, *Medicine*, *Investigation* and related Abilities as their generational limits allow, forsaking other concerns except insofar as some personal mastery might help them understand research subjects better.

Necromancy and *Thaumaturgy* provide the Necronomist's primary tools, while *Auspex* allows fuller data collection. *Vicissitude* allows Necronomists interested in matters of the physical heart to experiment widely; other Necronomists can take it or leave it. Necronomists seldom engage in combat, so other vampires don't grasp why followers of this Path like *Fortitude*. Supernatural endurance, however, lets a Necronomist engage in long-term experiments no mortal (or even weak vampire) could maintain, and since insight comes from the purity of extremes, Necronomists seek out *Fortitude* early in their studies.

The First Impulse

Some people always found death more interesting in life. Life consists only of what you see, after all; the great mysteries await beyond death. Seekers of insights into the ultimate mysteries often bring themselves to the attention of Sabbat observers. If they survive the early shocks of actually being part of the world beyond death, the new recruits may find in the Path of Death and the Soul what they always sought, unawares. In addition, some people attract such attention for sheer unemotional detachment from the world. Whether or not they had any interest in such matters before death, some of these recruits take to the Path and its support for calm study.

Path of Death and the Soul Hierarchy of Sins

Traits	Violations
Five	Showing a fear of Final Death; maintaining any attachment to the mortal world.
Four	Succumbing to frenzy; being guided by emotions other than the ones you currently study.
Three	Failing to kill when it would be useful; forsaking the pursuit of enlightenment for other satisfactions.
Two	Showing an aversion to death in any form; showing compassion.
One	Needlessly preventing a death; killing without studying the death and its aftermath.

The Path of Evil Revelations

The followers of the Path of Evil Revelations, who call themselves Corrupters and Slaves, teach that all vampires serve the greater powers of evil. Vampires are not their own masters, but agents of Hell itself. The vampire's only choice is to acknowledge and serve his infernal creators — to resist is to face destruction. The Beast is the demon given to each vampire in the Embrace. In the end, when Hell triumphs and the infernal lords stride through every realm of existence, vampires who obeyed their inner demons will reap rewards. The others… won't.

No Slave knows just how many demons exist, or whether, over time, new demons emerge in some mysterious process of creation. Demons don't tell their servants such things. Each Slave learns his particular part in the grand schemes of Hell — the specific vices he should promote and, in some cases, the virtues he should concentrate on undermining. The demons set some vampires to traveling wherever the opportunity to corrupt in a particular way may arise while other vampires must stay in one area and corrupt it in a variety of ways.

Keep in mind that Corrupters don't make all this up. Spiritual beings of great power and great evil *do* exist in the World of Darkness. Infernalism does allow material beings to contact demons, and a variety of rules systematize the process of cutting deals with demons. Demons never tell the truth except when it makes a good weapon, so bystanders need not assume that the Beast actually is a demon or that Hell's triumph is inevitable. Vampire skeptics face enough surprises already when infernal force presents itself to them.

The Sabbat and Camarilla hate the Path of Evil Revelations with equal fervor. Neither sect likes the idea of vampires binding themselves to demons or the destruction such creatures bring. Corrupters regard the sects as foolish and weak, obstacles for Hell's willing servants to overcome — by subversion and mastery if possible. The Path of Evil Revelations claims unique truth. Any moral code founded on rejection

of vampires' status as demonic servants is wrong, pure and simple. Adherents to other Paths find the Corrupters laughably pretentious, dangerously insane or both.

Vampires on the Path of Evil Revelations practice *Conviction* and *Instinct*.

The Ethics of the Path

• You serve Hell. Demons reward their loyal servants and punish rebels and incompetents.

• Persuade other vampires of the truth. When they resist, corrupt them so that they unwittingly serve demonic agendas anyway, then explain the rest of the story.

• Fight fiercely against all vampires who harbor desires to be good or honorable.

• Never speak the truth except to gain something that dishonesty can't get for you. Intrigue with other vampires and demons other than the one you serve; success justifies disobedience.

• The Beast is your master and ally. Exploit it always.

Following the Path

Infernalism in various forms is as old as the Curse of Caine. The current form of the Path reflects, like most Sabbat Paths, the influence of mortal thinking during the Inquisition and Renaissance. The idea of Hell as a political state in a grand war with Heaven developed only after the nation-state appeared as the basis of mortal politics. Likewise, the notion of an autonomous evil — neither in rebellion against the good nor in ultimately harmonious tension with it — shows the influence of an increasingly secular philosophy. The dwindling of popular belief in demons as personal entities pushed the Path into obscurity, and it remains an unpopular choice.

The Sabbat does its best to keep the Path unpopular. Sabbat Inquisitors hunt infernalists as diligently as any breathing Inquisitor ever did. Unfortunately for anti-infernalist officers, the sect's fundamental lack of concern over human mortal restraints makes Sabbat members easier targets than the Humanity-obsessed ranks of the Camarilla. Infernalism flourishes most successfully in nomadic packs since it's easier to maintain secrecy over infernalist practices in the short term.

The escalating terror of the Final Nights makes infernalism more popular. Corrupters find ready recruits everywhere they go now that no lesser form of support seems likely to survive. When even Antediluvians fall, what hope waits for young vampires except the comforts of Hell? The Inquisition works overtime without really making a dent in the new ranks of infernalists.

Slaves practice a variety of rituals. Different demons want different sorts of offerings: Some care a lot about ceremony, and others don't. The most important sacrifice is of the vampire's self, his free will, place in the community and morality. Everything else is secondary. Human sacrifice helps bind the vampire to the demon, so demons encourage it. They also encourage other sacrifices and even demand the absence of sacrifices when that might breed more fear of reprisals. Followers of the Path all engage in frenetic activity since Hell frowns on idleness and no demonic master *ever* guarantees unconditional support.

Corrupters don't create many childer: It's just inviting competition for demonic favors. Instead, they work through their own servants and dupes to get things done. Some turn back to mortal society while others specialize in corrupting their fellow vampires. Mortal-oriented Corrupters feed evils great and small. Every sin from petty theft to global terrorism can serve Hell's agenda. As with the Corrupter himself, what matters most in mortal pawns is that their souls turn to Hell. The actions that follow just make the inner change visible.

Hell receives all willing lackeys, so there's no particularly "typical" Slave. To do their work well, followers of the Path must be social creatures. A vampire who does not spread evil doesn't matter to Hell, after all. Hell demands obedience, and followers of the Path often find themselves ordered to suddenly give up things they valued or enjoyed and replace them with new objects of desire. Anything that might distract the vampire from his master's concerns must go. Longtime followers of the Path tend to become strange, disconnected, obsessed creatures.

Corrupters who prepare themselves thoughtfully develop *Occult, Subterfuge, Etiquette, Intimidation* and *Empathy*. Those who actively fight their masters' enemies also build up a range of combat Abilities.

Auspex and *Presence* are the most popular Disciplines for followers of the Path. Many also study *Dark Thaumaturgy*, a particular form of *Thaumaturgy* known only to their masters. *Dementation* became popular recently as the Malkavian clan showed just how influential the Discipline could be when used intelligently.

The First Impulse

Every generation of mortals includes some people willing to sell their souls. The Sabbat generally doesn't like such fools any more than the Camarilla does, but vampires already on the Path of Evil Revelations do recruit among like-minded humans. Most often, however, people who never really thought about serving demons in life respond to their first experiences as vampires with a chain of logic that leads straight to Hell. If they manage to avoid destruction at the hands of vampires who don't approve of infernalism, these recruits gravitate toward packs focused on the Path.

Path of Evil Revelations Hierarchy of Sins

Traits	Violations
Five	Ever acting charitably or honorably; skipping nightly devotions.
Four	Helping others except for your own advantage; failing to acquire power in the society you corrupt (mortal or Cainite).
Three	Developing your own interests; not cooperating with other servants of the same master.
Two	Passing up a chance to fulfill your master's goals; providing infernal concepts to others not on the Path.
One	Disobeying your infernal master; failing to corrupt other vampires and to destroy those who resist.

The Path of the Feral Heart

The followers of the Path of the Feral Heart, or Beasts, define themselves in terms of the Beast. As the ultimate predators, vampires stand outside all human social constraints. Civilization supports the weak — vampires aren't weak and don't need the support. Vampires should hunt when hungry and rest when tired. The Beast is only one part of the vampire's nature, but it's the most important part. The Beast tells the vampire when to act and when to remain calm. There's nothing wrong with either state, only with doing something at the wrong time.

The Path doesn't give any merit to stupidity. As sentient predators, vampires must use their intelligence as well as their instincts. Forethought sharpens the hunt, letting the vampire prey most efficiently. The Path rejects the trappings of civilization, including technology. The Curse gives vampires everything they need. Relying on the tools invented by prey makes the predator that much more dependent on prey, more like the prey, more prone to failure. Vampires hunt and kill and should do just fine without any trappings.

Vampires on the Path of the Feral Heart practice *Conviction* and *Instinct*.

The Ethics of the Path

• Survive. You can't do anything if you don't exist.

• Strike a balance with your Beast. Temper brutality with cunning, reason with instinct.

• Everything that exists is in some sense "natural." Civilization isn't bad because it's unnatural. Civilization is bad because it weakens you.

• Master your fears, including fire. You must be free to choose your course of action unfettered by terror.

• Your allegiances should be absolute. You owe total commitment to yourself and your packmates.

Following the Path

The Path of the Feral Heart has existed without much change for thousands of years. Gangrel pioneers created it, and it spread to other clans as they found themselves facing defeat and exile. Nomadic Sabbat packs often practice it.

Followers of the Path feel no urge to create a formal organization: They share insights and questions when they happen to encounter fellow adherents. A minority of Beasts serve the Sabbat as assassins and do very well indeed. The Path teaches vampires to kill carefully, in response to need, not caprice.

Beasts don't bother with fashion. If they wear clothes at all, they aim for functionality. Sturdy protective garb does the job. Nor do they bother with camouflage — Beast Gangrel let their animal features show. Beasts do pay constant attention to their environment. Bystanders notice them glancing around, smelling everything and listening for faint sounds. The Path pretty well precludes involvement in politics; Beasts hold no high offices in the Sabbat although some make good pack priests.

Country Gangrel outnumber all other followers of the Path. Some City Gangrel who style themselves urban predators follow the Path, along with small numbers of Ravnos *antitribu*, Nosferatu *antitribu* and a few in each of the other clans. The Lasombra and Tzimisce almost never commit to it, since they take civilization very seriously.

Physical or Mental Attributes come first for Beasts. Every Beast learns *Survival, Brawl, Dodge* and *Alertness*. Many also study *Animal Ken*, and some become formidable at *Empathy* thanks to their ability to pick up clues about mental states others try to hide. *Intimidation* often follows naturally from the Path's emphasis on cooperation with the Beast.

Followers of this Path find *Fortitude* and *Protean* indispensable. *Animalism* is useful to learn from lesser predators and for feeding. Many Beasts develop *Auspex, Obfuscate* and *Celerity* as well, since all three enhance a vampire's ability to hunt.

The First Impulse

Some people turn their backs on civilization in search of an imagined better existence in the wild. They may gather in small communes or may live altogether solitary lives, trying to purge themselves of the taints created by technology and population. Vampires on the Path of the Feral Heart love to recruit these sorts of people, offering them the opportunity to exist with far fewer shackles than any mortal can hope for. In addition, some people who moved happily through life turn to the wilderness after death to separate themselves from their lost existence. The Path of the Feral Heart helps them maintain internal discipline as they cut ties to sources of external discipline.

	PATH OF THE FERAL HEART HIERARCHY OF SINS
Traits	Violations
Five	Hunting with anything other than your innate powers; engaging in politics.
Four	Remaining near fire or sunlight except to finish a job; acting with unnecessary cruelty.
Three	Failing to hunt when hungry; failing to support your pack.
Two	Refusing to follow one's instincts; killing without need.
One	Refusing to kill to survive; killing for any reason other than survival.

THE PATH OF HONORABLE ACCORD

The followers of the Path of Honorable Accord call themselves Knights and focus on the society of vampires as a whole. The Curse makes vampires predators with a strong individualistic bias. Unrestrained, they'd destroy each other down to the very last Leech. Knights teach that honor — the rigorous enforcement of standards of nobility in conduct — holds the society of vampires together. Honor strengthens a vampire's ability to resist the Beast and provides the rules that allow vampires to coexist without having to fall back on the human morality they've abandoned.

The Path allows no room for mercy or sentiment. Honor is a matter of calculated rational choice. Knights carefully analyze the meaning of the commitments they make and the circumstances they face. Either they must act a particular way to keep their commitments, or not. If not, they enjoy complete freedom to decide how to act on any basis that suits them — raw self-interest usually dominates. Knights gradually lose track of notions like "friendship." They have allies and regular associates; trust plays no part in the Path. Nor does the Path require making any particular commitments, with a few specific exceptions. What matters is how Knights keep their word, not which particular promises they give.

Knights make prominent and reliable Sabbat leaders. As long as their superiors administer oaths of office carefully, Knights serve with less treachery or complicated side issues than almost anyone else in the sect. If their oaths require them to fight, Knights fight courageously because cowardice would betray the spirit of their commitment. If they swear to teach, Knights teach thoroughly and make sure their students learn. The problem comes when superiors offer oaths that don't require the Knights to restrain personal ambitions. Knights make great traitors, and rationalize their treachery as providing negative examples of just how important careful definition is when honor ties the society together.

Vampires on the Path of Honorable Accord practice *Conscience* and *Self-Control*. Keep in mind that this Path's version of *Conscience* does not include remorse, only concern for one's integrity.

The Ethics of the Path

- Honor every commitment you make. Your word defines who you are to everyone else.
- Never fear, or at least never show it. Duty takes precedence over your personal worries.
- Show respect to your superiors, loyalty to your equals and appropriate consideration to your lessers.
- Repay your debts in full.
- Support your comrades-at-arms in all endeavors except treachery.

Following the Path

The Path of Honorable Accord emerged from the medieval world, inspired by the same ideas that underlay the older Path of Chivalry without accepting human morality in any matter but honor itself. The decline of chivalry in mortal society also led to Honorable Accord losing ground to the Paths of the Renaissance era. The Sabbat civil wars brought Honorable Accord back to general attention. Knights committed themselves to the Code of Milan, becoming its first defenders. Many Knights identify themselves by an oath as "followers of the Code."

The Knights remained prominent throughout the sect schisms of the 19th and 20th centuries. They generally remained aloof from factional wars, defining their duty to the sect as a whole. In particularly contested regions, Knight often brokered cease-fires between rival factions. As pack leaders, they allow more experimentation than followers of other Paths: Any action that doesn't jeopardize the commitments of pack members to each other and the sect is fine with adherents of the Path of Honorable Accord.

Knights take a very visible part in *ritae* and ceremonies. Public reaffirmation of one's oaths allows the Knights to shine as the really trustworthy, serious members of the group… and also provide good opportunities for humiliating or punishing the unreliable fools around them. Other Sabbat members find Knights useful but scary and sometimes downright ridiculous. Only vampires with a suicidal urge actually laugh *at* Knights, though. For their part, Knights see everyone else as tools or obstacles. That includes mortal society as well as Cainite; where mortals may advance a Knight's oaths, she won't hesitate to use them, destroying them once the job is done.

Ventrue *antitribu* and Salubi *antitribu* dominate this Path. Nosferatu *antitribu*, Tzimisce uninterested in radical personal transformation and lucid Malkavian *antitribu* also find the Path a good match for their concerns. More and more Panders adopt the Path as they find it a good route to respect from the vampires around them. A handful of Camarilla elders — those who can keep their private lives well away from unsympathetic inquirers — practice the Path, making no effort to teach it, simply holding onto what they remember as their mortal ideals from 800 years ago.

The Path of Honorable Accord requires calm contemplation. A Knight must never act rashly. She should first consider her obligations and then evaluate the consequences of the options available to her. Hasty Knights

perish. Deliberate Knights also perish, but only when fighting on behalf of their commitments and when no lesser sacrifice can do justice to the duty.

Most Knights learn a wide range of combat Abilities along with *Leadership* and *Expression*. *Investigation*, *Law* and other research-related Abilities help Knights commit and act wisely. Knights who take office acquire relevant *Lores*.

More Knights learn *Fortitude* and *Presence* than any other Disciplines: *Fortitude* for surviving the rigors of duty, *Presence* for commanding proper respect. *Potence* helps in discharging martial duties. Salubri *antitribu* on the Path favor the martial side of *Valeran* and sometimes teach it to their fellow Knights.

The First Impulse

Some people want to be part of the winning team. They emerge from mortality with the knowledge that the Sabbat is the biggest winning team there ever was: No corporate acumen or political clout can begin to compete with the power of the blood. Having joined the winning team, they want to help it win. The Path of Honorable Accord gives structure to their desire. Some of these natural adherents were real winners in life, but some lost again and again and take their undead existence as a chance to forget all that and get it right this time.

Path of Honorable Accord Hierarchy of Sins

Traits	Violations
Five	Failing to uphold every precept your group teaches; failing to show hospitality to your allies.
Four	Associating with dishonorable individuals; failing to participate in group rites.
Three	Disobeying your leader; failing to protect your allies.
Two	Placing persona concerns above duty; showing cowardice.
One	Breaking your word; killing without strong justification.

The Path of Lilith

The followers of the Path of Lilith, who sometimes call themselves Bahari or Lilins, begin with a heretical view of Cainite history. According to the Lilins, the textual fragments that compose the Book of Lilith reveal the true story of vampires' origins. The tale begins not with Caine but with Lilith, Adam's first wife, whom he rejected because she claimed to be his equal. Exiled, she wandered the unfinished wilderness of the world. Out of her sufferings, greater than any we can imagine now, came a unique enlightenment. She built a garden of her own and taught herself to master those gifts that God had hoarded for Himself. When Caine received God's curse, Lilith stood ready to take him, comfort him and train him. Caine has never acknowledged the extent of his debt; most of his childer show the same lack of gratitude. Nonetheless, Lilith's heirs persist in seeking true wisdom for themselves and for the whole world.

The Lilins regard everyone, mortal and Cainite alike, as children trapped in an immature understanding of the universe. Everyone advances to a comfortable point and stops there, afraid of the challenges that lie ahead. Lilith taught Caine the way a parent must teach a rebellious child, the way her heirs teach themselves and others: Through pain. Only discipline forces the child to pay attention and persevere, resisting the temptations to turn aside. Adults deceive themselves into believing they've learned the important lessons. They're wrong. Compared to the vast scope of potential enlightenment, almost no one ever takes more than one step along the hard road. The Path of Lilith pushes its adherents to go further.

Pain marks every step. The Lilins seek to challenge their own limits. Fire walking, freezing themselves, impaling themselves on thorns and blades, starving themselves, feeding on poisoned blood, amputation — everything that shocks the body and mind might open a door of perception. Flesh imprisons the soul even after life stops, and Cainite have to work at least as hard as mortals to escape its limits. Outsiders see the Lilins as a bunch of masochists and sadists, but no outsider really understands the point. Pain isn't the end; it's a means of forcing fresh thought. If other means served, the Lilins would use them. In fact, the Lilins *do* pursue esoteric study, meditation and the like, resorting to pain at the point the other means fail.

While the Lilins don't pursue pain gratuitously, the Path allows no room for compassion in any ordinary sense. Enlightenment must come, whatever the cost. Let those who wish to remain ignorant remove themselves from the Lilins. Above all, Lilins drive themselves and each other, but they won't let others remain ignorant. Everyone needs to awaken to their full potential. The Final Nights give the Lilins an extra sense of urgency since they see absolutely no hope except the attainment of the heights Lilith reached long ago. If the Antediluvians rise and face only an ignorant horde, the world will not last. Pain must save the world.

Some individuals find themselves suddenly hearing a quiet song beneath all other sounds. The Hierophants — the priests and priestesses of the Path — call this the *ahi hay Lilitu* and diligently seek out its hearers. The song marks one's readiness to join the ranks… regardless of how the listener feels about it now.

Vampires on the Path of Lilith practice *Conviction* and *Instinct*.

The Ethics of the Path

- Accept every pain. There is no enlightenment without it.
- Freely give pain to seekers; freely receive pain from seekers. You do not follow this Path alone.
- Practice what you learn. The world depends on practice, not theory.
- Plant a garden that shows the power of your mastery over creation. Gather with your brothers and sisters to share your progress.
- Seek out those who, unknown to themselves, are now ready to join you.

Following the Path

The Path of Lilith is older than recorded Cainite history. Conflicting legends attribute its formalization to various Methuselahs; most stories agree that the key manuscripts came to light in Africa, but no details can be confirmed now. The ranks of Lilins have always been small — they rise in times of great crisis, then shrink again as the uncommitted fall away. (A few very clever outside observers look for rising numbers of Lilins as a clue that trouble brews somewhere.) The Path prescribes no specific rituals, so every community of Lilins develops complex ceremonies of their own.

The Camarilla ruthlessly persecutes the Lilins; their very presence raises unwanted questions about just how dead and buried the past is. The Sabbat doesn't support the Path's teachings but allows Lilins to remain as long as they serve the sect. This policy of tolerance may change as the Path grows more popular.

Lilins trade the knowledge they've won. They maintain loose networks of occult-minded individuals — not just vampires, but mortals, magicians and even ghosts sometimes prove useful. The Sabbat *does* frown on these exchanges, and Lilins who share too much risk harsh punishment. The Lilins often develop their own versions of *ritae*, with much more pain involved. It's impossible to catalog fully the range of Bahari practices because they never fully discard anything that once proved useful. Enlightenment could strike twice in the same way, after all.

Lilins alternate periods of frenzied activity, when they search endlessly for the next change and the next learning experience, with periods of quiet withdrawal, when they turn inward and try to collate what they've learned so far. The Path finds some adherents in every social class and group, and offers no barrier based on wealth (or its absence), gender or any other external marker. By the time they're done, Lilins generally retain few if any clues as to their original condition. Sustained torture burns away the features a vampire began with while deep insights change the vampire's demeanor. Many Lilins, though not all, favor elaborate vestments and props for their rituals, and this attention to ceremonial detail is one of the few traits the Lilins have in common.

No clan dominates the Path of Lilith, within the Sabbat or outside it. Sabbat followers include Tzimisce and Lasombra and *antitribu* from the Malkavian, Nosferatu and Toreador clans. A few Kiasyd practice it, as do Harbingers of Skulls who refer to their unseen high priestess Lamia. As noted above, some version of the Path also finds mortal and ghostly practitioners. More women follow it than men, and women seem to fare better on it, but the Path does not exclude men. Individuals make their own way toward the goal of completeness, and followers encourage each other even when their specific steps diverge greatly. The Path promotes a real, if peculiar, sense of community among people who share only the drive to break through all restraints that keep them finite and static.

Torture and *Occult* form the foundation of the Bahari standard set of Abilities. Many things can supplement them; *Lores*, academic and scientific

Abilities, *Investigation* and *Medicine* are all popular. *Linguistics* comes in handy when Lilins try to trace the work of their predecessors.

The Path's core teachings state that Lilith developed Disciplines within herself in response to the pain of evil. Her disciples emulate her with special attention to *Animalism, Celerity, Fortitude* and *Obfuscate*. *Vicissitude* provides pain without external tools, and packs of Lilins try to include someone who knows it. The handful of Ravnos who follow the Path enjoy tremendous popularity as *Horrid Reality* makes a wonderful teaching tool.

The First Impulse

The truth hurts, some people believe. Becoming undead hurt a lot; even a physically painless Embrace does involve dying and the trauma that goes with it, and the Sabbat seldom Embraces with regard for the personal comfort of recruits. Having begun their new existence in pain, they continue to seek further truths in pain. Some of these recruits were masochists or sadists in life, others dealt with pain no more intimately than the picking of a scab. The Path of Lilith draws more followers from those who never cared about pain in life than from those who already have experience trying to open their spiritual eyes through material suffering.

Path of Lilith Hierarchy of Sins

Traits	Violations
Five	Gratifying desires immediately; pursuing temporal wealth or power.
Four	Letting others remain ignorant about Caine and Lilith; inflicting pain on those not ready to learn from it.
Three	Refusing to participate in Bahari rituals; fearing death.
Two	Killing a living or undead being except in immediate self-defense; failing to seek out Lilith's teachings.
One	Shunning pain; failing to dispense pain to others who can learn something from it.

The Path of Power and the Inner Voice

The followers of the Path of Power and the Inner Voice, called Unifiers, take the rejection of their lost humanity to its extreme. They discard all desire for community, all interest in philosophical and theological matters, all intellectual and abstract pursuits in favor of one single goal: Power. Vampires, they say, exist to rule, and they shall set the example. Some night they'll rule the world. In the meantime, they rule as much as they can.

Unifiers focus on the tangible world around them. If they ever had a soul, it's gone along with their breath. Human beings and their petty desires don't matter since they all die. Purely personal satisfactions don't matter, either. What counts is the society of vampires, and the role Unifiers play in it. The ability to give orders and watch others obey them matters. Unifiers aim to command everything around them — political, economic, social and spiritual authority should all be theirs.

The Path of Power and the Inner Voice requires Unifiers to understand everyone. Would-be rulers must know why people obey, what drives them to rebel and how different forms of power work. Every aspect of human and vampiric nature comes into play, from the foundations of biology and occult history to psychology. Unifiers study both the surface mind and the subconscious, as well as the body they exist in. Particularly diligent followers of the Path zealously pursue competing theories of vampiric origins and development in hopes of creating the Cainite counterpart to human medical lore. Stupid power-seekers try to apply bigger sticks when obvious brute-force solutions fail. Usurpers know that command sometimes works secretly, and that very complex forces interact with each other each time subjects obey or reject an order.

Unifiers enjoy a great deal of respect, and even more fear, from other Sabbat members. Every successful follower of this Path shows herself both willing and able to use every means at her disposal to increase her power. As followers, Unifiers seek constantly to displace their superiors. As leaders, Unifiers tolerate no failure or dissent. Wherever a significant number of Unifiers gather, most of them soon end up either fleeing or dead. The abolition of mercy and compassion applies to one's fellow followers of the Path just as much as to anyone else.

Novices on the Path tend to practice overt forms of rulership, with fear and punishment as their tools. More sophisticated Unifiers realize that the best control is that which rules out the possibility of rebellion. Willing servants do things slaves and prisoners don't. An effective Unifier corrupts his followers until they can conceive of no existence without him. Offer them the satisfaction of all their desires and develop desires that only you can satisfy, and they're yours.

Vampires on the Path of Power and the Inner Voice practice *Conviction* and *Instinct*.

The Ethics of the Path

- Success justifies everything. Pursue mastery at all costs.
- Be sparing in rewards. Don't let subordinates count too strongly on your favor.
- Show respect to leaders who deserve it; replace those who don't.
- Never show weakness for fear. Appear stronger than you are and grow into your image.
- Use every tool at your disposal.

Following the Path

Nobody knows for sure just how this Path developed. The most common story attributes it to Lord Marcus of the Lasombra in the early 16th century. It certainly originated or took its current form in the Renaissance, but may have roots running back further. Unifiers gave prominent early support to the Sabbat; those who survive continue to lead it in the Final Nights. Unifiers choose their childer more carefully than many Sabbat members and are responsible for many mysterious disappearances of tyrants, politicians, prison camp directors and the like. In recent years the Path has gained many more adherents. The prospect of ever-escalating warfare inspires low-ranking Sabbat members to try to move up in the ranks so that they can give orders rather than take them.

Unifiers practice no Path-specific rituals and don't like to spend time around each other except when necessary. They do enthusiastically take part in war parties and hunts. Every opportunity to show mastery, like the Fire Dance, gives Unifiers the chance to humiliate others in public. A humble follower of this Path would be a contradiction in terms. Whatever the social background of a particular Unifier, confidence to the point of megalomania now drives her actions.

Some Unifiers develop extensive combat mastery; others don't. All Unifiers build Abilities such as *Leadership*, *Intimidation*, *Politics* and *Subterfuge*. *Empathy* and *Meditation* assist careful planners.

Dominate and *Presence* are the favorite Disciplines for followers of this Path. Everything else has its uses, and the Unifiers don't spurn any Disciplines as irrelevant.

The First Impulse

Some people want to rule the world and want to rule it without having to share it with others. Becoming a vampire shows them how much they didn't know about the real nature of power in the world. That's a learning experience. Now that they know about the night's society, they want to master it. If they manage to avoid destruction for excessive insubordination, recruits of this sort take readily to the Path of Power and the Inner Voice — at least, they do if they can refrain from arguing too much with their teachers. As with the Path of Honorable Accord, some adherents were winners and rulers in life, others just the opposite. The impulse to rule doesn't always go with prior success in exercising it.

Path of Power and the Inner Voice
Hierarchy of Sins

Traits	Violations
Five	Denying responsibility for your actions; treating loyal underlings badly.
Four	Failing to respect your superiors (except when they err); helping others when you gain nothing from it.
Three	Accepting defeat; failing to kill when it's in your interests.
Two	Submitting to others' errors; not using every effective tool of control.
One	Tolerating failure; declining an opportunity for power.

Chapter Five: Caine's Armory

Between the Lasombra and Tzimisce, the various *antitribu* and a handful of minor bloodlines, the vampires of the Sabbat practice most of the commonly known Disciplines (*Animalism, Auspex, Celerity, Dominate, Fortitude, Obfuscate, Potence* and *Presence*). Specific lines also know certain proprietary Disciplines that appear in **Laws of the Night** (*Chimerstry, Dementation, Obtenebration, Protean, Quietus, Serpentis* and *Vicissitude*). However, this is hardly the full extent of the powers that various Sabbat members boast. Several Sabbat bloodlines claim their own secret permutations of Caine's curse, and elder Lasombra, Tzimisce and Malkavian *antitribu* wield aspects of their respective Disciplines that are unmatched by those of any Camarilla vampire. The late, unlamented Tremere *antitribu* did add a handful of *Thaumaturgy* paths and rituals to the sect's arsenal, and these are still in the hands and grimoires of other blood magicians. The sect's few necromancers boast their own rites, and the mysterious Harbingers of Skulls have demonstrated their own mastery of the boundaries of life and death through the art known as the *Mortuus Path*.

Though many outside the Sabbat regard the sect's unique powers as the foulest arts of the undead, the Sabbat itself is all too aware of abilities that are even more blasphemous. Since its inception, traitorous infernalists have plagued the sect, vampires who would give over their very souls to demons for the promise of temporal power. Many times, this power comes in the form of lessons in blood magic, and the Sabbat knows these arts as *Dark Thaumaturgy*.

Dark Thaumaturgy

Though the Sabbat endorses many paths to power, dealing with demons is one that the sect has never approved of. Servitude to an infernal master, to the Sabbat's way of thinking, is no better than servitude to the Antediluvians — in some ways worse, as it places the Cainite under an influence that Caine himself

never accepted. Nevertheless, individual Sabbat vampires do seek out the quick road to personal power that demons provide. One of the most common forms of power that demons grant to vampires is a unique form of blood magic, and such paths and rituals are collectively known as *Dark Thaumaturgy*. Most Cainites refer to practitioners of this Discipline as infernalists.

Were a scholar of blood magic to compare the fundamental practices of *Thaumaturgy* to *Dark Thaumaturgy*, she would find few differences. Both are forms of magic that rely on the strength of Caine's Curse and the individual practitioner's vitae to power their effects. The primary differences lie in the philosophy behind the two Disciplines and the source of the requisite knowledge. Much like a history lesson from a devout neo-Nazi is inescapably colored by his perceptions, a blood magic lesson from a demon bears the biases of the infernal perspective on magical workings. With time, this taint affects the vampire's perceptions, his worldview, his physical form and even his very soul (which, by this point, he merely holds in trust for his demonic master).

The Sabbat loathes infernalists because their ultimate loyalty is not to the sect. Rather, it is to the demon with whom they made their pact for power. Though an infernalist's night-to-night actions may be in accordance with the Sabbat's goals, his master may call upon him at any moment to act on the demon's own agenda, regardless of how it conflicts with the actions and views of those around him. To an organization whose very existence is based on the principle of mutual loyalty, such betrayal is anathema. The recently expanded Sabbat Inquisition exists for the sole purpose of rooting out and destroying such traitors, and it is very, very good at this job.

Learning individual paths and rituals of *Dark Thaumaturgy* follows the same limitations as for *Thaumaturgy*, including the declaration of a primary path. However, the learning process is marginally easier, thanks to demonic tutelage. All *Dark Thaumaturgy* paths cost two Experience Traits for Basic powers, five for Intermediate ones, and eight for Advanced ones. All Basic rituals cost two Experience Traits, Intermediate rituals cost three and Advanced Rituals cost five. Note that *Thaumaturgy* and *Dark Thaumaturgy* are incompatible for the purposes of sharing rituals and primary path levels — a character with an Advanced rating in his primary *Dark Thaumaturgy* path but only an Intermediate one in his primary path of *Thaumaturgy* cannot learn Advanced *Thaumaturgy* rituals.

Players may not take this as one of their Disciplines at character creation. Even if you have every intention of coming into the chronicle as an infernalist (and where is your Storyteller if you are?), you must still make the bargain to start acquiring *Dark Thaumaturgy*. Furthermore, you may not learn simply by spending a couple of Experience Traits and calling it a *fait accompli* — your character must petition his dark master each and every time he wishes to advance on his path or learn a ritual. Doing so otherwise is to trivialize the dark pact and the fact that an infernalist is at the beck and call of a demon.

Dark Thaumaturgical Paths

Mechanically, *Dark Thaumaturgy* functions in the same manner as does *Thaumaturgy* (**Laws of the Night**, p. 176). To use one of the powers of an individual path, spend a Blood Trait and make any additional challenges or expenditures that the individual path calls for.

SUPERIOR DISCIPLINES:
THE FRONTIERS OF THE BLOOD

Cainites whose blood is of the Eighth Generation or stronger have access to Discipline manifestations that are orders of magnitude more potent than Basic, Intermediate, and Advanced powers. These are collectively known as Superior Disciplines, and they are further divided by the minimum generation that a character must have in order to learn them. As with Basic and Intermediate Disciplines, a character may not acquire a Superior Discipline until he has learned all of that Discipline's preceding levels, so a character wishing to acquire Ascendant *Dementation* must first learn Basic, Intermediate, Advanced, Elder and Master *Dementation*.

Past the Advanced level, the "path" of Discipline development forks. A character's individual Superior Discipline powers develop based on her own philosophy regarding that Discipline, as well as her precise needs. As a result, there are multiple possible powers for each level of a Superior Discipline. A character need not learn all the listed Elder-level powers of a Discipline in order to proceed to the Master level — she only needs to acquire one. Additional powers at the same level cost the same amount of experience as the first.

Additionally, it should be noted that a character is not limited to the powers listed here. Players and Storytellers are encouraged to work together to develop a new Superior power for a character whose mindset and needs do not match any of these.

Note that this chapter only presents Superior levels of Disciplines whose primary practitioners are Sabbat member clans or bloodlines. Superior levels of *Animalism*, *Auspex*, *Celerity*, *Dominate*, *Fortitude*, *Obfuscate*, *Potence*, *Presence* and *Protean*, as well as more *Thaumaturgy* paths and rituals, can be found in this book's companion, **The Camarilla Guide**. More detailed rules for creating elder vampires also appear in that book. After all, the Camarilla needs all the help it can get. Superior levels of *Chimerstry*, *Quietus* and *Serpentis*, as well as more *Necromancy* rituals, will appear in upcoming products.

A final word on these powers: some of them are truly horrific beyond the scale that any reasonable chronicle should ever see. Methuselah-level powers, in particular, are game-breaking devices. At the risk of stating the obvious, fifth-generation vampires are not intended to be player characters. They are akin to forces of nature, and the powers at their command should also be treated as such.

Level	Generation	Experience Trait Cost
Elder	eighth	12
Master	seventh	15
Ascendant	sixth	18
Methuselah	fifth	21

Caine's Armory

The Fires of the Inferno

With this path, you learn mastery over the very fires of Hell (or so you're told). Unlike a practitioner of *The Lure of Flames*, who spontaneously generates fire, you summon this sickly green flame by opening a tiny one-way portal to Hell. This path is extremely unsubtle and impossible to hide, but its eldritch flames are as impressive in effect as they are fearsome in appearance.

Fire from this path is supernatural in origin, and protection from mundane flames does not help its victims. Unless a power specifically protects against supernatural aggravated damage (such as *Fortitude*), it provides no special benefits when resisting *Fires of the Inferno*. Body armor does not absorb damage from this path, which instead goes straight to the target. These flames may, however, be extinguished in the same manner as any other fire (with holy water having more than normal effect, at Storyteller discretion). *Fires of the Inferno* uses the *Occult* Ability for retests. All powers of this path have a maximum range of the character's line of sight.

Basic Fires of the Inferno
Flash Blind

You may cause a brief flash of intensely bright flame to appear in front of a target's eyes. Though this power functions more as a distraction than an attack, it briefly disorients its victim, during which time you may launch an additional attack or take advantage of the confusion to escape.

To *Flash Blind* a target, make a Mental Challenge against her. If you win, she is dazzled and disoriented by the eruption of fire and automatically loses all ties until the end of the next turn. If she was using *Heightened Senses* to enhance her vision, the sensory overload blinds her for one hour (see the Flaw *Blind*, p. 116 of **Laws of the Night**).

Flame Lance

This power allows you to shoot a pencil-thin stream of intense fire. This appears as a perfectly straight line of bright green flame reaching from you to your target. Many practitioners of *Flame Lance* invoke this power by pointing at their intended target and twisting their wrists, defining the portal through which the flame erupts with the circle that their fingertip describes in the air.

To strike someone with *Flame Lance*, make a Mental Challenge that the target resists with her Physical Traits. If you win, she suffers one level of aggravated damage. You may use *Flame Lance* to ignite flammable inanimate targets, though it will not set flame to anything that your target is wearing.

Intermediate Fires of the Inferno
Ring of Fire

When you use this power, a foot-thick circle of flame erupts in a 10' radius around you. Smoldering lines appear on the ground inside this circle, inscribing a pentagram with you at its center. This fire reaches your own height, forming a wall of dancing flame through which any potential assailant must leap in order to reach you. The fire stays in place regardless of where you move, though you have no special immunity to it if you attempt to pass through it.

Spend a Willpower Trait to ignite a *Ring of Fire*. The circle erupts instantly, and anyone who is standing on its perimeter must win a Static Physical

Challenge against five Traits or suffer one level of aggravated damage. Before making this challenge, he has the option to declare whether he will move to the outside or inside of the ring after the test is resolved (we assume that no one will want to remain standing directly on the ring's perimeter, though particularly brave or stupid individuals may do so by expending a Willpower Trait). The *Ring of Fire* remains in place for the rest of the scene or until you are knocked unconscious, move out of line of sight of it or decide to release it.

Anyone who attempts to pass through the *Ring of Fire* must win a *Courage* Virtue Test against three Traits in order to summon the will to do so and takes one level of aggravated damage if he does step through it. You are not immune to damage from the fire, though you suffer no fear of it and may pass through it without the *Courage* Virtue Test.

Incinerate

You may inflict the very wrath of Hell upon an enemy. With a gesture and a glance, you create a three-foot wide circle under a target from which a column of flame erupts to consume her. This fire reaches the ceiling if you are indoors, and reaches 30 feet into the air outdoors.

To *Incinerate* your target, issue a Mental Challenge that she resists with her Physical Traits. If you win, she is unable to dodge before the ground under her erupts in fire. The initial blast does two levels of aggravated damage to her and anyone in contact with her. Your primary target is also on fire and takes one additional aggravated health level every turn until she extinguishes the blaze or perishes. A victim of this attack may use *Dodge* for a retest.

Advanced Fires of the Inferno

Furnaces of Hell

Your mastery of hellfire has surpassed mere point-targeting. With this power, you may engulf multiple opponents in simultaneous eruptions of fire. This power's effects resemble those of *Incinerate*, but the fires summoned with *Furnaces of Hell* are much more intense.

To throw open the doors of the *Furnaces of Hell*, spend a Willpower Trait and make a mass challenge against all your intended targets (you may affect as many targets as you have permanent Willpower), testing your Mental Traits against their Physical Traits. Anyone you beat in this challenge is subject to the effects of *Incinerate*, but the initial injury to each primary target is three levels of aggravated damage.

Stop, Drop and Roll

A character who is on fire must take an action to try to put herself out. This is resolved after all opposed actions take place. It requires a Static Physical Challenge against a number of Traits equal to three times the number of Health Levels of fire damage that the character was exposed to during the turn (*not* the actual amount of damage she took). If she wins, she extinguishes the flames (though she may re-ignite if she remains in contact with open flame). Players should roleplay this appropriately, though not to the extent of causing a false alarm.

The Path of Phobos

This path is subtle in most of its manifestations, and its effects are usually difficult to recognize as blood magic in action. This is because the *Path of Phobos*, rather than creating horrifying images or inducing artificial emotions, releases and magnifies fears that were already lurking within its victims' minds. While this path is not an overtly powerful one, many cunning infernalists prefer it as they can use its effects as a source of social and psychological leverage. It is all the more powerful because its illusions exist entirely within the victim's mind, and thus *Auspex* cannot penetrate them as it can the specters of *Chimerstry*. The *Path of Phobos* uses the *Intimidation* Ability for retests. All powers of this path require you to be within line of sight of your victim to apply them though some effects may persist after activation regardless of where your victim is.

The *Path of Phobos* is not without its drawbacks. Continued use of it often results in the infernalist sharing her victims' unearthed fears. You may use *Path of Phobos* twice per night without any danger. However, on the third and every subsequent use of a power from this Path, you must succeed in a Static Mental Challenge against a number of Traits equal to the number of times that night you have used the path. If you fail, you are afflicted with the Flaw *Nightmares* (**Laws of the Night**, p. 117) for the next week and you lose an additional Blood Trait for every night that this lasts. If you fail three such tests in the same night, you permanently gain the Flaw *Phobia* (**Laws of the Night**, p. 117). The Storyteller determines the object of this phobia; it should be related to the fears of one or more of the victims on whom you have used *Path of Phobos* during that night.

Basic Path of Phobos

Induce Fear

You can induce a mild paranoia in your victim. She feels as if she is being watched constantly. Menacing figures hover at the edges of her vision, never coming fully into view.

Make a Static Mental Challenge against your subject's permanent Mental Traits to *Induce Fear* in your victim. If you succeed, she is affected for the remainder of the scene. While under the effects of *Induce Fear*, she must make a *Courage* Virtue Test against two Traits to take any action that exposes her to her unseen stalkers. She is also down one Trait on all tests she makes in combat due to the distraction imposed by "having to watch her back."

Spook

The implicit terrors of *Induce Fear* become explicit with *Spook*. Your victim experiences minor hallucinations that portray an imminent attack that he will be powerless to resist. A police officer might see the flash of a gun barrel from the window of a burned-out apartment building while a Gangrel elder might hear the heavy footfalls of Lupines in war-form just around the corner. Whatever form these sensations take, they add up to the overburdening impression that your victim must flee at once lest he fall prey to whatever menaces him.

Issue a Mental Challenge. If you win, your target must leave the area immediately. Additionally, a Cainite victim of this power must win a *Courage* Virtue Test against three Traits or enter Rötschreck. The compulsion to avoid the area lasts for one hour; the frenzy subsides in five minutes.

Intermediate Path of Phobos
Terrorize

You can now summon illusions of your victim's worst fears that, to her, are indistinguishable from reality. No one else can perceive them, but they are immediate threats to her, and so omnipresent that they all but paralyze her. If she is afraid of heights, the floor seems to fall away from her; if she fears snakes, a hundred cobras slither into the room and surround her. You are not automatically aware of what fear you have unearthed with this power though you may be able to infer it from your victim's reactions by winning a Social Challenge (retest with *Empathy* or *Subterfuge*).

To *Terrorize* your victim, bid a number of Mental Traits equal to her number of *Courage* Traits and defeat her in a Mental Challenge. If she loses, she must either succeed in a *Courage* Virtue Test against a four-Trait difficulty or spend a Mental Trait to take any action except cowering in fear. *Terrorize* lasts for the rest of the scene.

Fear-Plague

Through this power, you may draw your subject's deepest fears out of his mind, examine them and hurl them back at him. They then haunt him at every turn, stalking his mind and denying him any sort of peace. A criminal might constantly hear police cars pulling up; a Pander who believes in occult conspiracy theories may see mysterious sigils scrawled on walls wherever he goes. These omens and experiences are so all-pervading as to seriously affect the victim's mental equilibrium.

To inflict *Fear-Plague* on a target, spend a Willpower Trait and defeat him in a Mental Challenge. If you win, he cannot spend Willpower Traits for any purpose that does not directly complement his Nature or directly affect him immediate chances for survival *as he perceives them*. These effects last for one week. Your victim must be within your line of sight when you activate this power though its effects persist regardless of where he is.

Advanced Path of Phobos
Leech of Fear

The diets of demons are many and varied. Some feed on blood like Cainites while others subsist on such diverse substances as the breath of infants or the remains of dead murderers. With this power, you may feed on other individuals' fears, drawing sustenance as if they were mortal vitae.

You may use this power on any given individual once per night. She must be within your line of sight, and she must be currently afraid of or intimidated by something or someone (though this power will not work if the fear is an artificial product of another *Path of Phobos* power). Spend the usual Blood Trait to activate *Leech of Fear* and make a number of Simple Tests equal to six minus your target's number of *Courage* Traits. Each such test that you win or tie is one Fear Trait that you may add to your Blood Pool. Fear Traits function exactly like Blood Traits, except that all unspent Fear Traits disappear at sunrise.

The Taking of the Spirit

Through this path's will-draining magics, you can strip mental stability, self-determination and even the very sense of self from your chosen victim. *The Taking of the Spirit* allows you, with time and practice, to reduce even the

strongest-willed individual to a mindless automaton who only exists to serve your will. You must be within line of sight of your target for all of the following powers to work. *The Taking of the Spirit* uses the *Subterfuge* Ability for retests.

Basic Taking of the Spirit

Mind Leech

The most basic power of this Path allows you to temporarily drain a small portion of a target's mental stamina. Your victim has no idea what causes the sudden listlessness she experiences; she only knows that she feels listless, drained, distracted and discouraged.

Make a Static Mental Challenge against a difficulty of the victim's Mental Traits. If you win, your subject must bid an additional Trait on all Mental Challenges for the rest of the scene. You may only successfully use *Mind Leech* on an individual once per scene, though multiple infernalists may all apply it to the same target.

Stigmatize

You may now probe deeper into your victim's psyche, impairing her ability to relate to other individuals. As with *Mind Leech*, your subject does not know the cause of her mysterious loss of social aptitude — she simply feels detached, antisocial and unable to relate to other people.

Make a Static Mental Challenge against a difficulty of the victim's Mental Traits. If you win, your subject must bid an additional Social Trait on all Social Challenges for the rest of the scene. You may only successfully use *Stigmatize* on an individual once per scene, though multiple infernalists may all apply it to the same target.

Intermediate Taking of the Spirit

Drain Resolve

Your ability to siphon away your victim's will has progressed to such an extent that you may impair her ability to regain self-determination. This power's psychological effects resemble those of deep depression. As in the case of the previous powers, *Drain Resolve* has no obvious source.

Within five minutes of a successful use of *Mind Leech*, issue a Mental Challenge against the same target. If you win, your victim must spend three Willpower Traits, not one, to refresh her Mental Traits. The target should roleplay the psychological effects, which last until the next sunrise.

Sap Will

With *Sap Will*, you may strike at the very heart of your victim's psyche, stripping away her very strength of self. This is not without its dangers as a particularly strong mind can turn your attack back upon you. Unlike the lesser powers of *Taking of the Spirit*, *Sap Will* is obvious to its victim as some sort of mystic attack.

Issue a Mental Challenge, bidding three Mental Traits. If you win, your victim loses a Willpower Trait. You may use *Sap Will* to drain no more than three Willpower Traits per night from any given target.

Advanced Taking of the Spirit

The Gift of Servitude

Though this path's lesser magics have the potential to temporarily weaken a victim, *Gift of Servitude* is the goal to which all students of *Taking of the Spirit*

eventually aspire. Through this feat of magical manipulation, you can bind your victim's will to your own, leaving him little more than an empty shell who follows your commands with perfect obedience.

Gift of Servitude will only work on an individual who has no Mental Traits left. Once you have prepared the target, spend a Willpower Trait and issue a Social Challenge. If you win, your target is affected as if you have bound him to you via the *Dominate* power *Conditioning* (**Laws of the Night**, p. 147). This lasts for one week. If you lose the Social Challenge, you may not use *Gift of Servitude* on that target for one full year.

Dark Thaumaturgical Rituals

To cast a *Dark Thaumaturgy* ritual, follow the same procedure as for casting a ritual from *Thaumaturgy*. Make a Static Mental Challenge with a difficulty dependent on the level of the ritual: five Traits for a Basic ritual, seven for Intermediate and nine for Advanced. The only exceptions to this are the two variable-level rituals below, whose difficulty is equal to two plus the number of Willpower Traits that the target demon has.

Basic Dark Thaumaturgical Rituals
Call Forth the Host (Variable Level)

This ritual's existence is no secret, for folklore has spoken of infernalists' ability to summon demons for untold centuries. It is taught in many forms, and the particulars vary widely. However, the one constant is that the ritual requires some form of sacrifice. Blood, souls, lives and unique material possessions are popular as are desecrated holy relics and items that have been used to perform acts of violence. The precise sacrifice depends on the nature of the demon in question (and is left to the Storyteller's discretion). You must also know the demon's True Name in order to summon it.

A successful casting of this ritual does not guarantee that you have a willing or loyal servant. It only indicates that you have brought the demon to this plane of existence. To bind the demon to your will, you must defeat it in both a Social Challenge (to convince it of your dominance) and a Mental Challenge (to impose your terms of service upon it).

If you lose the Social Challenge, you do not impress the demon with your transparent attempts at power and it either leaves or attacks you as it sees fit. If you lose the Mental Challenge, the demon returns to Hell rather than accept such unfavorable terms. If you are unfortunate enough to lose *both* challenges, the demon drags you back to Hell as it goes — make a new character. If you win both of these challenges, you must then expend a number of Mental Traits equal to the demon's Willpower Traits (see below) in order to finish binding it to your will. You may spend additional Mental Traits at this time to increase the length of the demon's service to you; see below. If you are unable to expend the full number of Mental Traits, the result is the same as if you had failed the Mental Challenge to impose your terms of service upon the demon.

If the entire procedure is successful, your demon is your loyal (though not blindly loyal) servant for a period equal to 24 hours, minus one hour per Mental Trait you had to expend to complete the binding, plus one hour for every *additional* Mental Trait you spent. At the end of this time, the demon vanishes in a flash of hellfire, returning to its infernal home. You must be careful to

phrase your commands very precisely as most demons summoned with this ritual are resentful and will only obey the letter of the order unless you placate them with very favorable terms of service. "Very favorable" depends on the demon in question, and the Storyteller is free to make you research it.

Bind the Interloper (Variable Level)

Infernalists are a fractious lot, and the purposes of one may lie against those of another. *Bind the Interloper* allows you to take control of a demon that another infernalist has summoned, turning it against its former master. The inducements you may use to achieve this end are varied, ranging from blood to material items to souls, and the precise forms of the ritual depend on what you believe will attract the demon's attention. You must also know the True Name of the demon in question and the name or face of the infernalist whom it serves. Finally, your *Dark Thaumaturgy* must be at an equal or greater level than that required to summon the demon in the first place (see below).

Bind the Interloper requires 15 minutes to cast for every Willpower Trait the target demon has. If the casting is successful, you have attracted the demon's attention. You must then defeat its current master in a Mental Challenge. If you win, the demon transfers its loyalty to you for the remainder of its term of service. If you lose, you lose three Willpower Traits and the demon's master receives a perfect mental picture of your face (though no other information concerning your identity unless the demon is on good enough terms with him to tell him) and the knowledge that you just tried to take his servant away from him.

Curse of Oedipus

By invoking the legacy of Oedipus, who tore out his eyes when he became aware of his crimes against his own family, you may inflict temporary blindness on a victim. You must know the face of your intended target, and you must concentrate on this image while inhaling the fumes from a burning stick of incense. When the incense is done burning, your victim receives the Flaw: *Blind* (**Laws of the Night**, p. 116) for five hours, minus one hour for every Trait of *Conscience* or *Conviction* he has (thus, individuals with five *Conscience* or *Conviction* Traits are immune to the *Curse of Oedipus*). During this time, the victim is overcome by grief for every wrong, real or imagined, that he has committed, and he weeps tears of blood (which can be deeply disturbing for mortals and a threat to the Masquerade for Cainites).

Video Nefas

The forces of Hell are everywhere, or so most infernalists believe. Accordingly, the sum of all knowledge is open to you if you can find the demon who knows what you want to learn. *Video Nefas* allows you to commune with an invisible messenger imp who whispers the secrets of the universe in your ear. Beware, though: this ritual causes the demons it commands to tell you the truth, but they will only tell you as much of that truth as you can force them to reveal.

To enact *Video Nefas*, write your question in black ink, using a sharpened bone as a stylus. Snap the bone in two, burn the surface that you wrote the question on and make five Simple Tests. The number of these Tests that you win or tie determines how much information your demon informants reveal to you. You may not declare retests for these tests though a generous Storyteller may allow you to perform Mental Tests to analyze the accuracy of the answers if you possess Abilities that relate to the subject of the question.

With one win or tie, you can learn the answer to a "yes or no" question. Two gives you a short sentence's worth of information. If you win or tie three times, you receive a short synopsis (three to five sentences). A complete answer, perhaps two or three paragraphs' worth, comes with four wins or ties. If you win or tie all five Simple Tests, you learn the complete truth behind the subject of your inquiry, perhaps even facts previously unknown to any mortal or Cainite.

Intermediate Dark Thaumaturgical Rituals

Felis Negrum

Rumors of Gangrel infernalists abound because of this ritual, which allows you to change yourself or another individual into a black cat. To cast *Felis Negrum* on yourself, you must have three whiskers from a black cat; to transform someone else, you will need the skin of a white cat. You must burn this material over a one-foot square of glass, then inscribe on the glass, in your own blood, the name of the individual you wish to transform (using one Blood Trait).

If you use this ritual on yourself, its effects last indefinitely, and you can return to your natural form whenever you wish. A ghoul or a mortal is transformed for 24 hours while another vampire is changed for 13 nights, less one night for every Morality Trait he has. If you cast this ritual on an unwilling recipient, you must defeat him in a Mental Challenge after a successful casting. This metamorphosis only changes the subject's physical form; it does not affect clothing or carried items.

A character in cat form loses his normal Physical Traits; they are replaced with one Trait each of *Agile*, *Energetic*, *Nimble* and *Quick*. His normal Social Traits remain, though he may have some difficulty applying them under most circumstances as he loses the power of speech. His Mental Traits also remain as normal. He is an exceptionally durable cat, however, as he retains his usual Health Levels, Disciplines and Blood Pool. A transformed vampire is a vampiric cat, complete with fangs, a lack of pulse or respiration and bite and claw attacks that do one Health Level of aggravated damage. The magic of this change renders the subject immune to *Dominate* and *Presence*, but *Animalism* affects him as if he were an actual cat.

Plague's Secret Domain

Although many Kindred consider themselves safe from mortal diseases, they overlook illnesses of the mind and heart. *Plague's Secret Domain* unlocks the secrets of these maladies, allowing you to inflict a morbid weariness on mortal and vampire alike. Casting this ritual requires you to intone a one-hour chant in front of a ritual fire in which you burn the corpse of a freshly killed mourning dove. At the end of the hour, you must extinguish the fire with two Blood Traits from someone pure of heart (five Humanity Traits), then spend any number of temporary or permanent Willpower Traits and defeat your intended victim in a Mental Challenge.

Once you have successfully cast *Plague's Secret Domain*, your target falls into a crushing depression, which she should roleplay. She is down two Traits on any Social or Mental Challenge due to listlessness and apathy, and is down three Traits (these penalties are cumulative) on any challenge that may result in her death. These effects last for one night for every temporary Willpower Trait you

Although an infernalist character learns *Bind the Interloper* and *Call Forth the Host* as Basic rituals, she may use them at any strength up to her level of mastery of *Dark Thaumaturgy*. The following Traits define the power of the demons that the infernalist may summon or bind at each level of strength. These Traits are restricted by exact level, rather than by Basic/Intermediate/Advanced classification: a character who only knows *Dark Thaumaturgy* at the first Intermediate level cannot summon a demon with the second set of Intermediate traits. The Storyteller should create a summoned demon using the following Trait suggestions and assign a Narrator to take its role.

Any demon has a number of Health Levels equal to its number of Physical Traits, and it suffers no wound penalties. A "killed" demon returns to its infernal home and may not be summoned again for a year and a night. A demon who displays Disciplines usually does so in accordance with its role in Hell, though the Storyteller is free to ignore these categories in favor of horror or dramatic effect. Tempters generally have powers of *Dementation*, *Dominate*, *Melpominee* or *Presence*. Warriors typically have *Celerity*, *Fortitude*, *Potence* or *Thanatosis*. Spies are versed in *Animalism*, *Auspex*, *Chimerstry* and *Obfuscate*. Of course, most demons of any mental capacity are versed in *Dark Thaumaturgy* though their knowledge may be theoretical rather than practical. Note that in no case are these actual Cainite Disciplines, merely demonic powers that simulate those Disciplines' effects (and without requiring Blood Traits: substitute Physical Traits for physical Disciplines and Mental Traits for mental Disciplines where Blood Trait expenditure is required). Any demon may have special strengths or vulnerabilities at the Storyteller's discretion.

Note that suggested power levels are given for demons summoned with any level of *Dark Thaumaturgy* through the rank of Methuselah. These are given for comparison purposes, for use in all-elder games and to demonstrate why very few infernalists attempt to summon and control such beings. Any demon summoned with any rank of Superior *Dark Thaumaturgy* would be beyond the capability of most troupes to resist, let alone defeat.

Basic Demons

Imp (cost: 1 Mental Trait): 6 Attribute Traits, 2 Ability Traits, 1 Willpower Trait.

Fiend (cost: 2 Mental Traits): 10 Attribute Traits, 3 Ability Traits, 2 Willpower Traits, 2 Basic Discipline powers.

Intermediate Demons

Shade (cost: 4 Mental Traits): 15 Attribute Traits, 5 Ability Traits, 4 Willpower Traits, 4 Basic Discipline powers.

Servitor (cost: 6 Mental Traits): 21 Attribute Traits, 8 Ability Traits, 6 Willpower Traits, 6 Basic and Intermediate Discipline powers.

Advanced Demons

Pit Lord (cost: 8 Mental Traits): 28 Attribute Traits, 13 Ability Traits, 8 Willpower Traits, 10 Discipline powers of Basic through Advanced levels.

Superior Demons

Elder: Minor Demon Noble (cost: 10 Mental Traits): 36 Attribute Traits, 21 Ability Traits, 10 Willpower Traits, 16 Discipline powers through Elder level.

Master: Lesser Demon Noble (cost: 12 Mental Traits): 45 Attribute Traits, 35 Ability Traits, 12 Willpower Traits, 24 Discipline powers through Master level.

Ascendant: Greater Demon Noble (cost: 15 Mental Traits): 55 Attribute Traits, 55 Ability Traits, 15 Willpower Traits, 36 Discipline powers through Ascendant level.

Methuselah: Demon Overlord (cost: 20 Mental Traits): 70 Attribute Traits, 70 Ability Traits, 20 Willpower Traits, 50 Discipline powers through Methuselah level.

spent and one lunar month for every permanent Willpower Trait you spent. A vampire whose depression lasts for one lunar month or more must win a *Self-Control* or *Instincts* Virtue Test against a difficulty of the number of permanent Willpower Traits you spent. If she fails, she enters torpor at the end of the ritual's duration. A mortal whose depression lasts a similar length of time must win the same Virtue Test or commit suicide when the ritual's duration expires.

Advanced Dark Thaumaturgical Rituals

Close the Ways

If your hatred of a given target — or at least your ill will — is great enough, you can wreak untold havoc upon his fortune. *Close the Ways* is the path to such doom. It is deceptively simple in its execution. To cast it, you must meditate naked while kneeling on a stone surface for six hours while 14 black candles burn down around you. At the end of this time, you extinguish all 14 candles with the palm of your left hand. As each candle flame goes out, speak the birth name of your target. You must also expend seven temporary and three permanent Traits each in the Social and Mental categories as well as a permanent Willpower Trait. If the ritual fails, you still lose the Willpower Trait, though not the permanent Attribute Traits.

Your victim suffers catastrophic bad luck if this ritual succeeds. First, all Influence expenditures require one more Trait than normal as strings don't pull as easily and pawns are difficult to contact and exert pressure over. Second, he treats all ties on Simple Tests as losses. Third and most damaging, he gains the *Cursed* Negative Trait, and anyone who knows of the curse may bid against him in *any* challenge. These effects persist for a number of months equal to the number of permanent Willpower Traits you possess after casting the ritual.

You may remove this ritual's effects should you so choose, as may anyone else who knows *Close the Ways*. This requires a one-hour ceremony conducted in a graveyard in which the individual lifting the curse cuts off his own left hand (incurring three levels of lethal damage) and expends a permanent Willpower Trait.

Into the Abyss

Although the wisdom of such a course of action is debatable at best, sometimes insanity is the only option. *Into the Abyss* is insane by most standards, even those of infernalists, for this ritual opens a portal to Hell itself. Some dark thaumaturges claim that this is the best way to commune with demons of great power while others tell stories of ancient treasures (or slumbering Methuselahs) contained in the depths of the infernal regions. Still others study this ritual as a last hope against the threat of capture.

To enact *Into the Abyss*, you must spend 24 hours, midnight to midnight, painting the sigils of power on a stone wall with the blood of children and a brush made from the hair of a white horse. Staying awake during the day requires one Static Mental Challenge for every hour of local daylight, with a difficulty of nine Traits minus the vampire's number of Morality Traits (retest with *Survival*). Once you have successfully cast the ritual, the portal opens and remains open for a number of hours equal to your permanent Willpower Traits. During this time, anyone can enter the portal. No one, including a demon, can leave Hell through it without your express permission.

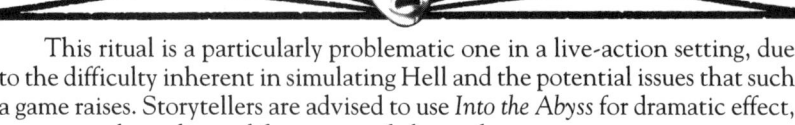

This ritual is a particularly problematic one in a live-action setting, due to the difficulty inherent in simulating Hell and the potential issues that such a game raises. Storytellers are advised to use *Into the Abyss* for dramatic effect, not as a garbage disposal for groups of player characters.

Superior Dementation

Elder Dementation: Lingering Malaise

While lesser Malkavians are only able to inflict temporary (though sometimes very long-lasting) insanity on their victims, your power to twist the psyche has progressed to such an extent that you can gift your subjects with permanent psychological shifts and dementia.

You must speak to your victim for at least a minute, describing in vivid and precise detail the derangement that you wish to inflict upon her. This may take place in the middle of an ordinary conversation if you wish; you do not have to explicitly state what you are doing until you make the challenge. When you have described the derangement in sufficient detail, spend a Willpower Trait and make a Social Challenge. If you win, your target receives one permanent derangement of your choice. You may only inflict one derangement per game session on any given target, though you may make multiple attempts until you succeed.

In the interest of fairness, it's polite to get Storyteller approval for any "non-standard" (i.e. "not published in a **Mind's Eye Theatre** book") derangement.

Elder Dementation: Shattered Mirror

Although some *Dementation* powers are subtle, initiating or promoting insanity, *Shattered Mirror* results in immediate and devastating effects. With but a glance, you can bestow your own psychological afflictions on another victim, spreading your own derangements like a psychological virus.

To inflict *Shattered Mirror*, make eye contact with your target, spend a Willpower Trait and one or more Mental Traits, and defeat her in a Social Challenge. Your victim receives *all* of your derangements and Mental Flaws for one night per Mental Trait you expended.

Master Dementation: Restructure

At this level of mastery, you may now rewrite the most fundamental aspects of a subject's mind, changing his very self-image and worldview. Victims of *Restructure* often compare the experience to a religious rebirth or a philosophical epiphany and state that their new mindset feels completely natural and they don't really understand why they used to act the way they did. Your target retains all his memories but may view his previous actions in a radically different light.

To *Restructure* a subject, make eye contact with him, spend a number of Mental Traits equal to his total number of permanent Willpower Traits and initiate a Social Challenge. If you win, his Nature changes to one of your choice, and your subject should roleplay his new mindset appropriately. This effect is permanent unless undone by another application of *Restructure*, though even such a restoration is hardly flawless due to the complexity of the effort.

If you lose the Social Challenge, including all retests, your victim may spend a Willpower Trait to initiate a Social Challenge against you. If he wins, *your* Nature changes to *his* Nature for the next lunar month.

Ascendant Dementation: Personal Scourge

This fearsome power goes beyond the psychological aspects of madness. With *Personal Scourge*, you may turn a victim's own mind against him in a psychic attack with explicit physical manifestations. In effect, he is torn apart by the force of his own will. His body erupts in violent stigmata — bruises, lacerations, punctures and abrasions appear over the surface of his skin as he sprays blood and howls in agony. Observers using *Aura Perception* see the victim's aura exude spiritual tendrils and lashes even as it swirls into the patterns of extreme psychosis.

To attack a victim with *Personal Scourge*, you must touch him or make eye contact, spend two Willpower Traits, and defeat him in a Social Challenge. For each of the next three turns, he makes a number of Simple Tests equal to his number of permanent Willpower Traits. Each test he loses is one level of lethal damage that he receives. During these three turns, he may take no actions other than thrashing, gibbering and howling in agony — this includes spending blood to heal himself.

Methuselah Dementation: Lunatic Eruption

Most Malkavians know of this power's existence, if only as a dim legend passed down through the clan. It has seen no confirmed use in the modern era, and the only reliable account of its appearance in past nights places a Malkavian Methuselah at the final battle of Carthage. *Lunatic Eruption* is a devastating area-wide psychic effect that triggers a massive orgy of destruction. Unconfirmed rumors from within the Black Hand state that one of the Seraphs knows, or has access to a master of, this power and has used it as a threat against the Camarilla in recent nights.

To activate *Lunatic Eruption*, spend eight Willpower Traits and make a Static Mental Challenge against a difficulty of 12 Traits. The entire city (or everyone in a radius of 30 miles if you are not in an urban area) falls into temporary insanity. Mortals riot, loot, rape and burn. Cainites go berserk or enter hunger frenzies, laying waste to all in their path and draining as many vessels as they can consume. Other supernatural beings suffer similar effects: Werewolves take their war forms and go berserk against any likely target, and magicians and fae revel in the sudden influx of wild power they receive. These effects persist until the next sunrise.

A Cainite who's caught in the "blast radius" must make a *Self-Control/Instincts* Virtue Test against a five-Trait difficulty. If she fails, she succumbs to the madness and instantly frenzies. Once she recovers from the initial frenzy, she is down three Traits on any further attempt to resist any other frenzy trigger for the rest of the night.

This sort of game-wide effect is best used as a background plot device. The Storyteller should convene an all-hands meeting (preferably at the beginning of the game session) in order to conduct the mass Virtue Test and to ensure that all players know what is happening to them and around them. It's hard to simulate a howling mob in live action, so player understanding of offstage events is key.

Mytherceria

The reclusive Kiasyd care little for the affairs of other Kindred, so reliable knowledge of their bastardized faerie powers is difficult to come by. Those few

Sabbat who have dealt with Kiasyd characterize their Discipline, *Mytherceria*, as a path of twisted perceptions — whether those perceptions be of the Kiasyd or of her unfortunate victims. In some ways, *Mytherceria* is similar to *Auspex* for its ability to reveal insights about the world; in others, it resembles *Dementation* in its ability to bring the sturdiest mind crashing down in madness. Few, if any, Kiasyd are willing to teach this Discipline to outsiders. They value the power that it gives them and fear that, were their abilities too well-known, the Sabbat's regard for their might could turn to mindless hunger.

Mytherceria users retest with the *Awareness* Ability. At the Storyteller's discretion, the specialized Ability *Faerie Lore* may augment or replace *Awareness* for this purpose.

Basic Mytherceria

Folderol

The first shroud of reality through which you see is that of untruth. This power's precise manifestation varies with each practitioner. You may weep or sweat blood, see the liar's tongue assume unnatural shapes or colors, or experience a crawling sensation on your hands or neck. Regardless of the trappings, the result is the same: you know a lie when you hear one.

When someone makes a statement that you want to assess, make a Static Mental Challenge with a difficulty of the subject's number of Social Traits, plus one for every *Subterfuge* Ability Trait he has. Success indicates that you know with absolute certainty whether or not the statement was true. You must be able to hear the statement as it is spoken (or read the speaker's lips if you are deaf), and you must make this challenge for each statement that you want to analyze.

Fae Sight

Your ability to view multiple levels of reality at once has advanced to the point that you can perceive all things fae as they truly are. With a small amount of effort, you can also scrutinize an area to determine if faerie magic was recently used there or if faerie beings were present.

The first part of this power is always in effect. No challenge is needed. You instantly recognize all fae beings as such. If you are viewing a faerie in a mortal body, you see the individual's true form with a ghostly superimposed silhouette of its "human" appearance.

To determine if an area held fae creatures or was subjected to fae magic within the past three nights, concentrate for a turn and expend a Mental Trait. Traces of faerie presence appear to you as faintly glowing footprints, runes or scorch marks. Interpretation of these signs may require one or more Static Mental Challenges, as determined by the Storyteller, but you can always tell whether or not the signs are actually there.

Intermediate Mytherceria

Aura Absorption

This power is virtually identical to the first Intermediate *Auspex* power, *Spirit's Touch*, and the same rules should be applied (**Laws of the Night**, p. 138). However, when you examine an object with *Aura Absorption*, you devour the psychic traces on it. Anyone who attempts to examine the same object with *The Spirit's Touch* or *Aura Absorption* after you have finished with it must

win a Static Mental Challenge against your permanent Mental Traits in order to glean any impressions.

Chanjelin Ward

You may create arcane glyphs that reveal your own altered perceptions to others. However, most individuals don't handle seeing reality the way you see it. While not directly threatening, these wards are sufficiently distracting that most characters who see them become disoriented, which may lead to other unpleasant complications. These wards may guard a single object, affect an individual who wears the clothing on which they are inscribed or fill an entire room with their effects.

To inscribe a *Chanjelin Ward*, spend one turn tracing the ward on the target object with your fingertip (if warding an entire room, spend 10 minutes tracing the ward on the floor) and make a Static Mental Challenge with a difficulty of seven traits. Success means that anyone touching the object or entering the room is down two Traits on all Mental Challenges for as long as she is in contact with the item or in the room. Additionally, she must win a Static Mental Challenge against a difficulty of nine Traits or become lost until someone leads her to familiar surroundings.

If the object you are warding is currently worn by another individual, make a Mental Challenge against her instead. Success inflicts the above effects on her, but no one else is affected by the wards unless they don the afflicted item.

A *Chanjelin Ward* lasts for one night. You may extend this at the time of creation by spending one Blood Trait per extra night. A victim is only affected by one *Chanjelin Ward* at a time. Any character who has *Chanjelin Ward* is immune to all *Chanjelin Wards*.

Advanced Mytherceria

Riddle Phantastique

Your study of "reality" has now progressed to the point that you have an innate knowledge of the underpinnings of the universe — though, to anyone who does not share your altered perceptions, this knowledge is closer to madness. You may share your unique insights with any one subject who can hear you ask your penetrating philosophical questions (and, of course, understand the language in which you are speaking). The *Riddle Phantastique* is so arcane that it can drive its victims to madness, even self-inflicted injury, until they solve it. Insanity is neither a sure solution nor a certain doom where the *Riddle Phantastique* is concerned. Some deranged minds are capable of unraveling it with ease while others are driven even farther into incoherence.

To inflict the *Riddle Phantastique*, speak to your victim and make a challenge that pits your Social Traits against her Mental Traits. If you win, the subject falls into a trance state as the complexities of your twisted logic ensnare her mind. She may take no actions while so entranced as all her concentration is devoted to solving the riddle.

Once per half-hour, the victim makes a Static Mental Challenge against a difficulty of your Mental Traits (retest with *Occult*, and she gains a number of free *Occult* Ability Traits, usable only for these retests, equal to the number of *Dementation* powers she has). Once she wins three such tests, she solves the riddle and breaks the trance. Every time she fails a retest, she tears at herself in spasms of

raging frustration, inflicting one level of lethal damage upon herself. At any time, you may tell her the answer to the *Riddle Phantastique* and end the trance. The same individual may be the target of *Riddle Phantastique* on multiple occasions as you have a virtually limitless supply of questions. For roleplaying purposes, you may want to have a supply of Zen riddles or advanced calculus problems on hand so that you can actually issue your enigma as an in-character statement.

Superior Mytherceria

Elder Mytherceria: Steal the Mind

Though it superficially resembles some forms of telepathy, *Steal the Mind* is a much more invasive power than those of Advanced and Superior *Auspex*. Many Kiasyd believe that their line's founder developed this ability from the memory-altering arts of his faerie brethren. At this level of mastery, your ability to perceive various aspects of reality is so advanced that you may plumb the depths of a subject's psyche for any memory he has — even those that he has repressed or someone else has erased with *Dominate*. This theft is temporary, for a victim's memories trickle through your fingers over the course of the night, but while you have possession of your subject's mind, he is little more than a husk.

To steal a victim's mind, make eye contact with him, spend a Willpower Trait, and initiate a Mental Challenge. If you succeed, you have full access to *all* of his memories. He becomes comatose or torporous, depending on whether he is mortal or Cainite. You may search his mind for anything that he knows, though Static Mental Challenges (with Storyteller assistance) may be necessary to find suppressed or erased information. You retain the victim's memories for one hour (unless you choose to give them back sooner), and may extend this time by spending Willpower Traits at the rate of one per additional hour. If you feel benevolent, you may choose to release your victim's mind at any time.

While you are in possession of your victim's mind, you gain a number of *Knowledgeable* Mental Traits equal to one-third the total number of Mental Traits he has (rounded down). However, you also receive an equal number of *Oblivious* Negative Mental Traits thanks to the distraction that holding two sets of memories in your head incurs.

Master Mytherceria: Absorb the Mind

While *Steal the Mind* allows you to pilfer a subject's memories, *Absorb the Mind* goes beyond even this impressive theft, allowing you to "borrow" portions of your victim's psyche, taking the fruits of his learning for your own. This procedure is less overtly invasive than *Steal the Mind*, for the subject is still able to function, but many of its victims consider it much crueler.

To absorb a portion of your victim's mind, make eye contact, spend a Willpower Trait and any number of Mental Traits, and initiate a Mental Challenge. If you win, you may take a number of Ability Traits from your victim equal to the number of Mental Traits you spent to activate *Absorb the Mind*. Your victim loses these Traits as if he had spent them for retests, regaining them normally at the next game session. You may spend these stolen Traits as if they were your own, but once spent (or at the end of the session, if you haven't spent them by then) they return to their rightful owner.

Ascendant Mytherceria: The Grandest Trick

According to Lasombra legend, the Kiasyd share a strong bond with the fae folk — strong enough to call upon the faerie blood that taints the bloodline.

The Grandest Trick is a bittersweet legacy of this blood, for it allows you to temporarily bring the faint traces of faerie heritage to the forefront of your blood, overwhelming Caine's curse for a few precious hours.

To perform *The Grandest Trick*, spend 10 Blood Traits and one or more Willpower Traits and make a Static Mental Challenge against a difficulty of 15 Traits minus your number of Morality Traits. If you succeed, you briefly shrug off the Curse of Caine and revert to mortality (including your pre-Embrace mortal appearance) at the next sunrise. You retain no vampiric qualities while mortal. You have no Blood Pool, and you lose access to all Disciplines except the second basic Mytherceria power, *Fae Sight*. You lose all Attribute and Ability Traits in excess of normal human maximums (10 Attribute Traits per category, a maximum of five Traits in any one Ability, and a maximum of six Willpower Traits; you decide which Traits to cross off). You do not actually lose all memory of being a vampire, though all of your experiences in unlife take on a hazy, dreamlike quality, and you must make a Static Mental Challenge against a nine-Trait difficulty to recall any specifics of Cainite existence. To outside observers, you appear a normal mortal, though your aura appears to be that of a faerie.

The Grandest Trick lasts for one hour per Willpower Trait you spent when you activated the power. When you have one hour of "mortality" left, you begin to feel a strange compulsion to seek shelter from sunlight. You are aware of your impending return to unlife, even if you are unable to recall any other aspect of your personal history. When this power's duration of effect expires, you instantly revert to your normal state of existence, regaining all Traits and Disciplines. Your Blood Pool contains 10 Blood Traits when this power wears off, regardless of how many you had left when you invoked *The Grandest Trick*. If you are killed while in mortal form, you die and may not be re-Embraced.

Necromancy

Though the Giovanni clan likes to claim exclusive mastery of necromantic blood magic, the truth is that *Necromancy* is something of an open secret. While it's not a subject that a Camarilla occultist teaches for cash, nor does a Sabbat priscus know necromantic rites to go with her *auctoritas ritae*, odds are that a truly dedicated Cainite scholar can find an instructor for the right price. *Necromancy* may be more common in the Sabbat than in the Camarilla, due in part to the interest that practitioners of the Path of Death and the Soul have in it. For that matter, *Necromancy* is largely held to be a more "acceptable" form of blood magic than *Thaumaturgy* as the former deals more closely with the undead condition. As with *Thaumaturgy*, *Necromancy* is hardly an organized field of study in the sect, and lessons are largely a matter of catch as catch can.

There are a few somewhat cohesive groups within the Sabbat which practice *Necromancy*, though none are large enough to be formal organizations of scholars in any sense. Some Tzimisce *kolduns* are versed in the *Ash Path*, which they use as a means of dealing with another family of spirits. A small but widespread network of Nosferatu *antitribu* and Sabbat-affiliated Samedi collaborate in using various *Sepulchre Path* arts for their own ends, most often the acquisition of priceless information. The Sabbat Inquisition and the Black Hand are both believed to use various rituals in their investigations and operations, though this is more rumor than fact. Finally, the recently arrived Harbingers of Skulls make use of their own unique permutation on the dark arts.

The Mortuus Path

The Harbingers of Skulls claim to have developed their proprietary *Mortuus Path* during their long sojourn in the Underworld. Of course, whether this is true or simply another one of the veils in which the Harbingers wrap themselves is a matter of some conjecture. Regardless, the Harbingers do have access to powers that no Giovanni has ever demonstrated or admitted to knowing. The *Mortuus Path* deals with the physical processes and manifestations of death as they affect the physical form.

The Harbingers learn the *Mortuus Path* as their primary *Necromancy* path. Once a Harbinger has attained the first Intermediate level of this path, he may begin to study the basic levels of another. Once he reaches the Advanced level of the *Mortuus Path*, he may raise his second path to the Intermediate level and begin to study the remaining paths, which he may not raise past the second Basic level until he has reached the Advanced stage of his second path. Though the Harbingers shouldn't be player characters, they have taught the basics of their art to a very few students, most of whom seem to have been selected for no identifiable common quality. As always with blood magic, the accessibility of these powers is wholly subject to Storyteller approval.

Basic Mortuus Path Necromancy

Reaper's Shroud

You may take on the semblance of a corpse or inflict this same transfiguration on another individual. The victim of this power resembles a cadaver in the advanced stages of deterioration — skin yellows and stretches, eyeballs shrink, and joints become stiff. Though the most obvious application of this power is as a temporary curse, some practitioners use it as a means of disguise or concealment or simply to terrify unsuspecting mortals.

If you wish to assume this form yourself, simply spend a Blood Trait. The change is instantaneous. If you want to inflict it on another subject, you must spend the Blood Trait and defeat him in a challenge of your Mental Traits against his Physical Traits. The subject of *Reaper's Shroud* gains the Negative Physical Traits *Decrepit* and *Lethargic* and the Negative Social Trait *Repugnant*. However, she also gains one free retest on any attempt to remain completely motionless (including attempts to be stealthy while not moving), and she is up three Traits on any challenge in which she attempts to intimidate or to inflict fear. The effects of this power last until the next sunrise or sunset, at which time they fade. A vampire can remove all these effects by spending two Blood Traits to reverse her body's deterioration.

Blight

With *Blight*, you can push a victim closer to the edge of her grave, spinning out the thread of her life by decades in a single moment. Your target suffers all the effects of advanced age: wrinkled and weathered skin, arthritic joints, fragile bones, poor perception and occasionally even mental impairment.

To inflict *Blight* on someone, touch her, spend a Blood Trait and defeat her in a challenge of your Mental Traits against her Physical Traits. Until the next dusk or dawn, your victim receives the following Negative Traits: *Decrepit, Sickly*

and her choice of *Delicate, Dull, Forgetful* or *Oblivious*. Additionally, a mortal victim of *Blight* risks cardiac arrest. Every turn that she engages in strenuous activity, she must win a Static Physical Challenge with a five-Trait difficulty or suffer a heart attack, the effects of which are left to the Storyteller's discretion.

Intermediate Mortuus Path Necromancy

Resume the Coil

This subtle but potent art allows you to defeat the effects of torpor, raising a slumbering Cainite from the sleep of ages. It is one of the few Discipline powers that a character can use while in torpor, though most practitioners have no particular desire to enter this condition on a regular basis. *Resume the Coil* is by no means a soothing experience to undergo as it awakens its sleeping subject's body with a sudden infusion of the very energies of death itself, much like an undead equivalent of cardiac shock paddles. Many recipients of this power have reported strange visions or near-Final Death experiences.

To activate *Resume the Coil*, spend a Willpower Trait and make a Static Mental Challenge against a number of Traits equal to 10 minus your target's number of Morality Traits. If you are attempting to awaken yourself, you must spend an additional Willpower Trait. If you are using this power on another individual, you must touch him. A vampire who entered torpor due to lack of blood awakens with one Blood Trait, and will not enter a hunger frenzy for the first hour after he arises.

True Death

A power whose benefits are not altogether certain or obvious, *True Death* is just what its name implies. For a brief period of time, you may cast off the Curse of Caine — but unlike other methods of attaining such a goal, *True Death* renders you both clinically and spiritually dead. Your body becomes an inert cadaver, indistinguishable from that of any other dead mortal, and it obeys all the laws thereof. Sunlight and True Faith have no particular effect on you, your blood is stale and unpalatable, and you exhibit no signs of life or unlife, lacking even an aura. However, your soul is trapped in an inanimate husk, and the only action you may attempt is awakening from this slumber.

You may automatically assume this form at any time. Awakening from it, however, requires you to expend two Blood Traits. While you are under *True Death's* effects, you have no access to any Disciplines, even "automatic" ones such as Fortitude. You do not, however, consume blood nightly, nor do you enter torpor unless you choose to. The only way your body can be externally distinguished from that of a deceased mortal is with extended observation over a period of years (beyond the scope of most games): You do not decay. However, if you have more than 10 Blood Traits in your Blood Pool and an enterprising medical examiner cuts you open, the excess erupts from the incision in a high-pressure crimson fountain (reducing you to 10 Blood Traits in the process).

Barring outside interference, you may remain "dead" as long as you like. Anyone attempting to drain or drink your blood may take you down to zero Blood Traits in your system but may not diablerize you, and the blood they remove is considered "generic" mortal blood. However, any damage to your uninhabited "corpse" that would kill a vampire with no special Disciplines of resilience does, in fact, inflict Final Death upon you. Decapitation is still fatal, as is total incineration.

Advanced Mortuus Path Necromancy
Mercy for Seth

Plague has always been one of humanity's greatest fears. With this power, you can visit such a fate upon your victims. This is a blood magic-generated effect and does not actually produce a virus or bacterium, but instead simulates the effects of such plagues with uncanny accuracy. Many Cainite elders who witness *Mercy for Seth* in action are uncomfortably reminded of the various plagues that swept through Europe in the 11th through 15th centuries. Symptoms include blackened and bloated skin, blood sweat, blood in bodily excretions, suppurating lesions, swollen glands, chills, fever and delirium. A mortal victim of this plague generally dies within 24 hours while a vampire sinks into torpor.

To apply *Mercy for Seth* to a target, you must touch him, spend a Willpower Trait and a Blood Trait, and win a challenge of your Mental Traits against his Physical Traits. A victim must make one Static Physical Challenge against a five-Trait difficulty every hour. If he loses, he takes one level of lethal damage (if mortal) or receives one Negative Physical Trait of *Sickly* (if Cainite). A vampire who accumulates a number of *Sickly* Traits equal to his number of Physical Traits sinks into torpor.

Mercy for Seth's effects cannot be cured through scientific/medical techniques, though various magical practices or herbal remedies may have some effect at the Storyteller's discretion. The "plague" leaves its victim on the third sunrise after it was inflicted, so a particularly hardy character may be able to stave it off long enough to walk away.

Necromantic Rituals

These sinister rites use the same system presented in **Laws of the Night** (p. 156). They originated with Sabbat practitioners of *Necromancy*, but they are not wholly exclusive to the sect. However, these secrets are anything but common, even within the Sabbat, and the Storyteller should feel free to treat them as even more difficult to acquire than sect-specific Thaumaturgical rituals.

Basic Necromantic Rituals
Eldritch Beacon

This ritual allows you to create a small token that makes the bearer stand out like a bonfire in the lands of the dead. Melt a green candle and mold its wax into a half-inch sphere. The bearer of this sphere, aware or otherwise, is down one Trait on any attempts to resist the powers of any ghost (Arcanoi, if you are using **Oblivion**). This effect lasts for one hour, plus one hour for every Blood Trait you expend when casting the ritual.

Puppet

Some Sabbat necromancers use *Puppet* to facilitate interrogations of the dead while others use it to shock the living (or the unliving) into cooperation. By smearing herb-laden grave soil across the eyes, lips and forehead of a subject, you prepare him for ghostly possession. For the rest of the scene, any wraith that attempts to enter the subject's body and take control of him gains one free retest.

Intermediate Necromantic Rituals

Din of the Damned

This ritual bears some similarities to *Call of the Hungry Dead* (**Laws of the Night**, p. 157) in that it makes the sounds of the Underworld audible in the physical realm. However, *Din of the Damned* affects an enclosed chamber, not an individual. Some necromancers use it to ensure privacy while others simply cast it for the psychological effect it has on those who encounter it.

To ward a room in this manner, draw an unbroken line of crematorium ash around its perimeter (you may go over doors and windows to allow entrance). Until dawn, any attempt to eavesdrop on events inside the room, be it mundane, technologically-enhanced or supernatural, requires a Static Mental Challenge against a nine-Trait difficulty. Failure means the listener is partially deafened by an unholy cacophony of ghostly screams and howling winds and receives the Negative Mental Traits *Oblivious x 2* for the rest of the night.

Peek Past the Shroud

Ergot is a black mold that grows on unharvested grain in cold, damp weather. In its natural form, it is poisonous and can cause hallucinations. This ritual allows you to enchant a handful of ergot to create a small amount of a substance that allows limited second sight. A successful ritual transforms a handful of ergot into three doses of a fine black powder. An individual who consumes one dose of this powder gains the benefits of *Shroudsight* (Basic Ash Path Necromancy, **Laws of the Night**, p. 154) for three hours. If you fail your initial Mental Challenge to cast the ritual and subsequently fail a retest, the ergot becomes highly poisonous. Any character (even a vampire) who ingests the product of such a critically failed ritual takes four levels of lethal damage. This cannot be used to create large amounts of toxin (in other words, no, you can't deliberately fail in order to manufacture poison; those who try may find themselves with large batches of inert sludge).

Advanced Necromantic Ritual

Chill of Oblivion

This potent rite allows a necromancer to infuse her body or that of a willing subject with the proverbial cold of the grave. This ritual has several benefits, though its risks are not inconsiderable. To enact *Chill of Oblivion*, the subject must lie naked on bare earth while a one-foot cube of ice melts on her chest (mortal subjects take three levels of bashing damage from the extreme cold). This takes an entire night (the ritual causes the ice to melt at a uniform speed regardless of the air temperature). Once *Chill of Oblivion* is completed, its effects last for one week.

An individual affected by *Chill of Oblivion* converts aggravated damage from fire and high temperatures to lethal damage. She may also attempt to extinguish any open flame with which she is in contact by spending a Willpower Trait and making a Static Mental Challenge against a number of Traits determined by the fire's size: three for a lighter or candle, five for a torch, eight for a bonfire, 12 for a room or 18 for an entire building. The Narrator representing the fire may attempt to overbid on this challenge.

While under *Chill of Oblivion*, the character's aura is laced with writhing black lines that appear as proof of diablerie to anyone not intimately familiar with this ritual. She also draws in heat from her immediate environment, giving her the Flaws *Touch of Frost* and *Eerie Presence*. Finally, the taint of the Underworld makes her appealing to malevolent spirits and susceptible to their arts; all such entities are up three Traits when using their powers on her (Dark Arcanoi, if you are using **Oblivion**).

Superior Obtenebration

Elder Obtenebration: The Darkness Within

Though the casual observer may mistake this power's manifestation for that of *Shroud of Night* (**Laws of the Night**, p. 164), your command of the very stuff of darkness now reaches far beyond simple summoning. The cloud of shadow that you produce with *The Darkness Within* is an extension of your tainted soul, and its touch drains both courage and life from its victims.

To assault someone with *The Darkness Within*, spend a Blood Trait and a Willpower Trait. A cloud of shadow pours forth from whatever orifice you choose. Most Lasombra expel this shadow from their mouths, though some cut themselves and let the darkness leak from the wound or command it to spring forth from other areas of their bodies. Whatever the precise source of this shadow, it rushes forward to envelop its designated target, covering him in an inch-thick shroud of liquid darkness. This power may target anyone within 50 steps of you.

While enveloped in this shadow, your victim suffers all the effects of *Shroud of Night*. If he has not previously experienced the effects of *Shroud of Night* or *The Darkness Within*, he must also resist Rötschreck with a two-Trait difficulty. Every turn, he must make a Static Physical Challenge against a five Traits difficulty; if he fails, the cloud drains one of his Blood Traits.

You must maintain total concentration to keep your victim ensnared. If you sustain an attack, the cloud immediately rushes back to you. However, if you voluntarily recall the cloud, you may absorb up to half the Blood Traits (rounded up) that it drained from its victim. This is considered the same as drinking from the individual in question for purposes of blood bonds and other blood-borne effects.

Elder Obtenebration: Shadowstep

Your kinship with the shadows is such that you can use one shadow as a portal to another by calling on the kinship that all darkness shares with its ultimate source. To use *Shadowstep*, you must be standing in a naturally occurring shadow—*not* one produced via *Obtenebration*. Spend two Blood Traits and make a Static Mental Challenge against a seven-Trait difficulty. If you win, you may shift your position up to 50 steps, so long as the point at which you end is within your line of sight and is also in a natural shadow. You are not considered to have moved "through" the intervening space in any sense — outside observers see your form briefly obscured by a flicker like moonlight through tree branches, with a similar effect at the point from which you emerge. Your clothes and personal possessions (up to half your body weight) travel with you. If you use *Shadowstep* as a means of Fair Escape, it occurs at the same speed as a normal action, which means an individual using *Alacrity* may be able to stop you.

You may bring one other person with you as you *Shadowstep*. This requires you to spend a Willpower Trait in addition to the power's other costs. If your

traveling companion is unwilling to move with you, you must defeat her in a Physical Challenge; if she wins, neither of you move.

If you wish to use *Shadowstep* to escape restraint, you must likewise spend a Willpower Trait and win a Physical Challenge against the item or person restraining you. If you're held by another individual, success means you slip out of his grasp. If you are chained to a wall, handcuffed to a bed or tied to railroad tracks, a Narrator decides how many Physical Traits your bonds have.

Master Obtenebration: Shadow Twin

You may breathe a twisted semblance of life into an individual's shadow, causing it to become a dark mannequin. During this dim servant's short life span, it is your loyal servitor, obeying your commands with as much accuracy as its necessary limitations allow.

To animate a shadow, make a Static Mental Challenge against nine Traits and expend one or more Blood Traits. If you win, the target's shadow takes on a life of its own for one hour per Blood Trait you spent — though it will last no longer than the next sunrise, regardless of how much blood you use to create it. It has all of its parent's Physical, Social, Mental and Ability Traits and six Health Levels (all Bruised for damage penalty purposes). It may invoke *Shadow Play* at the cost of one Mental Trait. A Narrator should depict the *Shadow Twin* for the duration of the night.

A *Shadow Twin* may move no farther than 50 feet from its parent, though it may become two-dimensional and slide up walls or under doors. It may engage in combat, though it takes half damage from physical attacks and double damage from supernatural attacks, fire and sunlight. It is normally under your verbal command, though you may release it to its parent's service if you so desire. If a Shadow Twin "dies," its parent loses one Willpower Trait.

You may animate a maximum number of *Shadow Twins* per night up to your number of Morality Traits.

Ascendant Obtenebration: Oubliette

Unlike the dungeon from which it draws its name, the *Oubliette* of *Obtenebration* has no opening, and thus it is inescapable unless the jailer wills it. It is a prison of pure abysmal shadow, summoned around its victim no matter where she stands. To the outside observer, a victim of this power appears to be drawn down a two-yard wide pool of darkness that forms under her in a second or less, sucks her in, ripples briefly as she passes its surface and then returns to imperturbable quiescence.

To entrap a victim in an *Oubliette*, spend five Willpower Traits and issue a Mental Challenge that your victim resists with her Physical Traits. If you win, your victim is encased in the *Oubliette* until you release her or until sunlight touches the portion of the *Oubliette* that remains in the physical realm. You may only summon one *Oubliette* at a time.

Your victim is transported to a frigid, unlit, unventilated, spherical chamber just large enough for her to touch both walls with her outstretched arms. If she is mortal, she suffocates in a number of minutes equal to her Physical Traits. If she is Cainite, she may use no powers of any Discipline of which she does not possess an Ascendant or Methuselah power. She may think as much as she likes, however; the calm surroundings and isolation give her two

bonus Traits on any Mental Challenge that she makes during this contemplation unless she has a phobia that the *Oubliette* would prey upon.

Methuselah Obtenebration: Ahriman's Demesne

No modern accounts of this power's use are in evidence, though several prominent Sabbat founders claim that Montano invoked it during his final defense of his sire. *Ahriman's Demesne* allows you to summon a great, billowing darkness capable of destroying all who stand within it. It is unclear if the cloud itself serves your will or if some darkling creatures within are your willing legions, but the end result is the same. When the cloud withdraws into you, it takes with it the bodies of all those who fell to its wrath, leaving behind their possessions — the only mortal remains this world will ever see of them again.

To summon *Ahriman's Demesne*, spend any number of Willpower Traits and concentrate for three turns. During this time, the cloud billows out from your hands and eyes and under your clothing, spreading throughout a radius of 50 paces like a cold black mist. At the end of the third turn, this entire area is considered to be under *Shroud of Night*. At the beginning of each of the next three turns, everyone in the area of effect who you wish to destroy must make a Static Physical Challenge against the number of Willpower Traits you spent invoking this power. If they lose, they take three Health Levels of aggravated damage.

At the end of the third turn of damage, the cloud collapses back into you. Anyone who died within it, whether the fatal damage came from *Ahriman's Demesne* or another source, disappears, though their clothes and belongings remain. You may not invoke this power again for the rest of the night.

Sanguinus

The unique Discipline of the Blood Brothers is a product of Tremere rituals and Tzimisce applications of *Vicissitude* that created the bloodline. *Sanguinus* allows a Blood Brother to share various parts of his body with any other member of his circle. This Discipline is grotesque, to say the least. Many of its powers evoke mindless terror in mortals. Any human who witnesses the effects of *Octopod* or *Coagulated Entity* must make a *Courage* Virtue Test against a two-Trait difficulty or flee in nauseated terror. *Sanguinus* uses *Empathy* for retests as it requires the Blood Brother to have a certain degree of rapport with his circlemates in order to function at maximum efficiency. Outsiders attempting to acquire the secrets of *Sanguinus* often find themselves at a disadvantage; many of the powers do not function as well without circlemates.

Basic Sanguinus

Brother's Blood

The bond that each circle of Blood Brothers shares gives that circle a unique physical, spiritual and mental link. The blood of one is the blood of all. You may exploit this link to heal the wounds that your brothers sustain, regardless of distance.

To use *Brother's Blood*, spend a Blood Trait as if you were healing one of own wounds and declare which member of your circle you are healing. You may spend five Blood Traits over the course of several turns to heal a circlemate's

aggravated wound. This Blood Trait expenditure counts against your per turn limit, not your target's.

Octopod

Expanding on the lessons of *Brother's Blood*, you may now lend limbs or external organs to your circlemates. This power is horrifying to watch, not only for the effects on the recipient but for the effects on the donor. Experienced Blood Brother circles often leave their weaker members a safe distance outside combat, and these individuals quickly come to resemble quadruple amputees as they pass their limbs to comrades in need. *Octopod* takes effect instantly and over any distance within line of sight; donated parts simply vanish from the donor and appear attached to the recipient.

To lend a limb, eye or ear to a circlemate, spend a Blood Trait. The loaned organ appears at the end of the turn, manifesting wherever the recipient wants it to appear. This power imparts no means of additional attack. However, an extra ear or eye gives two bonus Traits for resolving perception-based challenges for the appropriate sense; an extra arm gives two bonus Traits in close combat, and an extra leg gives one bonus Trait for close combat and two bonus Traits for any balance-related challenge. You may call the limb back whenever you wish. This power may only be used to lend external parts — you may not give away your brain or your heart. Any supernatural enhancements your limb has, such as *Feral Claws* or *Fleshcrafted* hooves, travel with it, as do any ornaments or jewelry, but clothing stays with you.

Intermediate Sanguinus

Gestalt

Though you normally share a low-level mental bond with your circlemates, *Gestalt* allows you to intensify this bond, giving your circle the equivalent of a temporary hive mind. While this power is in effect, you do not actually become one, though you share thoughts and your will is strengthened by those of your comrades.

To activate *Gestalt*, every member of your circle must spend a Blood Trait. A member who does not possess *Gestalt* himself must also succeed in a Static Mental Challenge against five Traits to join the link. If one member is unable or unwilling to spend the Blood Trait, the power does not take effect, though individuals who fail the Mental Challenge do not destroy the entire link, just their own connection to it. *Gestalt* lasts for the rest of the scene, even if you or another circle member are killed or rendered unconscious.

While this power is in effect, you enjoy several benefits. First and foremost, you are all in telepathic communication, requiring no effort and no Trait expenditure. Second, any circle member may sacrifice his action for the next turn in order to expend an Ability Trait, "giving" it to any other circle member who can use it for a retest on a challenge taking place during the current turn. Third, any attempt to use any mind-altering Discipline on any circle member is resisted by the highest number of the appropriate Trait that any individual in the circle possesses, though the individual target must still bid his own Traits to resist. For example, if Leon has three Mental Traits and is the target of a

Dominate attempt, he must bid one of his own Mental Traits, but ties and overbids resolve against the 14 Mental Traits that Leon's circlemate Rick has.

Walk of Caine

Drawing on your circle's link at both the sanguine and the spiritual levels, you may now increase the potency of your own vitae at the expense of a circlemate. Most circles use this power when only one member is embattled, donating the strength of their blood to him in order to allow him to perform fearsome physical feats or to heal massive wounds in a matter of moments.

To borrow a *Generation* Background Trait from a willing circlemate, make a Static Mental Challenge against a difficulty of five Traits. If your target is unwilling to give up this Trait, this power fails. If he is willing but does not know *Walk of Caine* himself, he must succeed in the same challenge. *Walk of Caine* lasts for the scene.

You may only borrow one *Generation* Trait from any one member of your circle, and you may not reduce your own generation past fourth. If you borrow a generation from a 13th-generation circlemate, he gains the Flaw: *Fourteenth Generation* until the power wears off. You may not borrow a generation from a circlemate who is already 14th generation. Any effects of your circle's blood that last past the end of the scene, including Embraces you perform or diablerie that you commit or that is committed upon you, use your normal generation rather than your altered one. For example, if you are usually 10th generation but reduce your generation to seventh and Embrace a childe, she will be 11th generation, not eighth.

ADVANCED SANGUINUS

Coagulated Entity

Stepping beyond mere sharing of blood, flesh and minds, you and your circlemates may now combine your very forms into one monstrous conglomeration of writhing muscle and jagged bone. While this makes you a likely target for any enemy attacks, you more than likely have the combined strength to shrug off most assaults as you shamble over any opposition. This power should be overseen by a Narrator as its effects on the surrounding scenery and mortals are rather severe. It is recommended that you work out a *Coagulated Entity's* Traits before play begins.

Every member of the circle who wishes to join the *Coagulated Entity* must be in physical contact with one another and spend three Blood Traits, taking no other action for three turns, though only one participating member must know this power in order to initiate the merge. At the end of the third turn, the unholy melding is complete. The component character with the lowest generation controls the entity's actions, though its actual generation is equal to that of the highest-generation member.

A *Coagulated Entity* enjoys the combined Physical Traits and Mental Traits of all its members. However, it gains a number of *Clumsy* Negative Physical Traits and *Witless* Negative Mental Traits each equal to half its total number of component characters, rounded up. Normal Social Traits are submerged, replaced by a number of *Fearsome* Social Traits equal to three times the number of members. The entity's Blood Pool holds 10 Blood Traits per member, though per turn expenditure is determined by the entity's generation. Its Disciplines are the highest level of any given Discipline that any circle member has attained, so if one member has Advanced *Potence*, a second has Advanced *Fortitude* and a third has Advanced *Auspex*, the *Coagulated Entity* has Advanced *Auspex*, *Fortitude* and *Potence*.

A *Coagulated Entity* may not be staked as it has too many hearts in inaccessible places. It has a normal range of health levels, plus two additional Bruised health levels per component vampire past the first. This power's effects last until the end of the scene or until the entity is destroyed.

Thaumaturgy

Sabbat vampires have never practiced *Thaumaturgy* widely. The Tremere *antitribu* were hardly numerous, even at the height of their power, and their recent disappearance nearly destroyed the sect's magical capabilities. The sect no longer has an organized group willing to provide rituals, instruction, research or support.

This is not to say that the Sabbat has lost all thaumaturgical knowledge — far from it. Many pack priests and Black Hand members practice the arts of blood magic for their general value. Many vampires who follow the Paths of Caine and Death and the Soul see *Thaumaturgy* as one more method of furthering their respective goals and studies. Several bloodlines, most notably the Tzimisce *kolduns* and the Serpents of the Light, have made attempts to organize and combine their knowledge, though no one group has yet matched the degree of proficiency that the Tremere *antitribu* displayed.

The following material is a collection of Sabbat-specific *Thaumaturgy*. While some outside of the sect will undoubtedly have learned or stolen these practices, such instances are more exceptions than rules. Thus, Storytellers should feel perfectly within their rights to deny any non-Sabbat character access to these paths and rituals. Most are products of Tremere *antitribu* research that took place after the bloodline split from its parent clan, though some are adaptations of arts that predate the Sabbat's inception. Camarilla Tremere are familiar with the existence, capabilities and appearances of most of the following techniques (Static Mental Challenge to recognize a "competing brand" of *Thaumaturgy* as not from the character's own sect, difficulty of seven Traits, must have Basic *Thaumaturgy* to recognize paths and a level of *Thaumaturgy* equal to that of a ritual to recognize it). Anyone who is foolish enough to display such powers in Camarilla circles comes under a great deal of unpleasant scrutiny.

Mechanically, these paths and rituals work in the same manner as "common" *Thaumaturgy* and use the basic rules on page 176 of **Laws of the Night**.

The Path of Mars

Unlike the Camarilla Tremere, the Tremere *antitribu* were never at liberty to pursue pure research in blood magic — all of their work was applied toward their sect's goals. This path, one of the first developed after the Sabbat's formation, is a directly martial one, which sets it apart from many utilitarian paths that happen to have martial applications. It is also a highly personal path as its user focuses the effects internally rather than externally, and no two students of the *Path of Mars* approach it with exactly the same attitude. Practitioners of this path tend to be adept at close combat and often complement it with knowledge of *Hands of Destruction* (**Laws of the Night**, p. 183). *Path of Mars* uses the *Occult* Ability for retests.

Basic Path of Mars
War Cry

The first technique you learn is that of focusing your will to fight. This enhances your courage and renders you less susceptible to mind-altering effects. However, this artificial strengthening of your will locks your emotions away from you while it is in effect, rendering you cold and distant. You activate this power with some symbolic gesture or outcry, be it howling a Rebel yell, murmuring a quick meditative chant, donning a stripe of war paint or inflicting superficial cuts on your face and chest.

For the duration of the scene, your *Courage* is increased by one Trait, and you automatically win all ties on Mental Challenges when resisting hostile Discipline effects. However, you are too focused on fighting — and winning — to consider others' feelings, and you gain the Negative Social Trait *Tactless* while under *War Cry*'s influence.

Strike True

Once you have learned to harden your will and subvert all weakness, you begin to gain the unity of purpose necessary to ignore all obstacles. This technique allows you a momentary flash of clarity as you strike an opponent, using your magic to enhance your perceptions and reflexes. Some thaumaturges invoke this power with a martial artist's *kiai* or a fencer's dramatic flourish, though others attack with perfect silence and no wasted motion.

Invoke this power when making a close combat (bare hands or a melee weapon) attack before you make the challenge. You gain one free retest on this attack alone. You may not make any other attacks this turn, though you can use multiple actions normally (to move or to ready a weapon, for instance).

Intermediate Path of Mars
Wind Dance

The clarity of vision that you learned to apply to your own attacks with *Strike True* can now be used to discern the strikes that others make against you. Though this grants you no supernatural knowledge of attacks that you are not aware of, you are much more able to evade those that you can see coming. If you have a "signature" invocation that you use to activate *War Cry*, you may well have a corresponding one for this power as well.

Once you have activated *Wind Dance*, you gain two extra *Dodge* Ability Traits for the duration of the scene (which may exceed your generation limits on Ability Traits in any one Ability). You may only activate *Wind Dance* once per scene and these Traits disappear if you do not spend them by the end of that scene — you may not "stack" multiple applications of *Wind Dance*.

Fearless Heart

This technique reaches beyond mere tricks of perception to subtly enhance your physical form. Though not as potent as the combat transformations of Disciplines such as *Vicissitude*, the advantage of *Fearless Heart* is that its application is largely undetectable. As with *Wind Dance*, many thaumaturges who employ this power summon it with more complex variations of the invocations they use for *War Cry*.

Once you have activated *Fearless Heart*, you gain the Physical Traits *Stalwart*, *Quick* and *Enduring* for the duration of the scene. You may not "stack"

multiple applications of *Fearless Heart*, but you may employ it in conjunction with *Wind Dance* or other Discipline powers that give you additional Traits.

Advanced Path of Mars

Comrades at Arms

Rather than bestowing more complex boons, the pinnacle of the *Path of Mars* allows you to share your benedictions with your packmates. You may bestow the effects of *War Cry*, *Wind Dance* or *Fearless Heart* upon any willing recipient by touching her and spending the usual Blood Trait to activate the power in question. You may give any combination of these effects to any number of recipients as long as you spend one action and one Blood Trait for each power and each character. Roleplay this appropriately, especially if your unique "style" for this path's lesser powers involves war paint or superficial injuries. All limitations for self-application of these powers also apply when applying them to others (e.g. no multiple *Wind Dance* applications on the same subject).

The Path of the Father's Vengeance

This path originated with the first Noddist Tremere *antitribu*. According to their claims, it is a blood magic method of directly manipulating the curse that God placed upon Caine. However, most non-Noddist scholars of the *Path of the Father's Vengeance* state that it is simply one more application of blood magic, albeit with trappings that certainly make it *look* like a primal tie to the vampiric condition and that the path's creators were probably inflating their own importance. This path's study is a hot topic of debate among Sabbat thaumaturges, as some Noddists, Bahari and Unifiers believe that claiming mastery over Caine's curse is dangerously close to heresy — or an aspiration to apotheosis.

Most Sabbat thaumaturges teach *Path of the Father's Vengeance* with a verbal component. Invocation of any power requires the thaumaturge to speak the portion of the Curse (or a related passage from *The Book of Nod*) that she is applying. There is no actual innate power in the words (though some thaumaturges claim otherwise); rather, they serve as a mnemonic focus to steady the caster's concentration. All powers from this path have a maximum range of the distance at which the caster's voice is audible without mechanical assistance. Apply common sense in determining this range — don't penalize the character if the player has laryngitis.

These powers only affect Cainites. They have no effect on Cathayans, mortals, ghouls, Lupines or any other beings. *Path of the Father's Vengeance* uses the *Occult* Ability for retests, though it may use the specialized Ability of *Vampire Lore* if the Storyteller so desires.

Basic Father's Vengeance

Zillah's Litany

Your blood, potent as it is now, will bond those who drink it, as you did, once a night for three nights. You will be the master. They will be your thrall, as you are mine.

According to commonly accepted Cainite prehistory, Zillah was Caine's wife. She was the first vampire besides Caine to undergo the blood bond as Caine used the harsh lesson that the Crone taught him to capture Zillah's eternal love.

Trade Secrets

The *Thaumaturgy* that's presented in **Laws of the Night** is "common" knowledge. It's widespread enough that both sects and several of the independent clans theoretically have access to it (though not necessarily *open* access). However, both the Tremere of the Camarilla and the disparate thaumaturges of the Sabbat have their own toys that they don't usually share. Magical espionage is a very lucrative business for those few individuals with the skill, courage and savvy to "liberate" guarded tomes and artifacts. Of course, both sides also make a point of stamping out wandering knowledge before it can spread too far.

In game terms, what this means is that acquisition of sect-specific *Thaumaturgy* from an opposing sect is *entirely* at the Storyteller's discretion and may involve a long-term project with some serious application of multiple Backgrounds. In addition, while the basics of vampiric blood magic are the same, each sect and clan has its own unique permutations. Think of it as the differences between competing brands of cars: a Corvette is built on the same engineering principles as a Mustang, but the parts aren't necessarily interchangeable. This translates into elevated experience costs for out-of-sect *Thaumaturgy* (a Sabbat character trying to learn a ritual or path from **The Camarilla Guide**, or vice versa, or an independent trying to learn something from *either* sect). Add one Experience Trait to the cost of Basic and Intermediate paths and rituals and two to the cost of Advanced paths and rituals.

Note that Sabbat thaumaturges have their own unique difficulties in learning even common or Sabbat-specific *Thaumaturgy*. The Tremere *antitribu* are gone, and their chantry library with them. They did share their secrets while they were present, but even this knowledge is far from widespread. Storytellers may take this as license to restrict or unilaterally ban *Thaumaturgy* from Sabbat chronicles — or to build entire plots around the acquisition or recovery of such knowledge. As always, do whatever is best for your game.

The passages from *The Book of Nod* that deal with this incident serve as a mnemonic device to focus your concentration, allowing you hazy impressions of any blood bonds or Vinculi to which your target might be subject.

To apply *Zillah's Litany*, you must speak the passages in question to your target. Make a Simple Test for each vampire to whom your subject is connected by blood bond or Vinculum. On a tie, you gain a hazy impression of the individual's face. If you win, you gain a face and the name by which the subject knows that individual, as well as a hazy psychic impression. A Narrator will most likely have to arbitrate this power's effects as your subject may not be aware of all her Vinculi.

The Crone's Pride

And Caine could do nothing but stare into her ancient eyes, desire her leathery skin.

The Crone is the mythic-historic figure who taught Caine the power of the blood bond by subjecting him to it. According to *The Book of Nod*, she was a creature of loathsome visage, horrifying to gaze upon and undesirable by even the coarsest standards. To apply a similar appearance to your target, you must recite a description of the Crone to her and defeat her in a Mental Challenge. If you win, she receives the Nosferatu clan disadvantage for the rest of the night, including the Negative Social Traits *Repugnant x 3*. She may not bid the Social Traits that are banned for Nosferatu (*Alluring*, *Gorgeous* or *Seductive*), nor do they count toward her total Social Traits for ties and overbids.

Intermediate Father's Vengeance

Feast of Ashes

You will drink only blood. You will eat only ashes. You will be always as you were at death.

With this power, you may invoke the final curse that God laid upon Caine, twisting your subject's hunger so that blood no longer sustains him. For the duration of this power, he gains no sustenance from vitae, but instead must consume ash for nourishment.

Make a Mental Challenge against your target. If you win, expend a number of Mental Traits. This is the number of nights during which he gains no Blood Traits from drinking blood. Instead, for every handful of ash he consumes, he gains one Ashen Blood Trait, which he may only expend to heal non-aggravated damage or to satisfy his normal nightly sustenance requirement. This may be any sort of ash: cigarette butts, the leavings of a campfire or even the remains of a vampire who has met Final Death.

Uriel's Disfavor

Then, for as long as you walk this earth, you and your children will fear the dawn, and the sun's rays will seek to burn you like fire where ever you hide always.

Purists argue that this power's proper name should be "Raphael's Disfavor," as it was that angel, not Uriel, who cursed Caine in such a fashion. Nevertheless, the current appellation remains. A victim of this power is afflicted with a vastly heightened sensitivity to any sort of light, even artificial sources that are normally harmless to most Cainites.

Make a Mental Challenge against your target. If you win, she gains *Uriel's Disfavor* for the rest of the scene. You may spend a Willpower Trait after winning the challenge to extend this to the rest of the night. While under the effect of this power, the subject gains the Negative Mental Trait *Oblivious* when in the presence of any light source brighter than a single candle. Worse yet, she sustains one level of aggravated damage for every turn that she is directly exposed to any bright light, such as a halogen flashlight, automobile high beams or nightclub strobes (Storyteller's discretion; a good rule of thumb is any light that would make you go "ouch!" if you looked directly into it from three yards or less).

Advanced Father's Vengeance

Valediction

Seek not the blood of thine own Elder. Seek not the blood of thy Sire's Sire. Seek not the blood that made thee Kin.

Though many Sabbat consider diablerie a sacrament or a duty, such behavior is in direct opposition to one of the few dictates that Caine supposedly laid down. The mere threat of *Valediction* is enough to give pause to those who are familiar with it. By invoking Caine's law against diablerie, you can strip all the benefits of that act from your victim.

You must spend three turns to speak the entire invocation of this power. On the third turn, make a Mental Challenge against your victim. If you succeed, spend any number of Willpower Traits. For that many nights, the subject returns to the generation she possessed at the time of her Embrace. She immediately loses access to all Traits that are in excess of her generation maximum (Storyteller's discretion as to which specific Traits the victim loses in each category). Her Blood Pool likewise shrinks; if she has more Blood Traits in her system than she can currently hold, she is unable to initiate any actions until she has finished vomiting up the excess blood at the rate of one Blood Trait per turn. If this shift in generation changes her access to high-level Disciplines, she is temporarily stripped of those powers.

Thaumaturgical Rituals

Most Sabbat-taught rituals, whether sect-specific or commonly known, are couched in some sort of pseudo-religious ceremony. Many require a certain amount of paraphernalia and elaborate incantations. Physical components also tend to be unsettling to mortal sensibilities; body parts of humans or animals are common, as are rare or precious substances and body fluids.

These rituals use the same systems as those in **Laws of the Night** (p. 185).

Basic Thaumaturgical Rituals

Blood Rush

With this ritual, you may experience all of the pleasure of feeding with none of the business of the hunt. This is particularly useful in staving off hunger pangs or preparing to deal with large quantities of spilt blood. While affected by *Blood Rush*, you gain one free retest to avoid frenzying over hunger or the smell or sight of blood. *Blood Rush* uses the fangs of a predatory animal as a focus, and you must carry these for the ritual to work. It lasts until the next sunset.

Dominoe of Life

Dominoe of Life allows you to assume one physical characteristic of mortality: normal human temperature, an appetite for solid food, automatic respiration or a pulse and a normal flesh tone. You may only replicate one of these features per casting, though you may "stack" them multiple times. *Dominoe of Life* requires you to carry a small vial of mortal blood on your person (at least 1/4 of a Blood Trait). It lasts until one hour after dawn.

Eyes of the Night Hawk

Through this ritual, you may transfer your perceptions into the body of a predatory bird. Until dawn breaks or you end the ritual, you see with the raptor's eyes rather than your own. You may exert no influence over the bird other than controlling its flight and its gaze — commanding it to attack a target or pick up an object is beyond your grasp (though it will follow its own instincts if it sees food or a threat).

Except for the behavioral restrictions mentioned above and the means of ending the ritual, the effects of *Eyes of the Night Hawk* simulate those of *Subsume the Spirit* (**Laws of the Night**, p. 135). Your raptor has the Physical Traits *Energetic*, *Quick* x 2 and *Resilient*. You may only use *Auspex* through it.

To end the ritual, you must touch the bird. You must also put out its eyes within one minute of ending the ritual or suffer blindness for three nights (note that such an act may cause a crisis of ethics, depending on your particular Morality). Some enterprising thaumaturges ghoul their raptors in order to produce reusable subjects who can regenerate their eyes over time. If you do not voluntarily end *Eyes of the Night Hawk*, it expires at sunrise and you face the normal consequences of not blinding your avian surveillance device.

Illuminate Trail of the Prey

By invoking the spirits of air and earth, you may command them to reveal the trail of an individual who you now pursue. Whether she is traveling on foot, on a mount or in a vehicle, your eyes perceive the path she took as a series of faintly glowing silver footprints. Your quarry is unaware that you are tracking her in such a manner unless she has some magical warning mechanism. Her trail will end at the first body of water through which she passes (though passing *over* it has no effect). The ritual's effects only last as long as you are directly on the trail — if you stop tracking to feed, sleep or make a phone call, the footprints fade.

To enact this ritual, you must have a starting point from which to work and you must know your target's true face. While reciting your invocation of the appropriate spirits, you must burn a six-foot length of white satin ribbon wrapped around a bone from the leg of a predatory mammal. When the ribbon is reduced to ash, the trail appears before you. This is not a foolproof method of tracking as the spirits this ritual commands are weak and capricious, but it does give you three free retests on attempts to track your quarry (most often using the *Investigation* or *Survival* Abilities).

Machine Blitz

For the most part, *Thaumaturgy* is hardly technological in nature, but this ritual stands as one of the rare exceptions to that rule. Through *Machine Blitz*, you may increase the level of chaos within a mechanical device to the point that it breaks down under the weight of its own complexity. This ritual can be used to affect any single machine more complex than a rope-and-pulley, including both mechanical and electronic devices.

To inflict *Machine Blitz*, spend one minute tracing a series of incorrect mathematical equations on the surface of the target device. For this, you must use a pencil-sized wand made of a bone from a mortal who was killed in a mechanical accident. If you successfully cast the ritual, the machine instantly stops working through what appears to be a normal system failure. A skilled repairman (a number of *Repair* or appropriate *Crafts* Ability Traits equal to your number of *Occult* Ability Traits) can restore the target to function with a Static Mental Challenge against a difficulty of your Mental Traits.

Recure of the Homeland

This ritual, which many Sabbat believe to be a Tzimisce innovation, allows you to create a muddy paste which can assist you in healing even the most devastating wounds. To prepare one dose, mix one handful of earth from the area of your mortal birth with two of your own Blood Traits. The resulting

paste (assuming you succeed in casting the ritual) instantly heals one level of aggravated damage when you smear it on the wound (or consume it, in the case of internal injuries). You may make any amount of this paste, as long as you have sufficient supplies of earth and blood, but you may only use it to heal one Health Level per night. Once you cast the ritual, the blood you use becomes part of the curative substance and is no longer considered blood for game purposes. Only you may benefit from the properties of this paste — to any other character, it is simply a glob of reddish mud.

Widow's Spite

By constructing a small ceremonial doll, you may inflict a distracting itch or ache on a target. This ritual holds little actual danger for its subject. Many Sabbat use it as a practical joke or a message of contempt, though some intrepid thaumaturges utilize *Widow's Spite* to probe a potential victim's defenses in preparation for a more devastating magical attack.

You must construct the doll yourself, and it must bear at least a vague resemblance to your target (no test required, but roleplaying this construction is encouraged). When you cast the ritual, the doll oozes a few drops of blood from the location that you want to afflict with the distracting sensation. If the ritual succeeds, the target receives the Negative Mental Trait *Witless* for the rest of the night. You may re-use the doll if you so desire, though it falls apart after the second time you fail in casting the ritual.

Intermediate Thaumaturgical Rituals

Clinging of the Insect

Through this ritual, you may imbue yourself with a mystical property of adhesion that mimics an insect's ability to climb vertical surfaces. Spend five minutes performing stretching exercises, then place a live spider under your tongue. You may then move on walls and ceilings at half your normal walking speed. This lasts for the rest of the scene or until the spider dies or leaves its place under your tongue. While keeping a live spider pinned under your tongue, you are down three Traits on any Social Challenge that requires you to speak well. Naturally, you should simulate the spider through Narrator notification or candy rather than using a real one.

Firewalker

Though no vampire in his right mind ever *plans* to come in contact with open flame, this ritual allows you to prepare yourself for situations where such an event might occur. To enact *Firewalker*, cut off one of your big toes (which hurts like hell and inflicts one level of lethal damage) and burn it over a wood fire, then smear the resulting ashes on the soles of your feet and the palms of your hands. For the next hour, make a Simple Test for each level of aggravated damage you take from fire. If you win or tie, that level of damage becomes lethal damage. You may cast this ritual on another vampire, in which case you must sacrifice one of your beneficiary's toes. Multiple subjects' toes may be sacrificed simultaneously in the same group ritual, up to a maximum number of subjects equal to your number of permanent Mental Traits. A character who is missing a big toe gains the Negative Physical Trait *Clumsy* due to the effect this loss has on his balance.

Mirror of Second Sight

Unlike most rituals, whose effects are short-lived, *Mirror of Second Sight* allows you to create a permanently enchanted item. You may imbue any circular mirror between four and 18 inches in diameter with the property of reflecting an individual's supernatural nature, if any, superimposed over her mundane image. To do this, you must etch the back of the mirror with a series of mystic sigils and bathe it in two of your own Blood Traits.

Once you successfully enchant the mirror, its reflections reveal all supernatural creatures for what they are. Vampires appear as skeletal husks of their physical selves, werewolves are shown simultaneously as men and beasts, ghosts are visible as misty outlines, changelings are masked with their faerie faces and mages bear luminescent auras. Mortals still look like mortals, however; this mirror will not detect a ghoul or a human who practices lesser sorcerous arts. Additionally, this mirror only reveals the "true forms" of individuals who are visible to the unaided eye — it does nothing to pierce *Obfuscate* or any other supernatural means of concealment save for showing images of ghosts who are normally invisible in the physical world.

ADVANCED THAUMATURGICAL RITUALS

Paper Flesh

This fearsome ritual allows you to strip a vampire of most of his supernatural resilience, leaving him as defenseless as an ordinary mortal. However, you must know his mortal birth name, which is much harder to learn of paranoid (or senile) elders than it is of innocent neonates.

To enact *Paper Flesh*, sketch your target's face on a sheet of unblemished white paper, using one Blood Trait of your own blood for ink (Static Physical Challenge against a difficulty of the subject's Social Traits, retest with an appropriate *Crafts* Ability). Then write his birth name across the image's forehead in black ink and cut the image's throat with a silver dagger. For the rest of the night, the subject loses any *Fortitude* he may have had except for *Endurance*, as well as all of the following Physical Traits: *Enduring*, *Resilient*, *Robust*, *Rugged* and *Tireless*.

If your target is a vampire who is of seventh generation or greater, he may retain one additional level of *Fortitude* and two of the affected Physical Traits for every generation he is above eighth. For instance, a sixth-generation target would retain both Basic *Fortitude* powers, the first Intermediate *Fortitude* power and four of the affected Physical Traits (assuming he had these powers and Traits to begin with).

VALEREN

The Salubri *antitribu* claim that *Valeren* is one of their former clan's oldest secrets, a Discipline of mystic martial prowess that the non-Sabbat Salubri perverted into a weakling's healing tool. Saulot, they claim, was a holy warrior, and they remain true to his heritage by practicing *Valeren*.

While this Discipline has some features in common with *Obeah*, the Discipline of the Salubri, it is its own distinct series of lessons, and its practitioners tend to regard it as one of their foremost weapons for their sacred battles. Like *Obeah*, *Valeren* does have a physical manifestation in the form of a third eye, which appears on any *Valeren* practitioner's forehead when he learns the first

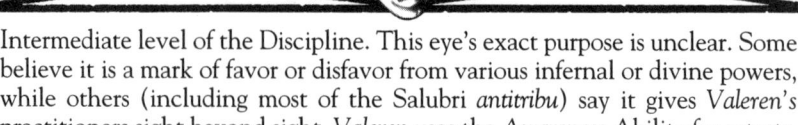

Intermediate level of the Discipline. This eye's exact purpose is unclear. Some believe it is a mark of favor or disfavor from various infernal or divine powers, while others (including most of the Salubri *antitribu*) say it gives *Valeren's* practitioners sight beyond sight. *Valeren* uses the *Awareness* Ability for retests.

Basic Valeren

Sense Vitality

This power functions exactly as the *Obeah* power of the same name (**Laws of the Night,** p. 158).

Anesthetic Touch

This power functions exactly as the *Obeah* power of the same name (**Laws of the Night,** p. 159).

Intermediate Valeren

Burning Touch

In a grim parody of the legends of saints' healing touches, you may lay hands on an individual to inflict excruciating pain. This power does no actual damage, but the subject feels as if he is being burned, flayed, impaled, eviscerated, dissolved or experiencing whatever other sensation you care to inflict. Some Salubri *antitribu* use *Burning Touch* as an interrogation tool while others simply apply it out of sadism. When you apply *Burning Touch*, your third eye glows with a dim, flickering red-orange light.

To apply *Burning Touch*, simply touch your victim and expend a Blood Trait. If you apply this power in combat, your victim suffers the penalties for being at the Wounded state of health for the rest of the turn. If he is already Wounded, he must defeat you in a Mental Challenge or suffer the effects of being Incapacitated for the rest of the turn.

If you use *Burning Touch* as an interrogation tool, you or your fellow interrogators gain one free retest on the next interrogation- or torture-related challenge you make against that individual. Recreational applications of this power are best left to roleplaying.

Ending the Watch

This power allows you to visit euthanasia upon a willing mortal. By simply laying your hand over your subject's heart, you may release her from the trials and turmoil of earthly existence.

To *End the Watch*, touch your victim and spend a Willpower Trait. The mortal must actively want to die; if she has any doubts about this desire, the power fails to work. However, if death is truly what she yearns for, her soul instantly flees her body. A mortal killed with this power may not be Embraced, become a wraith after death or have any form of *Necromancy* work on her soul or body. Medical or mystic examination will reveal the cause of her death to be sudden heart failure. *Ending the Watch* will only kill an ordinary mortal with no supernatural qualities — it has no effect on werewolves, changelings, wizards, ghosts, ghouls, mummies or any other supernatural being.

Advanced Valeren

Vengeance of Samiel

By invoking the legacy of your line's distant progenitor, the legendary holy warrior Samiel, you may strike with the devastating precision that he devel-

oped over centuries of battle. *Vengeance of Samiel* is an exhausting power to invoke, but its effects are unparalleled. Your third eye flares wide open when you invoke this power, emitting a hellish red glare, and you may close your normal eyes with no penalty to this attack.

You may only use *Vengeance of Samiel* when you are making an attack with your bare hands or a melee weapon and it is your only action for the turn. Spend three Blood Traits to activate this power. You may not use *Vengeance of Samiel* to augment an attack you make with another Discipline (such as combat *Bonecrafting*), though you may still use it with another attack-enhancing Discipline power that does not generate the attack in and of itself (such as *Feral Claws* or *Prowess*). Add your Mental Traits to your Physical Traits for the attack challenge, including bidding, tie resolution and overbidding. Your opponent may not evade this attack by declaring a retest with the *Dodge* Ability. If the attack succeeds, it inflicts an additional two health levels of the appropriate type of damage. If you use *Vengeance of Samiel* in an attempt to stake an opponent, you must win or tie only one Simple Test after the successful attack, as opposed to the two that staking usually requires (**Laws of the Night**, p. 204).

Superior Valeren

Elder Valeren: Blissful Agony

You may visit agony on an enemy that makes the torture of *Burning Touch* pale in comparison. This searing pain persists even after you remove your hand, and it is intense enough to kill weak-willed mortals and drive Cainites into frenzy.

To inflict *Blissful Agony* on your victim, touch him, spend a Blood Trait and defeat him in a Mental Challenge. For the rest of the scene, your victim is considered to be Wounded for purposes of wound penalties. If his condition actually reaches Wounded, he is considered Incapacitated.

If you wish, you may inflict lethal damage on an opponent, though you must maintain contact and spend one Blood Trait per health level to exercise this option. A Cainite may make one Simple Test per health level you inflict in this fashion; if she wins, she negates the damage. This damage heals normally for mortals, but vanishes at the next sunset for a vampire. If you inflict more health levels on a vampire than she has Willpower Traits, she must resist Rötschreck against a difficulty of your Mental Traits.

Superior Vicissitude

Elder Vicissitude: Chiropteran Marauder

Although this form bears vague resemblance to the more familiar *zulo* or *Horrid Form* (**Laws of the Night**, p. 189), it is even more capable and terrifying. *Chiropteran Marauder* allows you to assume the form of a horrid melding of human and bat forms. Your face gnarls into a hideous grimace while your arms shift into leathery wings bearing talons.

To take on this visage, spend three Blood Traits. You gain all the benefits of *Horrid Form*, as well as the ability to fly at speeds of up to 25 mph (*Celerity* does not increase this). You can carry aloft a maximum weight equal to that of your own body in this altered form, though your flight is rather awkward if you do so. You also possess bony claws at the end of your wings that have the same effect as *Feral Claws* (**Laws of the Night**, p. 169). You are down two Trait on

all perception-related challenges that deal with hearing but gain one bonus Trait on any vision-based challenges that deal with wits or perception. This form remains in effect for the scene once you invoke it.

Elder Vicissitude: Blood of Acid

This power's effects are exactly what its name suggests. You have permanently converted your vitae into a powerful organic acid. While this limits your potential applications of it, it also serves as a final line of defense against diablerie, as well as posing a formidable hazard to anyone who would engage you in close combat.

Each Blood Trait of yours that comes in contact with something other than you inflicts two levels of aggravated damage to that item or individual. Anyone who actually *ingests* your vitae receives *four* levels of aggravated damage per Blood Trait she drinks. This makes the creation of progeny or ghouls rather difficult and unpleasant, though not completely impossible.

Every time a penetrating attack injures you in close combat (stake, claws, sword, or any gunshot at five feet or less), make a Simple Test. If you win, you lose one Blood Trait of your vitae as it sprays toward your attacker. She, in turn, must make a Static Physical Challenge against a difficulty of five Traits. If she loses, she takes one level of aggravated damage (damage is lessened due to the dispersed spray).

This acid also affects any weapon or object that enters your body. Make a Simple Test every time this happens. A wooden object will be corroded to uselessness within five minutes if you win or tie while a metal or plastic item suffers the same fate on a win. Individuals who stake you are in for an unpleasant surprise as the concentration of vitae in your heart dissolves the stake in five turns (15 seconds).

If you assume *Bloodform* (**Laws of the Night**, p. 189), your blood only dissolves what you wish it to dissolve. Use this effect carefully as you may find yourself reacting away to nothingness if you decide to dissolve your way through the floor.

Master Vicissitude: Cocoon

Many ancient Tzimisce use *Cocoon* to sleep away the ages in safety and comfort. This power allows you to extrude an opaque cocoon from various bodily fluids, spinning it around yourself like the chrysalis of a vampiric butterfly. The cocoon solidifies within a few minutes and vaguely resembles a tough, fibrous coffin.

To spin your *Cocoon*, spend three Blood Traits and 10 minutes. It lasts as long as you wish, and you may emerge from it at no cost or effort. The cocoon blocks sunlight, and is somewhat flame-retardant, negating the first two health levels of damage per turn that you would otherwise sustain from fire. Any attacker making a physical strike against you must first defeat the cocoon's strength in a Static Physical Challenge against a difficulty of twice your number of Physical Traits. While within your *Cocoon*, you may still use mental Disciplines so long as you can meet the requirements (eye contact is right out under most circumstances).

Ascendant Vicissitude: Breath of the Dragon

Your mastery of your own flesh and blood is such that you can vomit forth your vitae even as you convert it to a highly combustible fluid that ignites in a

hellish flame as it leaves your mouth. You may purse your lips to direct this fire against one target or open your mouth wide to spray flaming droplets over an area. You are immune to this flame though not to secondary fires that it starts.

To attack a single target, spend a Blood Trait and defeat him in a Physical Challenge. If you win, he sustains three levels of aggravated damage and bursts into flame. In the next turn, he suffers an additional two levels of aggravated damage, and one more each subsequent turn until he extinguishes the flame or perishes. You may strike an individual at a maximum range of 100 feet (30 steps).

If you wish to incinerate an area, spend five Blood Traits. You may center the blast on any point in your line of sight that is within 100 feet (30 steps) of you. The radius of effect is 20 feet. Everyone within that area receives two levels of aggravated damage. All flammable objects within the area are ignited. Any victims must succeed in a Static Physical Challenge against a difficulty of five Traits to avoid being set afire as well; this does one additional aggravated health level per turn, as does remaining within the burning area on subsequent turns.

Methuselah Vicissitude: Earth's Vast Haven

This power hails from the time when the childer of Tzimisce were the undisputed masters of Eastern Europe, calling upon the line's strange bond to the earth of their ancestral homeland. It allows you to become one with your very domain, spreading your vitae, physical form and consciousness throughout all that you survey. You are virtually invulnerable in this form — nothing short of an explosion powerful enough to leave a mile-wide crater can harm you in any meaningful manner, and sunlight on your soil does nothing but stimulate plant growth.

To enter *Earth's Vast Haven*, spend six Blood Traits. You sink into the ground in a manner that is visually similar to that of *Earth Meld*. However, your form is spread throughout the ground in an approximate three-mile radius to a depth of six feet. While in *Earth's Vast Haven*, you require no blood for sustenance. You may exercise your mental Disciplines on anyone within your area of dispersion, as long as you may maintain the other requirements (eye contact is impossible, but anyone who is standing on bare earth within your area is assumed to be in physical contact with you). You may also initiate direct mental contact with anyone within this area at any time, using the rules for *Telepathy* (**Laws of the Night**, p. 138). You theoretically have complete awareness of all that transpires within your area of existence, though in practice your mind tends to wander when inhabiting such a vast space. If you decide to emerge from *Earth's Vast Haven*, you may re-form your normal body at any point within the power's area of effect.

If nuclear weapons are used on the area in which you reside (the only practical means of killing you available to modern technology), you suffer one to three levels of aggravated damage per explosion. You may not heal this damage until you leave *Earth's Vast Haven*. The explosions must be on or under the ground in order to harm you — even the most powerful air burst won't displace enough earth to do more than annoy you. Obviously, the effects of nuclear weapons are difficult enough to simulate in a live-action setting that they should remain plot devices.

Chapter Six: Midnight Dances

Ritae

The Sabbat has another side, one that contrasts the bloodthirsty façade that the average Cainite of any stripe sees — that of its spirituality. The *ritae*, or rites, remind believers of their common goals, reward them for success and punish them for failure. Regular performance of the *ritae* keeps pack members in harmony (or something like it) and focused on their goals.

There's no sect-wide standard for formality. Storytellers should decide on the tone they want for their chronicles and flesh out the *ritae* accordingly. If you want to go for the grand ceremonial feel, appropriate props and music can make a big difference. Even a couple of candlesticks, an altar cloth and a tape of Gregorian chants go a long way toward evoking the sense of a chapel dedicated to dark deeds.

Sabbat spirituality — and no, that's not a contradiction in terms — isn't tied to one single culture. Even the stodgiest cardinals reluctantly admit, the truths the Sabbat proclaims don't require that members practice a medieval Black Mass. A Sabbat ceremony might look like a gang hanging out, a corporate board meeting or a blood-cult pagan gathering. Beneath it all there's the same set of doctrines. As long as orthodoxy prevails in action, most bishops don't fuss too loudly about how packs celebrate.

Pomp, circumstance and abused liturgical Latin can convey a mystic sense, but there's a risk of turning into gratuitous blasphemy. Only a monster would trample someone's real religious beliefs for the sake of a game. Keep the game and life separate, and watch for danger signs that someone is taking his personal intolerances out of one arena and into another.

Performing the Rites

If you want priestly competence and power to matter in your chronicle, use these optional rules. If you'd rather keep it simple, just use the standard rules for tests associated with each rite. Again, these rules are strictly optional.

When a priest embarks on a rite, he makes a Social Challenge against a number of Traits equal to the number of participants. When a bishop or higher-ranked priest performs a rite with lower-ranked assistants, each assistant adds one Trait to the lead priest's Social Traits total. If the lead priest ties this test, participants receive no bonus or penalty during the rite. If the lead priest succeeds, everyone adds one Trait per level of the priest's Path rating to their own Traits for the purposes of tests. This bonus applies to all tests directly associated with the *ritus* — during Fire Dancing, for instance, it applies to a vampire's Physical Trait total for jumping the fire but not to trying to establish a psychic link to someone four blocks away.

If the priest fails the test, make two Simple Tests. If the priest wins at least one of them, the rite unfolds as usual. Otherwise, all participants suffer a one-Trait penalty on all related tests — if the priest is spiritually impaired, how can he hope to lead his followers appropriately? The priest has the option of canceling the rite. This automatically imposes the Negative Status Trait *Unfaithful*, which the priest can remove only by successfully performing two *auctoritas ritae* in the future.

Official (Auctoritas)

Everyone in the sect practices the *auctoritas ritae*. Each one gives expression to an important aspect of the Sabbat's mission and goals, and their universal exercise binds members together.

The Binding

On the night of the winter solstice, Sabbat members gather for a public reaffirmation of their oaths to the sect. Just as the Vaulderie unites members of a pack, the Binding ties together all the oath-taking vampires in the community.

The ceremony begins with a recitation of the group's interpretation of the Sabbat credo. Each group does this a little differently. Some work it out in liturgical form while others present each point in metaphorical language or in the form of a parable. Military-style gatherings shout out the credo in call-and-response style. Sometimes the recitation takes an hour or occupies just a few angry sentences.

Founded packs host nomadic packs, where possible, although the negotiations beforehand to allow safe passage seldom go smoothly (very few occasions could encourage such mutual restraint). Tradition calls for performing the Binding near water — a beach, riverbank or waterfall if possible, a fountain if there's nothing else. Water symbolizes the sect's implacable determination, eroding or flooding all opposition just as the Sabbat must in the end triumph completely.

Vaulderie and a separate oath to protect the sect's secrets to Final Death almost always follow the Binding. Major Sabbat war efforts also often begin at the Binding, exploiting the unity of purpose the *ritus* creates.

System: The Vinculum ratings of all participants in the *ritus* increase by one (to a maximum of 10), and remain elevated for the next month.

The Blood Bath

Sect leaders perform this *ritus* to confirm a vampire's appointment to a bishopric or higher office. All Sabbat members who can attend the Blood Bath do so; avoiding it unnecessarily may strike the new leader as an insult. Each participant in the *ritus* steps forward, kneels to the new leader, expresses praise for or confidence in the recipient and offers blood into a common vessel. The leading priest acts first, followed by attending sect leaders and then by everyone else present. The vampire receiving the new title offers a response of praise or advice to each vampire present, emphasizing her wisdom and how she benefits the Sabbat. He then bathes in the pool, and all participants drink from it. Sometimes the priest consecrates the pool as a Vaulderie, sometimes not.

Fervent Sabbat supporters often refuse to acknowledge leaders who cannot produce evidence of having undergone a proper Blood Bath.

System: Each participant must contribute at least one Blood Trait. If the pool is consecrated as a Vaulderie, follow the Vaulderie system.

The Blood Feast

The Blood Feast often accompanies other *ritae*; in some cities, the bishops celebrate this on its own. This *ritus* combines an opportunity for formal gathering with a stark celebration of vampires' predatory natures.

The Blood Feast itself is the vampiric equivalent of a formal dinner. The guests dine on the blood of captured men and women suspended over a dining table, bound to statues or otherwise immobilized.

Preparations begin well before the feast. For several nights before the feast, a specially constituted hunting party rounds up humans (and, when the opportunity arises, vampires outside the Sabbat). It's an honor to be chosen to take part in the hunt, and it takes great self-restraint to deliver the captured prey alive and as unharmed as possible. The hunters present their prey along with demonstrations of martial prowess and boasts of their exploits to the highest-ranking Sabbat member present. She receives each victim and gives the vampire who brought the victim a kiss of thanks of the forehead. Vampires then secure the prey safely until the night of the Blood Feast.

On the night of the feast, ghouls or low-ranking vampires arrange the prey at the Blood Feast's location. The nature of the meal makes tardiness a grave offense against hospitality; guests arrive early or on time. The presiding official dedicates the prey to the glory of the Sabbat and the participants in the *ritus*. She may deliver a Sermon of Caine at this time, depending on how self-controlled the participants are in the face of imminent feeding. The presiding official gets her pick of the vessels and draws first blood. Once she's begun, the guests set in.

Tradition calls for a minimum of one vessel per three participants in the Blood Feast. Some groups favor more. The ratio depends partly on how tidily

or messily the participants feed. Some groups feed directly from the vessels while others drain the blood into champagne flutes or other containers. The presiding official may mandate a particular method of feeding or allow diverse styles as she deems fit.

The priestly blessing at the beginning of the Blood Feast somehow intensifies the vessels' blood as it leaves their bodies; it gains double normal potency. The Sabbat hierarchy appreciates the merits of the Blood Feast but censures groups that engage in it too often. Too many kidnappings and gore-spattered meeting halls attract mortal attention even in thoroughly cowed cities.

System: The priest's ceremony at the start of the *ritus* transforms the blood of victims bound and presented for the Blood Feast. Each Blood Trait of a vessel so consecrated becomes two Blood Traits as it leaves the vessel's body. Vampires who drink the consecrated blood get the benefit of two Blood Traits even though it only occupies one Blood Trait's worth of capacity in their own bodies. Participants in the Blood Feast generally feel unusually energetic; the extra blood can take them beyond their normal generational limits for vitae. Any doubled Blood Traits unspent at the end of the third night after the Blood Feast collapse back into single Blood Traits.

Creation Rites

Outsiders assume that the Sabbat's "shovel party" is the standard way of making new Sabbat members. The sect knows otherwise. The process is inefficient; a lot of victims don't make it out. Many of those who do survive emerge permanently insane.

New recruits to the Sabbat don't join as full members until they've proven themselves in combat or intrigue. Until they complete the Creation Rites, they're on probation. They can be destroyed at any time for disobedience, creating childer of their own or even for getting in the way of their elders. The probation lasts at least for several days, often for weeks and goes on for years in areas with very strict leadership. A sire may require his childe to display her newfound strength and nature by performing in a test of his choosing before he considers her ready for the rite.

A priest administers the Creation Rites. She touches a flaming brand to the initiate's forehead and leads her in an oath of allegiance. The phrasing varies; the key points include loyalty to one's pack leader, to the chain of command and to the principles of the Sabbat as they've been taught to the recruit. Once branded, the initiate becomes a true member of the Sabbat, with all the risks and benefits that implies. The priest follows the branding with a Vaulderie.

Sires and packs often add celebrations or other rites of their own. Young urban packs perform gang-style initiations while dignified elders present their upper-class childer in formal gatherings. In their various forms, such supplemental commemorations both congratulate the new recruit and remind her that she is still at the bottom of the pile.

System: The branding requires the new recruit to succeed in a two-Trait Rötschreck test. A recruit who panics gets a second chance, albeit with a

substantial stigma for cowardice. Failing the test a second time brings immediate destruction.

See **Laws of the Night**, p. 224, for the shovel-party rules.

Some bishops like to form new packs in a special version of the Creation Rites. Each member of the pack-to-be gets drained and buried as if the victim of a shovel party, and must dig her way out. With the benefits of vampiric strength, a vampire undergoing re-creation must win or tie two out of three Simple Tests with the Narrator (rather than having to win two out of three). Like a mortal in the same situation, the vampire can spend Physical Traits for retests. When (and if) all the members of the pack emerge, their designated priest brands himself and the other members of the pack and leads them in a Vaulderie. Since there's always the risk of losing vampires in this process, bishops in areas of active conflict or reduced numbers of members frown on the practice.

The Festival of the Dead (Festivo Dello Estinto)

The Festival of the Dead occupies the entire second week of March; it's second only to the Grand Ball as an opportunity for participants to celebrate their trans-human abilities. All the Sabbat vampires in a city gather, setting aside usual disputes for the week of the Festival, and nomadic packs come into town to celebrate with their urban brethren.

The Festival begins as soon as the highest-ranking priest in town declares it underway. He gives a single instruction to the assembled participants: Revel. This is the time for vampires to set aside their normal restraints and find out just what they can do to themselves, to each other and above all to the mortals around them. Each night includes a Blood Feast and a celebration of the Vaulderie after the night's exertions, scheduled as late as possible given the need of the participants to settle down for the day.

In principle, the Festival's participants should act utterly without regard for anyone's concerns but their own. In practice, the world is still there even while vampires celebrate. The Sabbat uses the Festival partly to weed out the vampires who cannot distinguish between the freedom to choose their own course of action and consequences to their choices. Vampires who bring out mortal hunters or other supernatural beings in response to Festival behavior deserve what they get, the sect's teachers say.

Festival events vary widely. Fire Dancing takes place almost everywhere, often coupled with dances pairing vampires with unwilling mortal partners. Packs whose members know *Necromancy* often raise zombies to provide accompaniment. In many cities, packs compete to present reenactments of passages from the *Book of Nod* and Sabbat history. Vampires who fancy themselves great hunters set out on special hunts, going after specific sorts of victims — teen mothers, bald priests, married computer programmers or some other specialized category of mortal. Vampires with experience in butchery, surgery and the like oversee competitions to kill victims with a minimum of blood spilled or to remove of as many internal organs as possible while keeping the victim alive and conscious.

Presiding archbishops and bishops watch the various competitions and award victors with the right of drawing first blood at the next Blood Feast. In some cases, a particularly good performance wins the victor a promotion on the spot while an appalling failure may lead to demotion or to the loser becoming one of the next Blood Feast's vessels. Elders look with favor on competitions to hunt as widely and freely as possible without attracting mortal attention. Success in this sort of challenge requires developing and presenting a plausible cover story, such as a terrorist attack. The Sabbat hierarchy admires and rewards the ability to use mortal institutions without becoming tangled in mortal values or concerns like the Camarilla.

System: Resolve the various competitions as seems appropriate. The Festival is as much an occasion for roleplaying as for number-crunching. Note that many Festival sports require a fair number of Storyteller mortal characters, so plan ahead to have enough Narrator support.

Fire Dance

Fire is one of the great enemies to vampire, a danger to flee. The Sabbat believes in mastering that fear. In times of war, Sabbat vampires use fire as a weapon against their enemies. In between battles, they perform the Fire Dance to show their triumph over the weaknesses in their souls.

A priest can call a Fire Dance at any time, whenever she judges the pack in need of some morale boosting. Bishops generally celebrate a Fire Dance just before a War Party, bringing together all the packs who will fight in the upcoming assault. Given the Sabbat's emphasis on individual freedom, the convening priest never forces a vampire to take part in the *ritus* until she feels truly ready for it. Most vampires somehow find the resolve to participate anyway; their packmates do not tolerate cowardice, and too many refusals of the Fire Dance can get a vampire exiled or destroyed.

The convening priest lights a bonfire somewhere away from mortal eyes. Participants set a rhythm with drumming, chanting or other regular music. They circle the fire, working themselves into a trancelike frenzy. They close in on the flames until primitive instinct forces them away; some make obeisance to the fire as if it is a god they hate but still venerate. As each participant feels ready, she jumps through the flames. The more vampires make it through, the more they encourage (and challenge) the remaining participants to do so. Particularly devoted or entranced vampires jump again and again; some perform the most exotic stunts along the way. The *ritus* ends when every vampire has jumped.

Sometimes a vampire simply can't muster the courage to jump. Tolerant packs throw him through so as to honor the spirit of the occasion. Less tolerant packs slaughter him as an inferior breed or pin him down in the fire to help him overcome his weakness.

System: Once the fire's started and the revels begin, participating vampires must make a *Courage* test against two Traits to approach the fire. (Their trance state reduces the normal difficulty.) Actually jumping through the fire requires a Static Physical Challenge against five Traits. The Storyteller should increase the difficulty of complex maneuvers; if they work, the participant gains one or more bonus Social Traits for the rest of the night.

All participants who voluntarily leap through the fire get a bonus *Courage* Trait for the rest of the night and for three nights after that. This bonus can exceed the usual Virtue limit of 5.

Do not, under any circumstances, actually go leaping through bonfires. Use your imagination to capture a sense of the experience without the prop of real fire.

Games of Instinct

The Sabbat glorifies achievement. Thinking grand thoughts doesn't mean anything without action. Therefore, the ceremonial demonstration of one's physical, mental and social prowess is a religious act. The label "Games of Instinct" applies to all competitions in which participants compete against each other and the surrounding world in ways that exemplify the Sabbat's ideas.

Note that Games of Instinct do not include random carnage for its own sake. The Sabbat does not believe in the Masquerade as a goal, but sect leaders aren't stupid and know that there are very firm limits to how far vampires can go without bringing down massive reprisals. The Sabbat does not value stupidity and won't reward it, let alone treat it as a matter of spiritual importance.

The priest presides over each game, blessing the participants and instructing them in the terms of this particular game. The practice should resemble the ancient Olympic games in which participants demonstrated physical excellence as an act of worship. The games are vigorous, enthusiastic and often bloody, but never frivolous. Holy joy in one's superiority is far more than simple bloodthirst.

System: The specific mechanical aspects of a Game of Instinct depend on the nature of the game. All games share a specific feature. The winners of a game get a one-Trait bonus to one Ability they used during the game. This bonus lasts for two weeks of game time. A vampire can only enjoy this benefit for one Ability at a time, no matter how many games she participates in.

Some examples of common Games of Instinct:

• **Capture the Ductus.** This game pits two packs against each other. The priest designates territory, generally a few square blocks. Each pack aims to present the ductus of the other to the priest; the first pack to do so wins. Inflicting Final Death on any participant automatically costs the destroyer's pack the game (plus the rage of the offended pack). The priest has discretion in setting boundaries for mortal awareness. Particularly challenging games require that no mortal ever know the game's being played while other times, for games of terror, the priest actively condones displays of vampiric power.

• **The Rat Race.** At the beginning of the game, participants unleash one or more humans in a bounded, labyrinthine space — an actual maze, a factory district or someplace else with complex terrain. The humans get piles of weaponry capable of actually hurting the vampires. Then the vampires go in unarmed and hunt the humans. Each vampire who drains a human wins. It's "legit" to cripple or maim competing vampires, but not to torpor or destroy them. A more extreme form of this game requires vampiric participants to draw straws, with the one who gets the short straw becoming the designated victim. The vampiric variety seldom proceeds to Final Death except as a punishment (in which the draw of straws is usually rigged).

- **Rousing the Beast.** Each participant must dig up a victim of a failed shovel party. The participant must then immobilize and destroy his victim. Keep in mind that the victim emerges weak but in frenzy. The process of consecrating disinterment as a *ritus* somehow strengthens the victim, who regains one Trait per turn until at full strength and suffers half normal wound penalties.
- **The Spire.** The priest designates some target to climb that human beings cannot achieve without elaborate tools, such as the tallest skyscraper in the area. The participants must scale it using only their own bare hands and feet, their Attributes, Abilities and Disciplines. The first one to the top and back down wins. Climbing barehanded up modern buildings (stone, glass and metal, etc.) requires a Simple Physical Test every 10 feet or so. The difficulty varies, from six Traits for conveniently sized bricks up to 12 or more for sheer featureless walls. Using Disciplines stylishly doesn't guarantee a win, but earns the respect of competitors.

Grand Ball (Palla Grande)

The Grand Ball — Palla Grande to Sabbat elders and others who like to retain a European flavor to their *ritae* — marks the end of the Sabbat's year. On All Hallows Eve, all the vampires in the city gather for a two-part celebration. Some archbishops summon all the vampires in their territory to celebrate in a single city; others encourage separate celebrations in each city. In either case, attendance is not optional. Nomad packs converge on the nearest city holding a Grand Ball. The most renowned priest in the city (who may not be the highest-ranked) oversees the *ritus*.

The night before the Grand Ball, the presiding priest and her assistants prepare incense burners. The burners hold an exotic mix of herbs and chemicals designed to weaken mortals' willpower and skepticism and induce a mild hallucinogenic state in which acquiescence and belief come easily. As she blesses each burner, the priest adds a Blood Trait of her own to start the mix's transformation.

The first part of the Grand Ball takes place in public, often staged as a festival, a rave or some other gathering open to the general populace. The Ball's vampiric hosts generally put on a fancy spread in whatever idiom they choose, with the best music, plenty of free food and drink and so on. Almost all Grand Balls emphasize costumes, going beyond fancy wardrobe to include physical transformation through *Vicissitude* and the illusions of *Obfuscate* and *Chimerstry*. Each vampiric participant in the *ritus* adds a Blood Trait of his own to one (or more) of the incense burners. The air takes on a very slight pink tinge and all mortals in the area experience a mild form of the surrender that comes with the Embrace.

The second part of the Grand Ball takes place away from mortal eyes. The priest convenes a Blood Feast for the vampires of the area. Daring groups snatch their vessels from the nearby crowd or from the unlucky recipients of invitations to a "special private gathering" associated with the ball's public face. Sabbat communities who face more serious challenges from hunters or whose leaders believe in not creating unnecessary risks round up their victims for weeks beforehand. Sabbat vampires, retainers and ghouls who've committed flagrant offenses also become vessels for the occasion.

At midnight, individuals chosen by the presiding priest present a reenactment of an event from Cainite legend or history. In some cities, would-be actors compete for the priest's favor; in others, theatre duty is as much a punishment as a reward. Caine's murder of Abel outstrips all other topics in popularity, with the diablerie of the Tzimisce and Lasombra Antediluvians close behind. Gehenna scenes attract both favor and controversy, with some elders (and devout neonates) arguing that too much attention to future troubles undermines morale. Most theatre groups include some element of audience participation, seizing prepared targets for use as disposable props.

After the show, the archbishop or ranking bishop present receives the Blood Bath. The recipient reclines in a tub, pool or other large container. Attendants bleed out selected victims to fill the pool. Each vampire present contributes vitae to a Vaulderie cup, whose contents then join the mortal blood. The recipient maintains a steady chanting all the while, and takes in a bit of the essence of the other participants.

At the conclusion of the Blood Bath, the participants join the bath's recipient in a final pre-dawn dance, generally very noisy and almost always ending in a frenzied attack on the unfortunate mortals saved for the consummation of the *ritus*. In most cases, the participants collapse in the ball's private space and rely on ghouls to take care of guarding them and cleaning up during the following day. Over the next several days, vampires and ghouls charged with attending to the aftermath use a combination of lethal force, mental Disciplines and occasional Embraces to tidy up loose ends.

System: Grand Ball participants gain the benefits of the Blood Feast and Blood Bath as usual. In addition, they completely replenish their Willpower. Each participant must contribute at least one Blood Trait to the cloaking incense burners, and may contribute more. The recipient of the Blood Bath can make a Mental Challenge against any of the other participants; if she succeeds, the recipient can use any oracular powers the target possesses, like *Auspex* and some Thaumaturgical Paths, as if they were her own for the night. She does not gain fine control, seeing random moments of the coming year that warrant her attention. The Storyteller should feel free to make the resulting images symbolic and allusive, and to allow circumstances to render them null and void.

Monomacy

The Sabbat's internal disagreements don't always erupt into war, contrary to the popular opinion among outsiders. Most conflicts find fairly quick and fairly peaceful resolution, through a combination of actual persuasion, use of Status and the occasional push with Disciplines. When two individuals can't settle a quarrel, often their authorities, starting with the pack leader and priest, can. Sometimes all efforts at mediation fail. Monomacy provides the ultimate resolution: Combat to the death.

Monomacy isn't just a duel to the death. Through careful authorization of Monomacy, the Sabbat applies a limited form of evolutionary selection to its ranks. The duels purge individuals who were too physically weak or too crippled by bad ideas to make effective use of their abilities. The sect grows stronger as the weak and inefficient fall — better to lose them in an internal dispute than to suffer them in crises to come. Strong leaders and strong followers keep the sect strong as well.

Monomacy is a genuine *ritus*, not a right anyone can claim on their own. The Sabbat denies the opportunity to young, unproven recruits who don't appreciate the gravity of what they're doing. If everyone could get their leaders' blessings for the sacred duel, in short order most packs would lose all their members over trivial matters. The pack priest must formalize any effort at Monomacy. The challenger presents her claim to the priest and the target simultaneously. The priest decides whether the point of conflict warrants Monomacy, and if so, whether the priest will preside himself or appoint a substitute. If the priest is himself the challenged party, the ductus presides or refers it to another pack's priest.

The defender doesn't have to accept just because the priest approves. Declining involves some loss of status, since bystanders assume cowardice or some shameful secret must contribute to the refusal to take part in an important *ritus*. The defender encounters fewer hassles if the challenger is of much lower rank. Leaders can brush off even genuinely serious claims as just another case of a youngster being uppity.

When the challenger and defender belong to the same pack, it's easy to pick the right authority to arbitrate: Their pack priest does the job. Matters get more complex when the disputing parties belong to different packs. In theory, a bishop should hear such cases. In practice, most bishops feel they have better things to do with their time and respond unfavorably to all but the most urgent or illuminating claims. Rivals often do better to seek out the priest of a third pack, preferably but not always one they both know, and ask him to perform the *ritus*.

The definition of the *ritus* leaves the setting and method of combat open. As long as it satisfies the participants and the overseeing priest, it's fine. The challenger sets the time and place; the defender rules on weapons and other details. The defender can ask for the duel to be to first blood rather than Final Death. In such a case the loser faces exile. A defender who takes such a wimpy course of action loses respect whether he loses the duel or not. More impressive restrictions include fighting while blindfolded, fighting surrounded by fire, fighting only with out-of-clan Disciplines and the like. The priest declares the duel begun and finished. Priests and archbishops can declare a Monomacy null and void, but doing so for any reason short of proof of direct cheating by a participant invites new Monomacy-worthy challenges against the priest.

Sometimes Monomacy takes on strange forms. Lasombra elders may choose to duel with life-sized chessboard populated by living pieces, moved by threat or command. A famous conflict between a Tzimisce and a Ventrue *antitribu* ended in a Monomacy in which each took turns shooting one of the other's ghouls. The Tzimisce won when the last of the Ventrue's ghouls succumbed to his wounds and fell over.

The winner of the Monomacy gets his pick of the loser's possessions. This doesn't include diablerie unless the priest approves it as a term of the contest. Custom suggests but doesn't require offering a cut to the presiding priest.

Anything left over goes to the loser's packmates and any scavengers who can stake a claim.

Monomacy settles all sorts of serious disputes within the sect. Would-be ducti, pack priests and bishops bring out their grievances (and generally lose). Individuals contesting points of influence take it to a duel if their priest deems the issue important to Sabbat activity in the area. Rumor says that the current regent took her position after besting her predecessor in a simple no-weapons physical battle.

System: This *ritus* calls for very little mechanical adjudication. The form of the fight itself suggests what sorts of challenges the participants should make. The priest's player should emphasize the seriousness of the occasion with proper pomp and circumstance. This isn't just a rumble, it's a rumble with profound religious significance. Whatever theme and style a pack presents — urban gang, enthusiastic cult, disciplined military team or something else — should color the proceedings. The priest should feel at liberty to add plausible restrictions, perhaps postponing the battle to the next new or full moon or requiring the setting to incorporate sacred numbers.

Sermons of Caine

Caine the historical (or at least mythical) figure matters very much to some Sabbat members, not at all to others. Among the vampires who care enough to argue theology, some treat Caine as the biggest, oldest and therefore worst menace of all, while others find in him the example of true freedom and individuality. Vampires who do care about origins and do take Caine as their inspiration gather regularly to listen to teachings about him. This *ritus* renews their conviction and provides them with the shared attitudes and ideas to resolve disputes.

In some packs, the priest always delivers the sermon. In others, pack members share the duties. Each one in turn recites some favored passage from the *Book of Nod* and offers comments about its relevance to the pack's situation. Depending on the pack's preferences, the speaker may get an uninterrupted audience, or the rest of the pack may argue back. After the sermon, the priest may perform the Vaulderie. Enthusiastic pack members may continue the "discussion" until the approach of dawn.

Vampiric society has very few written records. The *Book of Nod* isn't a single text — it's a mass of fragments and an attitude about Cainite origins. Sabbat packs argue constantly about the best, truest or oldest phrasing of a passage, and about whether a passage belongs in canon at all. Some believers argue that the sect must establish a single authoritative reading and make sure everyone studies it. Others claim, with just as much fervor, that the spirit of the work transcends any specific text, so competing searches for illumination serve the sect's best interests. Arguments on these points sometimes destroy packs and fuel inter-pack wars.

System: This *ritus* doesn't really require any mechanics. If Storytellers want, they can ask for *Performance* tests to see how effectively a speaker communicates her point. Regular exposure to the Sermons of Caine might raise a participant's *Sabbat Lore*, up to a limit of one or two levels less than that of the pack priest. This *ritus* is primarily an occasion for roleplaying.

Vaulderie and Vinculum

The Vaulderie defines the Sabbat as a group. Vampires who partake show that they are part of the sect; vampires who refuse the cup can never really belong. The Blood Bond as Camarilla and independent vampires use it binds the subject as the slave of his regnant. It reinforces the static hierarchy of elder over childe. The Vaulderie makes the participants equal, uniting them in their shared cause. It also introduces a constantly shifting mosaic of relationships as the vampire who held another in highest esteem last night has a new target of supreme devotion tonight. The bonds don't erode; they do gain rivals of equal or greater intensity.

Simply mixing vitae isn't sufficient for the Vaulderie. The presiding priest must use a cutting tool and cup dedicated to this specific purpose. Priests generally decorate their tools with hieroglyphics and artwork that expresses their pack concerns. (Artisans who produce tools that express a pack's shared sense of self gain high status. The Sabbat never has enough creators to match its ranks of corruptors and destroyers.)

The priest takes her ritual tools, makes a cut in herself and drains out as many Blood Traits as she cares to contribute. Once the priest begins the ceremony, she passes the cup and tool to each participant in turn, who contributes as many Blood Traits as he chooses.

Contributing only one Blood Trait looks bad — do you have something to hide? Contributing five or more Blood Traits, except when duty requires, looks bad, too — are you angling for control? The ductus must contribute at least one Blood Trait per participant (down to a minimum of one Blood Trait remaining), and generally aims to put in more than anyone else as a show of dedication and primacy of place. Trying to put in someone else's blood, from a concealed pouch or other source, doesn't work. The cup erupts and splashes the blood everywhere. Everyone loses the blood they put in. The priest must start the ritual again, and the offender probably faces swift destruction.

The priest takes the filled cup and performs a simple ritual over it that merges the blood together. Real magic happens at this point. Even if the priest was chosen on the spur of the moment by packmates interested in renewing their Vinculum, a priest performing the ritual makes it work while someone not chosen as priest could perform the same ritual but get no results. The priest offers a brief blessing on each participant as she drinks from the cup. The ritual gives back to each participant as many Blood Traits as she put in.

Every Sabbat member takes the Vaulderie seriously. Even the most feral wanderers or rowdy urban punks settle down for this ritual even if they're never serious at any other time. This is what it's all about.

The Vaulderie generates the Sabbat's alternative to the blood bond, the Vinculum. Each vampire takes away from the ritual a special bond to some other members of the pack (or whatever group performs the ritual). In game terms, each participant has a Vinculum rating of 1-10 with each of the other participants. The stronger the bond, the more firmly the participants feel bound to each other. At the high end, the Vinculum ties individuals together even more tightly than the blood bond. Note that Vinculum ratings aren't symmetrical. Andrew can have a Vinculum rating of 6 to Bettina, indicating

a very strong attachment to her, while she has only a rating of 1 to him, indicating the minimum possible result from sharing the ritual.

System: The system given here supercedes that in **Laws of the Night**, p. 224.

The player of a vampire taking part in the Vaulderie writes the character's name on an index card to represent one Blood Trait added to the cup. Find a container big enough to hold the cards players contribute — a typical chalice will overflow. Don't carry the roleplaying of bloodletting to an extreme, and whatever you do, don't really drain any blood for this purpose (or any purpose in the game).

The player of the priest mixes the cards together, generally with some ritual. The level of ceremony depends on the group's preferences. The priest's invocation may be a simple "Grant us the strength to defeat all our enemies through unity of purpose" or a full-blown recitation from the *Book of Nod* about Caine's refusal to bow to God's threats. Likewise, the blessing can range from "Take courage to perform all your duties well" to complete Latin renderings of

Vinculum Ratings

Vinculum	Effects
10	You'll commit one-Trait sins for this individual; you'd give yourself and destroy others without hesitation.
9	You'll commit two-Trait sins for this individual, and will put yourself at substantial risk of permanent harm.
8	You'll commit three-Trait sins for this individual, and gladly spend your resources, influences and other assets on her behalf.
7	You'll commit four-Trait sins for this individual
6	You'll commit five-Trait sins for this individual. You respect her deeply.
5	You aid this individual as long as it doesn't put you at serious risk.
4	You aid this individual as long as it doesn't seriously inconvenience your own plans.
3	You aid this individual on matters of mutual interest.
2	You feel some general interest in this individual's well-being and don't deliberately get in her way.
1	You don't feel anything toward this individual, though the basic Vinculum makes it hard to plot her destruction. These feelings are artificial, created by the ritual. The vampire retains her own rational mind, but she gets compulsions that she must obey.

liturgical prayers adapted to the Sabbat's worldview. Each participant draws out one card for each one he put in. If you want to work with religious themes, choose your place carefully. Don't freak the bystanders and people not taking part. Save the funky stuff for private spaces.

The first time a vampire takes part in the Vaulderie, she gets a Vinculum rating of 1 toward every other participant, plus one for each Blood Trait she drank that belonged to a particular individual. In later performances of the Vaulderie, she makes a Static Challenge of her current Vinculum rating toward a particular individual against a total of one plus the number of Blood Traits she drank that belonged to that individual this time. If she loses the challenge, her Vinculum rating toward that individual rises by one. If she ties, her Vinculum rating remains the same. If she wins, she can (at her discretion) make two Simple Tests. If she wins both, her Vinculum rating toward that individual falls by one; otherwise it remains the same. Her Vinculum rating toward a fellow participant in this Vaulderie can never fall below 1. The player cannot spend Willpower or Traits for retests in these challenges.

Optionally, you may simplify proceedings. You can have each player test for her character's Vinculum rating toward everyone involved in the *ritus* by a single Static Challenge against the highest total of Blood Traits she drew. Keep in mind that this cuts out many layers of inter-personal intrigue that give Sabbat games an important part of their flavor. Discuss it with players before adopting it.

Vinculum ratings don't fade over time. Only a feat of will in the celebration of the Vaulderie lets a vampire break some of her ties to others. Packs that regularly celebrate the Vaulderie develop very close ties, and the Sabbat's elders retain a network of deep connections to each other. Rumor attributes a Vinculum-breaking ritual to Nosferatu *antitribu*, the Sabbat Inquisition or both. Allegedly, the Inquisition uses it to break ties between loyal Sabbat members and infernalists, but it is considered rumor at this point.

A character attempting to destroy another vampire to whom he has any Vinculum rating at all must spend two Willpower Traits. Acting less terminally against the interests of a vampire to whom he has a Vinculum rating of three or more requires spending one Willpower Trait, and acting against a Vinculum rating of six or more requires two Willpower Traits. The only exception is Monomacy performed under the supervision of an approved Sabbat official.

When a character with Vinculum ties to several individuals faces a choice between them, she draws on the Vinculum to settle her conflicting impulses. She makes an Extended Challenge of her Willpower against each of the Vinculum ratings involved (adding two to her Willpower when testing for the individual she favors most). Whichever individual wins the most successes in the challenge gets her loyalty in that situation. She may also simply go with whomever she has the higher Vinculum rating for, especially if the difference is two or greater.

The Vaulderie gradually breaks down blood bonds. A vampire seeking release from bondage must put in at least six Blood Traits and reduce himself down to one Blood Trait remaining. Taking in six points of Vaulderie-

consecrated blood negates the effects of one draught of an individual vampire's blood. Doing this three times, therefore, completely breaks a blood bond (and generates very strong Vinculum ratings).

War Party

The War Party puts Sabbat doctrine to practical use. Multiple packs compete for the blood of a designated non-Sabbat elder, with the winners getting the benefits of diablerie. Hunting elders isn't easy — they generally didn't survive all those centuries by being careless or stupid, after all. In addition, while rival packs seldom use outright lethal force against each other, they can and do sabotage each other's efforts with means that stop short of destruction.

A Sabbat member of bishop or higher rank declares a War Party after identifying an elder whose removal would benefit the sect. (Almost every non-Sabbat elder poses a threat to the sect in some sense.) Preparations usually include a Fire Dance, a Sermon of Caine and a Blood Feast or Vaulderie. The chief of the War Party — usually the highest ranking priest involved, though sometimes ducti or bishops lead more politically oriented hunts — addresses the assembled packs. He asks each ductus one of the few ritual questions that actually has a standard phrasing throughout the sect: "Do you come freely to war, and do you take up this noble cause, never resting until the blood of our enemy is spilled?" Each ductus answers with "We do!" After this expression of commitment, the War Party leader identifies the target and presents information that might help the hunt.

A ductus can decide to withdraw her pack from the challenge. She faces ridicule for this, and any packmates who call for Monomacy generally win approval on the spot. The packs who remain celebrate the rest of the night and embark on the hunt itself after rising from sleep on the following night.

The War Party makes every tactic legitimate if not automatically wise. Hunting packs can inflict whatever collateral damage they deem necessary on their way to the target, and when the destructive action shows courage and forethought, packs not participating in the War Party often help clean up the damage. In the final approach to the target's haven, competing packs often dispense with niceties like doors if they have members with the strength to break through barriers. Note that sometimes, brute force is very unwise. A well-protected target calls for approaches emphasizing stealth and treachery. Some War Parties last for weeks or even months rather than a few violent nights.

Only one member of the winning pack gets the full benefit of the diablerie, of course. Sabbat tradition generally recognizes success, and awards the kill to the first vampire to get her fangs into the victim. Pack members need not sit idly by, however. Tradition also endorses vigorous competition, and it's not uncommon for a hunt to end with only one pack member still mobile enough to actually commit the deed.

The target elder seldom acquiesces calmly to her fate. Entire city blocks sometimes collapse in rubble in the ensuing struggle. Depending on their personal styles, targeted elders may unleash Master-level Disciplines or potent bribes in various coins. Every so often, a winning pack gets a good enough offer to betray the Sabbat and defend the elder, though they usually don't survive long after that.

The War Party *ritus* comes to an end when the winning pack presents tangible evidence of their kill to the War Party leader. The leader accepts the token after examining it for signs of fakery and blesses the victors. All surviving packs gather for another round of revels as soon as news of the War Party's resolution spreads.

System: The individual vampire who actually diablerizes the target gets all the usual benefits of diablerie. The members of the winning pack get the temporary Status of *Martial*, which lasts until the next War Party, Grand Ball or Festival of the Dead. Particularly prominent targets like Methuselahs win permanent Status for the victors.

Wild Hunt

The Wild Hunt gives force to the Sabbat's emphasis on devotion. A member who betrays the sect's secrets risks this ultimate sanction.

A priest calls the Wild Hunt. Generally the highest-ranking priest in the vicinity does so, and she'd better have the support of her superiors before accusing another Sabbat member of treachery or face the same punishment herself. All loyal sect members in the area must hunt down the traitor and anyone, Cainite or mortal, to whom he may have given the information. Overzealous vampires who destroy a Wild Hunt target before interrogation risk Final Death themselves. The traitor's contacts are exterminated only after examination makes sure that they haven't spread the leaked information further.

The Wild Hunt seldom takes place in the risky and yet exuberant atmosphere of a War Party. Treachery exposes the whole sect to risk. Whatever preparatory rites take place, their priests perform them solemnly. Vaulderie is essential, and Fire Dancing usually accompanies it.

The vampire who captures the traitor and his contacts bring their prisoner back to some central meeting place for questioning. The ductus and priest, and any superiors who wish to take part, recite the traitor's crimes and use torture to extract confirmation. Hot irons, mutilation, *Vicissitude* and a multitude of other means come into play. Once the traitor confirms his sins and the Sabbat establishes the spread of his leaked secrets, torture becomes straightforward punishment, lasting as long as anyone involved has ideas about how to hurt the traitor. Vampiric collaborators also face torture while mortal allies generally meet quick, if painful, ends.

After tormenting the traitor, his former packmates throw his staked body onto a consecrated funeral pyre. An attending priest recites the *Book of Nod's* Chronicle of Caine to remind all involved that victory requires unity and that distrust makes unity impossible. Vaulderie follows to reestablish the bonds of mutual commitment.

System: Some regions practice the *ignoblis ritus* of Contrition, to allow traitors to make amends. Storytellers may allow the targets of a Wild Hunt to invoke this or not, at Storyteller discretion. For minor offenses, allowing contrition with punishment balances severity with the avoidance of hasty character death. More serious offenses should bring a more serious penalty:

The Sabbat is not a place where "do as you please" flourishes without qualification, and sometimes nothing short of character death makes the point clear. Never arrange a character's death lightly, but don't hold back when it's truly earned.

Low Rites (Ignoblis Ritae)

The "low rites" vary from pack to pack. Not all packs observe them; many packs that do acknowledge them put local variations and emphases on them. Storytellers can establish *ignoblis ritae* for their chronicles, and players should feel free to work up new low rites subject to review by their characters' superiors.

The Sabbat works from the bottom up as well as from the top down. In the war against the shadows of the past, innovation is one of the sect's key weapons. Characters should know that their innovations may well meet with favorable response. Sect leaders encourage new ways of putting existing principles into action, particularly in response to new situations.

Acceptance

Acceptance *ritae* mark an individual's induction to a pack, whether at the end of *auctoritas* Creation Rites, adoption of an existing Sabbat member separated from his old pack or as a reaffirmation of the pack's membership after a change of leadership. Each member of the pack acknowledges the newcomer with some personal token. Some packs offer vitae while others offer gifts, advice, favors or something else useful. There's no innate magical benefit in the Acceptance *ritus*, just the social bond. Many packs include a short oath in which the newcomer acknowledges his debt to the pack and the sect; in turn, his new packmates take an oath to treat him as an equal, with the same rewards for his successes and punishments for his failures that they all face.

Allegiance

The Allegiance *ritus* bridges the gap between formal creation of a new Sabbat member and her acceptance into a specific pack. The new vampire must prove herself familiar with the sect's ideals and capable of acting effectively. While in this transitional period, the vampire occupies a distinctly secondary position. She stands at the rear during *auctoritas ritae*, drinks last at the Vaulderie (and generally can't contribute her own blood) and cannot engage in discussion of the *Book of Nod*. Most packs administer a secret mark of some sort as part of the *ritus*, identifying the recipient as someone who's begun to win acceptance and not yet completed the process.

The trial period may last only a few weeks if the vampire proves remarkably capable or may stretch on for years. A vampire who never succeeds in impressing a pack enough to warrant Acceptance faces the threat of Final Death administered by her disappointed creators. Camarilla defectors spend more time under scrutiny and must complete tougher challenges of their new loyalty, often including attacks on their former comrades.

The Asp's Blessing

Sabbat teachings sometimes compare the sect to a snake. This *ritus* gives that metaphor tangible form. The priest raises a snake (almost always of some

poisonous species) before the pack and asks Caine's spirit to guide the snake's eyes and fangs. Each pack member must step forward to kiss the snake. If it bites back, the priest denounces the participant for concealed sins. At the end of the Asp's Blessing *ritus*, examination and Contrition *ritae* follow for all who failed the test of purity.

Contrition

The Contrition *ritus* is most likely to win promotion to *auctoritas* status soon; very nearly every pack practices it in some form. Sabbat members who've committed offenses against the sect confess their failings and accept any punishment short of Final Death. Minor failures earn no more than a beating and assignment to unpleasant duties. Breaches of sect security might win dismemberment and the restoration of just enough vitae to let the contrite vampire begin healing.

Packs vary in their willingness to accept repeated performance of the Contrition *ritus*, whether for the same offense again and again or for a diversified but sustained pattern of clueless conduct. Packs whose leaders show too much leniency face condemnation themselves. The sect is, after, all, at war.

Welcoming

The Welcoming *ritus* is, like Acceptance, a social occasion. Whenever two packs meet for a shared task, or a nomad pack enters a city, they have to establish some neutral space within which to become acquainted. The members of the packs name themselves and their homes. Vampires who recognize others with whom they have grievances promptly say so, and the packs' ducti and priests attempt to mediate the dispute. A short, non-lethal duel often follows just to let the disputing parties deal with it. The packs' leaders establish basic protocols governing access to havens and favored feeding grounds. All the packmates then reaffirm their loyalty to the Sabbat's twin emphasis on individual liberty and united action. In many areas, the pack leaders exchange blood; in areas with a very strong religious emphasis, everyone in the packs may immediately share the Vaulderie.

After the Welcoming *ritus*, pack leaders feel more comfortable making plans for whatever their common purpose may be.

Thanksgiving

The Thanksgiving *ritus* practices the giving of thanks in an old-fashioned, literal sense. Members of a pack gather and each tells a story about his exploits. He begins, "I thank Caine for his favor when I…." Then he recounts a recent accomplishment, aiming to show his particularly remarkable strength, cunning or other desirable characteristic. Exaggeration is routine in almost all packs that practice this *ritus*. Thanksgiving often precedes an esbat or other more formal occasion.

Martial

Martial *ritae* take many forms, all with the goal of mustering pack members' enthusiasm for and ability to take the endless war to their enemies. A Martial *ritus* generally involves some rhythmic activity to ease participants into a trance state. Music, dance and martial arts all enjoy widespread

popularity. Traditional (or neo-primitive) groups include body adornment, ritual scarification and the like.

Spilling of Blood

The *ritus* of the Spilling of Blood is one of several that never quite became *auctoritas* but is well-known throughout the sect. Vampires feeding together make a point of trading sips from their respective vessels with a ritual acknowledgement along the lines of "Hot blood that spurted from Abel at his time of death, sustain us for the will of the Sabbat."

Stealth

Packs about to embark on an assignment that requires silence practice the Stealth *ritus*, as do packs that simply wish to test their discipline. Participants bite out each other's tongues and spit the severed organs into a fire. This inflicts no lasting damage; the participants each spend a Blood Point to stabilize the wound. In some cases the ductus or priest refrains from participating so that he can give orders, while in others all pack members join in and communicate through hand signals and mental Disciplines.

Sun Dance

This *ritus* tests the participants' endurance and courage. The Sun Dance *ritus* always takes place during a full moon. Participants wear frightening costumes or body paint, hoping to intimidate others. The participants dance from the moment they waken after sunset until sunrise, gyrating around a symbolic inscription of a fiery sun. They then attempt to stay wake and in the open as long as possible during the new day. A Blood Feast generally follows the next night.

Some packs make provision to rescue participants who become too injured to seek shelter, while others don't. Sect leaders frown on this sort of pointless loss of brave members and encourage Sun Dance observers to keep bystanders at hand.

Tests of Pain

All of the various Test of Pain *ritae* challenge the participants' ability to remain functional in the face of severe pain. Some packs use Tests of Pain as part of their competition to choose new leaders; many packs include Tests of Pain along with Contrition *ritae* as punishment. The Trial by Stake is simple and widely practiced. The participant to be tested gets staked to a wall by a stake through his chest, mounted high enough that his feet don't touch the ground. Depending on the pack, he may remain there until packmates let him down just before sunrise, or he may have to tear himself loose and go on to perform other tests. The Trial by Fire subjects various parts of a participant's body to flame wielded by the pack priest. The Trial by Gauntlet requires the participant to make his way through parallel rows of packmates who beat him, sometimes with weapons, sometimes barehanded.

The range of Tests of Pain is nearly infinite. Pack priests generally develop a favored personal repertoire. Use Courage and Self-Control (or Instinct) for specific tests when the vampire's resolve is in doubt.

Truth Revealed

The Truth Revealed *ritus* hangs on the edge of *auctoritas* standing; its efficacy depends on the ability of the priest administering the *ritus*. A vampire under suspicion of dishonesty writes out a statement with her own blood. The priest takes the paper and burns it, usually in a ceremonial censer. If the smoke turns black, the statement was false while white smoke indicates truthfulness. Even when the priest does nothing special, the *ritus* produces accurate results more often than chance would allow. Sabbat scholars theorize that the ceremony taps into the latent mystic powers of the pack united in the search for truth. Priests who possess three or more levels of *Occult* or *Rituals* may make a Mental Challenge against the subject of the inquiry. If the priest succeeds, the *ritus* always generates the right color of smoke.

STATUS

The Sabbat takes Status very seriously indeed. The sect fights wars on all fronts, and in time of war, everyone fighting on the same side needs to know who gives orders and who carries them out. The war isn't just political — it's religious, involving fundamental questions of right and wrong, who may be saved or damned, when the world can or must end and so on. Individuals rise through the Sabbat's ranks on merit, proving themselves physically and mentally capable of wielding power. Status Traits honor their past achievements and show what others should expect.

Sabbat members gain Status more readily than most Camarilla members. They also lose Status more readily. As noted in **Laws of the Night**, Revised Edition, p. 222, the members of a pack acting in unison can strip a packmate of any Status Trait except those associated with matters of fact. See below for a summary of common Sabbat Status Traits and the ways Sabbat members qualify for them.

As the descriptions of particular offices emphasize, the Sabbat's masters lead rather than rule. They cannot hand down decrees with impunity; they must set the example of courageous action and penetrating insight. The religious and political goals of the secret favor pragmatic response. A good leader is the one who gets things done. If things don't get done, or get done badly, the leader is leading badly and runs the risk of being deposed. Even the eldest master of war and crusade gets little automatic respect. Long lists of past honors don't matter much in the face of tonight's needs.

The higher the rank a Sabbat member holds, the more of a proven record she must have. Nobody becomes bishop the night after she earns *Initiated* Status. Nobody loses a bishopric overnight in response to a single minor problem or allegation from a neonate, either. Deposing a high-ranking officer requires verifiable charges. Real failings are easier to prove than fraudulent ones, though sometimes trickery does work. The challenges facing the Sabbat from all sides generally ensure that every leader does in fact make some mistakes, and rivals need only keep a careful tally of the leader's errors. Rivals also generally strike deals with the leader's enemies or superiors (or both) so that when the current leader falls, the right candidate emerges as a plausible replacement.

The Camarilla generally sees the Sabbat as a mass of fanatics and berserkers only because the true depths of Sabbat sect politics happen where outsiders don't see them. Court and conclave schemes offer no more tangled morass of intrigue than the maneuverings around a new bishop's ascension.

What Status Means

Keep in mind that Status Traits quantify something that's hazy and subjective to characters in the World of Darkness. Status is fluid, personalized and subject to change without notice. If you'd prefer to run your chronicle without using the mechanics, go right ahead. The reality of Status — superior and inferior rank, plus acknowledgement of smart or foolish deeds — exists, and you can roleplay it out in lots of ways. The rules should serve the chronicle. Most particularly, in a sect as open to variation as the Sabbat, you have the freedom to present the world in terms that work for your players and characters.

Status for Sabbat

A Sabbat member can have eight Status Traits, plus one per level of Path rating. Note that Sabbat Status comes and goes far more rapidly than in the Camarilla, see **Laws of the Night**, p. 222.

Some Sabbat Status Traits reflect accomplishments that don't require the vampire to hold an office. Important Traits of this sort include:

• *Battle-Scarred*. The vampire was Wounded or Incapacitated while fighting enemies of the Sabbat.

• *Blessed*, *Devoted* and *Enlightened* all mark progress on a Path. A vampire with two levels in his Morality earns one of these Traits — which one depends on the views of his priest and pack about his particular standing. A vampire with three Morality Traits is eligible for a second of these Traits, and a vampire with four Morality Traits can carry all three.

• *Blooded*. The vampire killed another vampire in fair combat, and observers agree that it was a meaningful challenge (as opposed to a 6th-generation Methuselah devouring the 13th-generation childe created last night, for instance).

• *Enriched*. The vampire committed diablerie in accordance with sect practice (often because her Path recommends it).

• *Initiated*. The vampire went through Creation Rites and Vaulderie to the satisfaction of her new packmates and any higher-ranking vampires overseeing the process.

• *Undefeated*. The vampire has never lost a fair fight or Monomacy. Facing overwhelming odds that force flight doesn't invalidate this Status.

Storytellers should feel free to define more Status Traits that apply to a pack, all the packs in a bishop's territory or even to the sect as a whole. Just as the *ignoblis ritae* supplement the *auctoritas ritae*, "unofficial" Status Traits express the concerns of the leaders in a particular region. Make the style of the Sabbat in your region matter in Status along with rites and the general tone of your chronicle.

The packmates of a successful leader who steps down in honorable circumstances often grant him the Status he held as an officer. It's a display of satisfaction with how he did his work. Superiors generally let these gifts of Status stand; removing them shows disapproval almost as directly as a slap in the face.

The Sabbat also defines a number of standard negative Status Traits. (As with positive Status Traits, feel free to add more that suit your chronicle.) A Sabbat member may possess two of these at any given moment. Recently awarded negative Traits displace older ones as far as game mechanics go, though Sabbat members retain their memories of what went wrong and can act on those memories even without game mechanics prodding them along. A vampire can earn the removal of the Trait by twice successfully completing whatever task it was he failed at to earn the negative Trait in the first place: A failed priest removes *Untrustworthy* by performing rites correctly twice; a *Dangerous* vampire goes on two hunts without making trouble for packmates and so on.

• *Dangerous*. This Trait goes to vampires who endanger packmates for stupid reasons, particularly while on a hunt or other *ritus*-related mission. Most packs only give it to those who do things like shooting packmates or standing around to argue with flamethrower-wielding soldiers; strict packs give it simply for creating a risky situation.

• *Ignorant*. The vampire cannot remember some essential tenet of the Sabbat as explained to her time and time again. Most often this Trait goes to a vampire who says something like "Well, maybe some of the Antediluvians are okay."

• *Slow*. This Trait goes to any vampire who gets overtaken by humans, whether in a pursuit on foot, by vehicles or some more exotic means of travel.

• *Untrustworthy*. The vampire failed in the performance of some key duty of his position. This may go to a priest who "botches" a *ritus* but may also go to some other leader for an explicit violation of his duties.

• *Vain* (also known as *Cocky, Full Of Himself* or comparable terms). The vampire claims mastery of some field she goes on to fail publicly at, preferably in an impressive or even physically dangerous way. This Trait commemorates acts of unsuccessful hubris.

The Privileges of Office

Higher-ranked officers can exercise the privileges of those beneath them, except as noted in each office's description. Thus archbishops can do everything bishops can; cardinals can do everything archbishops can, and regents can do everything cardinals can. The Sabbat ranks ducti, priests and abbots equally. Templars and prisci occupy special positions somewhat outside the chain of command and have only the powers listed in their respective descriptions.

Ductus

Every Sabbat pack has a ductus, its leader. The importance of the title varies from pack to pack. Sometimes the ductus holds real authority, whether by fear, charisma or some other means of getting her packmates to do her will. In other packs it's just there because superior officers want someone to blame when the pack screws up. A ductus who consistently gets her pack into trouble eventually gets destroyed, from above or below.

The ductus calls her packmates to esbat, or pack meeting, in which the pack discusses its affairs. Members who've earned rewards get them now, and members who've earned punishments face judgment. The ductus divides up responsibilities like haven defense and corpse removal as seems wise to her — some ducti reserve jobs for themselves while others spread the load around as much as possible.

The ductus may not be the eldest member of the pack. If she isn't, she needs some other edge, like most ferocious, most skilled in an impressive Discipline or best stocked with blackmail information. Most packs go through a phase of choosing the most personable or charming member as ductus. A few disastrous and wholly avoidable defeats cure the urge.

When rank becomes absolutely critical, the ductus is considered "more equal than" all others in the pack — she has distinguished herself somehow and earned responsibility for (and some authority over) the pack, which most ducti can bring to bear should a matter of pack policy come into question. The wise ductus, of course, listens to her pack, resorting to rank only when others refuse to see the strength of her arguments.

• The ductus automatically gains the Status Trait of *Feared* when taking office, and this can never be permanently removed while she remains ductus.

• The ductus appoints and removes the pack's priest.

• The ductus can grant or remove permanent Status Traits from pack members at a cost of one temporary Status Trait each. Each grant of Status after the third permanent Trait costs the ductus one permanent Status Trait of her own. It costs nothing at all for the ductus to grant the Status of *Initiated* to new recruits.

Pack Priest

The priest takes care of his packmates' souls just as the ductus takes care of their bodies. The priest sets the tone for the pack's values and priorities. What do pack members value most highly? What angers them most? How do they deal with losses and setbacks? The priest's teachings provide the answers.

The priest must know all the standard *ritae* since the ductus and bishop conduct inspections for pack orthodoxy. The priest also has freedom to invent new *ritae* for the pack's own use. The popular ones spread, earning favor for the priest and the enlightened leaders who let him experiment while unpopular ones bring disfavor on the idiot and the fools who let him out of his cage.

Every pack has at least one priest. Large packs and packs led by ducti who really care about the religious side of the Sabbat may have two. If the ductus becomes unable to lead, the priest acts as *pro tem* pack leader until the pack chooses a replacement or the bishop appoints a new ductus. Even while the ductus leads on other matters, the priest carries a tremendous responsibility. He must teach his packmates to resist frenzy and steer them away from infernalist temptations. Most priests, though not all, forsake Humanity in favor of one of the Paths of Enlightenment. Some priests encourage their packmates to adopt the same Path while others encourage any system of morality that doesn't undermine the pack's goals.

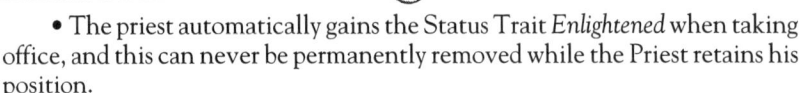

• The priest automatically gains the Status Trait *Enlightened* when taking office, and this can never be permanently removed while the Priest retains his position.

• The priest can give or remove the following permanent Status Traits, each at a cost of one temporary Status Trait of his own: *Blessed*, *Devoted* and *Enlightened*. The priest uses these Traits to mark the rise (and fall) of his packmates' spiritual insight.

• The priest's performance of the *ritae* modifies the results available to the pack, as discussed on page 140.

Abbot

The office of abbot goes in and out of fashion. In the Final Nights, it's favored mostly by bishops and archbishops who like large packs. In regions that appoint individuals to the office, the abbot takes charge of maintaining a pack's haven and food supply. The abbot must scout out possible locations, deal with security threats, find ways to dispose of the bodies and keep the pack rested and fit for all their various duties. Converts from the Camarilla describe the abbot's duties as a combination of the work of seneschal and scourge.

• The abbot automatically gains the Status Trait of *Loyal* when taking office, and this can never be permanently removed while she retains her position.

• The abbot can ignore one Status held by packmates whose actions jeopardize the haven. This only applies to immediate threats, like leading police pursuers back to the haven.

Templar/Paladin

Bishops and higher-ranking officers can appoint bodyguards and personal agents for tasks that require force and finesse. The Sabbat as a whole maintains few standards for the position, not even having a single title for it. Templar and paladin refer to the same category of special service. Templars have a variety of duties, all related to combat or protection in some fashion. Most look over the personal safety of the officer who appointed them. Some monitor pack leaders' performance and intervene to solve problems, then punish the leader who screwed up. The Inquisitors employ templars with them as enforcers during their travels and trials.

Templars cannot join the Black Hand. Membership is seen as a conflict of interests as the paladins are encouraged to eschew factional agendas. In theory, a templar pays attention only to his specific duties at the present time. In practice, every templar has other issues in mind as well, and the sect simply tries to reduce the unnecessary complications.

Templars are used extensively by sect leaders, though some may belong to packs during periods of inactivity or have been honorably discharged from their duties in times when their leaders have no need for bodyguards. Ex-templars enjoy widespread respect. Packs in their vicinity compete to recruit vampires with a history of such prominent service and to treat them well after recruitment.

• The templar automatically gains the Status Traits of *Respected* and *Ominous* when taking office, and this can never be permanently removed while he retains his position.

- The templar can disobey an order from an officer lower-ranked than the one who appointed him, as long as it's disobedience in the line of duty. If the templar's superior refuses to support the templar, then normal Sabbat justice takes its course.

Bishop (always of a specific city)

The bishop presides over the Sabbat population of a small to mid-sized metropolitan region, or an expanse of smaller settlements that doesn't strike Sabbat leadership as big or important enough to warrant an archbishop. Large cities without archbishops run under a council of all the bishops in the area.

Many bishops once served as priests. It's not a requirement, however — skillful ducti also go on to hold bishoprics. Rising to the rank of bishop marks a vampire's entrance into the serious realm of sect politics. New bishops are almost always less than two centuries old and generally know only some of the matters they must now make decisions about. Priests with profound insights into the *ritae*, for instance, may know nothing about administration and security issues while expert warriors may lack any experience in detecting the early signs of heresy and infernalism. The council of bishops lets each of the new leaders consult with peers and learn through observation.

Clueless bishops don't last long. The cardinal of the region oversees the bishops' council, and most cardinals tolerate few serious mistakes. The often fractious nature of pack debates means that bishops must constantly intervene to forestall disaster while worrying that the wrong action taken or left undone could mean their own destruction. A bishop enjoys less maneuvering room in which to demand obedience: The bishop must negotiate as well as command.

A bishop may command as few as two packs, or as many as a dozen. The Sabbat tries to keep bishops from getting too overloaded with duties, but the ongoing crises sometimes make it necessary. One unlucky attack on a Camarilla city can leave a region devoid of leaders above the level of ducti and priests, for instance. So can a successful investigation into infernalism (where "success" may involve the conviction and punishment of political enemies who weren't actually dealing with demons). In peaceful times, bishops groom their heirs with extensive training and preparation and discussion beforehand with archbishops and cardinals about their own plans. In the Final Nights, being chosen as bishop more often comes as a complete surprise, with training after appointment.

Bishops answer directly to cardinals, whose justice may have severe consequences if an errant bishop refuses to mend his ways.

- The bishop automatically gains the Status Traits of *Feared* and *Proven* when taking office, and these can never be permanently removed while she retains her position.
- The bishop can appoint and remove ducti and priests.
- The bishop can appoint templars. To promote a pack member to templar rank, the bishop must spend a temporary Status Trait of her own.
- The bishop may choose to lead *ritae* in which she participates; she must choose an appropriate surrogate when she declines. (Declining too often

suggests cowardice and makes a good start for accumulated charges of dereliction of duty.)

• The bishop leads the packs under her jurisdiction against the Sabbat's enemies. She can delegate some responsibilities to templars, ducti and chosen war leaders, but as with *ritae*, too much refusal or reassignment undermines her authority.

• The bishop can strip a Sabbat member of the Status of Initiated in response to serious violations of the Sabbat's governing code. At that point, only the individual bonds of Vaulderie protect the outcast from immediate destruction. This costs the bishop one temporary Status Trait of her own.

• The bishop can set terms on which roving packs enter her jurisdiction. She cannot refuse passage to packs who acknowledge her authority and take part in *ritae*; she can restrict their ability to act independently while residing in the area.

Archbishop (always of a specific region)

The archbishop rules over the city, or at least that's the general idea. The cardinal for the region appoints an archbishop to the lead the Sabbat in a city the cardinal believes needs a more experienced individual in charge or where a council of bishops hasn't done well.

Archbishops always come from the ranks of bishops. Nobody gains responsibility for all the affairs of a city until he's learned how to handle all aspects of Sabbat routine. The new archbishop takes office already solidly grounded in Sabbat beliefs and practice. He's proven himself in battle and shown himself capable of attending to his followers' spiritual needs. He's probably not equally competent in all fields, but he's at least not so incompetent that he got punished severely in lower positions.

The archbishop doesn't look after the well-being of mortals. Sabbat strongholds tend to be blighted, crime-ridden hellholes where nobody notices a few more dead bodies. The people of the town live in fear, but are too scared, exhausted or depressed to flee. The Sabbat has no tradition of Masquerade: As long as Sabbat behavior doesn't bring down massive mortal retaliation, it's fine. Highly visible displays of vampiric power usually merit punishment — not because they're wicked, but because they're bad tactics. In the era of mass media, the Sabbat has to restrain its more zealous members from behavior that wouldn't have mattered when cities were more isolated. (Some Sabbat enthusiasts favor social and technological collapse for precisely this reason.) The archbishop sets the tone for his city.

Most archbishops take office sometime in their second century of unlife, and few make it to 300. Competition and the endless war take their toll. A handful of archbishops are much older, running back to the Sabbat's founding or even before, and they exercise tremendous authority in the sect regardless of their nominal rank.

Every priest can create *ignoblis ritae* on her own, and superiors can intervene only in cases of extreme doctrinal divergence. The archbishop can recommend *ignoblis ritae* that impress him to packs in his jurisdiction and even suggest them for elevation to *auctoritas* status. In addition, the archbishop takes the lead in setting the style of ritual observance for all the packs he leads. Priests

and bishops act very slowly (if they know what's good for them) when contradicting the archbishop's preferences for level of formality, aesthetic presentation and the like.

The archbishop is also the spiritual authority of her city. Many archbishops were pack priests before attaining their positions. Archbishops officiate at many of the *auctoritas ritae* of their city's Cainites, and they often develop personal, local or regional *ignoblis ritae* as well. In the end, the archbishop supervises the spiritual, and therefore civic, health of her city.

- The archbishop gains the Status Traits of *Feared*, *Proven* and *Relentless* when taking office, and these can never be permanently removed while he retains his position.
- The archbishop appoints and removes bishops and lower-ranked officers in his jurisdiction.
- The archbishop can create and remove templars; this costs him no temporary Status Traits.
- The archbishop can strip a vampire in her jurisdiction of the Status of *Initiated* and grant the Status of *Hunted*. This costs the archbishop one temporary Status Trait of his own when changing the status of a bishop and one permanent Status Trait when changing the status of another archbishop or superior. Vampires who know that a target is *Hunted* can use it as a Negative Trait while resisting efforts by the outcast to call on Vinculum bonds for aid. Casting out an archbishop or cardinal without very good reason leads to the offending archbishop's own destruction.
- The archbishop can temporarily strip priests under his command of one or more Status Traits for inappropriate performance of the *ritae* — that is, for performing them in a style the archbishop doesn't like. In cases of gross deviation, the archbishop may spend a temporary Status Trait to grant the Status of *Questionable* or *Unreliable* to the priest, and (at the archbishop's discretion) to the ductus and other participants. No Sabbat member may rise through the ranks without convincing an archbishop or superior to remove the negative mark; it takes heroic displays of merit to earn release unless the archbishop himself comes into disgrace, in which case his successor undoes most negative grants.

CARDINAL (ALWAYS OF A SPECIFIC REGION)

What archbishops do for cities, cardinals do for states and whole countries. The cardinal coordinates all the archbishops in her jurisdiction, directing them as the great war requires.

Like her subordinates, the cardinal exercises both political and spiritual authority. The balance depends on the cardinal's own inclinations. Every successful cardinal must advance the sect's goals (or, in areas of particularly intense opposition, at least not let the sect's interests suffer) and see to it that healthy religious dispute remains within the bounds of Sabbat orthodoxy. Some cardinals emphasize themselves as generals and warriors taking their people into heroic battle. Others fancy themselves master tacticians and devise cunning plans that their followers carry out. Still others see themselves as the guardians of the true Cainite faith, putting up with administrative chores as the price of leading the masses toward the ultimate freedom of the soul.

Regardless of her particular style, every cardinal enjoys the mixed fear and devotion of her subjects. The vampires she commands must know that she punishes failure and rebellion by any means she deems appropriate, up to and including Final Death, just as she rewards success and innovation.

The cardinal bears personal responsibility for the crusades in her region. The territory assigned to her includes many cities that the Sabbat does not control. She must see to it that they come under the sect's direction. Experienced in the various means of warfare, she's expected to use them all, not just the ones she's personally fond of. A successful crusade usually takes years to plan, with reconnaissance (updated constantly), contacts with potential allies inside the target zone, as well as contingency plans. The cardinal needs to oversee the planning while keeping her (theoretically) devoted followers busy enough in the meantime. Inevitably, she must delegate responsibility for many aspects of the process, and the failure of her chosen agents generally forms the basis of charges for her own removal.

Most cardinals have been vampires for at least three centuries by the time they take office, though there are prominent exceptions. Many cardinals, even in the Final Nights, took part in the Anarch Revolt as well as the Sabbat's various civil wars. The successful cardinal has to appease her peers and superiors, offering evidence that her unfolding plans make sense and offer a reasonable chance of success. Simultaneously, she must rein in her own enthusiasm for the sect's ultimate triumph and keep her followers from prematurely ravaging the cities they dominate so thoroughly as to provoke mortal response.

The cardinal's subjects usually don't see her often, except during the annual *ritae* and in moments of great crisis when she must take a personal role in leadership. Even advocates of individual supremacy need a chain of command, and bishops and archbishops handle routine matters. If the cardinal gets involved, the situation is by definition unusual and generally unfortunate for whoever attracted the cardinal's attention.

• The cardinal gains the Status Traits of *Ominous*, *Proven* and *Superior* upon taking office, and these can never be permanently removed while she retains her position.

• The cardinal can appoint and remove archbishops (at the cost of one of her own temporary Status Traits), templars and lower-ranked officers (at no cost to herself).

• The cardinal can remove a vampire's *Initiated* Status and impose the Status of *Hunted* without cost to herself. She may also punish priests with the removal of one or more Status Traits without cost to herself.

• The cardinal may spend a temporary Status Trait to grant the Status of *Favored* to chosen agents — infiltrators, strategists and the like. Anyone who punishes or destroys a *Favored* member of the Sabbat faces automatic Monomacy against the cardinal unless there's an extremely good reason for the action.

Priscus

The priscus generally has held offices in the past and may in the future, but the rank of priscus doesn't require other position in the Sabbat's hierarchy. Prisci act as advisors to the regent, cardinals and archbishops (and occasionally to lower-ranked officers). The priscus generally holds a great deal of influence, both in the form of favors owed by current officials and in the fundamental coin of the sect, respect for individual achievement.

The priscus sometimes acts independently, with or without the approval of the official he's advising. More often, he provides information and training to younger vampires. Above all, the priscus helps the vampire he aids to make most effective use of the weaknesses presented by the sect's enemies of the moment. Sometimes the job involves surgical strikes to study military defenses, sometimes espionage, sometimes ideological warfare to sow confusion and plant seeds of thought that the Sabbat can exploit later. Many prisci were lords or military strategists before becoming vampires, and their experience serves the sect. Often, a crusade's success or failure depends on vital information, such as what defenses a prince can call upon or which influential vampires might sympathize with the Sabbat. This is the priscus' true purpose: to maximize on the flaws of the others through proven strategies.

The "generation gap" in the Sabbat shows very prominently in members' reaction to prisci. No vampire has ever become a prisci with less than 200 years of service to the sect, and most are twice that old. The Sabbat's elders generally feel that prisci are reaping their due reward for long service; younger members often think that prisci coast on past glories at the expense of the vampires who go out and get things done now. The truth of the matter is that young vampires rarely see the prisci in action. Devoted as they are to the regent and her support, much of the prisci's responsibilities keep them out of contact with the foot soldiers of the sect. These young Cainites aren't completely incorrect, however. The consistory does resemble an aristocratic "court," as the vampires who comprise it (including some cardinals) play at their own Jyhads. In a nutshell, the priscus' role is to ensure the Sabbat's long-term success through good advice and careful planning. Prisci typically maintain the social structure of the Sabbat as well — a priscus' patronage is required to become an archbishop, for example, and the consistory selects its own members from lesser ranks of the sect.

• The priscus automatically gains the Status Traits of *Confirmed*, *Feared* and *Infamous* upon taking office, and these can never be permanently removed while he retains his position.

• Only a priscus can appoint or remove another vampire as priscus. This costs one of the acting priscus' own temporary Status Traits and usually happens only after all prisci in the area agree. The appointment to priscus rank always comes with assignment to a particular Sabbat leader. (The priscus may change the affiliation when all parties agree or when the original leader perishes or loses office.)

• The priscus can spend a temporary Status Trait to ignore an order given by any vampire of lower rank than the one the priscus serves.

• The priscus can use his Status Traits for retests in Mental Challenges directly related to the advice he's giving his leader — testing an infiltration plan, for instance, or scouting out saboteurs.

Regent

The regent directs the entire sect, drawing on the support of her advisors to guide the whole Sabbat toward ultimate victory. In theory, she holds absolute power. In practice, subordinates often distort or just plain "lose" orders they refuse to accept, and the regent's power depends on her personal base of support. Ideologically driven young vampires (and a few elders) make their rejection of the regent's authority a point of doctrine: They accept the Sabbat's ideals and feel that no personal leader is compatible with the sect's founding principles. Less thoroughly independent vampires simply don't trust a high and remote commander to understand what their immediate situation may require or forbid.

The regent is necessarily an old vampire, chosen from the ranks of cardinals by exhaustive competition, and generally spends much time in torpor. The night-to-night governing of the sect depends on how her subordinates carry out the overall vision she gives them and how much of their own goals they mix in. While awake, the regent must spend much of her time meeting with sect leaders to hear their reports and lay out the grand strategy for coming conflicts. Details come only after multiple layers of filtering, and a sensible regent assumes that she doesn't know everything about what's going on. The routine struggle to preserve her position against rivals also consumes a lot of attention, which further requires the scattered limbs of the sect to make their own way as best they can.

The regent's nightly affairs consist primarily of entertaining sect luminaries, hearing progress reports, plotting against other vampires (both in the sect and out) and deciding which tactical or strategic maneuvers to make. Add to this list the incessant cultivation of influences, moving and counter-moving to keep one's enemies at bay, presiding over *ritae* and weathering the countless intrigues inherent to centuries among the undead.

• The regent gains the Status Traits of *Feared, Infamous, Proven* and *Supreme* upon taking office, and these can never be permanently lost while she retains her position.

• The regent can appoint and remove cardinals at the cost of one of her own temporary Status Traits. (In turn, the cardinals acting in unison appoint and remove the regent.) She can appoint and remove lesser officials at no cost to herself.

• The regent can use her temporary Status Traits for retests in Mental Challenges related to her role as sect leader: Detecting plots against her, giving instructions and so on.

Titles

What follow are a few of the titles used by the sect, as well as common forms of address. While the titles themselves are male, the forms of address reflect the bearer's gender; female forms of address are given in parentheses if they differ from the masculine. Players and Storytellers should feel free to create their own titles and pack names as well — Brother Logan of the Grave Revenant Families Ciphers has a certain ring that Logan the Tzimisce from Pack Number Three seems to lack.

Revenants

In the early Middle Ages, a consortium of Tzimisce elders systematically infused *vitae* into the blood of selected families of Eastern European nobility.

Over the course of several generations, the revenant lineages emerged: Human beings, mortal men and women, with vastly extended lifespan and innate affinities for some vampiric Disciplines. Revenants manufacture a unique variation of *vitae*, sufficient to support their limited abilities even though it's too weak for Cainite purposes. Some theorists believe that magical forces in the revenant families' homeland contribute to maintaining revenant powers; arguments on the subject consume many a long night.

The original experiments produced more than a dozen revenant lineages. Some perished during the Inquisition and Anarch revolt. Two merged with surviving families through intermarriage and lost any distinct identity. Rumors say the Ducheski and Rustovitch lines broke away from the Tzimisce to serve other masters. Matching rumors credit Assamites, Setites, Giovanni and

Title	Similar Titles	Form of Address
Regent	None	Our Most Distinguished Excellency
Cardinal (Always associated with a specific region)	High Lord (Lady) His (Her) Eminence	His (Her) Eminence
Priscus	Grand Master (Mistress), Monsignor	Very Reverend Sir (Madam)
Archbishop (Always associated with a specific city or region)	Archdeacon, Father (Mother) Superior	His (Her) Excellency
Bishop (Always associated with a specific city)	Deacon, High Father (Mother)	His (Her) Excellency
Templar/Paladin	Lord (Lady)	Sir (Lady)
Ductus	Lord (Lady), Sergeant, Chief	By Title
Priest	Father (Mother), Master (Mistress), Minister	Reverend Sir (Madam)
Pack Member	None	None, though sometimes Brother (Sister)

Tremere with creating their own revenant lines. In any event, four revenant families serve the Sabbat in the Final Nights.

The revenant families make Sabbat packs seem humane and psychologically balanced by comparison. Incest runs rampant in all of them. So do pedophilia, cannibalism and bestiality. Necrophilia and more esoteric vices turn up fairly regularly. Revenants who deal with mortal society gravitate toward the most extreme political, religious and social views they can find, contributing to the monstrous image such groups receive. Many revenants follow Paths of Enlightenment rather than Humanity, and they actually start off with advantages in this direction. Unlike most vampires, they grow up surrounded by the evidence of trans-human forces and powers, and they're sharply aware of how different they are from the mortals around them. A revenant may pass for normal more easily than a vampire can simply because the revenant has breath and a pulse, but the revenant shouldn't expect to please many people with his perspective on the human condition.

The Revenant Condition

In most respects, revenants follow the same rules as other ghouls: assign a revenant 6/4/3 Attributes, 5 Abilities, 5 Backgrounds and five freebie points. A revenant starts with one Trait in each of the Virtues and divides another five points between them. (See "Path," below, for revenant morality.) Most revenant characters are a few decades old. With Storyteller approval, players may buy extra age at the cost of one freebie point per full century. While revenants naturally acquire many deficiencies of mind, body and spirit, the seven-point limit on Flaws and Negative Traits remains in effect for revenant characters. Revenants also have the following unique features:

• **Vitae.** Each revenant produces one Blood Trait of weak vitae per night. This is much weaker than Cainite vitae (even that of the thin-blooded). It cannot create other ghouls, help in Embracing a drained corpse or create blood bonds. It allows the revenant to use his Disciplines, heal injuries and boost Attributes temporarily. Each revenant has a Blood Pool of 10 Traits, plus one for every full century he's been alive. Revenants have no generation; they cannot *Dominate* Cainites, cannot diablerize and cannot be diablerized.

• **Powers.** The revenant family lineage provides each revenant with a set of "in-clan" Disciplines and a family weakness comparable to clan weaknesses. Each revenant begins with one level in one of the family's Disciplines and can learn more for the "out of clan" costs (4 experience points for basic Disciplines, 7 for intermediate and 10 for advanced; revenants cannot learn Disciplines above the advanced level). A revenant can only learn the first level of each Discipline, plus one per full century: a 300-year old revenant can learn the second intermediate level of each family Discipline.

• **Paths.** Each revenant begins with one Trait in a Path (or, occasionally, Humanity, if the family allows it). Most revenants progress at about one Trait per full century.

Creating Revenants

The details of revenant family creation vary; no clan does it quite like any other. All the various methods draw on common principles, and in terms of game mechanics, they all work similarly. Note that these rituals all take a very long time to work. They appear in most chronicles as part of the background unless the chronicle involves extended downtime.

Each of the following rituals is an Advanced Thaumaturgical Ritual, requiring the usual cost in experience points to learn. Finding a teacher for them is generally hard. Very few vampires who know how to create revenant families survive in the Final Nights.

Stimulation of the Male's Essence

You work a change in the vitae of a male human who's been ghouled by a member of your clan. The subject male may thereafter mate with a female subjected to *Stimulation of the Female's Essence* (see below). Any offspring of the union carry revenant potential. Spend two Blood Traits to enact the ritual, plus one per year you maintain the stimulation.

Stimulation of the Female's Essence

You work a change in the vitae of a female human who's been ghouled by a member of your clan. The subject female may thereafter mate with a male subjected to *Stimulation of the Male's Essence* (see above). Any offspring of the union carry revenant potential. Spend two Blood Traits to enact the ritual, plus one per year you maintain the stimulation.

The chances of ghouls reproducing are vanishingly small. The participating ghouls must win (not tie) a series of three Simple Tests against the Storyteller, plus one per generation of the vampire(s) performing the *Stimulation* rituals, for a potential fertilization to succeed and come to term. The resulting child manifests one Discipline chosen at random from the creating clan's in-clan list, and one chosen at random, generally tuned to some aspect of the parents' psychology.

Protection of the Revenant Essence

You reinforce the revenant nature of each child born to properly prepared parents, manipulating its vitae to develop more intrinsic sympathy with its somewhat vampiric nature. This is an extended process, requiring a full year of operation upon and instruction of the child. You must perform the ritual before the child reaches puberty, or it reverts to being a normal ghoul. Spend two Blood Traits at the consummation of the year-long ritual. Children subjected to this ritual retain the two-Discipline limits described above, but reproduce more successfully upon mating with their own kind. The participants must win (not tie) a series of three Simple Tests against the Storyteller, plus a number of tests equal to half your generation.

Perfection of the Revenant Essence

This ritual only works on third-generation and later revenants whose parents and grandparents were all born as revenants. You perform a final set of vitae manipulations that bring the full potential of the revenant into expression. Like *Protection of the Revenant Essence*, this requires a full year with the child before it reaches puberty. Spend two Blood Traits at the end of the year. If you succeed in the ritual, the child manifests a third Discipline (the first child to do so sets the pattern for the family, and all subsequent offspring develop the same set of Disciplines) and develops the range of revenant features described above. Perfected revenants reproduce fairly easily upon mating with each

other; the participants must win or tie three Simple Tests against the Storyteller.

The nature of the rituals vary from clan to clan. Most clans perform debased versions of fertility rites when enchanting female ghouls and dark oath-swearing rituals involving swords (or impalement) when enchanting male ghouls. The Tzimisce sometimes bury children being subjected to *Protection* or *Perfection of the Revenant Essence* in mounds of corpses for a day to infuse a post-mortem spirit and drive out some of the taint of mundane existence.

The process of revenant creation necessarily involves a great deal of inbreeding. That's one reason it takes so long. The vampiric creators must constantly weed out the most defective individuals so as to keep the whole revenant family from collapsing into disease and madness. The difficulties here combine with the naturally low birthrate of potential and actual revenants to explain why most efforts at creating revenants end in failure.

No new ghoul lineages can join a revenant family once the first child successfully undergoes *Perfection of the Revenant Essence*. In the earlier stages, fresh ghouls can be brought in through stimulation of their respective essences and mated so as to create offspring suitable for *Protection of the Revenant Essence*. Some revenant families, especially the Bratovitches, kidnap and mate with outsiders. This doesn't produce revenant offspring, since the non-revenant parent lacks any of the necessary preparatory steps and doing them now wouldn't change anything. It's just one way to pass the time. They almost always destroy the non-revenant offspring in short order, often by feeding such children to real members of the family.

Bratovitch

The Bratovitches are the most rural, not to mention bestial, of the four families. They maintain rural estates in very remote countrysides, as far as possible from civilization. Within their well-secured boundaries, the Bratovitches breed hellhounds and other abnormal creatures with which they venture forth to hunt Lupines and the other enemies of the Sabbat. Apart from these hunts, Bratovitches generally leave their estates only to act as guides for nomadic Sabbat packs and to kidnap brides and studs.

The family fulfills every stereotype of inbred, homicidal rural monsters and adds unique wrinkles of its own. North American Sabbat vampires describe Bratovitch enclaves as "like *Deliverance*, except not so nice" while the family's ancestral holdings in Poland strike visitors as gatherings of cavemen with the latest firepower. Bratovitches don't care what others think about them. They like being able to wrestle down every animal they can raise and being able to have sex with just about every orifice those wrestled-down animals provide. The Sabbat seems to the Bratovitches like a bunch of big nasty uncles and aunts — neat and impressive but not around that much.

Most Bratovitches live in rural North America, in mountain valleys and long deserted stream channels where their pets have room to graze. The South American settlements are mostly new — less than a century old — and growing slowly but steadily. The Polish homestead maintains a fairly constant

size, and has largely escaped the social upheavals of the post-Communist era since it was never part of the society at large to begin with.

The family isn't exclusively composed of hicks, despite being rural. The elders include many scholars of vampiric affairs, including some of the Tzimisce's most valuable research assistants on breeding projects. Established Bratovitch settlements maintain well-stocked libraries. Bratovitch children generally get eccentric and ill-balanced educations, but those who want to pursue book lore can develop a first-rate mastery of selected fields.

No Bratovitches follow Humanity. It just doesn't work for them. The other Paths of Enlightenment all occur with roughly equal frequency, and some scholarly minded members of the family preserve Paths that the Sabbat generally abandoned long ago.

Disciplines: *Animalism, Potence, Vicissitude*

Weakness: Bratovitches are psychotic and unstable. They take a two-Trait penalty in all tests related to resisting frenzy and suffer a one-Trait penalty on all social interactions with normal people.

Hellhounds

The Bratovitches perform extensive breeding and vitae manipulation of dogs to create special war-hounds for the Tzimisce and other members of the Sabbat. The art of hellhound creation is a combined Discipline requiring mastery of both basic levels of *Animalism* and *Vicissitude*, so only Bratovitches over 200 can actually create hellhounds from regular dogs. Breeding existing hellhounds requires no special Disciplines, just a lot of courage and the ability to fix up the inevitable wounds.

Hellhounds have the following statistics: 10 Physical Traits, no Mental or Social Traits, *Alacrity* and *Swiftness* (*Celerity*), *Endurance* and *Mettle* (*Fortitude*) and *Prowess* and *Might* (*Potence*). A hellhound's bite inflicts two levels of aggravated damage, and its claws inflict one level of aggravated damage each. A hellhound possesses the equivalent of four levels each of *Brawl* and *Dodge* for retest purposes. Most hellhounds have the same health levels as vampires and 10 Blood Traits, though a few are stronger or weaker.

Hellhounds come in a variety of breeds, most heavily mixed. Whatever their canine ancestry, they look mean now.

Grimaldi

Before their bargain with the Tzimisce, the Grimaldi family ran merchant houses throughout the Italian city-states of the 12th century. They retain their flair for business, and are the most "normal" of the remaining revenant families. Most of their excesses fall within the general scope of self-indulgent behavior on the part of the very, very wealthy.

Grimaldi children grow up confident that they deserve the best and that they'll get it. They study at the finest schools and play with the most impressive toys. As they mature, Grimaldis take on positions of increasing corporate or political responsibility. The family knows the dangers of power without competence, and family members start their climbs on ladders to power *outside* family holdings. Once they've demonstrated their ability, then they take an appropriate place within the systems the family controls.

The Grimaldi family retains its connections to Italy; under their own name and a dozen other lineages the family's married into, Grimaldis hold offices at city and provincial levels. They sit on the boards of directors for firms in many industrial sectors and serve throughout the Roman Catholic hierarchy. There's no real "center" to the family. Wherever family interests took past generations, there's a current concentration of family influence, from Goa to New York.

This spread of the family serves visible goals as well as a secret agenda known only to family elders. The Grimaldi family leaders believe that the family survives only because of Tzimisce patronage. Should the Tzimisce ever withdraw their protection, forces inside and outside the Sabbat would slaughter the family and seize its assets. The elders therefore quietly work on contingency plans. Chosen agents negotiate with representatives of the Camarilla Ventrue and the Giovanni, discussing the terms under which those clans would find the family valuable enough to protect.

If news of these talks ever became public, the Tzimisce *would* immediately withdraw their patronage and let the slaughter begin, so the elders involved keep the matter secret from everyone else. Partly as misdirection, partly simply because it makes good sense, they do encourage their heirs to make ties with the other Sabbat clans, particularly the newcomers, so as to strengthen bonds that might prove useful in future calamities. The negotiating elders also keep themselves away from direct contact with Sabbat vampires, to avoid the risk of inadvertent revelation.

Grimaldi traditionally follow the Path of Honorable Accord or the Path of Power and the Inner Voice. In every generation, a handful follow the Path of Caine as best they can, given their inability to commit diablerie. This century, many Grimaldi have chosen to remain on the Path of Humanity, much to their elders' distress. The advocates of the "humane" Grimaldi movement explain that in an era of telecommunications, it's harder to hide signs of moral monstrosity. The Paths, the advocates say, reflect the opportunities and luxuries of a bygone age and are just bad business now. The Tzimisce who monitor the family find this development distressing and cultivate supporters of less humane strategies in the younger generations.

Disciplines: *Celerity, Dominate, Fortitude*

Weakness: All Grimaldi are blood bound to a Sabbat vampire of bishop rank or higher at puberty. The Sabbat started doing this to ensure the family's loyalty in its extensive dealings with mortal society at large. It became a habit, a sign of reaching adulthood in the eyes of the family and sect. The Sabbat rarely makes use of these blood bonds. The family elders planning for defection regretfully regard their heirs bound to Tzimisce officials as acceptable losses: Better to sacrifice the individuals blood bound recently enough that they would have to obey Tzimisce orders than sacrifice the whole family for their sake.

Obertus

The Obertuses survive on the basis of knowledge rather than wealth or raw power. They deal with the Sabbat at large as little as possible, maintaining regular contact only with a handful of Tzimisce scholars. When they become revenants, the Obertus family served as librarians and clerics in the northern reaches of the

Byzantine Empire. They congregated in the Tzimisce strongholds in eastern Europe for several centuries, then spread to the Americas with the Spanish and Portuguese empires. In the Final Nights, most of the family lives in New England and Canada's eastern provinces. The family maintains smaller enclaves in South America, particularly in Brazil, and in eastern Europe.

On all continents, the Obertuses prefer to live in small towns well removed from commerce and other distractions. They enjoy the freedom to engage in their own pursuits free of distractions, without wishing to be as cut off as most Bratovitches. The Obertus family ethos promotes stable, secure, comfortable living conditions as the foundation for the exhaustive, perennially innovative search for secret knowledge. Obertuses compete with each other to understand the unseen things of the world, all the hidden forces that shape the world outside mortal perception. Some enclaves train generation after generation to study a single subject, like poltergeists or the cryptozoology of suburbia; others try to encompass under one roof a wide range of expertise. The Tzimisce find little of this knowledge directly useful but appreciate the value of basic research. The next tremendously useful weapon in the War of Ages could appear in almost any context — after all, the Vinculum was once just a theoretical exercise in blood magic.

The Obertus elders have a secret project of their own, more devious and independent than the Grimaldi elders' scheme. The elders believe that revenants, and in particular *Homo obertus*, constitute a new species destined to replace *Homo sapiens*. The first evolutionary steps have been artificial, driven by Tzimisce manipulation. The Obertuses must find some way to make the revenant transformation happen naturally, or at least without requiring vampiric participation. To establish a proper context for this master goal, the family elders sponsor covert examination of many variations on the Embrace and ghouling. They capture Camarilla and independent Kindred from time to time and (more rarely) arrange the disappearance of Sabbat vampires who go to ground in Obertus-controlled towns. So far, results are patchy, consisting mostly of long lists of ways to make an Embrace or ghouling fail. The elders feel hopeful that the key breakthrough may come at any time.

Disciplines: *Auspex, Obfuscate, Vicissitude*

Weakness: The Obertuses were bred for intellectual ability without regard for stability, and are prone to psychological disorders. Each Obertus suffers at least one derangement of an intellectual nature. Most Obertuses suffer from the Obsessive/Compulsive Derangement, but characters may develop others with Storyteller approval.

Zantosa

The Zantosa family were and remain aristocrats, wealthy lords of the social scene. They remain prominent in Eastern Europe and spread, over the centuries, across the Atlantic. The family's leaders never cared much for direct power and worried about money only so far as necessary to maintain their lifestyle. Lifestyle itself has always been the Zantosa concern. The Zantosas exist, they tell each other, to widen the boundaries of human experience until one day they'll have done everything a human being can do. They keep the people around them stirred up in pursuit of the new, always seeking some fresh

sensation not yet made routine and therefore safe. The Zantosas set the standards others try to imitate.

Living on the edge carries certain risks, of course. Some Zantosas lose their standing after getting caught in some behind-the-scenes crime like blackmail or graft. Some members of the family choose the wrong partners for their exploits and face the legal and social hassles that come with accusations of pedophilia, necrophilia, sexual assault and other behavior most people haven't yet learned to accept. Many Zantosas become so addicted to a particular habit (or drug) that they become boring, locked in a single routine, no longer capable of or interested in innovation. In particularly tragic cases of self-inflicted tedium, the family quietly slaughters the offender to impress upon relatives the importance of remaining the master of one's habits rather than their servant. Few of the Zantosas' social partners *trust* the family, and like all experimenters, the family must avoid becoming so obnoxious that they lose the audiences they need to complete the great work of experience.

The Zantosas have dealt with several of the clans from their first generations as revenants. The Toreador *antitribu* tend to like the Zantosas, trading insights and taking turns acting as subjects in group activities. The Ventrue *antitribu* regard the Zantosas as particularly decadent jesters who reinforce the *antitribu* interest in preserving old power relationships inside new social forms. More recently, the Serpents of the Light and the Zantosas have entered into close association, mingling cultural, religious and purely aesthetic explorations.

It's been several generations since the presence of Zantosas could make or break a party in New York or Prague. Most of the family members now exist in fairly small sub-communities, dealing only with a handful of lineages that share the Zantosa fascination with extremes. Some Zantosas of the last two generations build elaborate false genealogies for themselves and then enter into high society as newcomers interested in "picking up the Zantosa legacy where those old fellows left off." The family elders frown on this, fearing that pointless deceptions could crumble and do harm to elaborate deceptions that actually do advance family concerns. Zantosa children learn from their nannies and mentors never to waste an action: If it's worth doing, it's worth doing in a way that makes an impact on someone.

The New York branch of the family suffered a severe setback in 1997, one that's had repercussions elsewhere. Two dozen family members, all in good standing with the family (that is, practicing the right sorts of perversions and degradations), suddenly found themselves denounced by family elders and executed. Sabbat inquiries produced the explanation that the elders uncovered a nest of infernalists. The Zantosas frown on dealing with devils since devils tend to want to impose their own aesthetics and interfere with the family pursuits. The Sabbat Inquisition apparently found the answer satisfactory since no vampiric investigation took place. Similar nests of infernalists turn up from time to time in other Zantosa communities; in each case, the Sabbat Inquisition pronounces itself satisfied with the Zantosas' own response.

Only the family elders know the real story. From the very beginning of the family's revenant experience, the elders have guarded the body of a Tzimisce elder in very deep torpor. The body came with the first sizable contingent of Zantosas to settle in New York and slept away the centuries there. One night, without any sort of warning or disturbance, the body disappeared. The infernalist story is an after-the-fact explanation for mysterious deaths inflicted on elders who helped tend the body at some point. Quiet inquiries with the Obertus (a painful matter for the Zantosas, who hate to admit the usefulness of anyone so boring) and occultists outside the Sabbat produce no clues as to the identity of the presumably reawakened vampire.

Most Zantosas pursue the Path of Cathari; many succeed in maintaining very high ratings in it, thanks to the family's accumulated wisdom in such matters. More necrotically inclined individuals pursue the Path of Death and the Soul. One rural Zantosa enclave whose members deal regularly with the Bratovitches specializes in the Path of the Feral Heart, to the embarrassment of their relatives. No Zantosa admits to practicing the Path of Caine, despite persistent rumors of Noddists in the family and the demonstrable use of blood and vitae for more recreational ends.

Disciplines: *Auspex, Presence, Vicissitude*

Weakness: Nothing in Zantosa family training prepares its members to resist interesting temptations. Whenever a Zantosa faces what looks like an interesting and intense pleasure, she must make a *Self-Control* or *Instinct* test, generally against a difficulty of three Traits, to avoid wandering off to pursue it instead of what she had been working on. Zantosas cannot spend Willpower to resist supernatural enticements as long as there's a pleasurable component involved (bear in mind that Zantosa notions of "pleasure" aren't like most people's).

Szlachta and Vohzd

The Tzimisce excel in the creation of highly specialized ghouls. Clan lore includes the techniques for creating the *slzachta* (guardian ghouls) and the *vohzd* (war ghouls). The Tzimisce make no particular effort to keep their techniques secrets; the requirements, including *Vicissitude* and extensive practice, exclude anyone outside the clan. A non-Tzimisce would-be student who wants to learn may or may not meet with a favorable response, depending on the whim of the Tzimisce elders she meets, but it's not usually due to a need for secrecy.

The processes for both *slzachta* and *vohzd* creation require the vampire to know *Bonecraft* and to possess at least two levels of the *Crafts* Ability with a focus in *Body Crafting*.

Playing Specialized Ghouls

Neither *szlachta* nor *vohzd* make suitable player characters. Specialized ghouls undergo a level of distortion and transformation that renders them effectively mindless in normal terms — they possess even less independent consciousness than someone subjected to *Conditioning*. Specialized ghouls should only be Storyteller characters, and when they do appear in your chronicle, emphasize their alien nature.

Szlachta

The *slzachta* serve as soldiers, bodyguards and sentries. Each *szlachta* emerges from its creator's laboratory unlike any other, since the process requires handwork. Some features are fairly standard despite the variations.

A typical *szlachta* has spikes, armored plates or both. The Tzimisce creating the ghoul removes all unnecessary fat, or transfers it to areas where extra padding might come in handy, such as over vital organs. Most Tzimisce replace the ghoul's entire skin with something tougher while some add on extra layers to create whole-body calluses or otherwise increase the ghoul's capacity to resist wounds. Almost all *szlachta* possess armored sensory organs with increased sensitivity, so as to make better observers.

To reduce the ghoul's automatic resistance to modification, most Tzimisce starve their subjects before setting to work. Some creators outright attack their creations-to-be, using injury to further weaken the target body's defenses.

Each of the following transformations requires a successful Mental Challenge against the target's current health levels (the creator may use *Body Crafting* for a retest) and a Physical Challenge with *Bonecraft*.

• **Armor.** The target gains one health level of all-body armor or two levels of armor for one specific part of the body (head, torso, arms, etc.). If the creator wins both challenges, the armor adds no Negative Traits; if the creator ties, the armor works as usual but the target gains the Negative Trait of *Heavy*. After the third level of *Heavy*, the *szlachta* can carry no more armor.

• **Organic Weapons.** The target does an extra level of lethal damage with each strike in hand-to-hand combat. Depending on the creator's taste, the weapons might be spikes, fangs, exuded poisons or something else. (Note that most poisons don't work against vampires; the creator should plan based on the circumstances she expects her creation to face.) If the creator ties either challenge, the target gains the Negative Trait of *Clumsy*; after the third level of *Clumsy*, the target cannot engage in tasks requiring fine manipulation and can receive no more weaponry.

• **Enhanced Sense.** The target gains the equivalent of one level of the *Acute Sense* Merit (see **Laws of the Night**, p. 112). If the creator ties either challenge, the target also gains a 2-Trait penalty on all uses of one of its other senses. A creator attempting to compensate for such deficiencies must use this process to undo the flaw before attempting to boost the impaired sense. This requirement can, given bad luck, turn into an endless spiral of sensory degeneration. It's one of the most common reasons creators destroy otherwise satisfactory *szlachta*.

• **Enhanced Speed.** The target can take two extra steps during combat movement. This change involves lengthening the target's legs and changing the ratio of upper limb to lower limb length as well as modifying leg and hip joints. If the creator ties either challenge, the target becomes imbalanced and must win or tie a Simple Test to avoid falling over when it comes to rest after a period of motion. Each additional level of this complication requires the target to win or tie another Simple Test when stopping. After developing the need to perform three Simple Tests every time it stands still, the target can receive no more speed enhancements.

- **Programmed Ability.** This modification is a combination of preparing specialized physical features and mental condition; the creator must know *Conditioning* as well as the basic requirements for creating *szlachta*. The target gains two levels in one ability related to its basic nature, such as a weapon skill or Alertness. If the creator ties either challenge, the target also develops the Fugue Derangement (see **Laws of the Night**, p. 213). Each additional level of this complication subtracts 1 from the target's Mental total for the challenge to resist the fugue state. After getting a 2-Trait penalty, the target cannot receive further ability programming.

The creator can attempt one modification per night, plus one for each level of *Body Crafting* she possesses beyond the two required to make *szlachta* at all.

Szlachta in Play

Szlachta remind young vampires of H.R. Geiger paintings come to life. Guardian ghouls lack most normal facial features and cannot easily express the limited range of emotions they do feel. Creators who turn captured mortals into *szlachta* and send the new ghouls as weapons against the mortals' allies do make sure to leave a few distinctive features visible. People who knew the *szlachta* recognize it upon succeeding in a Static Mental Challenge against four Traits. The horror of identifying a former friend or ally under these circumstances requires a 3-Trait *Courage* test to resist the impulse to flee.

Unless you happen to have players who are skilled contortionists, it takes costuming, props and a measure of imagination to portray *szlachta* in a game session. Dark clothing, presented in low light, helps hide the player's own body contours. Also, never underestimate the effects of careful posture — look into how stage actors portray characters like the Elephant Man and Shakespeare's Richard III.

Vohzd

Few vampires make *vohzd* anymore, just as few vampires build castles anymore. The titanic war ghouls come from an age when the Tzimisce strode the Carpathian landscape as absolute masters, free from fear of mortal hunters or even vampiric rivals. In the age of organized vampire hunters, satellite imagery and portable anti-tank weaponry, war ghouls create more problems than they solve. Since vampires seldom completely abandon any practice once they take it up, a handful of creators do continue to make *vohzd* in the Final Nights.

Almost all *vohzd* are team projects. It takes time and effort to reassemble components into the final form, and teamwork reduces the risk of components going bad, suffering accidental damage or otherwise wasting the creator's work.

The construction of a war ghoul begins with at least 15 regular ghouls, whether human or animal. The creators force them all to drink each others' blood in a Vaulderie-like ritual. (If you need rules for this, require the creators to win Mental Challenges with *Intimidation* or some Discipline suitable for issuing simple commands.) The creators then disassemble their targets with *Vicissitude*, sometimes using *Thaumaturgy* for assistance. To simulate the effects of *Vicissitude* surgery, keep track of the damage that the creators would normally inflict with *Fleshcraft* and *Bonecraft* attacks. The target takes no actual damage from this manipulation; when it reaches zero health levels, it

comes apart in surgically tidy components. These pieces of ghouls generally survive in storage for about one night per level of the creator's *Body Crafting* ability — less in adverse conditions, more in places with provision for storing organic materials like meat.

Vivisected ghouls provide one component each for sensory purposes — each head yields up just one useful set of sensory organs — along with two useful limb components, and a number of "general" components equal to half their health levels. General components provide the skeleton, musculature and internal organs necessary to make the new amalgamated organism work properly.

"Component" as a term reflects the Tzimisce attitude toward their work. When describing these pieces of people and animals in play, reinforce the idea that each component is a still-living piece of an organism. It pulses slowly; eyes stare blindly; fingers and toes twitch without conscious control. The mystical properties of *Vicissitude* and *Body Crafting* produce seamless barriers of flesh over the points where one body part was severed from another. The resulting masses *shouldn't* live at all. Storytellers should feel free to require *Conscience* or *Courage* checks for bystanders to remain calm in the presence of *vohzd* creation in progress. Prop cards don't do justice to the experience. Very minimal props can add a lot, such as cardboard boxes covered with appropriate photographs to illustrate the body parts involved.

Once the creators have their initial set of components, they begin reassembling bits. The *vohzd* automatically develops *Potence* and *Fortitude* equal to twice the highest level possessed by any of the ghouls providing components. Its blood pool also equals twice the largest blood pool of any of the component ghouls. *Vohzd* generally move at half normal human speed (one step walking or two steps running per action).

The creators must decide on a single individual to act as the *vohzd's* controller. The war ghoul has scarcely any mind to speak of, and responds only to commands of three words or less from the controller. Tzimisce war leaders generally starve their *vohzd* before a battle and then point the hungry war ghouls at enticing *vitae*- or blood-rich targets. The *vohzd's* mindless, alien condition makes it immune to *Animalism*, *Dominate* and *Presence*.

Each of the following transformations requires the creator to make a Physical Challenge with *Bonecraft* to insert the components correctly. Failure renders the component useless; the creator must discard it and try again.

• **General framework.** Two general components fused together give the *vohzd* one health level. Keep track of the total health levels of the work in progress and follow this progression: Healthy, Bruised, Wounded, Incapacitated, Healthy, Bruised, Wounded. A *vohzd* with five health levels (from 10 general components) has Healthy, Healthy, Bruised, Wounded, Incapacitated. A *vohzd* with 10 health levels (from 20 components) goes all the way through the cycle and starts over again, ending up with Healthy, Healthy, Healthy, Bruised, Bruised, Bruised, Wounded, Wounded, Wounded, Incapacitated. The *vohzd* must have at least as many components dedicated to general framework as it has components allocated to specific purposes.

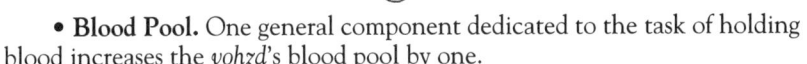

- **Blood Pool.** One general component dedicated to the task of holding blood increases the *vohzd*'s blood pool by one.
- **Disciplines.** Two sensory components taken from ghouls who knew *Fortitude* or *Potence* provide the brain matter and lingering soul traces to raise the *vohzd*'s level of one of those Disciplines by one.
- **Movement.** Four limb components increase the *vohzd*'s walking speed by one step per turn, up to a maximum of twice normal human speed. Yes, these are multiple legs.
- **Arms.** Two limb components provide the material for one arm and the necessary attachments. This is a standard human-type arm, doing one level of bashing damage. Each extra limb component included in this step can add one of the following: The ability to inflict Lethal damage, the ability to inflict one extra health level of damage or increasing the limb's reach by three feet.
- **Armor.** Three general components provide enough raw material to give the *vohzd* one level of armor, as long as it has 10 or less health levels. Add another two general components for every 10 health levels after that.

Each creator can attempt one modification per night, plus one for each level of *Body Crafting* she possesses beyond the two required to make *vohzd* at all.

Vohzd in Play

Vohzd horrify everyone who sees them, and it takes time to get used to them. Anyone seeing a *vohzd* for the first time must make a *Courage* test against five Traits to avoid running in terror. Each time a character succeeds in overcoming her fear of the war ghoul, reduce the difficulty of future tests by one Trait; when the difficulty falls to zero, the character finally takes such things for granted. A point of Willpower allows a retest on these challenges.

Vohzd often include multiple arms spread more or less evenly around the main torso. A *vohzd* gets one attack to its front, one to its rear, and one to one side or the other. Depending on how much of a head its creator gave it, these labels may be fairly arbitrary; assume that "front" is the direction the *vohzd* last moved, in the absence of more permanent physiological markers. Each arm beyond the second on that side of the *vohzd* adds two bonus Traits in combat; each leg beyond the second adds one bonus trait in close combat.

Presenting *vohzd* in your chronicle is very easy to do poorly. A bunch of players under a sheet and shuffling around seldom looks horrifying. Expect players to need to use their imagination to fill in the gaps, whatever you decide to do. A group of players wearing similar dark colors, roped together or moving in coordination and given the benefit of backlighting can create a startling impression if nobody gets the time to examine them in detail. Mannequin parts are unfortunately expensive, but if you have connections to someone in retail supply or other suitable source, extra arms and legs waving at the edges of the mass can be very startling, particularly if they're clothed like the people holding them.

Keep in mind that *vohzd* are *big*. Their creators store them in barns and remote valleys, not closets or phone booths. As far as your game space allows, arrange a suitably large area for the *vohzd* to occupy.

Chapter Seven: Urban Legends

Storytelling a Sabbat chronicle is something that should be approached with more preparation than average. Sabbat material is frankly adult, filled with shocking themes, disturbing sights and a streak of amorality that can be misunderstood without proper acclamation. This is not the place for the inexperienced or immature.

Because the vampires of the Sabbat are seen as callous, inhuman beasts, they are often given minor plots in live-action roleplay, complete with a three-digit body count. While such games are occasionally amusing in the same way that, say, a shoot 'em up arcade game is amusing, they are rarely a basis for a long-term storyline. The Sabbat can be challenging to portray, but challenges provide some of the most rewarding play. In this chapter, we'll be giving you some ideas and suggestions to help you run your own Sabbat chronicles.

If you are about to venture into the realm of Storytelling for the first time, you will certainly find it helpful to read the chapter on Storytelling in **Laws of the Night** if you haven't already done so. It will give you all the basics about bookkeeping, theme, mood, structure and plot, and it will help you make more sense of what you'll be reading here. For those who are already familiar with the ins and outs of Storytelling, prepare to take the next step into something a little larger.

The Really Important Stuff

It should go without saying that Sabbat chronicles delve into the darkest parts of the psyche. This is the place where you start conjuring up some very nasty demons, figuratively speaking — complete disregard for human life, glorying in atrocity and an utter lack of what are considered normal values such as compassion. Storytellers in Sabbat chronicles take on more than just plots and themes. It is vitally important for a Storyteller to always be in touch with her players and doubly so with Sabbat material. Is one player getting unnerved by the material, another one taking things a little too seriously, or are there Masquerade problems? Guess what — they're yours to deal with.

Players who are getting unnerved by Sabbat material can be fairly easy to spot — they have trouble joining in the games or *ritae*, even when their characters are being

ridiculed, or they seem enthused to be with the game until things start getting hairy. Touch base with the player in question and ask if things are all right. Don't pry or push, but make it clear that you're open to what he has to say. Once you learn what the problem is, ask him for suggestions about what he'd like to do about it. Consider other things for the player to do — it's unlikely he wants to chuck the *whole* game, just parts of it. Is he interested in the spirituality and social interaction? Encourage him to hang out with the Noddists and priests. Is someone going out of her way to harass him? Discipline the errant player. Is someone handling sensitive material, such as religion or sex, inappropriately? Lay down the law on treating the game with respect. This is supposed to be fun, and when players are uncomfortable about the material, then they aren't having fun.

On the flip side, there are those who think a Sabbat chronicle is an excuse to go completely wild. These are more than just "gun bunnies." They do everything in their power to shock their fellow players, from juvenile gross-outs to excessive profanity to profoundly insulting others' beliefs. Not a few take up infernalism for fun and profit and take pleasure in killing other characters. When confronted with their behavior, they claim that they're merely acting in the spirit of the chronicle — it's adult material, they say, and if you can't stand the heat, you better stay out of the kitchen. Such behavior is hardly the hallmark of the mature player. Don't tolerate this a minute longer than you see it. Such behavior is dangerous to your other players and to your chronicle, both from a story point of view and from a more mundane view. You don't want these jokers to be what non-players see of your game. If they can't treat mature material in a mature fashion, don't hesitate to throw them out.

Lastly, there are those matters which are sometimes termed "Masquerade" problems. This is when the real world and the game world collide, with unpleasant results. A case in point occurred at a convention where a Sabbat chronicle was being run. Two players, in character at the time, were overheard by a maid discussing the vivisection of a hotel worker. The maid was naturally disturbed and brought it to the attention of management, who subsequently came looking for the convention staff. People don't treat such things as murder, torture and the like lightly, not in these days of domestic terrorism. Be extremely careful where you play and where you discuss your game. Sabbat themes and material sound frightening to the average listener and can lead to panic when people aren't entirely aware of the situation.

These aren't meant to put a damper on your fun; they're meant as a safety net so you can keep having fun without getting hurt. Respect the material and your players, and everyone will have a good time.

Sabbat Chronicles

The plots, themes, goals and drives of a Sabbat chronicle are very different from those of a Camarilla story. Sabbat ideology demands a more straightforward approach to matters — at least, on the surface. A Sabbat chronicle is not merely a morass of combat in an urban hellhole setting with some "nasty bits" thrown in. A Storyteller who approaches it thusly is cheating the players (and herself) of the chance to tell some very unique and exciting stories.

Fresh Meat

One of the most rudimentary and yet compelling elements of the Sabbat is the theme of brotherhood. All Sabbat characters are expected to be, or to soon become, members of a pack. These packs are small cells of individuals, pressed

together through circumstance and, occasionally, choice, dedicated to their own goals as well as the goals of the sect. Though the Vaulderie and Vinculum provide some artificial ties of closeness, there are still squabbles between "brothers and sisters," no differently than among mortal siblings (with the exception that mortal siblings don't call on supernatural powers to put someone through a wall for disagreeing with them).

When a new character enters the chronicle, some thought must be given toward her "pack." Is she nomadic? Founded? Is she the lone survivor of a recently fallen pack? It's extremely unusual for a Sabbat to be without a pack for more than a few weeks. During that time, characters should be antsy and strained. Only through the repetitive bond of the Vaulderie are they safe from the overwhelming power of the Antediluvians and their blood bond.

The pack structure allows you a convenient method to integrate new characters into the venue. By placing an inexperienced player in an established pack, the Storyteller allows the pack to teach its "fledgling," and the new player is instructed by more experienced players. If one member of the pack has a reason to be involved in an ongoing plot, the rest of the pack will almost certainly become involved — willingly or not.

Intrigue

Although the Sabbat is theoretically bound together with a single overwhelming blood bond, the actual strength of that bond varies from individual to individual — even from month to month. At the moment when a character is relying on the total support of their pack, a traitor may break through the confines of the Vinculum and stab the metaphorical knife into the back of those who trusted him. Remember, also, that the Sabbat is a place of brotherhood, however enforced, and it can hamstring as often as it helps. At the moment when a character's revenge is about to be complete, he could find himself unable to strike.

A total disregard for mortal life does not mean a disregard for *all* life. Characters should have goals, dictated by their backgrounds, their Paths and, more importantly, by the constraints of the sect. As the game develops, look for plot points that can create intrigue between characters. Are there two Noddists looking for the same, one-of-a-kind occult item? Do you have several members on the Path of Power and the Inner Voice striving for position and rank? There's nothing wrong with conflicting goals, so long as one remembers that loyalty to the sect should always come first — or at least, it should always appear to come first. If you seem to be loyal, then you are treated as such. If you appear to be the strongest, or the most capable, then your position is more stable. It's all about appearances, from the archbishop trying to look like she's completely in command to the newest Pander recruit who's trying desperately to show off how tough she is.

The Sabbat is not merely a sect of fanatics anxiously awaiting the next excuse to start a killing spree. It is a motley of liars, manipulators and powermongers who further their personal goals and ambitions in the name of "the good of the sect" amidst devout believers and wild-eyed rowdies. Making this key distinction changes a Sabbat game from an excuse for mass slaughter to something with much more depth.

Setting

Many Sabbat games begin with the description of a horrific setting. No one knows how anything got there or why, but it's assumed that this is how things are done in the Sabbat: "You enter the chamber and see the mutilated bodies of five adults hanging from the ceiling. Their blood drains slowly into a large pool below. The dripping is the only sound you hear." While the inhumanity of the Sabbat is a theme that should be brought out, the players are going to become more jaded than their characters unless some real thought is put into the backdrop.

Think creatively. Why is this particular scene here? What purpose does it serve? What should the characters and players be getting from this? Consider the scene described above. If thrown into the middle of the evening to "liven things up," it may go to waste — just one more act of mindless brutality to which you don't want your players to become jaded. On the other hand, it can serve your story by enhancing some part of it. Perhaps it's the remains of an interrupted Blood Bath (so where is the recipient of the bath?). Better still, perhaps it's an illustration of a particular Sabbat bishop's cruelty or of some Toreador *antitribu's* latest work.

From a physical standpoint, a Sabbat game need not mean that all your games take place in grungy alleys or nightclubs of thundering music. The chosen gathering place may reflect the bishop's taste for meditative silence and study, or a pack may be hosting the gather and has set the tone of the place by putting out trophies of their successes and achievements. Set up lights with red bulbs and lay out dark bed sheets to indicate pools of blood when it's time for a more frightening scene, or set up colored cellophane to show where a ceremonial bonfire is burning.

Themes New and Old

The Sabbat has many opportunities for exciting and involving storylines that can be easily inserted into a long-term campaign. Below, you'll find some examples and ideas to get you started. These are by no means the only stories you can tell in this venue. Use your creativity, your imagination and the stories that your players write as backgrounds for their characters to create and intricate and involved setting. Does one of your Brujah *antitribu* have a mortal enemy in the Camarilla? What if the Lasombra's old flame on the other side had become attached to that character, but neither party knows?

There are several themes that are most appropriate for a Sabbat chronicle and can be highly useful when planning a story for your assembled characters. Theme is the most important part of your story — it is the organizing principal, the thread that ties together the errant parts into a unified whole. However, the Sabbat is a game about the absence of humanity and a group of individuals who have willingly given up their humanity. Alter common themes to accurately reflect the setting.

Here are a few examples, using the themes mentioned in **Laws of the Night**, with some slight modifications:

Love — The Sabbat is usually no place for love, although the heightened blood bond of the Vinculum can substitute. Love, even if created by an artificial source, can alter actions and create tension. What would we sacrifice for love? When the Vinculum becomes too strong, will a pack willingly separate in order to follow the commands of their leader? Worse, what if a packmate was guilty of some terrible crime against the sect? Would his loyal (and loving) packmates cover up the crime or answer for it themselves in order to free him?

Hate — Hatred runs strong in the Sabbat, particularly when it is thrust outward, toward the members of the Camarilla and other threats. How can hate be used to drive the character's motivations? What if two individuals who hated one another were forced to Vaulderie and gained a blood bond to one another? How will they resist the call of blood in order to fulfill their grudge?

Betrayal — When a member of the sect breaks the rules, it is the responsibility of the entire Sabbat to hunt her down. Use betrayal themes to bring warring factions together and give them a single enemy to dedicate their combined efforts against. At what price will a character's betrayal affect those who were once close to her?

Revenge — Any creature as long-lived as a vampire is bound to have made enemies, both inside and outside of the sect. When those enemies come to take their revenge, they will not stop at the individual, but will seek to annihilate those closest to her as well. Further, when a pack is formed, the enemies of a single member become enemies of the pack, and, as such, can provide a single goal for the characters to attain together. The pack is a strong support for player interaction, particularly when your game relies heavily on the theme of revenge.

Rebellion — Rebellion is one of the most dangerous themes in the Sabbat. The various political factions can be used to great advantage, forcing characters to choose between their loyalty to the sect and their dedication to the ideal of true freedom. Unlike the Camarilla, where revolutions are usually bloody affairs, the Sabbat must handle them with increasing delicacy and intrigue, especially where the Vinculum is concerned.

Morality — Alternately, the theme of morality can be the theme of anti-morality, and the price paid for escaping the bonds of humanity. What happens when the leadership of a certain area forces characters to accept an alternate Path of Enlightenment? What if the chosen Path of the archbishop is Cathari in a region predominated by Power and the Inner Voice? Who determines the correct Path and to what effect?

Building a Story

All good stories come in stages, from the carefully plotted beginning to the epic ending of the tale. Many of these focus heavily on conflict, either interpersonal feuds or full-scale wars, and in the Sabbat, such conflicts are often quite violent. Because Sabbat chronicles can be violent in nature, players and storytellers alike should be prepared to adjust their plotlines for a constantly changing character base. Still, the basic plot structure — opening, climax and denouement — provides milestones for the story that you're creating, whether the story's climax comes in the form of a valuable clue or the defeat of an enemy's guardian.

One good example of a Sabbat storyline, particularly one in which both sides of the story can be played, is the siege. Whether a Sabbat force has decided to wrest a city from Camarilla (or anarch) control, or the Sabbat is fighting against a Camarilla invasion of their territory, the siege plotline offers character development, action, intrigue and deception — in short, opportunities for stories.

Overall, establishing the timing and pacing of a single story and the stages of a more epic plot are very similar. In fact, when you are dealing with a large-scale plot, it is best to think of it in terms of a series of smaller events, to help give perspective and make an enormous task a little easier. In the Siege example, the Storyteller creates a larger story arc, which the players interact with (and may affect) though smaller vignettes and scenes.

Opening

First, spend time researching your chosen city, whether it is the actual city you are running your game in or a separate location. If you and the players are familiar with the location, challenges and benefits of a particular setting will become important to the plot. Los Angeles, for example, is a much different location for a siege than Charleston and will have a much different feel and pacing. Spend some time preparing the introduction to your story: Has the local cardinal declared war on the Camarilla in this city or are the the character's combined packs proving their worth to the Sabbat by assaulting a known Camarilla haven? Are the characters present because of duty or coincidence? A briefing on the city's current Cainite politics and organization, however brief or vague, gives the players a starting place for roleplaying. Further, if characters are interested in running brief preludes, arrange scouting missions that detail certain areas of the city or gather important information they can disseminate at the opening game.

During the latter stages of the opening, the Storyteller should make every effort to establish the enemy's strengths, weaknesses and ties within the city. Once the characters know who and what they are fighting, they can begin to understand the importance of their actions and generate new ideas to propel the siege forward. Scouting parties become raiding parties, striking against valuable positions within the city and tearing down Camarilla bastions. Internal debates and arguments within the sect become significant power struggles, determining the path of the siege. Two courses of action may be equally valid, but who has more political clout to force her ideas through? And don't forget that the enemy can strike back — setbacks and losses mark this time as much as wins and triumphs.

Climax

When the players have done a significant amount of research into the difficulties facing them, they are ready to confront them. Such actions determine the climax of a story — the assault, and the victory (or failure) against opposition. This is your story's high point, the point toward which your players have been traveling. In a siege storyline, the initial climax might be the first major battle against the Camarilla. Powerful forces, from prisci to the Black Hand's seraphim, may be involved in the battle — even if they choose to engage the enemy from behind a deceptive screen. Characters may battle for position, using their victories as leverage against weaker opponents, or may use the battles against the Camarilla as a convenient excuse to take care of another enemy.

The battle may be a single tremendous fight or, more likely, a series of waves as the Sabbat sends in packs of shock troops to break down the Camarilla's defenses. The siege will need infiltrators to tear apart the Camarilla's bonds of loyalty from the inside even as War Parties gather to destroy the city from the outside. Conversions are forced, defenses shattered, allies lost, and the story races headlong to the penultimate confrontation with the prince and her strongest allies.

If the opening of the story was sufficiently intriguing, and the characters are already involved in the plot, there should be little need for you to guide the climax. Player involvement is always stronger than Storyteller character commands, and when characters are initiating subplots, give them plenty of leash to run on; they'll take care of themselves just fine.

Denouement

After the climax, the story winds down. Players and characters alike gather to count the dead and honor the living. The Sabbat has either won the city or lost the siege. Tensions begin to ease, and story pieces begin to come together. It is important that both players and characters understand the resolution of the plot; they should feel as if they have accomplished something, as if they have somehow made an impact on the world around them. Remember to note the parts of your plot that your players missed — such openings can create all new plots.

There will certainly be new struggles within the sect to fill positions suddenly emptied by war and to claim power within the new hierarchy. Those packs who wish to set up permanent residency within the city must claim their territories, and there will be heartfelt farewells for those that seek to move on.

Subplots

Propaganda can serve an important purpose in a Sabbat chronicle. One odd fact about most players is their ability to solve conflicts (which, after all, are often the focus of stories). However, occasionally players can take their drive to bring peace a bit too far. The Sabbat is a dangerous place, and promises and political concessions are not easy ways to mollify enemies. A good storyteller will keep relations between the Sabbat and the Camarilla in constant turmoil, using small plot twists to throw the two factions against one another, at least in the background. Although war does not have to be a major theme in the plotline, it is a constant thought in the minds of all Sabbat vampires and should be recognized as such. The Storyteller should maintain walls of propaganda and misinformation, attacking the base philosophies of both sects so that no possibility of reconciliation is possible.

The internal corruption within the Sabbat provides for constant minor subplots and conflicts. Corruption eats at the very heart of the sect, dissolving it from within as well as without. The Lasombra and Tzimice fight for control, as the less populous clans ally and struggle against one another. The rise of the Panders has thrown the hearts of the inner courts into turmoil, and the friction between jealous leaders can lead to constant power struggles between their domains. Although loyalty and freedom are the sect's catchwords, too often leadership becomes the iron fist of rulership, and being considered disloyal is enough to ensure one's destruction.

Occult ties, particularly through the more unusual bloodlines and backgrounds of the sect, also make interesting and unusual subplots. Certainly, the Lasombra have been deeply involved in church politics almost from the inception of Christianity; their vaults are crammed with the prizes of hundreds of years of infiltration, from relics to texts to forgotten lore. The Tzimisce cling to the mystic ties of their homeland while the Kiasyd and Harbingers of Skulls probe into the mysteries of this world and the next. Though the Sabbat flaunts and brags of its superiority, they are well aware that there are mysteries and secrets beyond their reckoning. If nothing else, the recent loss of the Tremere *antitribu* has convinced them of that.

Conflicts

Sabbat stories, like all good plots, should revolve around conflict. Heroes need antagonists, and even villains have enemies. Most stories take the hero out of the ordinary world and place her within an alien landscape, trusting on her

actions to define her purpose and nature. The World of Darkness provides the setting; the Sabbat provides the goals and drive. Still, a character is partially defined by her enemies, so we've provided a few sketches of ideas and opponents that often come into a Sabbat chronicle. Many of these are *large* story hooks: a war with the Camarilla won't vanish after a single individual is killed — even if it is the prince, nor will werewolves casually forget that their Kinfolk were murdered during Sabbat *ritae*.

THE SABBAT AS HEROES

Difficult as it may be to imagine, the Sabbat are heroes in their environment. They believe that their fight lies against an opponent that wishes to destroy the world. They see the Camarilla as pawns of a greater power, and, not unlike the American colonists, they fight against the might of an established group that claims power by no recognized right. With each victory, they free the vampires of the Camarilla from the Jyhad by conversion or death.

While some players prefer to be the villain or anti-hero of the story, many players do want to be the heroes. Even in a Sabbat chronicle, players should be given opportunities for their characters to behave in a heroic manner, defending their comrades, goals and beliefs. One of the ways to accomplish this is by creating a city background for your players that gives them a natural enemy: the Camarilla. Restoring a city to Sabbat control can involve conversion, battle and other exciting adventures, and is a good place to begin a long-term Sabbat chronicle. It can be a refreshing change of pace to be on the other side of the fence, knocking down the things you were busily building up in another chronicle.

This is not to imply that you should destroy another game — turning players against each other in such a manner could create hard feelings. It is more equitable to create a completely new story for your Sabbat game, separate from any Camarilla games you may have running at the same time. On the other hand, some players enjoy the struggle against an unpredictable, living opponent and may be interested in dividing their player base among the two sides. In this case, your job as Storyteller will be to keep all lines of information and reaction open and ensure that players can understand and cope with the loss of a favorite character to the actions of a predatory member of the other sect.

SABBAT VERSUS ANARCH

The anarchs provide prime recruiting ground for the Sabbat. The Camarilla is not unfounded in its fear of Sabbat infiltration though local anarch ranks. But more than that, the anarchs can be a devastating wild card in a war between the sects, tipping the balance at critical moments. Whether the chronicle takes place within an anarch city, or the anarchs are friendly to the sect, a chronicle of this sort is certain to have significant upheaval and opportunity for conflict. The mindset of most anarchs (dedication to personal freedom) is supported by the Sabbat, but most anarchs spit on the Vaulderie as simply a dressed-up blood bond.

Betrayal of one stripe or another is often a theme in anarch-Sabbat plots. They may be easy to infiltrate, but how easy are they to convert? Many anarchs are aware of the Sabbat's brutal and unwanted attempts to convert them and will resist any Sabbat presence in their city to their utmost. Also, the Camarilla often uses rumors and false Sabbat infiltrators to encourage wars between the anarchs and the Sabbat, wars that can only be beneficial to the Camarilla. Finding the real traitor in a nest of them can be a dangerous and intriguing race against time.

Sabbat versus Camarilla

For centuries, the forces of the Camarilla have stood in violent opposition to the goals of the Sabbat. Where the Sabbat seeks to destroy the Antediluvians, the Camarilla dismisses them as myths. Where Cainites consider the Beast to be a gift of Caine that destroys their weakness, the Kindred embrace their humanity. There is no room for compromise. Ultimately, the Sabbat has one goal: to destroy the Camarilla and to convert or slaughter those who insist on following its tenets.

The ancient battle against the Camarilla can be fought on a number of different fronts. Events can center around street fights, but infiltration and conversion attempts can also provide storytelling opportunities. A city in turmoil (from Praxis struggles or clan wars) can appear the perfect wounded target for a crusade. It is also possible, and makes for interesting plot twists, if both sects are minor powers in a city held by anarchs, werewolves or even hunters. Such a situation might force the two sects to find ways to work together in order to defeat the more dangerous enemy. How does the alliance hold? What happens after the enemy is finally vanquished?

The Siege

A subset of the Sabbat/Camarilla plotline, the siege tactic revolves around open warfare over some trophy, typically a city or important geographical area. Involving the characters as large groups can be difficult when you are running a live-action game. After all, there are typically 20-30 players, and only one of you. While Narrators or Storyteller assistants can be helpful fix to this problem, the most important thing you can do as a Storyteller is to create a plotline that encourages character interaction and shared goals, taking some of the burden off of you. It can't be stressed enough that your players often give you the greatest motivational tools in their own character sheets. Read through their histories, find characters who are converts from or had earlier brushes with the Camarilla (for good or bad). Perhaps they're still sensitive to a humiliating loss at their enemy's hands, or a convert left behind a lover who could be leading the defense.

If the siege is going to be run against a city peopled solely with Storyteller characters, then you should take care to create believable antagonists with goals and initiative. These characters will become the villains to your players, so make them motivated, dangerous and above all *real* in their own right. A good way to give antagonists depth is to locate a personality test and take it while thinking as your lead antagonist. These can lend some flashes of insight into character, or give small details about how the antagonist might react to certain situations.

Young versus Old

The Sabbat is founded on the idea that the oldest Cainites in the world are corrupt, treacherous and use the younger generations as pawns in a great game of power that spans continents and nations. Therefore, it is not inconceivable that the newer members of the sect feel a certain amount of resentment toward those of greater age and power. Diablerie is a common practice; those of lower generation may be at risk of losing their immortal lives to feed the ambition of a younger vampire.

Also, the anachronism common among elder members of the sect can be a stumbling block to their younger companions, particularly when there is a war to be fought. The difference between fighting with guns and swords is monumental, and an elder who has become hidebound or unable to adapt will swiftly find himself outmaneuvered. The youth know well that the motto is "adapt or die" if they want to

survive this war, and they will not hesitate to use whatever new weapon Fate puts into their hands. So who will adapt? Will the elders learn in time that they must change to survive? Or will the young find themselves in a headlong race to keep up with the latest, only to risk becoming obsolete themselves?

Sabbat versus Itself

Possibly the greatest number of Sabbat plots comes from internal sect maneuverings. No outside force is needed to spark conflict between the sect's many paths and factions; even less is needed when characters add their own personal goals and desires to the mix. The sect is hardly a unified one, despite the best efforts of the leadership. It is a cacophony of voices, all screaming to be heard, and each one believes the louder it screams, the more likely it will be to achieve its goals.

Clans squabble with each other for a greater share of power and respect. Panders get in the middle of whatever they can in an effort to prove themselves once and for all. Lasombra and Ventrue *antitribu* often circle each other, two clans of kings and not enough thrones for them all. The violent Brujah *antitribu* press for more strikes against their enemies, railing against the cautions of more conservative clans. A simple fight for power in a city or between two clans can grow radically in scope if one side suddenly chooses to pull out the cards of sect unity and brotherhood.

The various Paths within the Sabbat contain their own plotlines. A member of the Sabbat who has started on the Path of Power and the Inner Voice will have difficulty coping in a city led by a radically hedonistic Catharist. Other Paths, as well, will come into conflict with one another when their goals are at odds, whether because of doctrinal disagreements or a sly antagonist.

Nomadic versus Founded

The nomadic bands of Sabbat are considered one of the banes of the sect, despite their occasional use as scouts, and founded packs often resent their presence. During the Sabbat civil wars, nomadic packs were frequently assassinated, destroyed for their power or influence or used as fodder between warring factions. Many of the packs who are currently nomadic are survivors of that era, and as such, have not forgotten their treatment at the hands of those they called "brother."

Nomadic packs are an unbalancing influence on a city and can create strife between formerly peaceful factions. They come in, cause trouble and vanish effortlessly, leaving the founded packs to clean up their messes. For this very reason, nomadic packs are rarely treated with the same respect as founded packs. Disrespect breeds resentment, which in turn breeds treachery and deceit — after all, though the founded packs of a city celebrate the Vaulderie with one another, those who are simply traveling through have no such enforced loyalty to the city nor to the Sabbat leadership that holds sway there. They are only loyal to themselves, and may ignore certain rituals, commands and restrictions placed on founded packs. Add a little background conflict to this, and the tension can become a powder keg waiting for the match.

Typically, a single nomadic pack causes little or no difficulty to a city with a major founded Sabbat presence. One idea might be to have several nomadic packs driven into the city by an outside force and compelled to live within its confines, rankling both their wanderlust and the stability of founded packs in the city. Nomadic packs are also frequently home to some very unpleasant practices (infernalism among them) — how long can the pack keep their secrets when each night in the city may bring them closer to discovery?

The Black Hand

As we've already mentioned, the Sabbat is a place of great internal conflict. Add the members of the Black Hand and the Inquisition, and the already-volatile mix grows that much more exciting. The Hand has always been trusted by the Sect and once saved the Sabbat from falling to civil war. However, that trust only goes so far in the eyes of the archbishops and cardinals who secretly fear the Hand's military might and wonder when loyalty to the sect is superceded by loyalty to the Hand. The Hand is only called upon in times of great need; once active, they may not be willing to relinquish control to a leader they see as "weak." Yet, if the Hand is kept from power, the Seraphim may lose influence and strength in the Sabbat. They must maintain a delicate balance of fear and respect and continue to influence the sect from their position in the rear of the column.

The Inquisition's goals are not quite so subtle. If infernalist taint threatens the sect in a city, political niceties fall by the wayside. The seizure of the city and the bloody purge that follows can shock even those who call themselves beasts. Unlike the Hand, which maintains a working relationship with the political leaders of the sect, the Inquisition is comprised of fanatics who will allow nothing to come between themselves and their enemy. Their goal is to see the sect cleansed of the cancer that rots it from within. However, even such "pure" motives can be corrupted — how many purges have swept up victims innocent of the charge of infernalism but not of the sin of interfering with a powerful bishop?

When a plotline involves either of these two very powerful factions, the Storyteller should be cautious not to overpower the characters and their goals. Like a visit from a Camarilla archon, the arrival of one of these mighty beings should be suitably momentous and rare. Use them sparingly on stage and let the occasion (and the plot it furthers) unfold on a grand scale.

Loyalty and Freedom

The conflict between the sect's two founding principles, freedom and loyalty, is a story always waiting to be told. Although the sect does everything it can to unify these two beliefs, the road can be a difficult one. Many Sabbat demand total freedom, seeing it as the ultimate goal of the sect. They refuse to take orders from *anyone* — even the regent — and the Code of Milan simply undermines everything they seek to achieve. Understandably, the Loyalists are a significant problem to those who seek to keep the Sabbat together under the umbrella of authority. If the Sabbat is to survive, the balance between loyalty and freedom must be maintained.

There are many ways to throw the delicate balance of power out of whack and thus open up new stories. A sudden attack on the city slaughters nearly all of the most vocal Loyalists, and the Ultra-Conservatives suddenly advance to power — a little too conveniently… Do the characters adjust their views to the liking of the new administration or is there more here than meets the eye? Or could it be that open rebellion on the part of Loyalists causes turmoil in the sect, allowing the Camarilla or other enemies to take advantage of the chaos — which enemy should be dealt with first?

Descent Into Hell

Infernalism is a disease within the Sabbat. The sect finds demons and their methods to be repulsive and anathema to all it stands for. Personal freedom does not mean selling oneself into slavery. Unfortunately, there are many younger members who are power-hungry, discontent with their position at the lowest ranks and eager to explore *any* avenue that offers them a quick route to power. Without Humanity to guide them, and often with only a basic understanding of vampiric Morality, temptation proves irresistible. If a vampire is found guilty of infernalism, the outcome is always the same: execution. The method varies from place to place and often relies on the whim of the Inquisitor-General, but the final result will be just that — *final*. Meanwhile, the Inquisition hopes the monster didn't do too much damage before they discovered her, but who can really tell where such a creature's influence begins or ends?

So, what makes someone desperate or greedy enough to throw away sect beliefs for demonic offers? Who makes the better target — the self-righteous, the underdog, the power mad or the ignored? What kind of damage can an infernalist do among the packs or the power structure? How far can one infernalist's legacy reach?

Non-Cainite Enemies

Mortals, Garou, even fae, all abhor the inhumane practices and butchery of the Sabbat. There are very few other creatures of the World of Darkness that the Sabbat can call friends, or even allies. There are many reasons why these groups might cross paths with the Sabbat, but what happens when they do?

Mortal hunters can cause no end of trouble for the Sabbat, forcing them to re-evaluate the belief that they are "superior beings." The vampires of the Sabbat are certain of their superiority to the Children of Seth and go out of their way to prove it in their rituals and games. The arrival of a particularly capable group of hunters should shake them out of complacency. Perhaps they are skilled outsiders who were drawn by some particularly spectacular breach of the Masquerade, or maybe they're the mortal Inquisition who has had the city under observation for some time. A more intriguing possibility is to see how the Sabbat try to maintain control when the mortals of a sect-controlled city become motivated to clean up their town. If the kine are struggling to throw off the yoke, is it possible to force them to go back under?

Garou and Sabbat clash on several fronts. Garou Kinfolk aren't immune from becoming targets when a pack goes scouting for Blood Feast vessels, and the Sabbat stink abominably of the Wyrm to even the most casual observer. Both groups are used to fighting against the odds, both revere honor and strength, and both adhere to the belief that humans are worthless except as breeding stock or food. Some whisper that Black Spiral Dancers and Sabbat have joined forces on rare occasions, but most Garou discount such tales as campfire stories.

Even the most heartless Unseelie can find the Sabbat lust for blood and cruelty to be too much, despite similar views on individual freedom, and Seelie fae abhor everything the Sabbat stand for. When the Sabbat target those they believe "weak," weakness in their eyes could be anything changelings value, such as compassion, joy or creativity. Rumors abound of unholy unions between the Shadow Court and the Sabbat. Their denizens often share similar views on the weakness of mortals, not to mention enjoying the same guilty pleasures, although few are willing to brave the gathers where the answers might be found.

Ritae

The *auctoritas* and *ignobilis ritae* are the rituals and customs that bind the Sabbat together. For many vampires, these are the times of their unlives when they feel closer to their heritage as vampires and closer to the greater family of Cainites that surrounds them. Using the *ritae* is a fine means of setting the stage for players and characters. For players, it's a complete immersion into the Sabbat world and values. For characters, it's a chance to get the blood racing (so to speak) and reconnect with their heritage.

One of the best ways to draw both players and characters into the setting of a game is to create interesting *ritae* and encourage every pack to develop their own games and rituals. The Sabbat hierarchy encourages spirituality in its members and encourages the development of new *ritae* as well. The *ritae* of a particular pack highlight the pack's qualities that others may admire or scorn. Many players love pomp and circumstance, and given time and space, they will create some amazing events for your chronicle.

Rogue's Gallery

The Sabbat isn't a homogeneous mass of vampires all spouting the same naughty words from between clenched fangs while posing in the latest rumble-worthy garb. The characters given here are all fairly typical: They'd fit in with the population of many Sabbat strongholds. They don't even come close to exhausting the range of possibilities. If you use them in your own chronicle, alter sex, appearance, behavior and whatever details need to change to suit your stories. Use these characters as starting points, not as barriers to your own innovation.

Note: The Ability levels presented here reflect a "conservative" reading of the rules and the assumption that characters can still attempt tasks that require Abilities they've used up. The characters just don't get retests anymore. If your chronicle imposes more limits or simply includes characters who routinely have more Ability levels, adjust the totals for these template characters to match.

Archbishop

Background: You earned your position a few decades ago after long, hard service in difficult circumstances. Older than the government of the country you dwell in, you've followed your region through multiple cycles of revolt and reform. Mortal society holds very few surprises for you. The political and social cause of perfect individual freedom first drew you to the sect, and you remain more interested in the social side of the Sabbat than doctrinal issues. Still, you can sustain debate on the fine points of all the major Paths and the theological implications of various divergent philosophies; your bishops learn quickly not to confuse a subject's secondary importance to you with ignorance. Soon there will.

Roleplaying Hints: You've proven yourself fit for your job. You hope to prove yourself fit for higher rank than this. Since your own success depends on the performance of those beneath you, you make sure they've got the resources they need to do well, the training to use their resources, rewards for doing good work and harsh penalties for failure. You can count the vampires you actually trust on one hand, but you have stable, mutually profitable relationships with your associates, and that counts for something.

Clan: Lasombra
Nature: Architect

Demeanor: Survivor
Generation: 7th
Embrace: 1715
Apparent Age: Middle-aged
Physical: Agile, Energetic x 2, Ferocious, Quick x 2, Tough x 2
Social: Charismatic x 3, Commanding x 3, Diplomatic, Intimidating x 3, Witty
Mental: Attentive x 2, Creative, Dedicated x 2, Knowledgeable x 3, Observant x 2, Vigilant x 2
Abilities: Alertness x 2, Brawl x 3, Camarilla Lore x3, Etiquette, Expression x 2, Fire Dancing x 2, Intimidation x 3, Investigation x 3, Leadership x 4, Occult x 3, Politics x 4, Rituals x 4, Sabbat Lore x 5, Streetwise, Subterfuge, Survival x 2
Disciplines: Dominate 4, Fortitude 1, Obtenebration 6, Potence 3, Protean 3
Backgrounds: Contacts x 5, Herd x 2, Resources x 3
Virtues: Conviction 4, Instinct 3, Courage 5
Path of Enlightenment: Power and the Inner Voice 4
Willpower: 14
Status: Battle-Scarred, Blessed, Blooded, Enlightened, Initiated, Ominous, Proven, Superior

BISHOP

Background: You are first among equals in your city. You're not the oldest, but you proved most adept at using your early fascination with Sabbat spirituality to build a network of alliances that left your opponents isolated. Your rapid rise through the ranks ended at this level, and until you learn to take the sect's enemies more seriously, you'll probably go no further. You excel at settling disputes between your followers and rousing them to action; you need to learn about strategy and develop an understanding of your opposition.

Roleplaying Hints: The best moment of your life was your last. You rejoice in no longer being human and dream of the time when all the kine bow before you for your pleasure. You know, beyond any shadow of a doubt, that the Sabbat must and shall rule the world. To prepare for the glorious triumph, you keep the vampires around you united. Different Paths, different styles… it's all fine as long as it serves the Sabbat. Nothing matters but the sect.

Clan: Ventrue *antitribu*
Nature: Fanatic
Demeanor: Visionary
Generation: 8th
Embrace: 1794
Apparent Age: varies
Physical: Brutal x 2, Dexterous x 2, Nimble x 2, Resilient x 2, Tireless x 2
Social: Charismatic, Commanding x 2, Empathetic x 2, Expressive, Ingratiating x 2, Intimidating x 2, Persuasive x 2; Tactless [N]
Mental: Astute, Creative x 2, Dedicated x 2, Discerning, Intuitive, Patient x 2, Shrewd x 2, Wily
Abilities: Athletics x 2, Brawl x 2, Empathy x 3, Fire Dancing x 5, Investigation x 2, Intimidation x 2, Leadership x 3, Occult x 2, Politics, Rituals x 4, Sabbat Lore x 3, Subterfuge, Survival
Disciplines: Dominate 4, Fortitude 3, Presence 5, Vicissitude 2

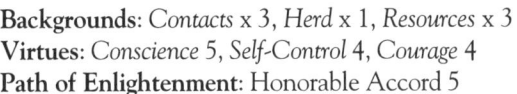

Backgrounds: *Contacts x 3, Herd x 1, Resources x 3*
Virtues: *Conscience 5, Self-Control 4, Courage 4*
Path of Enlightenment: Honorable Accord 5
Willpower: 10
Status: *Blooded, Devoted, Enlightened, Enriched, Feared, Initiated, Proven*

Templar

Background: It takes strength to do the dirty work that makes the sect run. You aren't just physically tough. You have the mental discipline to keep focused in the midst of confusion and deception and the force of will to intimidate would-be opponents into capitulation. You've taken bullets for the bishop, stalked would-be defectors through sewers and penthouses and perched for nights on end in surveillance assignments. The bishop has fewer secrets from you than he might imagine.

Roleplaying Hints: This is your next step up from pack leader, and you're out to do a good job. You don't care about administration; you care about the sect, and you do your part to make it work. Big theoretical questions hold no appeal to you; you're looking at the issues at hand. Do the job and let others get out of your way.

Clan: Nosferatu *antitribu*
Nature: Perfectionist
Demeanor: Bravo
Generation: 10th
Embrace: 1927
Apparent Age: 30
Physical: *Dexterous x 2, Enduring x 2, Energetic, Ferocious x 2, Quick x 2, Resilient, Vigorous x2*
Social: *Callous, Commanding x 2, Intimidating x 3*
Mental: *Astute, Attentive x 2, Cunning, Disciplined, Patient x 2, Rational, Vigilant, Violent*
Abilities: *Alertness x 3, Athletics x 2, Brawl x 3, Dodge x 2, Drive, Firearms x 2, Intimidation x 3, Investigation x 2, Security, Stealth x 2, Streetwise, Subterfuge x 2, Survival*
Disciplines: *Animalism 1, Fortitude 3, Obfuscate 3, Potence 4*
Backgrounds: *Contacts x 2*
Virtues: *Conscience 1, Self-Control 5, Courage 5*
Path of Enlightenment: Humanity 1
Willpower: 10
Status: *Battle-Scarred, Blooded, Initiated, Ominous, Respected, Undefeated*

Ductus

Background: You didn't seek out your position: Your pack pushed it on you with the support of the bishop, after a series of disastrous failures wiped out many of your pack's veterans. You saw yourself as more of a scholar. Much to your surprise, you thrived as a leader. Now you just hope you won't get promoted out of this position. You like your pack and guide them through a steady stream of successes. Your followers eat well, rest securely, and from time to time, strike a blow at one of the sect's enemies. Not long ago you planned and executed the successful assassination of an autarkis elder your pack located passing through

town. You decided that intrigue suits you and yours, and you're trying to persuade the bishop to let you undertake some covert operations in the city the archbishop has marked for the next crusade.

Roleplaying Hints: The world chewed you up, swallowed your joys and dumped you on the streets. Payback time. The bitches and sons of bitches can never suffer too much. You take great pleasure in making mortals hurt in ways that they can't cure and can't stop. Your second great pleasure is helping others escape the bonds of the human condition. Some of them have gone on to pass you in the hierarchy, and that's fine. Let them have sect power; you're satisfied with your lot.

Clan: Brujah *antitribu*
Nature: Fanatic
Demeanor: Curmudgeon
Generation: 9th
Embrace: 1933
Apparent Age: 70
Physical: *Enduring x 2, Robust x 2, Rugged x 2, Tireless x 2; Lame [N]*
Social: *Charming, Commanding x 2, Eloquent x 2, Empathetic x 2, Expressive x 3, Intimidating x 2, Persuasive; Condescending [N]*
Mental: *Attentive x 2, Clever, Cunning x 2, Dedicated x 2, Insightful x 3, Wise*
Abilities: *Alertness x 2, Animal Ken, Brawl x 2, Dodge x 2, Empathy x 3, Etiquette, Expression x 3, Firearms, Intimidation, Leadership x 2, Medicine, Occult, Security x 2, Survival x 2*
Disciplines: *Celerity 5, Fortitude 2, Potence 2, Presence 4*
Backgrounds: *Allies x 3, Contacts x 3*
Virtues: *Conviction 4, Instinct 4, Courage 3*
Path of Enlightenment: Cathari 4
Willpower: 9
Status: *Battle-Scarred, Blooded, Enriched, Feared, Initiated, Undefeated*

Priest

Background: When you were alive, you seemed to be just one more working-class woman attending your local evangelical church. One night the survivors of a pack from a failed crusade sheltered in your basement and discovered that all on your own, you'd reinvented most of the trappings of classical infernalism. Beneath your calm exterior, you were angry enough at the world to try everything your could think of that might summon demons. The survivors consulted briefly and offered you the Embrace. You accepted. Now you throw yourself without reserve into the spiritual side of the Sabbat. Who cares about politics? You want to see humanity crushed and the worthy few, yourself included, elevated to supreme power. God Himself can't hide from you forever. When you find Him, you'll pull Him down and crush him, too. In the meantime, you train yourself and your packmates to make fullest use of your blessed nature.

Roleplaying Hints: They're all going to get what's coming to them. You'll see to it. You're halfway to union with the First Rebel, the man who showed by his example how to exist free of subservience and fear. You love your condition and wish to help those around you do the same. By yourself you were nothing, but these wonderful people helped you find your way. In return, you owe them all the counsel you can provide. Alarmists say the Final Nights are here. If it's time for the consummation of the war, you'll make sure your troops go into battle blessed and ready.

Clan: Malkavian *antitribu*
Nature: Architect
Demeanor: Celebrant
Generation: 8th (originally 11th)
Embrace: 1940
Apparent Age: 40
Physical: *Brawny, Brutal, Energetic x 2, Ferocious x 2, Stalwart x 2, Tenacious x 2*
Social: *Charismatic x 2, Commanding x 2, Dignified x 2, Eloquent x 3, Ingratiating x 2*
Mental: *Astute, Attentive, Dedicated x 2, Disciplined x 2, Vigilant x 2, Wise x 2*
Abilities: *Alertness, Brawl, Empathy, Etiquette x 2, Fire Dancing x 2, Firearms, Hearth Wisdom x 2, Intimidation, Leadership x 2, Medicine, Occult x 2, Rituals x 3, Sabbat Lore x 2, Survival*
Disciplines: Auspex 3, Dementation 4, Fortitude 1, Obfuscate 1
Backgrounds: Contacts x 2, Mentor
Virtues: Conviction 5, Instinct 3, Courage 3
Path of Enlightenment: Caine 3
Willpower: 10
Status: *Battle-Scarred, Blessed, Devoted, Enlightened, Enriched, Initiated*

Grimaldi Fixer

Background: You could settle down, hold one job and get comfortably rich if you wanted to. You prefer to move around and deal with fresh situations as they come up. This temperamental quirk makes you valuable to your family and to the Sabbat. After living in a town for a few years, you usually know everybody who matters in a crisis. The vampires, revenants and ghouls you bail out of crises seldom see you doing very much, they just notice you on your cell phone or stopping in to visit a few offices, and then the crisis goes away. You know how to settle fears through a combination of calm words, carefully phrased promises and great quantities of money.

Roleplaying Hints: You get things done. That's the long and the short of it. Your family and the vampires can't rule the world if everyone's in jail, on the lam or dead, and you're the guy that keeps them at liberty. Cleaning up messes may seem like lower-class janitor work, but you don't mind: It's always a fresh chance to see how people tick when all their usual props fail. You'd never mention this part, but if you ever do decide to settle down, you'll have a whole lot of favors to collect.

Clan: Grimaldi (revenant family)
Nature: Caregiver
Demeanor: Survivor
Apparent Age: Early middle age
Physical: *Agile, Brutal x 2, Enduring, Ferocious x 2, Rugged x 2, Tireless*
Social: *Charismatic x 2, Charming, Commanding x 2, Diplomatic, Elegant, Expressive, Magnetic*

Mental: *Astute, Clever, Creative* x 2, *Determined, Insightful* x 2, *Knowledgeable, Reflective*
Abilities: *Alertness* x 3, *Brawl* x 2, *Camarilla Lore* x 3, *Computer* x 2, *Dodge* x 3, *Drive* x 3, *Empathy* x 3, *Etiquette* x 3, *Expression* x 2, *Finance* x 3, *Firearms* x 2, *Intimidation* x 3, *Investigation* x 3, *Law* x 2, *Leadership, Medicine, Occult, Politics* x 2, *Repair, Rituals, Sabbat Lore* x 4, *Security* x 2, *Stealth* x 2, *Streetwise* x 3, *Subterfuge* x 3
Disciplines: *Celerity* 2, *Dominate* 2, *Fortitude* 2
Backgrounds: *Allies* x 3, *Contacts* x 5, *Influence: Bureaucracy* x 4, *Influence: Finance* x 4, *Influence: High Society* x 2, *Influence: Legal* x 4, *Influence: Police* x 3, *Influence: Street* x 3, *Influence: Transportation* x 4, *Influence: Underworld* x 4, *Resources* x 4
Virtues: *Conscience* 3, *Self-Control* 4, *Courage* 4
Path of Enlightenment: Honorable Accord 4
Willpower: 8

Zantosa Socialite

Background: You make it a point to know everyone worth knowing and to turn that knowledge to the advantage of the Sabbat. When the time for a major *ritus* approaches, you make a few calls and line up a few wealthy people that nobody will miss. When a war party needs information on a target's influence in mortal society, you make discreet queries as to who's showing the little signs of unearned favor. You supply mortals with interesting substances in their blood for pack parties and know how to line up the latest musical acts for public shows.

Roleplaying Hints: It's a grand existence. You get the best of both worlds — neither mortal nor vampire can experience as much as you do. You're in the perfect position to make the world what you know it should be, and the best part is that others will pay you to help twist their souls. Every favor you do lets you push the recipients that much further from the light.

Clan: Zantosa (revenant family)
Nature: Monster
Demeanor: Bon Vivant
Apparent Age: Late 20s
Physical: *Agile, Graceful, Lithe, Quick, Resilient*
Social: *Charming, Commanding, Dignified, Diplomatic, Elegant, Magnetic, Persuasive, Witty*
Mental: *Astute, Cunning, Determined, Insightful, Knowledgeable, Vigilant, Wily*
Abilities: *Alertness, Athletics* x 2, *Drive, Empathy* x 3, *Expression* x 2, *Finance* x 2, *Firearms, Intimidation, Investigation, Occult* x 2, *Performance (singing)* x 3, *Security, Stealth, Subterfuge* x 3
Disciplines: *Auspex* 1, *Presence* 1, *Vicissitude* 1
Backgrounds: *Allies* x 2, *Contacts* x 3, *Fame* x 2, *Herd* x 2, *Influence: High Society* x 3, *Influence: Occult* x 3, *Influence: Political* x 2, *Resources* x 5
Virtues: *Conviction* 3, *Instinct* 3, *Courage* 3
Path of Enlightenment: Cathari 2
Willpower: 6